"YOU'D MAKE A FOOL OF ME, WOULD YOU?"

Lord St. Simon said furiously. *"Diablillo!"* He grabbed her hands as they lunged for his face, wrenching her arms above her head, grabbing her chin with his other hand, holding her head steady on the moss. "You'd serve me such a trick, would you? Let me tell you, *mi muchacha,* that it'll take more than a devious bandit to get the better of me."

Tamsyn twisted her body sideways, but he swung himself over her, straddling her.

"Espadachín!" she threw at him again. "I may be a bandit, but you're a brute and a bully, Colonel. Let me up."

"No."

The simple negative stunned her. She stared up into his face that was now as calm and equable as if they were sitting in some drawing room. He looked positively comfortable.

Her astonished silence lasted barely a second; then she launched a verbal assault of such richness and variety that the colonel's jaw dropped. She moved seamlessly within three languages, and the insults and oaths would have done an infantryman proud.

"Cease your ranting, girl!" He recovered from his surprise and did the only thing he could think of, bringing his mouth to hers to silence the stream of invective. . . .

Violet

JANE FEATHER

BANTAM BOOKS

NEW YORK   TORONTO   LONDON   SYDNEY   AUCKLAND

VIOLET

A Bantam Book / July 1995

All rights reserved.
Copyright © 1995 by Jane Feather.
Cover art copyright © 1995 by George Bush.
Insert art copyright © 1995 by Pino Dangelico.
No part of this book may be reproduced or transmitted in any form or by
any means, electronic or mechanical, including photocopying, recording,
or by any information storage and retrieval system, without permission in
writing from the publisher.
For information address: Bantam Books.

ISBN 0-553-56471-4

Published simultaneously in the United States and Canada

Bantam Books are published by Bantam Books, a division of Bantam Dou-
bleday Dell Publishing Group, Inc. Its trademark, consisting of the words
"Bantam Books" and the portrayal of a rooster, is Registered in U.S. Patent
and Trademark Office and in other countries. Marca Registrada. Bantam
Books, 1540 Broadway, New York, New York 10036.

PRINTED IN THE UNITED STATES OF AMERICA

RAD   0 9 8 7

This one's for Kate and Jo:

*I see it's written by a lady, and I want
a book that my daughters may read.
Give me something else.*

PUNCH, 1867

Violet

Prologue

THE SMALL PROCESSION WOUND UP THE STEEP MOUNTAIN path, leaving the French border behind as they headed toward the Spanish mountain town of Roncesvalles, the outriders sheltering beneath wide hat brims from the broiling afternoon heat. Inside the heavy, lumbering coach the atmosphere was stifling, the air so thick and hot it was like a suffocating blanket, making every breath an effort.

The two women leaned back against the leather squabs, the elder, veiled and gloved despite the heat, fanned herself and moaned softly, occasionally dabbing at her lips with a lavender-scented handkerchief. Her companion slumped in a corner, her back drenched with sweat, the dark taffeta of her gown sticking to the squabs. Her hat lay on the seat beside her, and she'd thrown off her veil long since. Her face was pink and hot, beads of perspiration gathered on her forehead, trickling down the side of her nose. Her hair, the color of summer wheat, clung damply to her small head, and her violet eyes were languorous under drooping lids.

"Oh, my dear Lord, will this journey never end?" the elder lady murmured.

The young lady didn't reply, knowing the question to be rhetorical. It had been asked every few minutes since they'd boarded the coach that morning. She regarded her companion with a degree of contempt. It was certainly hot and uncomfortable, but since Miss Henderson had been adamant in her refusal to draw back the leather curtains blocking the windows of the coach, enclosing them in this airless oven for reasons of propriety, as if there were anyone but a goatherd to look in on this mountain pass, Cecile Penhallan could find no sympathy for her sufferings.

If her duenna carried a little less flesh, she'd find it more bearable, the girl reflected, idly diverting herself with the image of Marianne Henderson's rolls of white flesh melting in the heat like butter in a pan.

It was hardly an uplifting image, and she closed her eyes. It was too much effort to keep them open.

The crack of a rifle shot, the plunging halt of the horses, brought her upright, flinging aside the leather curtain as her duenna screamed.

"Oh, it's brigands. I know it is. We'll be robbed. Attacked. They'll take our virtue . . . oh, my dear Miss Penhallan, what will your brother say . . . ?"

"La, ma'am, I doubt Cedric believes I'm still in possession of my virtue," Cecile observed, peering through the window aperture. "And who's to say he's incorrect," she added mischievously, her eyes alive and glowing, her previous languor banished. Above the babble of the outriders, the curses of the coachman, came a clipped, commanding voice that cut through the cacophony like scissors through silk.

"Oh, Miss Penhallan, how—" But whatever the lady

was about to say was lost as she slumped in a dead faint, sinking slowly in a crackle of starched taffeta to the floor of the coach.

The door of the coach was pulled open. "*Señorita,* I am desolated to discommode you, but I must ask you to descend," the same voice said courteously in heavily accented English. A hand reached in—an ungloved hand with a massive square-cut ruby on the little finger.

Cecile placed her own small white hand, similarly ungloved, in the one that had appeared. She felt the rough swordsman's calluses on the palm, and the strong brown fingers closed over hers, drawing her forward out of the coach into the blinding white sunshine.

She looked up into a bronzed face, dark eyes like a hawk's fixed on her countenance, a strong mouth set in a firm, intimidating line, long black hair caught in a ribbon at the nape of his neck.

"Who are you?"

"They call me El Baron." He offered a mock bow.

"Oh," Cecile breathed. This was the robber baron— the brigand whose name mothers used to frighten their children into obedience. The undisputed ruler of the mountain passes between Spain and France. And he was the most beautiful creature Cecile Penhallan had laid eyes on in all her seventeen years.

Gazing up at him, losing herself in the black eyes, she understood that she had been waiting for this meeting since she'd first felt the strange stirrings of her body, the unsettling energies that had driven her to defy her brother, a mocking defiance that had led to her present exile.

The baron was returning her scrutiny, and a light flickered in his eyes, then sprang into flaming life. And Cecile knew that her own eyes reflected the flame and gave it back to him. She moved closer to him as if drawn by an invisible string, unaware now of the scene around them, the pawing horses, the terrified outriders surrounded by the band of brigands, who sat their horses easily, bandoliers over their shoulders, rifles casually resting on their pommels. They made no threatening moves, but there was no need to. Their very presence was intimidation enough.

"Come," El Baron said. It was a command, but it was also a simple statement.

Catching her around the waist, he lifted her onto the back of a powerful chestnut with a white blaze on his forehead and swung up behind her.

"Sit back," he said. "You have nothing to fear, *querida*."

"I know," Cecile replied simply, leaning back against the broad chest as his arms went around her and he gathered up the reins. "Where are you taking me?"

"Home," he said.

Cecile glanced back as the horse moved forward, surefooted on the narrow climbing track. Marianne had recovered from her swoon and was leaning out of the window, one mittened hand fluttering frantically at her departing charge, a strange gibbering chatter of protest coming from beneath the veil.

Cecile chuckled. "Poor Marianne." She raised her hand in a jaunty salute. It was the last glimpse Marianne Henderson ever had of her—indeed, the last glimpse anyone who'd known Cecile Penhallan before she encountered El Baron ever had of her.

The band of brigands drew back from the coach as their leader's mount broke into a trot. They offered a mock salute to the trembling outriders and the still gibbering Miss Henderson and turned to follow their leader and his captive, leaving Miss Henderson's virtue as intact as the leather satchel of money stashed beneath the seat of the coach.

This had been no ordinary highway robbery, but they left with what they'd come for.

Chapter One

THE AIDE-DE-CAMP'S BOOTS CLATTERED ON THE WOODEN stairs as he hastened toward the commander in chief's private office at headquarters in the town of Elvas. Outside the door, however, he slowed, adjusted his stock, pulled down his tunic, smoothed his hair. The Peer didn't look kindly on untidiness, and he had a savage tongue when he chose.

"Enter!" The command rasped at his knock, and he pushed open the door. There were three men in the large drafty room—a colonel, a major, and the commander in chief, standing by the fire blazing in the hearth to combat the damp chill. It had been raining for five days, a relentless, drenching downpour that made life hell for the infantry digging trenches around the besieged town of Badajos just across the Spanish border.

The aide-de-camp saluted. "Dispatches from intelligence, sir." He placed a sheaf of papers on the desk.

Wellington grunted acknowledgment and moved from the fire to glance through them. His long, bony nose twitched in disgust. He glanced up toward the two

officers beside the fire. "The French have taken La Violette."

"When, sir?" Colonel, Lord Julian St. Simon held
out his hand for the document Wellington was proffer-
ing.

"Yesterday, apparently. Cornichet's men surrounded
her band of ruffians outside Olivenza. According to this,
they're holding La Violette in a military outpost outside
the town."

"How reliable is this?" The colonel's eyes flickered
over the dispatch.

Wellington shrugged and shot an interrogatory
glance at the aide-de-camp.

"The agent's one of our best men, sir," the aide said.
"And the information is so fresh, I'd lay any odds it's
correct."

"Damn," muttered Wellington. "If the French have
her, they'll wring every scrap of knowledge out of her.
She knows how to navigate every goddamned mountain
pass from here to Bayonne, and what she doesn't know
about the partisans in the area isn't worth knowing."

"We'd better get her out, then," the colonel drawled
as if it were a foregone conclusion, replacing the dispatch on the table. "We can't allow Johnny Crapaud to
have information we don't have."

"No," agreed Wellington, stroking his chin. "If La
Violette's already shared her knowledge with the
French, then we'll be at a significant disadvantage if she
can't be induced to give it to us too."

"Why do the French call her that?" inquired the
major. "The Spanish call her Violeta, too."

"It's the way she works, as I understand it," Colonel
St. Simon said, a sardonic note in his voice. "Or rather,
plays . . . the proverbial shrinking violet. She's always

to be found hiding behind the activities of the large partisan bands. While the French army is concentrating on guerrilla activities, the little violet and her band are flourishing in the background, causing merry mayhem where least expected."

"And feathering her own nest while she's about it," Wellington remarked. "She's said to have no time for the armies of either side, and while she'll assist the Spanish partisans, she expects to be paid for her help . . . or at least to be put in the way of a little profitable pillage."

"A mercenary, in other words," the major said, with a grimace of distaste.

"Precisely. But I gather the French find even less favor with her than our good selves. At least she's never offered to help the French, for any price." The commander in chief kicked at a falling log in the hearth.

"Until now," observed the colonel. "They may be offering her the right price at this moment." He was a big man, broad-shouldered, deep-chested, with a pair of startling blue eyes beneath bushy red-gold eyebrows. His hair was a thick mane of the same color, an unruly lock flopping over a wide forehead. He carried himself with all the natural authority of a man born to wealth and privilege, a man unaccustomed to questioning the established order of things. A cavalry officer's pelisse was cast carelessly over his scarlet tunic, a massive curved sword sheathed in a broad studded sword belt at his hip. He surged with a restless energy, seeming too big for the confined space.

"I've heard it said, my lord, that the name also comes from La Violette's appearance," the aide-de-camp ventured. "I understand she resembles the flower."

"Good God, man!" The colonel's scornful laughter

pealed through the dingy room. "She's a ruthless, murdering bandit who, when it suits her whim, chooses for a price to put her dubious services at the partisans' disposal."

Discomfited, the aide-de-camp shuffled his feet, but the major said briskly, "No, St. Simon, the man's right. I've heard it said, also. I gather she's a diminutive creature who looks as if you could blow her away in one puff."

"Then she'll not hold out long once Major Cornichet starts his gentle persuasion," Wellington declared. "He's a vicious, arrogant brute with a taste for interrogation. There's no time to lose. Julian, will you take it on?"

"With pleasure. It'll be a joy to balk Cornichet of his prey." The colonel was unable to hide his enthusiasm for the task as he clicked his booted feet and his spurs jingled. "And it'll be most satisfying to put an end to the games of this shrinking violet. She's played too long, enriching herself at our expense." A look of distaste crossed the aristocratic features. Julian St. Simon had no time for mercenaries. "I'll take twenty men."

"Will that be enough to storm an entire outpost, St. Simon?" the major inquired.

"Oh, I don't intend to storm it, my friend," Colonel, Lord St. Simon said, grinning. "Stealth and trickery —a little guerrilla warfare of our own, if you take my meaning."

"Then go to it, Julian." Wellington offered his hand. "And bring back this flower so we can pluck her petals ourselves."

"I'll have her here in five days, sir." The colonel left the room, currents of energy seeming to swirl in his wake.

Five days was no idle boast, as the commander in chief was aware. Julian St. Simon, at twenty-eight, had been a career soldier for ten years, and he was known as much for his unorthodox methods as for his invariable success. It was held as a fact of life in the mess that St. Simon never failed at a task he set himself, and his men would follow him into an inferno if he asked it of them.

The French outpost was a huddle of wooden huts and tents in a small wood outside the walls of Olivenza. The rain poured down from the leaden skies and dripped from the branches of the trees, soaking the canvas tents and streaming through the spaces between the wooden slats of the huts in a relentless torrent.

La Violette, known to her own people as Tamsyn, daughter of Cecile Penhallan and El Baron, sat huddled on the wet earthen floor in the corner of one of the huts. A rope attached to a plaited leather collar around her neck secured her to the wall. She inched sideways to avoid a persistent trickle of water funneling down a grooved slat and down the back of her shirt.

She was cold and hungry, cramped and wet, but her eyes were sharp with speculation, her ears straining to catch the low-voiced conversation through the drumming of the rain. Major Cornichet and two fellow officers were eating at a table in the center of the hut. The smell of garlic sausage and ripe cheese set her saliva running. A cork was pulled, and she could taste on her tongue the rough red wine of the region. A wave of hunger-induced nausea washed over her.

She'd been held like this for two days. They'd thrown her half a loaf of bread early this morning. It had landed in the mud beside her, but she'd brushed it off and devoured it, tipping her head to catch the rainwater funneling in the groove above her. At least there was no shortage of water if she was prepared to forage for herself, and so far she had suffered nothing but discomfort and the humiliation of her position.

A little humiliation and a degree of discomfort were nothing. Tamsyn could hear the baron's voice. "*Hija,* you must learn what can be endured and what must not; which battles are worth fighting and which are not."

But when would the softening up cease? When would they start seriously? She could simply give them what they wanted, of course, probably even demand a price for it. But this was a battle worth fighting for. She could not aid the French, betray the partisans, without betraying her father's memory. So when would it start?

As if in answer to her silent question, Major Cornichet stood up and strolled over to her. He looked down at her, one hand stroking the curled waxed mustache above a cruel mouth. She met his gaze as fearlessly as she could.

"*Eh, bien,*" he said. "You will talk to me now, I believe."

"About what?" she returned. Her mouth was dry, and despite the cold and the wet, she felt hot and feverish. The daughter of El Baron was no coward, but you didn't have to be a coward to fear what she must now face.

"Don't try my patience," he said almost affably. "We can do this without pain, or we can do it with. It matters not to me."

Tamsyn folded her arms, rested her head nonchalantly against the wall at her back, ignoring the trickle of water, and closed her eyes.

The rope attached to the collar was suddenly jerked hard, and she was hauled to her feet, the collar pulling tight against her throat as the colonel jerked upward again and she came up on her toes, fighting for breath.

"Don't be a fool, Violette," Cornichet said softly. "You will tell us in the end. Everything we wish to know and much that we don't if it will stop the pain. You know that. We know that. So let's spare ourselves the time and the trouble."

She wouldn't be able to hold out. Not forever. But she could endure for some time.

"Where is Longa?" The soft question hissed against the monotonous backdrop of the drumming rain.

Longa led the partisan bands in the north. His guerrillas were wreaking havoc on Napoleon's forces with their darting forays, their sneak attacks coming out of the blue, harassing struggling columns, picking off stragglers, laying waste to the land so there was no foraging to be done for an army that survived off the land as they marched.

Tamsyn knew where Longa was. But if news of her capture could reach the guerrilla leader before she broke, then he would be able to disappear. She had to pray that someone was aware of it, that the news was even now traveling to Pamplona. Her men had scattered in the ambush—those who hadn't been killed—all except for Gabriel. And where was Gabriel? Somewhere in this wretched hole, if they'd left him alive. Perhaps he was even now breaking free. It was impossible to imagine that giant oak of a man held captive by ordinary human bonds. And if Gabriel freed himself, then he would come for her.

She had to endure.

The rope slackened and she came back on her feet again, but the colonel's hand was on her shirt. Instead of ripping it, he unbuttoned it slowly and deliberately.

Her skin was now icy as she saw the knife he held in his other hand. Bitter nausea rose in her throat. Of all things, she dreaded the knife the most. Could Cornichet know that? Know of her invincible terror at the sight of her own torn skin, her own crimson blood escaping . . . . Black spots danced in front of her eyes, and she clung to consciousness with every last fiber of her being.

One of the other men came over, smiling. He moved behind her and pulled the shirt from her as the last button came undone. He grasped her wrists, dragging her arms behind her so that her breasts were pushed forward. Rough rope cut into her wrists. She could feel the soft tremble of her breasts on her rib cage.

"Such a pity," murmured Cornichet, moving the knife around the small swell of her right breast. "Such delicate skin. One wouldn't expect it of a brigand, a thief and a plunderer." The tip traced the circle of her nipple. "Don't make me do this," he said, cajoling. "Tell me where Longa is."

She said nothing, trying to take her mind away from the hut with the flickering candlelight and the ceaseless drumming of the rain; trying not to feel the cold flat of the knife, pressed now against her breast so that the edge was sharp on her flesh, but not yet cutting.

"You will tell me where Longa is," the colonel continued in the same almost pensive tone. "And then you will describe the passes through the Guadarrama heights —the ones you and your friends use."

Still she said nothing. Then she was spinning on the end of the rope as the man behind her whirled her to face the wall. The rope was pulled tight, and she came up on her toes again as they fastened it to a hook much higher on the wall. She felt the knife on her back now, and it was worse, much worse, when she couldn't see it. The tip scribbled down her spine, and she waited for the first nick. It would be a slow flaying, she knew; innumerable little cuts, drawing beads of blood until the stream flowed.

There was a strange smell. For a second Tamsyn didn't recognize it as she fought the terror for control, waiting for the next touch of the knife. Someone coughed behind her. Her breath caught in her throat. The tightness of the collar and her fear . . . but, no. It was smoke. Thick black smoke creeping under the door. Oily, sullen smoke billowing through the hut, defying the rain. Acrid, choking smoke.

Cornichet cursed, whirling toward the door. One of the others was there before him, wrenching it open. He fell back before the black rolling cloud.

A bugle sounded. An impudent clarion call. And then chaos broke out. In the choking smoke men struggled with black-clad wraiths who seemed to appear from nowhere, swords drawn. The sharp crack of rifles mingled with the curses and exclamations. A scream of pain.

Tamsyn tried to swing herself on her toes away from the wall, but with her hands bound she could get no leverage and could only imagine what was going on in the acrid darkness behind her. Her mind was racing as she tried to think of some way of capitalizing on this amazing piece of good fortune. But strung up as she was, there seemed nothing she could do to help herself. Could it be Gabriel causing this chaos?

Then miraculously the rope holding her to the wall parted. The tension was abruptly released, and she fell to her knees.

"Get up!" a voice said in English. A knife sliced through the bonds at her wrists.

Tamsyn wasted no time questioning her good fortune. She struggled to her feet, choking as the greasy black smoke curled around her.

"Quickly!" the same voice commanded. "Move!" A hand in the small of her back propelled her forward.

There was something irritatingly peremptory about her rescuer, but circumstances didn't lend themselves to protest. Her eyes stung with the smoke, and her lungs heaved. She ducked sideways away from the propelling hand to catch up her shirt, glimmering white on the floor at her feet. She thrust her arms in the sleeves before covering her mouth and nose with her forearm, then staggered forward, that hard hand in her back again, pushing rather than guiding her toward the door.

All around her, men swayed, cursed, coughed, fought for the door. Outside it was hardly better. Every hut seemed to be smoldering, sending greasy clouds into the rain, and men ran hither and thither grabbing up possessions, shouting orders.

Again the bugle sounded and she recognized the note of retreat. The man still pushing her forward bellowed, "The Sixth to me." Then her feet left the ground and he was carrying her, running with her through the mud and the rain and the confusion, dodging blue-uniformed Frenchmen.

Men wrapped in dark cloaks were racing to a clearing where twenty horses pawed the ground and whickered, the whites of their eyes showing as they smelled smoke.

Colonel St. Simon threw his light burden upward onto the back of his charger and was up behind her in almost the same movement.

"Gabriel!" the girl shouted incomprehensibly. "I

must find Gabriel." Taking the colonel by surprise, she hurled herself sideways, landing neatly on the balls of her feet.

St. Simon had no time to think. He leaped from his horse and plunged after his prize as she darted into the darkness. He caught her before she'd gone more than a few yards, his hand closing over her wrist.

"Goddamn it! Where the hell do you think you're going?"

Tamsyn couldn't see him clearly, was conscious only of the shape and mass of his body in the shadowy, flickering darkness. Again his tone set her hackles rising, but remembering that whoever he was, she owed him some considerable debt, she bit back a sharp rejoinder and spoke with impatient moderation.

"Thank you very much for rescuing me from such an uncomfortable situation, sir. I don't know why you should have done so, but I'm truly grateful. However, I can manage perfectly well now, and I must find Gabriel." She tugged at her captive wrist.

An uncomfortable situation! She called seminaked, strung up by the neck, facing the slow agony of the knife, an uncomfortable situation! And she was thanking him as if she believed either he'd acted out of pure altruism or her rescue was a coincidence. In any other circumstances St. Simon might have found such a wild misapprehension amusing.

Flame shot up in the air from somewhere in the encampment, and a burst of rifle fire punctuated the confused shouts and bellows. Julian heard one of his own men yell urgently from the clearing behind them. This was no time to be bandying words with La Violette. His grip on her wrist tightened as she fought to break his hold.

"You seem to be laboring under a misapprehension," he declared, unclasping his heavy black boat cloak with his free hand. "You are now a guest of His Majesty's Army of the Peninsular, my dear girl. I trust you'll find our hospitality quite satisfactory."

With a flick of his wrist he set the cloak whirling through the air. It swirled around the slight twisting figure, capturing her limbs in its folds. Her stream of invective was cut off abruptly as he swaddled her tightly in the garment and scooped her into his arms again, turning her head against his chest.

Tamsyn had had time to see the scarlet tunic and the insignia of a colonel before the cloak enfolded her, and her nose was now pressed against gold braid and glittering buttons. Her situation seemed to have changed dramatically for the second time in as many minutes, and if she was still being held by soldiers, it couldn't have changed that much for the better.

Her rescuer turned captor mounted, apparently unhampered by his burden. An order rang out in the clearing, and the small group of black-cloaked figures wheeled their horses and melted into the darkness.

Tamsyn realized rapidly that struggling against the swaddling folds was futile. The arm holding her was an iron band, preventing her from twisting away from the broad expanse of scarlet chest, and the horse beneath her was pounding the ground at such a speed that it would be suicidal to attempt to fling herself from his back, even if such a thing were possible.

She let her body relax while her mind raced. What did the English want with her? The same as the French, presumably. Would they use the same tactics? Goddamned soldiers—they were the same savage animals whatever uniform they wore. Blue, red, green, black. And gold braid and epaulets made no difference either.

Her mind filled with the nightmare images of that hideous night when the soldiers had come to Pueblo de St. Pedro. Her ears rang with the screams, and the hot reek of blood was in her nostrils as vividly as if she and Gabriel, helpless, were watching the massacre again. . . . Where was Gabriel?

The thought that Gabriel was still in the hands of the French while she was being carried away God knows where by an English cavalry officer banished the ghastly images under a clear wash of fury, and she fought against her bonds with a sudden desperate energy.

The arm tightened around her, a hand pressed against her scalp, forcing her face into his tunic so that she gasped for air. It was an effective way of discouraging her struggles.

Tamsyn lay still again. This mad ride would end at some point, and she'd do well to preserve her energies for an escape then. She focused her mind on possible courses of action once she felt solid ground beneath her feet. Some pompous, peremptory English cavalry officer would be no match in wits or speed for La Violette. She knew this territory like the back of her hand, and she was a past master at getting out of tight corners.

Julian could feel the currents of energy surging through the seemingly fragile bundle he held pinioned against him. Even when she was lying still and apparently compliant, he sensed determination and purpose. La Violette was a law unto herself, as her father, El Baron, had been, and she'd proved expert at outwitting the cumbersome mechanisms of two armies when she went about her profitable and lawless business. Julian had no intention of dropping his guard simply because at the moment he had this brigand's spawn physically secured.

The cavalcade reached the bank of the Guadiana and halted. There was no sound of pursuit, only the rushing water of the river. The night sky was black as pitch, and it was impossible to tell in the dark whether the river could be safely forded at this point.

"Sergeant!"

"Sir." One of the black-cloaked figures separated itself from the men and rode up to the colonel.

"We'll bivouac here until dawn and then look for a ford. Let's see if we can find some shelter from this blasted rain. Try those trees." The colonel gestured with his whip to an isolated clump of trees on the plain.

The sergeant gave the order and the cavalcade cantered off, the colonel following, his brow furrowed as he considered what he was to do with his captive once they were on the ground.

The copse yielded a deserted wooden shack, half its roof intact, and a ruined barn. The men of the Sixth were accustomed to bivouacking in the most unpromising circumstances. During the four-year struggle to drive Napoleon out of Spain and Portugal, the broiling summers and freezing, rain-swept winters in the Iberian Peninsula inured a man to ordinary discomforts. The horses were tethered under the trees, and men gathered sticks to make fires in the shelter of the barn walls. Even wet wood could be coaxed to produce a sullen flame with the dry tinder they all carried with them.

The colonel swung down from his horse, still holding his presently unresisting captive, and strode into the shack.

"Light a fire in 'ere, sir, an' you'll be snug as a bug in a rug," the sergeant pronounced, following him inside.

"The men 'ave got dry tinder left from the attack on the Froggies, an' I reckon a pannikin of tea wouldn't come amiss."

"Sounds wonderful, Sergeant," the colonel said somewhat absently. "Post pickets around the wood. We don't want the fires drawing unwelcome attention."

He glanced down at the figure in his arms. La Violette had turned her head away from his chest as his grip had changed, and he found himself looking into a pair of dark eyes in a heart-shaped face. She returned his scrutiny with an expression of mild curiosity that could have lulled a less cynical man into a false sense of security.

"What now, English Colonel?" Her English was so faintly accented, it would take a sharp ear to detect it, he thought in surprise.

"You speak good English?"

"Of course. My mother was English. Are you going to put me down?"

"If I do, will you give me your word you'll not attempt to run?"

A glint of mocking laughter appeared in her eyes. "You'd accept the parole of a brigand, English Colonel?"

"Should I?"

She laughed aloud. "That's for me to know and you to find out, Colonel."

There was something unpleasant beneath her mocking laughter. A wealth of antagonism that struck Julian as almost personal. Obviously it had slipped the brigand's mind that her present comfort was dependent upon his goodwill.

"Thank you for the warning," he said dryly. "I'll heed it." He glanced around the small, inhospitable

space. "I suppose I could utilize that neat collar Cornichet put on you and secure you in that fashion."

Tamsyn pulled herself up sharply. This was not a man
to mock, clearly. A different attitude was required.

"That won't be necessary," she said swiftly, her eyes
suddenly soft and conciliatory. "Please put me down,
Colonel. How could I possibly escape with all your men
around?"

Quite a little actress, La Violette, Julian thought with
a grim inner smile. But that little-girl-lost look wasn't
fooling him. "I'll put you down with pleasure," he
drawled. "But you'll have to forgive me if I take certain
precautions. Sergeant, bring me a length of rope."

Tamsyn cursed her stupidity. Clearly she'd underestimated this particular example of the flower of Wellington's cavalry. She'd allowed her anger to get the better
of her and indulged her contempt and loathing for the
entire pompous, conceited breed with their gold braid
and their buttons, but it seemed this colonel was not
quite as blind and stupid as her prejudice had dictated.

She was set on her feet, her limbs still immobilized by
the tight folds of the cloak.

"Do seat yourself, *señorita*," the colonel invited, his
voice as smooth as silk. "The floor is a trifle damp, but
I'm afraid my hospitality is somewhat limited at present." He took the length of rope the sergeant handed
him, and when Tamsyn didn't immediately avail herself
of his invitation, he placed his hands on her shoulders
and pushed her down.

Resistance was again futile. Tamsyn didn't fight the
pressure but folded herself onto the floor, leaning
against the wet wall. It was a horribly familiar position,
and she reflected dismally that she'd been flipped from
the frying pan to the fire with remarkable ease. She

waited grimly for him to fasten the rope to the collar she still wore, but to her relief, he bent and hobbled her ankles and then tied the free end to the buckle of his sword belt. The rope was long enough to allow him to move around the small space while effectively restraining his prisoner, but it was nowhere near as uncomfortable or as hideously humiliating as to be tethered by the neck.

With her hands free she was able to loosen the folds of the cloak, and it was always possible she'd have the opportunity to untie her ankles if this sharp-eyed colonel dropped his guard, or fell asleep. She reached up to unbuckle the loathsome leather collar and threw it as far from her as she could.

The colonel raised an eyebrow but said nothing and made no attempt to retrieve the collar. Presumably, he preferred his own methods of restraint. Tamsyn huddled into the cloak and settled down to await developments.

A small fire crackled now under the roofed half of the hut, and the sergeant had balanced a pannikin of water over the flames. An oil lamp flickered, throwing grotesque shadows as the colonel loosened his tunic, unfastened his saddlebags, rustled through the contents. Tamsyn could hear shufflings and low voices from outside as the men settled into their own makeshift camp.

Her mouth watered as she watched the colonel unwrap a loaf of bread and a packet of cold meat. The sergeant was making tea, wetting the precious leaves in a mug so they were thoroughly infused before pouring on the rest of the boiling water.

These English certainly knew how to see to their comforts, Tamsyn reflected. Even in such dismal and unpromising circumstances.

Julian ate his supper with relish. He took the mug of

tea from the sergeant with a word of thanks, and the man went outside to join the men bivouacking under the trees. The colonel studiously avoided looking at his captive as he drank thirstily and with obvious enjoyment. He'd decided that La Violette could go hungry for a salutary period. It might improve her attitude.

"What did you tell Cornichet?" he asked suddenly.

Tamsyn shrugged and closed her eyes. For some reason her usual resistance was deserting her, and she felt remarkably like crying. She wanted a cup of tea. More than food. In fact, she thought she could kill for a cup of that hot, steaming, reddish-brown liquid, so strong it would make her tongue curl. "Nothing."

"I assume they'd only just started on you."

She didn't reply.

"What did he want to know?"

"What right do you have to take me prisoner?" she countered. "I'm no enemy of the English. I help the partisans, not the French."

"As long as there's some profit in it for you, as I understand it," he said, his voice a whip crack in the dim hovel. "Don't pretend to patriotic loyalty. We all know where La Violette's interests lie."

"And just what business is it of yours?" she demanded furiously, forgetting her hunger and fatigue. "I've done you no harm. I don't interfere with the English army. You trample all over *my* country, behaving like God-given conquering heroes. All complacence and pomposity—"

"Hold your tongue, you!" The colonel was on his feet, his eyes blazing. "The blood of Englishmen has watered this damnable peninsula for four interminable years, doing the work of your countrymen, trying to save you and your country from Napoleon's heel. I have lost more friends than I can count in the interests of your miserable land, and you speak against those men at your peril. Do you understand that?"

He towered over her, and Tamsyn tried not to flinch. Suddenly he swooped down on her, his hand catching her chin, turning her face to the flickering lamplight. "Do you understand?" His voice was very quiet, but his fury was a naked blade in the bright-blue eyes, his close-gripped mouth a hard, thin line.

"The English have their own reasons for being here," she retorted, forcing herself to meet his eye. "England couldn't survive if Napoleon held Spain and Portugal. He'd close their ports to English trading, and you'd all starve to death."

They both knew she spoke the unvarnished truth. There was silence. He still held her face, his own very close to hers, and she could feel the bruising indentation of his fingers on her chin and the warmth of his skin. He seemed to fill her vision, to expand before her eyes until he was all she could see, and their miserable surroundings, even the dull spurt of firelight, vanished into the shadows.

Julian found himself looking at her, examining her properly for the first time as his surge of righteous anger died beneath the truth of her counterattack. Pale hair like corn silk formed a close-cut cap around a small head, a roughly chopped fringe wisping on her forehead. Her eyes were almond-shaped, thick-lashed, and deep purple beneath arched fair eyebrows that gave her a rather quizzical air.

"Good God, comparison with a violet wasn't just whimsy," he said slowly into the tense silence. "But you belong to a rather thorny species, I suspect."

His fingers tightened, and for a moment his mouth

hovered over hers so that Tamsyn could feel his breath
on her lips and the sense of inhabiting some space and
time that held only the two of them intensified. When
his mouth met hers, it felt inevitable, and she was sliding
down into a warm, musky darkness bounded by the
scent of his rain-wet skin, the rasp of stubble against her
cheek, the firm pliancy of his lips on hers.

Then the trance was shattered, and she jerked her
head away, bringing her hand up to smash against his
cheek. *"Bastardo!"* Her voice shook. *"Batard!"* She spat
the words at him. "You rape your prisoners, do you,
English Colonel? I thought it was only your English
foot soldiers who indulged themselves in such fashion.
But I imagine they take example from their officers."

The depth of her rage, the power of the hatred that
lay beneath it, stunned him for a minute. He stared at
her, his hand unconsciously pressed to his stinging
cheek. Then suddenly he took her face between both
hands and brought his mouth to hers again, this time
with a bruising force that crushed her lips against her
teeth and forced her head back against the wall.

When he released her, she didn't move, her face a
pale shape in the gloom, her eyes dark pools.

"In future you won't confuse a mutual kiss with violation," he declared, his voice tight, his anger directed as
much at himself as at the girl. He couldn't imagine what
had possessed him. He made it a rule never to amuse
himself with women connected even tenuously with
any of the armies marching through the Peninsula. "You
ever insult me in that fashion again, *mi muchacha,* and I
won't answer for the consequences."

A shiver ran through her, and still she didn't move
and she didn't speak. Julian stood looking down at her,
and now he saw the blue shadows of exhaustion on the

paper-thin skin beneath her eyes, the fine lines of endurance on the drawn countenance. She'd been a prisoner of the French for two days. When had she last eaten? Slept?

She reminded him of a bruised flower.

Dear Lord! He was falling victim to an attack of sentimental fantasy, he thought disgustedly, but he turned to the fire and refilled his mug with tea. "Here."

She took the mug, still without speaking, but he saw how her fingers trembled as they curled around the warmth, lifting it to her lips. A shudder of pleasure rippled through the slight frame as the hot liquid slipped down her throat.

He broke bread, slapped two thick slices of cold mutton onto a crusty hunk, and handed it to her. Then he turned to tend the fire, withdrawing his attention from her so she could eat in relative privacy, despite the rope that fastened her to his sword belt.

As he rubbed his hands over the small flame, he realized that the rain had stopped. After seven days of continual downpour, the relentless drumming had ceased. He glanced up at the sky visible above the roofless half of their shelter. A faint, misty aura showed through the clouds. Fine weather would expedite the siegeworkings outside Badajos. Besieging a city was wretched work and made the men restless and dissatisfied. They'd all be glad when this one was over and done with.

He glanced over his shoulder at the girl. She'd put the empty mug on the floor beside her and was huddled into his boat cloak, her eyes closed.

For such a very thorny violet, she looked remarkably vulnerable and powerless. Nevertheless, Colonel, Lord St. Simon decided he'd stay awake for what remained of the night.

Chapter Two

TAMSYN AWOKE AFTER TWO HOURS. AS ALWAYS, SHE MOVED from sleep to waking without any transition. Her mind was clear, her body refreshed, her recollection of the events that had brought her to this place perfectly lucid. Except . . . except that she couldn't understand what had happened to cause that first kiss. It made no sense. She loathed and despised all men wearing a soldier's uniform, and yet she'd kissed this one, a man who with no justification held her captive in this muddy squalor. She'd kissed him and she'd enjoyed it. Her enjoyment had so shocked her that she'd lashed out at him with a violent injustice that she knew had earned his rough retribution.

She opened her eyes and looked across at the English colonel. He was sitting beside the fire, a horse blanket around his shoulders, his head drooping on his chest. The fire was still alight, though, so presumably he hadn't been asleep for long.

Her hands were clasped in her lap under the boat cloak. Keeping her eyes on the hunched, slumbering figure, she slid her hands down her leg, feeling for the knotted rope at her ankle. If she didn't move her feet, the tension and play of the rope would remain the same, and her captor would feel no change in his end.

"Don't even think about it." His voice was cool and crisp, and he raised his head, his eyes sharp and bright in the dawn light. If he'd been asleep, he slept like a cat, Tamsyn reflected glumly.

She pretended that she didn't understand what he meant. "I need to go outside," she said with a casual yawn and a stretch, adding acidly, "I assume I may do so."

"I have no objection," he returned blandly, getting to his feet. When she was standing up, he gave the rope a little jerk of encouragement. "Come. We don't have all day."

Tamsyn cursed him under her breath as she gingerly stepped after him with her hobbled feet, out into a balmy dawn.

The sky was cloudless, the sun a glowing red ball on the horizon, and the air smelled fresh and clean. The copse was filled with birdsong, and the men of the Sixth were waking, putting pannikins of water over the fires, seeing to the tethered horses. They cast curious glances at their colonel and his prisoner as the two walked away from the bivouac toward the river.

"You should find sufficient privacy behind those rocks," the colonel observed, gesturing toward an out-crop on the riverbank. "The rope is long enough for you to be one side and me to be the other."

"You are so considerate, Coronel."

"Yes, I believe I am," he agreed with a careless smile, ignoring her caustic tone.

"What is it you want of me?" she demanded. She'd asked the question last night, but matters had become somewhat confused, and there'd been no clear answer.

"Wellington wishes to speak with you," he returned. "Therefore, I am taking you to headquarters in Elvas."

"As a prisoner?" She gestured to the tethering rope. "Why should this be necessary for a simple conversation?" Her voice dripped sarcasm.

"Would La Violette accept an invitation from the commander in chief of His Majesty's Army of the Peninsular?" he retorted in the same tone.

"No," she said flatly. "I have no time for armies, whatever side they fight on. And the sooner this country is rid of you, the better." She glared into the red ball of the rising sun. "You have no more business interfering with the affairs of Spain than Napoleon. And you're no better than he is."

"But, unfortunately, you need us to drive him out," he said, hanging on to his temper. "And Wellington needs some information from you, which, my dear girl, you are going to give to him. Now, pray make haste." He gestured impatiently to the rocks.

Tamsyn didn't immediately move. This English colonel was all too complacent, like the rest of the breed. She gazed at the river for a moment, then said, "I would like to bathe. I seem to have been sitting in mud for days."

"Bathe?" Julian stared at her, taken aback at this abrupt switch of subject. "Don't be absurd. The water will be like ice."

"But the sun's warm," she pointed out. "And I've been bathing in these rivers all my life. I only wish to dip myself once in the water, just to wash off the worst of the mud." She turned pleading eyes on him. "What harm can it do, Colonel?"

He hesitated, words of denial on his lips, but before he could speak them, she plucked at her shirt and ran a hand through her short hair. "I'm filthy. Look at my hands." She held them out for his inspection. "And my hair's disgusting. I can't bear to be in my own skin! If I must converse with your commander in chief, at least allow me some dignity."

Her wrinkled nose and disgusted grimace amused him, despite his anger at the sweeping contempt of her earlier remarks. She *was* undeniably filthy. He knew the miseries of it himself; after days of marching through every kind of weather, sleeping on muddy ground and under hedgerows, a man couldn't get the smell of his own body out of his nostrils. His task was to bring her to headquarters at Elvas. But he could grant reasonable requests without jeopardizing that task.

"You'll freeze to death," he said. "But if you wish to, then you may—for two minutes."

"My thanks." She kicked off her shoes and then regarded him expectantly. "May I untie the rope? It'll tighten unbearably if it gets wet."

"You may," he agreed. "But if you attempt to run from me, my friend, I'll catch you, and you'll walk to Elvas tethered to my stirrup."

Anger flashed across her eyes, turning the deep purple almost black, and then it was quickly banished. She shrugged as if accepting his statement and bent to unfasten the rope. She tugged off her stockings, unfastened her britches, and pushed them off, kicking them to one side. Clad in thin linen drawers and her shirt, she turned to walk down to the river.

Suddenly Julian sensed the current of energy surging through her, just as he had done when he'd held her on his horse yesterday. Purpose and determination were in every taut line of her body. He caught her arm. "Just a minute."

He looked at the river. At the far bank. The water was fairly smooth, but there was a telltale ripple of an undercurrent a few feet from the near shore. It was unlikely she could swim to the other side . . . unlikely, but not impossible. This was La Violette, after all.

"Take off the rest of your clothes."

"What! All of them? In front of you?" She looked outraged, and yet somehow he wasn't convinced by this display of maidenly modesty.

"Yes, all of them," he affirmed evenly. "I doubt even you will take off from the far bank stark naked."

"What makes you think I could swim that far?" Her eyes widened in innocent inquiry. "It must be a good half mile with a strong undertow. I'm not that good a swimmer."

"You'll have to forgive me if I choose not to believe that," he responded as evenly as before. "If you wish to bathe, then you must do so in your skin. Otherwise, perhaps you would do what you have to behind the rocks and we can return to the camp."

Chagrin darted over her face. A mere fleeting expression, but he saw it and knew he'd been right. La Violette had had some thoughts of escape.

Tamsyn turned away from him and unfastened her shirt. Damn the man for being such a perspicacious bastard. It would have been simplicity itself to swim to the opposite shore, and she wouldn't have had far to go before she found help from some peasant farmer. But tramping the countryside in a soaked shirt and drawers was one thing. In her bare skin was a different matter altogether.

Her mind raced over alternatives, her eyes skimming across the riverbank, looking for anything helpful. The terrain was relatively flat and mossy, and she could run

like the wind if she had a decent start. A hundred yards
away the ground rose toward a small hill crowned with a
tangle of bushes and undergrowth. If she could reach
there, she could go to ground like a fox before the
hounds. No English soldier would be able to find La
Violette on her own territory.

She dropped the shirt to the ground, loosened the
string at the waist of her drawers, and kicked them off.
St. Simon had been correct in assuming his prisoner was
a stranger to modesty unless it suited her purposes to
feign it. She was no convent-reared hidalgo maiden and
had grown up in the rough-and-tumble of a bandit encampment, where she'd made an early acquaintance
with the facts of life. Besides, at this moment she was far
too occupied with the glimmer of a plan to give a moment's thought to the colonel's eyes on her body.

Gathering up her discarded garments, she folded
them with care and placed them on the ground close to
the rock. It was a tidy little gesture that struck St. Simon
as a trifle incongruous. But before he could work out
why it should trouble him, she turned to face him, her
feet slightly apart, arms akimbo, naked except for an
intricately worked silver locket on a slender chain.

"Satisfied, Colonel?"

For a moment he ignored the double-edged question
that threw a contemptuous challenge. His eyes ran
down the lean, taut body that seemed to thrum with
energy. He realized that the illusion of fragility came
from her diminutive stature; unclothed, she had the
compact, smooth-muscled body of an athlete, limber
and arrow straight. His gaze lingered on the small,
pointed breasts, the slight flare of her hips, the tangle of
pale hair at the base of her belly.

It was the most desirable little body. His breath

quickened, and his nostrils flared as he fought down the torrent of arousal. He must be losing his mind, to have put himself in this situation. Why the hell had he even considered allowing her to bathe in the river? But he had and it was too late now.

Emotions under control again, he raised his eyes to her face and saw with a certain grim satisfaction that his scrutiny had discomfited her. There was less certainty in her challenging stance, and her eyes slid away from his. It was some recompense for his own unbidden response.

"Perfectly," he drawled. "I find myself perfectly satisfied."

Anger chased discomfiture from her expression, and she took a step forward so that for a second he thought she was going to strike him again. If she did, she would regret it.

Tamsyn read the message in his eyes and in the almost imperceptible readying of his body. The impulse to lash out at him died as rapidly as it had risen as she reminded herself that she was wasting time. Her plan was now fully formed, and engaging in this disturbing battle of wits was both futile and distracting. She turned without a word and walked to the edge of the high bank.

Julian watched as she stood poised above the water. The back view was every bit as arousing as the front, he reflected dreamily. Then she rose on her toes, raised her arms, and dived cleanly into the swift-running river.

He walked to the edge of the bank, waiting for the bright fair head to surface. The water flowed strongly, and the rippling undertow was a wide band about five feet from the bank. A kingfisher flashed deepest blue as it dived into the swift surface and emerged with a fish sparking silver in the rays of the rising sun. But there was no sign of La Violette. It was as if she'd dived and disappeared.

His throat tightened in alarm. Could she have become entangled in the treacherous weeds he could see waving in thick dark-green fronds just below the surface?

Could she be swimming underwater to the far bank? His eyes darted to the neat pile of clothes. They were still there on the ground by the rock. He'd taken care of that escape route. His eyes raked the surface of the water. There was nothing. Not a sign. How long since she'd dived? Minutes.

He was pulling off his boots, tearing at the buttons of his tunic without conscious decision. He flung his sword belt to the grass, yanked off his britches and his shirt, and dived into the river as close as possible to where he believed his prisoner had gone in.

He surfaced, teeth chattering in the icy waters that poured down from the snow-covered Sierra. No one could survive in this temperature for more than a couple of minutes. He stared at the smooth, unbroken surface of the river, shaking the water from his hair. Nothing. She'd disappeared as completely as if she'd never existed.

Again he dived, pushing through the forest of reeds, his eyes open, looking for a pale limb, a flutter of hair that would show where she was trapped.

Tamsyn surfaced on the far side of the rocks as soon as she heard the splash as he entered the water. She too was shivering with cold, her hair a dark, wet cap plastered to her head. But there was a triumphant gleam in her eyes, and a grin curved her blue lips. It had been a gamble that he'd go in after her without a moment's consideration, but her mother had told her many laugh-

ing tales of the so-called and frequently misplaced chivalry of English gentlemen. This English colonel was
clearly no exception to the rule.

She leaped onto the bank, hidden by the rocks from
the swimmer on the other side, and shook the water
from her body with the vigor of a small dog. The sun
struck warmly on her icy flesh as she darted sideways to
grab up the neat pile of clothes.

Julian came up for air, numbed with cold, knowing
that he shouldn't stay in the water another minute, yet
forcing himself to go down for one more look. As he
prepared to dive, he glanced toward the bank and saw a
pale shadow against the rock, and then it was gone. It
was no more than a formless flicker, but he knew what
it was without even thinking.

His bellow of fury roared through the peaceful early
morning on the banks of the Guadiana. A curlew
screamed in imitation, and a flock of wild ducks rose
from their nesting place in the reeds, wings beating in
alarm as he waded through the water to the bank.

Tamsyn swore to herself and picked up her heels,
racing across the flat mossy ground toward the small
brush-covered hill. She didn't attempt to put on her
clothes, simply clutched them to her wet bosom. It was
sheer bad luck that he'd seen her, but she calculated she
had enough of a start. He still had to scramble onto the
bank, and she had to be fleeter of foot than a lumbering
large-framed soldier.

Julian, however, had been a sprinter in his school
days, and his long legs ate up the distance between
them. He was running in blind fury, at himself for being
so gullible, and at his quarry for making such a fool of
him. He never failed at anything he set out to accomplish, and he wasn't going to be defeated in this instance

by some flowerlike, diminutive, tricky, plundering, pillaging, mercenary bandit.

He was gaining on her, the icy river water turned to sweat on his bare skin, but she had almost reached the hill, and he knew that if she could attain the undergrowth, his chances of finding her were small. He and his men could beat the brush for hours, but he knew from experience how the guerrillas could disappear into this land without trace.

Tamsyn's breath was coming in gasping sobs now as she neared the rising ground. She could sense rather than hear her pursuer, his footfalls, like her own, were lost in the soft wet moss of the riverbank. But she knew he was closing on her. With a last effort she hurled herself up the slope, and then her foot caught in a sinewy tangle of thin roots creeping over the surface of the earth.

She fell to her knees with a cry of annoyance that changed to a shriek of alarmed fury as Julian hurled himself forward and his fingers closed over her ankle. She hadn't realized he was that close. Desperately, she kicked back with her free foot, but he hung on grimly, even when her foot bashed his chin. Her hands scrabbled at the sinewy roots, trying to get sufficient purchase to pull herself free, but he'd caught her other foot now and was hauling her backward, down to the flat ground. Her fingers slipped on the roots and she lost her hold, tumbling down as he pulled her, the bare skin of her belly and breasts rasping over the ground, pricked by twigs and tiny stones.

"Espadachín!" she raged, twisting onto her back, her fingers curled into claws, reaching for his face. "You're hurting me!"

"You'd make a fool of me, would you?" Lord St.

Simon said furiously. "*Diablillo!* Crafty, tricky god-damned little monkey!" He grabbed her hands as they lunged for his face, wrenching her arms above her head, grabbing her chin with his other hand, holding her head steady on the moss. "You'd serve me such a trick, would you? Let me tell you, *mi muchacha,* that it'll take more than a devious bandit to get the better of me."

Tamsyn twisted her body sideways, trying to bring her legs up to lever against him, but he swung himself over her, straddling her, sitting on her thighs with his full weight so she felt hammered into the ground, arms and head pinioned, her body flattened.

"Espadachín!" she threw at him again. "I may be a bandit, but you're a brute and a bully, Colonel. Let me up."

"No."

The simple negative stunned her. She stared up into his face that was now as calm and equable as if they were sitting in some drawing room. He looked positively comfortable. She could feel the wet wool of his drawers prickling the skin of her thighs. *He* hadn't gone into the water stark naked.

Her astonished silence lasted barely a second; then she launched a verbal assault of such richness and variety that the colonel's jaw dropped. She moved seamlessly within three languages, and the insults and oaths would have done an infantryman proud.

"Cease your ranting, girl!" He recovered from his surprise and did the only thing he could think of, bringing his mouth to hers to silence the stream of invective. His grip on her wrists tightened with his fingers on her chin, and his body was heavy on hers as he leaned over her supine figure.

Tamsyn choked on her words beneath the pressure of

his mouth. She heaved and jerked beneath him like a landed fish waiting for the gaff. Her skin was hot, her blood was boiling, there was a crimson mist behind her closed eyes, and his tongue was in her mouth, a living presence within her, probing and darting, and her own tongue wouldn't keep still but began to play in its turn.

Everything became confused. There was rage—wild rage—but it was mixed with a different passion, every bit as savage. There was fear and there was a sudden spiraling need. Her body was liquid fire, her mind a molten muddle. Her arms were still held above her head, his mouth still held hers captive, but the hand left her chin, moved down between their bodies, caressed her breast, reached down over the damp, hot skin of her belly. Her loins of their own accord lifted, her thighs parting for the heated probe, sliding within her so that she cried out against his mouth.

His fingers played upon her and his flesh moved within her, deep, smooth thrusts that carried her upward onto some plane where the air crackled, and fire and flame swirled around them. And then she was consumed in a roaring conflagration in which her body no longer had form or limits, when she flowed into the body that possessed hers with such unfaltering, unerring completeness that the boundaries of her self no longer existed, and amid the blazing glory of this extinction was the terror of annihilation.

Julian came to his senses slowly, aware first of the warmth of the sun on his back, then the breathing, living softness beneath him. He gazed down into her face. Her eyes were closed, her skin flushed, lips slightly parted. He still held her wrists above her head; his other hand was braced beside her body. He gazed at her as if he could make sense of what had just happened . .

and then the warmth of the sun on his back became cold steel.

He couldn't see it, but he knew the feel of a sword against his skin, the press of the rapier tip along his backbone. He couldn't see the man behind him without turning his head, but he could feel the warmth of a stranger's flesh, the rustle of breath that brought the fine hairs upright on the nape of his neck.

"Say your prayers, man. You have thirty seconds to make your peace with your Maker." The voice had the soft lilt of the Scottish Highlands, but it carried the chill of the grave. The rapier tip moved against his ribs, pressing into the taut skin, ready for the home thrust that would pierce his back and then his heart.

Julian experienced pure terror for the first time in his life. Facing death on a battlefield was nothing like this. That was a hot and hasty matter of luck and fate. This was execution, cold and slow. And for some reason he knew there was nothing he could say or do to alter the fact of this approaching death. Although he had no idea why it should have come out at him from the warm early morning on the heels of a glorious passion.

"No!" The girl beneath him spoke with sudden urgency, coming out of her trance, her eyes shooting open, awareness flooding back into their dark-purple depths.

"Gabriel. Gabriel, *no!*" She tugged at her still-captive hands, and Julian released them. She pushed against him, struggling to sit up, but he couldn't make another move without the deadly tip of the rapier sliding into his body, so he stayed between her thighs, thinking amid his terror of how ludicrous he must look, of how it was the stuff of farce to face death in such a position.

"Gabriel, it's all right." Tamsyn was speaking with desperate intensity, knowing the speed and the deadly fury of the giant standing over the colonel. He believed she'd been hurt, and it was his life's work to protect her and avenge her hurts. She owed the English colonel some grief for the way he'd treated her since he'd rescued her, but not for what had just happened between them. It was an act of insanity for which they were both responsible, and he didn't deserve the death Gabriel was waiting to hand out with the detachment of a man who'd lived all his adult life by the sword.

"Gabriel, nothing happened that I didn't wish for." She spoke now slowly and carefully, but the urgency of her message was still clearly to be heard.

Julian's blood ran cold, hearing it. She knew his executioner, and she was as afraid as he was of what the man would do. He remembered how she'd flung herself from his horse when he'd rescued her from Cornichet, saying she had to find Gabriel. It seemed that Gabriel, whoever he was, had found her.

"You were running mighty fast for someone who wanted to be caught, little girl," the voice at the end of the sword said slowly and full of doubt. The cold steel tip remained pressed against Julian's bare back.

Tamsyn thought rapidly. How to explain something she didn't understand herself. "It's very confusing, Gabriel." She fixed the man's gaze with her own. "I can't explain it, but truly nothing happened that I didn't wish for."

A silence that seemed to Julian to last an eternity was abruptly broken by a roar of laughter. The cold tip of steel left his back.

"Och, little girl! And what would El Baron say to see you rolling in the grass like a wanton milkmaid?"

" 'Things happen, *hija*,' " Tamsyn said, her voice slightly shaky as she tried to sound humorous. She thought the danger was over, but you could never be absolutely certain with Gabriel.

The colonel inched away from her, easing himself from between her thighs and away from the sword, whose tip now rested lightly on the ground beside his hip.

Tamsyn sat up. "You know that's what he would have said, Gabriel. He would have given one of his shrugs and smiled at Cecile as he said it."

The laugh boomed again. "Och, aye, lassie. I reckon y'are right, at that." He stared at Colonel, Lord St. Simon with a curiosity that was not exactly friendly, but neither was it threatening. "So who's your gallant, little girl?"

"Good question." Tamsyn regarded the colonel quizzically. His immediate danger was over, but with Gabriel's arrival she herself now had the upper hand, and the thought of a little revenge was very tempting. "We haven't been formally introduced as yet. But he's a colonel in Wellington's army."

Julian said nothing until he'd managed to pull on his sodden undergarments, discarded somehow in that crazy conflagration. He felt a little less vulnerable with them on, but not much. The new arrival was a giant oak of a man with massive limbs, bulging muscles beneath his jerkin, graying hair caught in a queue at the nape of his neck. His complexion bore the blossoming veins of a man fond of his drink; his washed-out gray eyes were sharp, however. Crooked teeth gleamed in a wide, full-lipped mouth, and he handled a two-bladed broadsword as easily as if it were a kitchen knife.

"If you wish a formal introduction, Violette, I'd prefer to make it in my clothes," St. Simon said dryly.

"Make yourself decent, little girl," the giant instructed, keeping his eyes on Julian. "The colonel and I will discuss a few matters while he dresses." He gestured with his sword along the bank to where Julian's clothes lay.

Julian shrugged acceptingly. The ball was no longer in his court, but he had twenty men a quarter of a mile away, and the situation would change as soon as he was in a position to do something about it. With the appearance of nonchalance he strolled back to his clothes, La Violette's defender walking beside him, his great sword still unsheathed but his expression bland, his pale eyes mild.

Julian was not, however, disposed to relax. He had the unshakable conviction that the giant's mood could change in the beat of a bird's wing.

Tamsyn scrambled into her clothes, casting half an eye along the bank where the English colonel was dressing, Gabriel leaning against the rocks, idly tracing patterns in the grass with the tip of his sword as they talked.

It had been many months since she'd succumbed to such an impulsive fit of passion. She knew, because she'd been told often enough, that she shared her mother's devil-may-care impulses, and the passion that ran deep in the veins of both her parents had flowed undiluted into their only child. She had been taught to regard such bodily hungers without prudery. They were perfectly normal among adults and should be satisfied without guilt. But she didn't think El Baron or Cecile would have regarded that wild encounter with approval. One didn't fraternize with the enemy.

And soldiers *were* the enemy . . . a personal enemy.

The images flooded in again, the screams, the steaming reek of blood. Her father standing in the midst of a yelling circle of men in the tattered uniforms of many nations, their faces twisted with the rapacious viciousness of greed, their senses drunk with blood. His great sword slashed from side to side but they kept on coming; shot after shot pierced his body, and it seemed to the two powerless watchers on the heights that he couldn't still stand there alive with the blood spurting from the holes in his body—and yet still he stayed on his feet and bodies fell beneath his sword.

Cecile lay in the shadows, dead by her husband's hand, a small black smudge on her forehead, where his merciful bullet had entered. El Baron's wife wouldn't fall victim to the rapine hungers of a vile mob of deserting soldiers. And his daughter too would have joined her mother in death if she'd been in the Puebla de St. Pedro that dreadful day, instead of hunting with Gabriel in the hills.

Slowly, she blinked away the images, put the anger and grief behind her. She'd led her own small band since that day. Those who'd escaped the massacre and others who'd joined them, all were prepared to follow El Baron's daughter as they aided the partisans, tormented the French, avoided direct contact with the English, and took what payment came their way.

Until that double-dyed bastard, Cornichet, had set his ambush. Tamsyn had no idea how many of La Violette's band had escaped the French in the pass, but she had been their target. The baron had long ago entrusted his daughter's safety in his own absence to his most trusted comrade, and Gabriel had fought beside her and for her. But one man, even a giant, was no match for fifty. They'd both been swept up like spiders before the broom.

But what was done was done, and bewailing the past was pointless. It was now a question of making the most of their present situation. There must be some advantage to be gained from it. There was always an advantage if one looked for it.

She tucked her shirt into the waist of her britches and walked toward the two men, carrying her shoes and stockings, enjoying the feel of the cool, mossy turf beneath her feet.

The colonel's bright-blue eyes rested on her as she approached, and Tamsyn's scalp lifted, her heart quickening. What was done was done, she told herself firmly. That moment of madness was in the past. It had nothing to do with the present situation.

Chapter Three

JULIAN FASTENED HIS SWORD BELT AT HIS WAIST. ARMED, HE felt immeasurably more secure, although the giant's sword was unsheathed, and the colonel was certain the man would be as fast and deadly with his weapon as any soldier he'd encountered.

The girl was walking toward them along the bank, carrying her shoes and stockings for all the world as if she were on a picnic by the river. He still couldn't get his mind around what had happened between them. His anger and injured pride at the ease with which she'd outsmarted him had turned into something else. Something darker and more powerful than simple lust, so that he'd lost all sense of reality, of duty, of purpose in a scrambling tangle of limbs and the heated furrow of her lithe body.

And it had lost him his prisoner and almost his skin. His fury at himself was boundless.

He had quickly dismissed the possibility of calling to his men. They'd not hear him from the woods, and they certainly couldn't get to him quickly enough to support him in a fight with Gabriel and his broadsword. La Violette, however, was unarmed—Cornichet had seen to that—so he had only one serious opponent to contend with.

"Colonel, Lord Julian St. Simon, he calls himself," Gabriel declared as Tamsyn reached them. "Quite the aristocratic gentleman." He picked his teeth with a fingernail, his mild eyes regarding the colonel with the same dispassionate curiosity. "It seems you owe him a favor, little girl, but I daresay you consider it paid."

Tamsyn flushed at this barbed comment and said swiftly, "Not in the way you mean, Gabriel. We'll leave what happened back there out of any negotiations."

"Negotiations?" Julian's eyebrows quirked. "Now, what could that mean, Violette? But, forgive me, I assume you have some other name. Since we're performing formal introduction . . ." He offered a mock bow and the tension in the air between them crackled. His body still retained the memory of hers as his brain fought to banish all such memories, and he knew it had to be the same for the girl, for they'd taken that mad flight together.

"I'm called Tamsyn," she replied. "If it matters to you." She shrugged, but both the gesture and the carelessness of her tone lacked conviction.

The name was as much of a puzzle as its owner. "Oh, it matters," he assured her, adjusting his hastily tied stock, his fingers now moving in leisurely fashion through the linen folds. "Tamsyn. That's a Cornish name."

"It was my mother's choice. How do you know it's Cornish?"

"I'm a Cornishman myself," he responded. He was surprised at the sudden flash in her eyes, almost as if someone had lit a candle there.

"Are you?" she said casually. "I believe my mother's family were Cornish aristocrats too."

The colonel's rather heavy eyelids drooped. His eyes were hooded, his voice a casual drawl. "Forgive me, but what was a Cornish aristocrat doing in a Spanish bandit's bed?"

Gabriel moved, the mighty sword lifting. "Watch your tongue, Englishman," he said softly. "You insult my lady at your peril."

Julian raised a hand in placation. He didn't know whether the man was referring to La Violette, who was certainly no lady by any of the standards he understood, or to her mother, but in the face of the broadsword and the fierceness in the giant's eyes, instant retreat struck him as the only option. "Forgive me. I meant no insult to a lady." He laid a slight inflection on the last word. "But surely it's an understandable question."

"Perhaps, but it's hardly your business, sir," Tamsyn said coldly. "It's no business of any soldier." The bleakness of her expression startled him. The dark-violet eyes were looking through him, and there were ghosts in their depths.

But of course, La Violette had taken over her father's band at his death. Julian had heard some story of a raid on El Baron's mountain village by one of the rogue groups of deserters, composed of disaffected soldiers from the English and French armies, who rampaged through the Peninsula, looting, raping, murdering without qualm.

Gabriel had moved ominously closer, and he judged it politic to change the subject. "You mentioned negotiation, Violette." It seemed a more appropriate name in present circumstances. His eyebrow lifted again in question.

"There'll be no negotiating with a damned soldier," Gabriel said harshly. "Come, little girl. Since you owe the man your life, we'll grant him his. But let's be out of here, now."

"No, Gabriel, wait." Tamsyn put her hand on his arm. "We owe Cornichet," she said slowly. There was a gleam in her eye now, a slight twist to her lips. The confusion had dissipated, and her feet were back on solid ground. Cornichet had killed her men, quite apart from his treatment of her, and he should pay for that. She couldn't expect the English colonel and his men to engage in unprovoked battle with the Frenchmen—the rules of war forbade such a personal encounter. But they could help her to have a little vengeful fun with Cornichet.

"The English milord wishes me to talk a little with his commander. I might be willing to hear what Wellington has to say, without agreeing to anything in advance, of course. But I'd wish for something in exchange."

Gabriel was silent, and Julian recognized now that the man's role was not that of decision maker. St. Simon might have to watch his neck with the bodyguard, but matters of leadership were the province of La Violette.

"In exchange for what, exactly?" he asked, keeping his voice neutral.

She shrugged. "Why, in exchange for my company to Elvas, of course. I make no promises about what I might be willing to discuss with Wellington, and I'll require your assurance—the oath of a Cornish gentleman . . ." Somehow she invested the words with a wealth of derision. "Your assurance that no attempt will be made to coerce me. I will come willingly and I will leave when I wish."

Julian wanted to take her by the shoulders and shake the derision from her eyes, make her swallow the dripping contempt in her voice. What possible right or justification did she have for doubting his honor?

"And if I give those assurances," he said frigidly, "I'm to assume you'll accompany me of your own free will?"

Tamsyn smiled. "In exchange for a small service, sir, yes. I give you my word. *My* word, Lord St. Simon, is given rarely and is the more precious for that."

He didn't think it was his own personal honor she was impugning; he was tarred with some brush from her past. There was much here that he didn't understand, but he didn't need to understand this unlikely spawn of an Englishwoman and a Spanish bandit to accomplish his mission. "And the service, *señorita*?"

Her smile broadened and her eyes danced. "Cornichet's epaulets, my lord."

Gabriel's booming laugh rang out again. "Lassie, ye've more tricks in you than all the monkeys on the Rock of Gibraltar."

Tamsyn chuckled, but her eyes remained on the colonel. "Well, sir? You have twenty men. Gabriel and I will join you. Between us we should be able to dock the French colonel of his insignia."

Julian was astounded. "Good God, girl, this is a war, not some bloody game." Her eyes were sparkling, her mouth curved in a wicked grin, but the mischief was belied by the determined set of her chin and a steely glimmer behind the sparkle.

"I'm aware of that, Colonel," she said. The laughter left her face, and suddenly he was chilled by the grimness of her expression, the cold flatness of her voice. "And Cornichet won't consider it a game, either, when he's obliged to show himself to his men in the disgraced uniform of a cashiered officer.''

It was certainly a neat revenge. Such mortification would be a bitter pill for the arrogant, brutal Cornichet to swallow. But how could he justify lending his men for such a trivial purpose?

Julian stared out at the river, his mind working furiously. He'd promised Wellington he'd bring La Violette in five days to Elvas to have her petals plucked. He could do it comfortably if they left now. His twenty men were needed at the siege of Badajos. To go off on some devil-may-care avenging jaunt to humiliate Cornichet was a waste of time and manpower. But if he didn't agree, then La Violette would be lost to him, and for the first time in his career he'd have to return to headquarters to report failure.

His pride wouldn't permit such a thing. It was as simple as that. The girl held all the cards, therefore he had no choice but to play the hand she dealt him. And if he allowed himself to admit it, the thought of outwitting the barbaric Cornichet again and serving him such a trick held its appeal, even if it was an appeal more suited to the youth and boyish amusements of a junior lieutenant than of a full colonel, who was also one of Wellington's intimates. But it was well-known that Julian St. Simon had a devious mind and preferred the trickery and cunning of undercover warfare to the brute force of the battlefield.

Cornichet and his men were presumably still in some disarray outside Olivenza half a day's ride away, repairing the damage to their smoldering outpost. If they could get the business over with swiftly, with some hard riding they could still be back at Elvas within the five days he'd set himself.

His mind raced on, examining and discarding possibilities. Somehow they'd have to extract Cornichet from his men.

"Very well," he said with a shrug of resignation. "It's against my better judgment, but you hold the cards. But if you join with us, Violette, then you do so under my command. Is that agreed?"

Tamsyn shook her head. "No, milord colonel. Gabriel and I operate as free agents, as do all partisan bands when they work with your army. But we'll not be at cross purposes, I assure you."

She spoke the truth. The guerrilla bands lent their services to Wellington's army when they chose, but they operated under their own command. This band consisted only of a diminutive girl and her giant bodyguard, but La Violette obviously didn't consider that a factor.

"I'm thinking that we should surprise him at night," Tamsyn continued, not even pausing to consider that the English colonel would object to her condition. "He usually retires at around midnight, and he's generally foxed, but he always goes around the pickets. We can ambush him. Then . . . swish, swish!" She chuckled, drawing her hand through the air in two slashing motions. "It's a small enough revenge for what he did to me, let alone what he intended to do. But I'm not overly vindictive," she added with a cheerful grin.

"Is that so," St. Simon muttered. "You could have fooled me. I'd have thought losing his captive and having his camp burned around his ears would have been enough for most people."

"But that was not *my* revenge," Tamsyn pointed out, sounding surprised that he couldn't see the difference. "Taking me for yourself was your mission. It had nothing to do with making Cornichet pay for what he'd done to me and my men. Not to mention Gabriel.''

"Och, don't count me in this," Gabriel said comfortably. "I had my revenge, little girl. I broke a few heads on my way out of there. They'll not forget Gabriel McFee in a hurry."

"But there's Gilles and Pedro and Joseph and Stefan . . .''

"Aye, I've not forgotten." The giant held up his hand to halt the list of their fallen comrades. "I'm with ye, lassie.''

"Well, if that's settled, perhaps we could get on with it," Julian said impatiently, glancing up at the sun that was now well risen. "The problem is mounting you. You'll have to ride with me, Violette. But we don't have a mount among us that could take the weight of your man in addition to one of mine.''

"Dinna fash yourself wi' that," Gabriel said with an easy smile. "I've my own mount, and the lassie's is tethered over yonder." He gestured to the high ground.

"You have Cesar?" Tamsyn exclaimed. "You brought him out of there?"

"Sure, I did, little girl. I'd not leave him behind. Shame on you for thinking such a thing.''

Tamsyn reached up on tiptoe and kissed him. "I don't know how you did it, but you're a miracle worker, Gabriel. Let's go and fetch them." She turned to the colonel. "We'll meet you in your bivouac.''

St. Simon hesitated, reluctant to let her go off with her giant bodyguard, yet unsure what he could do to prevent it.

"I gave you my word," she said, her chin tilting, her eyes flashing. "Do you doubt me, milord colonel?"

He remembered the sardonic challenge she'd thrown

at him the previous night about whether he could trust the parole of a brigand. She'd offered no assurances then, and he'd chosen not to trust her. Why he should now trust the honor of a self-confessed bandit, thief, and mercenary he didn't know.

He shrugged again. "It makes little difference whether I do or not." Turning on his heel, he strode off to the small wood and the camp.

"I hope ye know what y'are doing, lassie," Gabriel observed as they walked rapidly along the bank. "El Baron would have had no truck wi' soldiers. Going off to Wellington's headquarters like this. It's not right." He shook his head, his queue swinging against his shoulders.

"I haven't said I'll tell them what they want to know," she pointed out.

"And what makes ye think they can be trusted not to squeeze it out of ye?"

"Oh, I believe milord colonel can be trusted to keep his word," she said airily, then broke into a run. "Oh, there's Cesar. And you have my rifle, and my knife. However did you get them back?"

Gabriel snorted. "Piece o' cake, lassie. They were a dozy lot, and once I'd broken a few bones, they weren't goin' to stand in my way." He tossed her onto the back of the milk-white Arabian steed before mounting his own charger, an ugly brute whose massive shoulders and powerful hocks looked well up to the weight of his huge rider.

"Besides, I have a plan," Tamsyn went on as if there'd been no interruption. She settled into the saddle and pulled the stallion's ears affectionately. "I think this milord colonel might prove useful, if I can buy his services."

"Useful to do what?" Gabriel's tone was wary. He knew from experience that her plans were rarely simple. "Buy them with what?"

Tamsyn smiled and said mysteriously, "All in good time, Gabriel."

Unreassured, but resigned, he held his peace, and they cantered back along the river, turning into the trees.

The men of the Sixth were packed up and ready to leave, standing beside their horses as the fires were put out. Julian whistled at the sight of La Violette's magnificent mount, whose Mameluke training was as obvious as the Arabian blood.

"I should imagine you had a fight to wrest that beast from Cornichet," he observed to Gabriel as they rode up.

"Ye could say that," Gabriel said, shrugging off his fight with six brawny French infantrymen. "But I had a cudgel and my broadsword. And thanks to yourself, there was enough smoke around to create some difficulties for them."

Julian ran his hand along the Arab's creamy neck, inspecting him with a cavalry officer's expertise.

"Cesar was a gift from my father on my eighteenth birthday," Tamsyn volunteered, pleased at the colonel's knowledgeable admiration for her pride and joy.

"A supreme animal," Julian said with an ironic smile. He saw that she had a knife in the sheath at her saddle and a long rifle attached to the pommel, a bandolier slung across her chest. He'd seen women armed in this way many times among the partisan bands, but the contrast of the weapons with La Violette's diminutive fairness was startling. And yet it was obvious from her easy posture that she was perfectly at home bristling with arms in her high saddle of magnificently tooled leather.

"Plunder from some Spanish grandee's stud, no doubt," he added, his ironic smile unwavering.

"A Turk, as it happens," she retorted. "He was crossing the Sierra Nevada with a complete stud and a mule train laden with gold and emeralds. My father relieved him of everything, I believe."

"Och, little girl, such lies!" Gabriel exclaimed. "El Baron had his own stud, Englishman. It was renowned throughout Spain and Portugal, and men came from all over to buy a colt, but the baron would sell only to those he chose. I've seen grown men weeping and carpeting the ground with gold for one of his horses, but the baron wouldn't budge if he took agin a man."

"Such a vivid imagination you have, *señorita*," St. Simon murmured, glancing at Tamsyn, who was looking annoyed at Gabriel's intervention.

"Not as vivid as yours, Colonel," she snapped.

He shrugged. "I suggest you devote your imagination to a plan for exercising your vengeance on Cornichet. Let's get going. I've no desire to waste any more time than necessary on this ridiculous expedition."

He swung onto his mount and called, "Sergeant, give the order to move out."

Flushed with anger, Tamsyn drew aside with Gabriel as the cavalcade trotted out of the clearing. For two pins she would have turned Cesar and galloped in the opposite direction, and there wasn't a cavalry officer under the sun who could have caught her. But her old life was over now, brought to an end first by the massacre in Puebla de St. Pedro, and then by Cornichet's ambush. Now she must plan a future, and the English colonel had somehow woven himself into that future. She needed his help in this little matter of Cornichet, but the large picture was beginning to take shape in her mind, and Colonel, Lord Julian St. Simon rode through that canvas. A Cornishman who seemed to be in the right place at the right time—although whether he would put it that way himself was open to question. A question to be answered when they reached Elvas, once Cornichet had paid his dues.

Chapter Four

SIX HOURS BROUGHT THEM TO THE OUTSKIRTS OF Olivenza. Tamsyn and the colonel had exchanged no words, and she'd ridden with Gabriel in the manner of the partisans, keeping apart from the English soldiers, riding in the hills alongside the road. Gabriel, like the phlegmatic magician he was, had produced bread, cheese, dried dates, and a wineskin of rioja from his saddlebags, and they'd eaten in the saddle as they were accustomed to doing.

Julian had kept an eye on them through his glass as they rode in the distance, but as they reached the town, the two of them rode down to the cavalcade of soldiers.

"Beggin' yer pardon, Colonel, but this seems like a rum deal to me," the sergeant muttered. "I wouldn't want to meet that bleedin' great bloke in a dark alley."

"No," Julian agreed, feeling that he owed the sergeant some explanation. "But they say La Violette always has her price, and if this little junket is the cost of bringing her to headquarters, then we must pay it."

He hadn't told the sergeant how it had happened that he'd left the bivouac with a firmly tethered prisoner and returned alone to be joined by the girl armed to the teeth on her Arab, accompanied by a gigantic bodyguard. His men could draw what conclusions they wished. They were soldiers accustomed to the strange fancies of their officers and to obeying incomprehensible orders.

"We should wait until dark before approaching the outpost," Tamsyn declared, trotting up to him. She squinted up at the dimming ball of the setting sun. "Gabriel is going to reconnoiter, to make sure Cornichet's still there."

"You may do as you wish, Violette. But my men and I will reconnoiter on our own account," he said icily. "I don't commit my men to an action on the basis of someone else's observations."

Tamsyn shrugged. "As you wish, milord colonel. But it seems a great waste of energy. I'll lay odds Gabriel is better at this sort of thing than any English soldier."

"You are, of course, entitled to your opinion." Julian turned his mount aside, signaling that his men should follow him, and they trotted away from the road and into the wood surrounding the town.

Pompous ass! Tamsyn shook her head in irritation but followed with Gabriel. In a small clearing in the cool, dim seclusion of the woods, they halted. The colonel gave soft-spoken commands to his scouts, and the two men dismounted and disappeared into the undergrowth.

"Might as well let 'em do it," Gabriel said with a cheerful shrug, pulling out his wineskin. He threw back his head, and the dark-red stream arched from the neck of the skin and into his mouth.

"Colonel?" Aware of Julian's eyes on him, he offered the skin courteously.

"Thanks." St. Simon took a welcome draft of the robust wine. As he handed it back to Gabriel, Tamsyn intercepted the skin and deftly drank herself.

Her teeth flashed pearly white as she opened her mouth and tilted her head back. Julian found himself gazing with rapt fascination at the graceful curve of her throat, the little movements as she swallowed the wine, the ruby stream pouring unbroken between her parted lips. The short cap of her hair was almost white in the gathering gloom, contrasting with the gold of her skin and the dark fringe of her eyelashes. She was like some barbarian maiden, he thought, sitting her magnificent warhorse with her rifle and her bandolier, one brown ungloved hand gripping the reins, her serviceable britches and shirt mud splattered, her boots of soft cordovan leather shabby and well-worn like the favorite riding boots of someone who spent most of her life in the saddle.

And yet there was something delicate about her too. Something distinctly flowerlike.

He dismissed this whimsy with a disgusted head shake and tore his eyes away from her. "Sergeant, the men may dismount and take a break while we wait for the scouts. They should eat, but we'll be lighting no fires."

"Aye, sir." The sergeant gave the order and the men dismounted with relief. It had been six hard hours riding over ill-paved roads, and there was much stretching and cursing as they opened saddlebags and made what supper they could with cold provisions.

Gabriel and La Violette, however, remained on horseback, looking as comfortable as if they were in armchairs. Not for the first time Julian thought that the hard English saddles with their low pommels were a poor exchange for the high-cushioned Spanish type.

The scouts returned within the hour. The French under Cornichet were still in the encampment, about half an hour deeper into the woods, busily repairing the damaged huts. They had doubled the pickets, however, and another raid would be more difficult. Not least because the night promised to be clear and pleasant, and they wouldn't have the advantage of drenching rain and thick cloud cover.

Julian frowned. He was not prepared to lose any of his men over a personal vendetta. This would have to be done with stealth, not by force. "Sergeant, keep the men here. Keep your ears open, and be ready to come up in support at the first sound of trouble."

He turned to Tamsyn. "You," he said, pointing an imperative forefinger, "and Gabriel, come with me. If we can't do this with the three of us, then it won't be done."

Tamsyn considered this. It seemed as if he were reneging on the bargain, but the bright-blue eyes were like diamond chips, the forceful mouth tight, the jutting chin set, and it rather looked as if this was the best she was going to get. But the colonel was no lightweight. She'd had ample evidence of his physical strength, and though he couldn't compete with Gabriel, he cut an impressive figure, exuding an internal power that made him an opponent to be reckoned with. And at least his men would be there to cover their retreat.

With an equable nod she dismounted, slinging her rifle over her shoulder. "We'd best approach on foot."

They crept through the undergrowth, Julian, his scarlet tunic once again concealed beneath his black boat cloak, astonished at how Gabriel, despite his size, seemed to flit and melt into the brush. Tamsyn was like a fawn, her feet barely touching the ground, hardly crushing a blade of grass as she passed. He was not as practiced at this guerrilla warfare and felt like some clumsy great ox beside his companions.

They halted about fifty yards from the encampment, where they could see a patrolling picket. Another man joined him after a minute, his rifle resting against his shoulder. They spoke together and resumed their march in opposite directions.

Staging an ambush along the picket lines was not going to be easy. "How about the latrines?" Tamsyn whispered, her eyes shining wickedly in the now-full dark. "When Cornichet pays his nightly visit, we could be waiting for him. He's a creature of habit. Every evening at around eleven he goes to the jakes, taking a glass of cognac with him."

"How do you know?" Julian peered at her in the gloom, infected, despite his attitude toward this time-wasting and dangerous jaunt, by the wicked mischief emanating from the slight figure at his elbow.

Tamsyn grimaced. "I spent two and a half days tethered in his cabin, Colonel. I had ample opportunity to observe his routine."

"Do you know where the jakes are situated?"

She nodded. "I was permitted to use them—twice a day," she added with a hiss of fury, remembering the discomfort and humiliation of her imprisonment.

Julian offered no response. If one played in a dirty world, one risked falling into the slime, and he didn't think La Violette was asking for sympathy. "So where are they?"

"The far side of the encampment, dug about ten feet within the picket line, but set apart from the main camp."

"Lead on, Violette." His expression was wry. Of all the crazy exercises he'd been involved in, this one took the prize. But this Spanish-Cornish bandit clearly had a fertile imagination when it came to devising the downfall of her enemies. Cornichet's plight would be almost as ludicrous as his own that morning, caught while taking his pleasure between the smooth thighs of a passionate plunderer.

Gabriel was grinning, much amused by Tamsyn's plot. But he too had suffered at the hands of Cornichet and his men.

They crept around the picket line. A twig snapped beneath Julian's boot, and the sound seemed to echo in the silence. Immediately Tamsyn cupped her mouth with her hands, and the haunting call of a nightjar filled the wood. Gabriel nodded his approval and Julian cursed his clumsiness.

The smell of smoke and smoldering embers still lingered in the air, and the wood was very quiet, its wildlife fled from men and fire. The trees were still leafless, and the crescent moon shone through the branches with an alarming brightness, but Gabriel and Tamsyn hugged the silvered trunks of trees, slithered on their bellies through bushes, and Julian followed them as they crawled and darted from dark patch to dark patch until they'd circled the outpost, and the faint odor of sewage wafted from beyond the picket line where the latrine trenches were dug.

"The officers' latrine is at the far end, closest to the camp," Tamsyn whispered, her voice a mere breath on the air. "Their section has a canvas cover—as if what they do is any different from the common soldier," she added with derision.

"I should imagine you were glad enough of the privacy," Julian observed dryly, and was rewarded by a quick, rueful grin of acknowledgment. She was an infuriatingly opinionated girl, he reflected, but at least she knew when to yield an issue.

A staccato hail rang out from the picket line, and they dropped to the ground behind a thornbush. Tamsyn, squashed between the two men, slowly raised her head to look over the bush. There was another shout from the camp, and the colonel abruptly pushed her head down into the dirt.

"They haven't seen us," she protested in a fierce whisper, struggling against the pressure of his hand. "They're changing pickets."

"Your hair in the moonlight is like a damn torch," he hissed against her ear. "Cover it with that bandanna you're wearing."

Tamsyn pulled off the dark kerchief at her throat and tied it over her head. It was annoying to be reminded of this elementary precaution by someone she considered a mere novice at this game, but she couldn't quarrel with the instruction.

"It takes the picket about three minutes to patrol his section," Gabriel whispered. He'd been concentrating on the activity at the picket line throughout the exchange between the colonel and Tamsyn. "Long enough for one of us to get across."

"I'll go first," Tamsyn said. "You follow, Gabriel, and the colonel can come last."

"No." Julian stated. "You'll come between us. That way, if anything happens and you're caught, we'll be able to attack from both sides."

"Surely the same applies to either of you?"

"You're the one Cornichet wants," he snapped. "And having winkled you out of there once, I'm damned if I'm going to lose you again. It's bad enough indulging you in this ridiculous whim without jeopardizing my own mission more than I can help."

For a second Tamsyn debated with herself. He couldn't stop her if she simply launched herself across the ground. Gabriel would follow, and they could manage without help from this damned supercilious colonel. But he did have a point. Pride warred with common sense, and the latter won.

She made no response, merely hunkered down behind the bush, frowning fiercely. Julian gave Gabriel a nod, and as the picket turned at his post to march down the line, the giant leaped forward. He clung to the bare ground, but he was visible for a terrifying few moments under the moonlight; then he disappeared into the shadows beyond the picket line.

The two left behind waited, unmoving. The picket returned and left. Tamsyn didn't wait for the colonel's nod. She darted across the space, crouching low, a diminutive flying figure, and then she too disappeared into the shadows.

Julian waited alone, no longer concerned with the military merits of this exercise. Now that it was begun, all his concentration was on successful completion. His moment came, and he moved out of concealment and ran, conscious of his sword bumping against his hip. His foot caught on a stone and he almost tripped, cursing his clumsiness, but in the full regalia of a cavalry officer he was more encumbered than his companions.

"Over here." Tamsyn's hissing whisper beckoned him from the gloom, and he dropped to the ground beside the other two behind a woodpile. The camp was surprisingly quiet for this time of night, but they could hear subdued voices from the scattered tents and huts, an occasional burst of laughter, a shout of complaint.

"Let's get in place." Tamsyn moved forward on the words, but again Julian caught her arm, his fingers hard, his eyes glinting in the darkness.

"Same order as before."

She acceded in silence, and they waited while Gabriel threaded his way through the trees to the humped canvas shape of the officers' latrine and disappeared behind it.

"You, now."

The English colonel seemed to think he was in charge, but there was no time to stop and argue the toss with him. Tamsyn flitted away, cherishing the thought of revenge on Cornichet. It was worth putting up with a little of the English milord's autocratic manner to achieve it.

At precisely eleven o'clock Colonel Cornichet emerged from his hut, a glass of cognac in his hand. He paused and looked up at the sky, smelling the freshness of the air. Now that the rain had stopped, the English siege of Badajos would move apace. His own force was too small to go to the support of the citizens and garrison of the town, but if he hadn't lost La Violette, he'd now be in a position to mop up a few of the local partisan bands, and a map of the passes they used through the mountains would have been an invaluable contribution to the struggling French armies.

He'd planned and almost pulled off a neat coup that would have brought him the congratulations of his superiors and almost certainly a promotion. Something that would have taken him out of this godforsaken land before the miseries of summer came down on them. Instead he'd been outwitted by the English, who were now presumably in possession of all Violette's vital information.

A disgruntled frown drew his eyebrows together as he strode through the camp, making his accustomed tour of the pickets in a dour silence that none of his men chose to break, before he turned and walked purposefully toward the latrines.

"There he goes," an infantryman observed sotto voce to a companion. "Old man's regular as clockwork." A ribald response brought a guffaw from both of them as the colonel pushed aside the canvas curtain and disappeared from view.

He was preparing to make himself comfortable on the wooden slats resting over the trench when the tip of a knife poked through the canvas wall at the side of the enclosure. He stared, for a moment unsure what he was seeing, and then the canvas split with a harsh rending, and to his eternal astonishment the small face of La Violette appeared in the opening.

"*Bon soir,* Colonel Cornichet." Her white teeth flashed in a far from friendly smile, and the serviceable knife she held pressed into his throat. "We have a little unfinished business, you and I. Don't shout," she added softly, seeing him gather his wits. "If you open your mouth, my friend here will blow your brains to kingdom come."

Cornichet gazed stunned to where Gabriel's pale eyes regarded him with deceptive mildness from behind the girl. The muzzle of a rifle jutted through the torn canvas.

"*Sacré bleu,*" the colonel muttered at this apparition, as he fumbled desperately with his dropped britches, trying not to move his head against the tip of the knife.

"It's not a pleasant sensation, is it, Colonel?" the girl said, still smiling, but her eyes were as flat and cold as violet stones. The knife pricked, and a bead of blood formed and trickled down to stain the white folds of his stock.

Cornichet's Adam's apple moved convulsively, and the tip of the knife slid upward, pressing into the soft skin beneath his chin. He gave up trying to adjust his dress and stood immobile, sweat gathering on his forehead.

"There's an old saying, Colonel. Do as you would be done by," La Violette continued. "And something else I recall about the sweetness of vengeance." The knife tip traced a circle on his skin.

"For God's sake," he whispered hoarsely. "If you're going to do it, then get on with it."

She shook her head and her eyes made him shiver, but before she could say anything, St. Simon spoke with brusque impatience from the darkness behind her.

"In the name of goodness, girl! You're as bad as a cat with a mouse. Let's be done with this and get out of here."

Cornichet stared, dumbstruck as a tall cloaked Englishman pushed the colonel's tormentor aside, thrusting her behind him. He held a cavalry sword in his right hand and looked thoroughly exasperated.

"Forgive me, Cornichet. But there's something I want from you." His sword flickered twice, so quickly the Frenchman had scarcely time to draw breath, and the rich gold braided epaulets fell with a splash into the latrine trench.

"And his buttons," La Violette demanded from the darkness.

Julian sighed. "Your pardon, Cornichet, but I struck a bargain with this vengeful wretch." Again his sword flicked, and one by one the colonel's gold tunic buttons with the Napoleonic eagle stamped on them followed the epaulets into the latrine.

Cornichet seemed to be struggling with his senses, his eyes popping, his jaw working, but before he could gather himself together, his visitor had jumped sideways, back through the ripped canvas, and suddenly he was alone in the small odiferous space. If it weren't for the hole in the canvas and his own denuded uniform, he could almost believe he'd dreamed the whole mortifying episode.

Then he grabbed up his britches, yanking them to his waist, bellowing, *"A moi . . . à moi,"* as he burst out into the encampment.

Men came running from all sides, and the irate colonel screamed instructions and garbled explanations as he fumbled with the waist of his britches, his buttonless tunic flapping open.

Julian realized that Gabriel had vanished as they dived into the woods, hearing the uproar behind them. "We have to split up," Tamsyn shouted as they raced neck and neck through the undergrowth. "If we separate, it'll be much harder for them to follow us."

"I'm not letting you out of my sight," the colonel gritted, seizing her wrist when she ducked sideways.

"I gave you my word!"

"I'm still not letting you out of my sight. Now, run, girl!"

"What do you think I'm doing?" she demanded crossly. "And if you had a brain between your ears, milord colonel, you'd realize that my horse is with your men, and I'll be damned if I'm about to leave him with you."

"I believe in added insurance" was the cool response.

"You don't know the first thing about guerrilla warfare." It was the last word from either of them on the subject as they pounded onward, heedless of any noise or tracks they might be making. Speed was all that counted.

Confused shouts came from behind them, and rifles cracked erratically. Someone yelled in pain, and there was a roar of fury.

"Sounds like they're shooting each other," Tamsyn gasped with a gleeful little chuckle. "They don't know what they're looking for. Just imagine Cornichet trying to explain what happened. . . ."

"Stop gloating and save your breath," Julian ordered, although his own lips twitched at the image of the usually immaculate colonel with his waxed mustaches standing in his drawers and his desecrated tunic trying to describe his encounter in the latrine.

A bullet whined over their heads, and suddenly all desire to laugh abandoned them. They were drawing close to the outskirts of the wood where the colonel's men awaited them, but close wasn't good enough with bullets clipping one's ears.

Tamsyn veered sideways, dragging the colonel with her, pushing through what looked to him to be an impenetrable tangle of prickly bushes, but somehow a path revealed itself, although the bushes tore at their clothes.

Then they broke free into the clearing. The sergeant, hearing the uproar, had the twenty men of the Sixth mount, swords in their hands, ready to charge whatever might come at them. Tamsyn scrambled onto Cesar's back just as Gabriel crashed through the undergrowth, his broadsword in his hands. He raised a hand in greeting, his expression as benign and untroubled as always, and swung onto his own charger.

"The men are spoiling for a fight, sir," the sergeant

said, stroking the hilt of his sword. "Reckon they deserve their fun."

Colonel St. Simon shook his head. "There'll be fighting aplenty at Badajos." He wheeled his horse, ordering his men forward with an upraised hand.

The cavalcade galloped from the clearing just as a small group of pursuing French burst through, but they were on foot and could do nothing but watch in frustration as their quarry disappeared into the darkness.

St. Simon drew level with Tamsyn's milk-white Arabian. He noticed that she had a long scratch on her cheek from the thorny bushes they'd encountered on their retreat, but it didn't seem to bother her.

How the hell did she manage to claim kinship with some Cornish family? It was the most extraordinary thing, if true. He caught himself looking for signs of English blood in her complexion. She didn't have the olive skin, black hair, and dark eyes of the typical Spaniard; but fair skin, pale hair, and violet eyes, while more typically English, were not unheard of among Spanish families. On balance, there was nothing in her appearance to confirm or deny her claim. This hybrid had inherited some vigorous characteristics from somewhere, though, characteristics more likely to be associated with the robber baron than some demure English maiden . . . ruthlessness and arrogance, to name but two.

"I trust you're satisfied that I've fulfilled my side of our bargain?" he said with an ironic twist of his mouth.

"Perfectly, milord colonel," she responded. "And don't pretend you didn't enjoy it, because I could see how your eyes were twinkling."

"I'm very sure my eyes never twinkle," the colonel said, revolted at such an image.

"Oh, but they do," she assured him with a grin, her perfect teeth glimmering in the moonlight. "You've just never been looking in a mirror at the right moment."

There seemed no adequate response to this, so he changed the subject. "I'll rest the horses when it's absolutely necessary, but other than that, I don't intend to stop until we reach Elvas."

"Cesar has a great deal of stamina," she said placidly. "And he was well rested in Cornichet's camp."

"You, on the other hand, are very short of sleep," he observed.

"I can sleep in the saddle. I've often done so." She cast him a sideways glance. "Don't worry, milord colonel. I'm perfectly prepared to uphold my end of the bargain. And I've never yet dropped out of the line of march."

Once again he could detect the currents of energy surging through the slim, upright figure. She was radiating purpose and determination, and he was instantly uneasy. Whenever he'd sensed that determined energy before, La Violette had been up to no good.

Chapter Five

THE STEADY BOOMING OF THE GUNS BESIEGING THE WALLS OF the Spanish town of Badajos drowned all other sound as the cavalcade approached the town standing on a hill in the midst of a flat plain. The sky was metallic, clouds hanging low over the gray earth, creating a uniform colorlessness, broken only by the scarlet tunics of the cavalrymen.

Julian, riding ahead of the troop, was watching Gabriel and Violette, as usual riding off to one side on slightly higher ground. He couldn't hear what they were saying, but from their gestures it seemed they were engaged in some altercation. The girl was gesticulating fiercely, her body, fluid in the saddle as she made her points. The giant Gabriel in contrast seemed to exude a rocklike obstinacy, occasionally shaking his head in a sharp, brief negative.

They were a two-hour ride from headquarters in the Portuguese border town of Elvas, and Julian would be bringing in his flower just within the five days he'd set himself. Unfortunately, he wasn't bringing in a submissive, intimidated prisoner ready to have her petals plucked, but a vigorous, self-determining mercenary who might be induced to sell her secrets, but certainly

wouldn't meekly divulge them for the asking. It would
be interesting to see what Wellington made of her . . .
and of his colonel's part in the play.

Julian grimaced. He'd have to find an explanation for
how he'd lost his prisoner and had to agree to a negoti-
ated settlement. The truth was far too mortifying. He
could only hope that the brigand would keep her
mouth shut about that riverside madness.

He became aware that the two were cantering toward
him. Gabriel was not looking happy; the girl's expression was neutral. They reached him and turned their
horses to ride alongside him.

"While I'm gone, I shall hold you responsible for the
bairn, Englishman," Gabriel announced gruffly, his
hand, in what seemed to Julian very pointed fashion,
resting on the hilt of his massive broadsword.

"Gone? Gone where?"

"Never you mind, but you're responsible, mark that
well."

Julian shook his head with a half laugh of disbelief.
"You expect me to be responsible for the actions of La
Violette? Good God, man, I know my limitations."

"Not her actions, but her safety," Gabriel declared
before Tamsyn could voice her own indignation.

"And I suppose it doesn't occur to you that one has
something to do with the other?" Julian said acidly.

"I am responsible for my own actions," Tamsyn said
impatiently. "And my own safety. Gabriel, you're being
an old woman."

"El Baron left your safety in *my* hands." There was a
mulish set to the giant's mouth. "And if y'are going off
on this frolic on your own, little girl, then I'll keep faith
with your father as I see fit." He glared at St. Simon.
"So, English Colonel, any harm comes to one hair of

her head, and I'll cleave your head from your shoulders."

Tamsyn raised her eyes heavenward. "No harm is going to come to me in the English headquarters, Gabriel."

"No, that I'll guarantee," Julian said, deciding to ignore Gabriel's extremely unfriendly threat. "For as long as she's a guest of headquarters. But if she steps outside Elvas, then it's out of my hands. I'm no nursemaid."

"And I don't need one," Tamsyn snapped. "Or a bodyguard. Do be off now, Gabriel. The sooner you go, the sooner you'll be back."

"And I've your word you'll not move from Elvas until I return?" He glowered, clearly very unhappy.

"You have it." She leaned over and lightly brushed his cheek with her fingertips, her smile soft, her eyes warm. "Don't fret, now. I'll be quite safe, and you know this has to be done."

Gabriel sighed. "If you say so, little girl." He wheeled his charger and cantered away, raising a hand in farewell.

"Poor Gabriel, he really doesn't want to go," Tamsyn said, still with that fond smile. "He can't bear to let me out of his sight, not since . . ." She stopped, her eyes clouding, the smile vanishing.

"Since . . . ?" Julian prompted.

Tamsyn shrugged. "History, milord colonel." She shaded her eyes, gazing across the plain to the walls of Badajos. The ground beneath them was shaking now with the bombardment, and the whine of shells from the returning French fire could clearly be heard.

"Where's he going?"

Again she shrugged. "Just to fetch something. We're getting close."

It seemed that Violette had said all she intended to about Gabriel's mysterious journey. He nodded. "We're concentrating the bombardment on the bastions of Santa Maria and La Trinidad."

"How soon does Wellington expect Soult to get here from Cadiz?"

"You are well informed," he said with an ironic raised eyebrow. The impending arrival of the French marshal to relieve Badajos was one of Wellington's main anxieties.

"Of course. I fight this war, too, Colonel."

"You fight for your own gain," he said bluntly.

Her eyes flashed. "As does your army, sir. Only the partisans fight simply for their country, and I fight with them."

"You deny you sell your services?" he demanded.

She gave him a look of supreme contempt. "To those who can afford them, I sell them. To those who can't, I give them. Sound business principles, milord colonel. And war is business, as you damn well know. Men get rich in wartime."

"Profiteers," he stated in disgust.

"And what are you in it for, English milord?" she asked with the same contempt. "Nothing as vulgar as wealth, of course. So what is it? Glory . . . honor . . . rank?"

Julian made no response. It was true he pursued all those goals, but he fought for the honor of his country, for loyalty and patriotism. He wasn't going to explain such concepts to a mercenary who would only mock them.

They were skirting the trenches now outside the walls, and the sound of the bombardment was deafening. Tamsyn's Arab was skittish, tossing his head, lifting his feet high, seeming to pick his way with delicacy over the soft, rain-soaked ground. The cavalry horses, on the other hand, were untroubled by the noise and the uneven terrain and plodded steadily on.

When a shell burst a few feet from them, throwing up a spume of mud, Cesar whinnied in high-pitched fright and plunged sideways. Julian automatically reached for Tamsyn's bridle to steady the animal.

"Take your hand off!" she commanded with such ferocity his hand dropped immediately. Expertly, she brought the animal under control, speaking to him softly in Spanish, and when he was quiet, turned again to the colonel, her eyes spurting flame. "How dare you presume to touch my bridle?"

"I'm sorry." He was genuinely taken aback by her fury. "I'm used to riding with my sister. She's not a natural rider, and I have to be on the alert all the time."

"Well, I am *not* your sister," she declared, still furious.

"Fortunately, in the circumstances," he murmured, unable to help himself, a wicked glimmer in his eye.

Tamsyn glared at him for a minute, then went into a peal of laughter. "How right you are, Colonel. There are some vices too heinous even for mercenary bandits."

His amusement, misplaced as it was, died as quickly as it had arisen. "We will not speak of that incident again, if you please," he said with an awkward formality.

Tamsyn glanced sideways at his set face, and a mischievous smile twitched her mouth. "You'd not wish your commander in chief to know you'd been dallying with a prisoner, I daresay."

"No, damn you, I would not!" he snapped.

"And you wouldn't wish it to occur again?" she mused. "How unflattering of you, Colonel. I confess I would enjoy a repetition."

"Forgive my bluntness, but I would not," he stated flatly, turning his horse aside. "Sergeant, you and the men may leave us here and return to the brigade. I intend to cross the river by the east pontoon."

"Right you are, sir." The sergeant barked an order to the troop behind him, and they cantered off toward the city of tents forming the army's encampment between the Guadiana and the siegeworks. The colonel and his companion rode along the river bank toward one of the pontoon bridges connecting the siegeworkings with headquarters at Elvas.

Tamsyn nodded to herself. Somehow she didn't think the colonel was telling the truth. How could anyone, having once enjoyed that explosion of ecstasy, not hanker for more. Cecile's voice spoke in her memory, soft with sensual laughter, telling her daughter that lovemaking was an appetite that grew whereon it fed. Tamsyn could hear the baron's answering chuckle, see his dark hawk's eyes fixed on her mother's face as if he would devour her.

A familiar wave of sorrow washed over her. She didn't resist it, simply waited for it to recede. The grief was for her own loss, since it was not possible to imagine two such joined souls as separated, even in death.

They crossed the pontoon into the small town of Elvas, the guards coming to attention as the colonel passed. The cobbled streets were thronged with soldiers in the green tunics of riflemen or the scarlet of infantry and cavalry; aide-de-camps hurried between command posts; laden commissary drays lumbered through town on their way to supply the troops in the trenches. Cesar

shied as a mangy dog darted out of an alley pursued by a
tribe of ragged urchins.

"That animal is too high-strung for his own good,"
Julian observed as Tamsyn soothed the horse.

"He's not accustomed to towns," she said, reacting
with asperity to this criticism of her beloved Cesar.
"He's not used to being surrounded by people. But he'll
carry me without flagging for a hundred miles along a
mountain track, and he'd outrun any beast you have in
your stables, and over any terrain, milord colonel."

"Doubtless." He contented himself with the dry observation, wishing she wouldn't call him that, it had
such a sardonic ring to it.

He turned his horse aside into the stableyard at the
rear of Wellington's headquarters. "Presumably that
sensitive beast will behave himself with the grooms
here?"

"Cesar has beautiful manners," she retorted, swinging down to the cobbles with an agile movement that
belied her fatigue. A groom came running over, his eyes
wide at the sight of the magnificent Arab.

"Eh, that's a beauty an' no mistake, sir," he said
admiringly to the colonel, his eyes darting curiously to
St. Simon's unusual companion.

"Yes, but he's high-strung," the colonel said. "So be
careful with him. I don't want to find myself looking for
a replacement."

"You wouldn't find one," Tamsyn declared, handing
the reins to the groom. "He's unique." She stroked the
animal's neck, murmuring incomprehensible sounds
that clearly soothed the horse. "Take him away," she
said to the groom. "He'll be quiet enough now."

"Let's go." St. Simon spoke with an abrupt brusque-

ness. He turned and strode toward a flight of outside
stairs at the rear of the wooden building.

Tamsyn followed, aware of her fatigue now as an
almost deadening exhaustion. She was in no fit condition to negotiate with Wellington. She needed food and
sleep before attempting the audacious task she'd set herself. A lot would depend on what kind of man the
English commander in chief proved to be. From what
she'd heard, he was of volatile temperament except on
the battlefield, capable of flaying his own senior officers
in one breath and offering the most urbane and civilized
conversation in the next. He was also known to have a
fondness for the female sex. Whether she could capital-
ize on that remained to be seen. Filthy and bedraggled as
she was at the moment, Tamsyn doubted she would
create a favorable impression.

At the top of the stairs the colonel opened a door,
and they entered a square landing at the head of an
internal staircase. The space was set up as an office, and
a harassed brigade-major, sitting at a deal table, looked
up from the mountain of paper in front of him.

"Colonel." He came to his feet, saluting. "The Peer
will be glad to see you, sir."

"Fretting, is he?" Julian returned the salute, glancing
toward the closed door behind the aide-de-camp.

"Something chronic," the man said with a rueful
grin. "We tried to blow up the dam the Froggies constructed outside the San Pedro bastion and didn't get
anywhere, and old Soult's on the march." Unable to
hide his fascination, he scrutinized the small figure
standing just behind the colonel and said, "He'll be glad
of some good news for once."

"Mmm." The colonel contented himself with the
brief mumble. "Keep an eye on her," he said shortly,

ignoring Tamsyn's swift indrawn breath, and strode to the door, knocking briskly before entering.

Tamsyn strolled over to a window at the head of the stairs and perched on the broad sill. She regarded the brigade-major thoughtfully. "Does English hospitality run to a glass of wine . . . or even water? Riding for two days is thirsty work."

The man looked dismayed, casting a quick glance around as if for assistance.

Tamsyn sighed. "Contrary to appearances, I'm here of my own free will. I assure you I'm not about to run away, and there's not the slightest need to 'keep an eye on me.' "

"But the colonel—"

"To the devil with the colonel," she said crossly. "He's in a bad mood, that's all. Now, could you please bring me something to drink?"

The brigade-major rose to his feet, his expression still uncertain. The girl didn't carry herself like any prisoner he'd come across, and the instruction to keep an eye on her was fairly vague . . . and it was certainly true that Colonel, Lord St. Simon hadn't looked to be in the best of tempers.

He compromised by locking the door to the outside stairs, reasoning that she couldn't use the inside staircase without alerting him, and went downstairs to summon an orderly to bring a carafe of water.

While she waited, Tamsyn looked down on the street. Her observation seemed merely idle, but in fact her eyes were taking in everything, assessing the mood and efficiency of the soldiers as they went about their business. Elvas at the moment closely resembled El Baron's almost military encampments in the mountain villages where she'd grown up, and she knew what she was looking for. On the whole, the atmosphere seemed buoyant, as if the men were comfortable with their present military operation. Of course, the men at headquarters would have a different viewpoint from those entrenched in the parallels before Badajos. Investing a town was generally a grim, frustrating business, and Badajos was holding out much longer than it had any right to. And the longer it held out, the more savage would be its taking.

Tamsyn shuddered, her mouth twisting in disgust. She knew that the old feudal rules of warfare still applied. If a besieged city surrendered in a gracious and timely fashion once it was clear it couldn't hold out, then its conquerors would be magnanimous. If it didn't, it was assumed its inhabitants asked for what they would get when the victorious besiegers poured through the breaches.

Soldiers, she thought. Savage beasts, whatever uniform they wore, whatever righteous cause they would tout. They were all the same.

The aide-de-camp came back, followed by an orderly with a carafe of water and a glass. Tamsyn turned from the window, and the power of the unfocused loathing in her violet eyes made them both draw back for an instant. Then it was gone, and she accepted the glass with a neutral nod of thanks.

Within the commander in chief's sanctum it was warm, a fire burning in the grate against the dullness of the day. Wellington poured wine for himself and St. Simon. "So you wrested her from Cornichet's hands. Much trouble?"

"Not too much." Julian sipped his wine. "At least not at that point."

Wellington raised an eyebrow at this caveat but didn't

pursue it. He moved to stand in front of the fire, his back to the cheerful glow. "How much had she told them?"

"Nothing. We arrived in the nick of time . . . quite literally." He explained briefly how he'd discovered La Violette. "We were away from there with no casualties and made camp a few hours later."

He paused. He was coming to the tricky part of his narrative. "The next morning the girl had personal needs to attend to. I escorted her beyond the camp to the river where there was an outcrop of rock. She was tethered by the ankle to my sword belt." He drank again. Wellington remained silent.

"She has a giant of a bodyguard. A Scotsman. He managed to escape from Cornichet's camp under cover of the fire we'd set. He followed us, and I'm afraid he sprang out at me while I was waiting for Violette to . . ."

"Quite so." Wellington waved a hand in comprehension. "He disarmed you?"

Julian nodded morosely. "I was a damn fool." *If you only knew how much of a fool.*

"But you still brought her in?"

"Yes, with my assurance that she's free to leave whenever she chooses; but she's prepared to sell her information for the right price."

"Which is?"

Julian shook his head. "As yet, she hasn't said."

"And this gigantic bodyguard?"

"She sent him off on some errand. He's to find her here on his return."

"A mysterious mercenary," mused the commander. He rubbed his backside meditatively in the fire's warmth, his eyes resting on the colonel's countenance.

He could read the man's chagrin, his sense of having failed in his mission, although by any standards it was only a technical failure. But Julian St. Simon didn't tolerate failure from anyone and least of all from himself.

"Let's invite her in," he said after a moment. "Hear what she has to say."

Julian nodded and said slowly, "By the way, she's not quite what you might expect. She's half-English. By some extraordinary quirk of circumstance her mother was Cornish, or so she claims. And gently bred into the bargain."

Wellington whistled. "A gently bred Englishwoman bedded with a notorious brigand! It's beyond belief."

"I agree. But why would she invent such a tale?"

Wellington scratched his long, bony nose. "No reason that I can think of."

Julian shrugged his own incomprehension. He strode to the door and opened it. "Violette."

Tamsyn slid off the windowsill and came over to the door, leaving her empty glass on the brigade-major's desk. She cast the colonel a sideways glance as she brushed past him into the presence of the commander in chief.

Wellington inclined his head in a slight bow of greeting, his eyes running over the small figure in her shabby, mud-splattered britches and boots. She still wore her bandolier, her rifle slung over her shoulder, the knife at her belt. And yet, despite this, he thought there was something almost forlorn about her. She seemed very young and very alone as she stood there regarding him with an indefinable air of challenge.

"I understand you have something to sell me," he stated.

"If the price is right," she agreed.

"And what is your price?"

Tamsyn shook her head. "Forgive me, but I'd like time to rest before we begin to negotiate. I don't know as yet exactly what you wish me to tell you."

She cast St. Simon another sidelong glance, one so redolent of sensual languor that it took his breath away. "Perhaps the colonel could show me where I may rest for a while."

Abruptly his body sang with memory, his blood flowing hot and swift. *God's grace, but she could become an addiction.*

He had to get away from her, from the dangerous temptation in those wicked violet eyes, in that lean, compact little body.

He'd brought the girl in, his task was over. How Wellington conducted the negotiations was none of his business.

"You'll have to excuse me, I must return to my brigade," he said frigidly, turning to leave. As he did so, the girl suddenly swayed on her feet, her hand reaching blindly for something to hold on to.

"What is it?" He'd reached her in one stride, encircling her with his arm. Immediately she leaned into him, a tiny, vulnerable figure against his own physical breadth.

Tamsyn closed her eyes, keeping her head bowed against his tunic to hide her satisfaction. Cecile hadn't been exaggerating about the English gentleman's foolish chivalry. She wanted Lord St. Simon at her side throughout her stay in Elvas, and she was quite willing to resort to trickery to achieve that purpose.

"What is it?" he repeated. "Are you ill?"

"I'm just very tired," she said, her voice weak. "I'm sorry . . . so silly of me, I feel quite faint."

"Come to the fire." Wellington was all concern and consideration. "Take a glass of wine, that'll revive you." He poured a glass, looking worriedly over his shoulder as the colonel half carried the girl to a chair by the fire.

"Here we are." Wellington handed her the glass. "Drink it down, now . . . that's the ticket." He nodded approvingly as obediently she sipped.

She raised her head and smiled at him, a faint, tremulous little smile. "So kind . . . thank you, sir."

Julian was still leaning over her, one arm at her back. Suddenly he withdrew it as if he'd been scalded. The little *diablillo* was up to her tricks again, he was convinced of it. He moved away and stood resting one arm along the mantelpiece, regarding the drooping, bravely smiling bandit with a sardonic glare. What the devil was she up to?

"Julian, we must find her a comfortable billet at once. I'll ask young Sanderson what he can come up with." Wellington bustled to the door to consult with the brigade-major, whose main task was to fix and contrive and organize for his commanding officer, however bizarre the circumstances.

"What are you up to?" the colonel demanded softly. "You're not fooling me with this swooning-maiden act, Violette."

Tamsyn raised her eyes, her expression hurt. "I don't know what you can mean. I can't even remember when I last slept in a bed. I'm exhausted."

She had every reason to be, and yet he remained unconvinced.

"Sanderson . . . a remarkable young fellow . . . knows just the billet, hard by the hospital." Rubbing his hands, Wellington came back to the fire. "He says there's a pleasant woman there who'll attend to you, my dear. And when you've rested, you'll dine with me and m'staff."

His eyes rested on her face, and they were sharp and shrewd despite his apparent geniality. "We'll discuss how we can assist each other a little later."

"You're too kind, sir," she said with a weary smile.

"Julian, you'll see her settled and bring her back here to dine," the commander in chief said, suddenly brisk.

"I really should return to my brigade, sir."

"Yes . . . yes, of course. But later, man, later."

There was nothing for it. Julian sighed and acceded with a curt nod in Tamsyn's direction. "Come."

She rose to her feet a little unsteadily, but Lord St. Simon seemed to have lost his chivalrous instincts. He remained standing by the fireplace, his unwavering gaze as sardonic as before. Oh, well, Tamsyn reflected with an inner shrug, she'd achieved what she'd intended for the moment. Wellington regarded her with sympathy rather than hostility, and the colonel was still at her side.

She offered Wellington another feeble smile of thanks and tottered to the door, the colonel on her heels. Her demeanor changed once they were outside, the door firmly closed behind them. She glanced up at her companion with a mischievous wink.

He inhaled sharply, then spun around to address the brigade-major. "Lieutenant, where am I to find this lodging?"

"A widow called Braganza, sir," Sanderson said. "The whitewashed cottage beside the hospital. I've sent an orderly to alert her, so she'll be expecting you." He stared with now unabashed curiosity at Violette. "She speaks only Portuguese. Does . . . does . . ."

"Yes, of course I do," Tamsyn said with a touch of impatience at what struck her as an absurd question. She'd spent her life roaming across the borders of Portugal, Spain, and France.

Julian said nothing, merely strode ahead of her down the stairs and out into the street. Tamsyn had to run to catch up with him. "Don't go so fast, I really am exhausted."

"You may pick some other gull for your tricks," he said tautly. "I don't know what the devil you're up to, and I don't give a damn. The sooner I can wash my hands of you, the happier I shall be."

"Temper, temper," Tamsyn murmured. "I wish I knew what I'd done to arouse it. It seems most unjust to me, but then I suppose you're one of those people of uncertain temper who vent their frustrations whenever the whim takes them. I've heard of such people, although I count myself fortunate that until now I haven't had many dealings—"

"Have you finished?" He interrupted this meandering muse, unsure whether he wanted to laugh or scream his vexation to the four winds.

"I hadn't," she said, sounding aggrieved. "But if you don't care for plain speaking . . ." She shrugged.

"On the contrary," he declared, tight-lipped. "I'm something of an exponent myself. Do you wish to hear a little?"

Tamsyn didn't answer. She sidestepped a puddle with an agile leap that made nonsense of her claims to exhaustion and said cheerfully, "That must be the widow's house up ahead on the left. It's the only whitewashed one on the street."

Senhora Braganza, well accustomed to the sight of

women partisans, showed little amazement at Tamsyn's appearance. Insisting they inspect the accommodations, she showed them upstairs to a small whitewashed chamber under the eaves.

"This will do beautifully," Tamsyn said, interrupting the widow's voluble description of the chamber's amenities. "All I need is a bed. And hot water."

The widow returned downstairs to see to the water, and Julian, who'd been standing by the window looking out on the street in front of the cottage, said brusquely, "I'll be on my way."

"Oh, don't be in such a hurry." Tamsyn went swiftly to the door, leaning against it, barring his way. She smiled at him. "Why so prudish, milord colonel? We have the time, we have even a bed."

"I do not have the inclination," he declared harshly. "Move aside."

She shook her head, that mischievous smile in her eyes again. She tossed her rifle onto the bed and with a deft movement shrugged off the bandolier, letting it fall to the floor. Then her hands were at her belt and he seemed powerless to move, watching as if only his eyes were alive, imprisoned in a body of stone, as she pushed off her britches and began to unbutton her shirt. The small, perfect breasts were revealed, their rosy crowns pertly erect. She moved away from the door and stepped toward him, her eyes never leaving his face.

He put his hands on her breasts, feeling how they filled his palms. He gazed down at the delicate tracery of blue veins beneath the milk-white skin. The pulse at her throat was beating fast, and the intricate silver locket quivered against her flesh.

Tamsyn didn't move, merely held herself still for his

touch as his hands slid down her rib cage, spanned the slender waist, slipped to her back, his fingers insinuating themselves into the waist of her drawers, creeping down over the taut roundness of her buttocks.

"Goddamn it, girl," he said, his voice husky in the quiet, dim room. "Goddamn it, girl, what are you doing to me?"

"It's more a case of what are you doing to *me*?" she said as his hands squeezed her backside, pressing her against his loins where his flesh thrust iron hard against the constraint of his britches.

The sound of heavy footsteps laboring up the wooden stairs outside broke his enchantment. The mist of passion left his bright-blue eyes, and he pulled his hands loose from her skin as if she were a burning brand.

And then he was gone from the room, brushing past Senhora Braganza as she toiled up the stairs with a steaming copper jug, and out into the lowering afternoon filled with the incessant sound of the bombardment.

He walked fast to the stables to reclaim his horse, and the groom quailed at the blue blazing light in the colonel's eyes beneath the thick red-gold eyebrows, and the close-gripped mouth in the grim set of his jaw. He rode out of Elvas and into the encampment to his own tent and the reassuring sanity of his own men. He must be losing his mind. She was a grubby, manipulative, unfeminine, mercenary hellion, and she stirred him to the root of his being.

Tamsyn watched him from the window as he strode down the street as if all the devils in hell were on his heels. "How very ungallant of you, milord colonel," she murmured to herself. "Whatever can you be afraid of? Not of me, surely?"

A tiny smile quirked her lips as she turned from the window to discuss with the widow Braganza the sorry condition of her clothes.

Chapter Six

"WHERE'S OUR GUEST, JULIAN?" THE COMMANDER IN CHIEF asked as the colonel entered his apartments before dinner that evening.

"I've sent Sanderson to escort her here," Julian said, nodding a greeting to the five men, all members of the commander in chief's staff, gathered to join Wellington for dinner.

"So what d'you think of her, Julian?" Major Carson handed him a glass of sherry. "We're all agog."

"I wouldn't trust her any farther than I can throw her," St. Simon stated flatly.

"Considering what a tiny little thing she is, that would be quite a distance." Wellington laughed at his own witticism, the sound remarkably like the neighing of a horse.

Julian's smile was dour. "You fell for that little act she put on this afternoon."

"Act?" Wellington raised an eyebrow.

"Trembling and swaying and tottering all over the place. She was exhausted, I grant you that. I don't suppose she's had more than a few hours' sleep in the last five days, and that mostly in the saddle, but swooning . . . La Violette . . . pull the other one." He took a disgusted gulp of his sherry.

"You don't like the lady, Julian?" Brigadier Cornwallis said with a grin.

"No, I dislike her intensely. And I have to tell you, Cornwallis, that 'lady' is a vast misnomer. She's a duplicitous, mercenary, untrustworthy vagabond."

There was an instant of silence at this brief but comprehensive denunciation; then Colonel Webster said, "Ah, well, Julian, you never did take kindly to being outsmarted."

You don't know the half of it. But Julian contented himself with another dour smile and said, "Not to mention being dragooned into charging across the countryside to remove Cornichet's epaulets."

"What?" There was a chorus of exclamations, and the colonel obliged with a brief narrative that had everyone but himself chuckling.

"Uh . . . excuse me, sir." Lieutenant Sanderson appeared in the doorway.

"Well?" Wellington regarded him with a touch of irritability. It was clear the brigade-major was alone.

"La Violette, sir, she—"

"She's not run off?" Julian interrupted, snapping his glass down on the table.

"Oh, no, Colonel. But she's asleep, sir, and Senhora Braganza couldn't awaken her."

"Perhaps we should let her sleep, then," Wellington suggested.

"Oh, she's not asleep," Julian stated. "It's one of her tricks. I'll have her here in fifteen minutes." With that he strode from the room.

"Well, well," murmured Colonel Webster. "I can't

wait to meet our guest. She seems to exercise a most powerful effect on St. Simon."

"Yes," agreed the commander in chief, frowning thoughtfully. "She does, doesn't she?"

Senhora Braganza greeted the irate colonel's arrival with a voluble flood of Portuguese and much hand waving. Julian, who had a smattering of her language and relatively fluent Spanish, divined that the "poor child" was sleeping like a baby and it would be a crime to awaken her. The partisans could do no wrong among the local populations of Portugal and Spain, and it rather seemed as if the widow was prepared to do battle to protect the sleeping one upstairs.

Julian was obliged to move her bodily aside as she defended the bottom of the stairs. He went up them two at a time with the senhora berating him on his heels. He flung open the door to the small chamber under the eaves and then stopped, something holding him back.

Moonlight from the single round window fell on the narrow cot where Violette lay. She slept on her back, her hands resting on the pillow on either side of her head, palms curled like a sleeping child's.

Julian closed the door in the face of the still-be-wailing widow and crossed soft-footed to the cot, where he stood looking down at her. Her face in repose had a youthful innocence that startled him. The dark, thick-lashed crescent of her eyelashes lay against the high cheekbones, the smooth, suntanned skin stretched taut across the bones. But sleep softened neither the firm line of her mouth nor the determined set of her jaw.

"Tamsyn?" He spoke her given name softly, unaware that it was the first time he'd used it.

She stirred, her eyelashes fluttered, a soft murmur of

protestation came from her lips. But there was something about the response, about the speed of it, that convinced him absolutely that she had not been asleep . . . that she'd been aware of his scrutiny.

His lips tightened. "Get up, Tamsyn. You're not fooling me with this playacting."

Her eyelashes swept up, and the deep-purple eyes gazed up at him with such a blend of sensual mischief that he caught his breath. Without taking her eyes off his face, she drew up her feet in a sudden swift movement, caught the covers, and kicked them off, baring her body, creamy in the moonlight. She smiled up at him, quirking an eyebrow, passing her hands over her body in unmistakable invitation.

Julian gasped at the sheer effrontery, the naked sexuality of the invitation. An invitation that he fought with clenched muscles to withstand. When he finally spoke, his voice grated in the lushly expectant silence.

"I will give you ten minutes to be ready to accompany me to the dinner table. If you're not dressed by then, so help me, I'll carry you through the streets just as you are." Then he turned and left the room, aware that he was almost running as if the devils of enchantment would still reach out and haul him back.

Tamsyn swung off the cot and stretched. It was strange, but the English colonel was behaving unpredictably. In her experience men didn't refuse such invitations. Especially when as far as the colonel knew, there were no strings. He couldn't possibly guess what she was planning for his—or rather, their—immediate future.

Her protective landlady had provided her with clean undergarments, stockings, and a shirt. They were of rough homespun rather than the fine lawn, linen, or silk

Tamsyn was accustomed to wearing next to her skin. El
Baron's daughter had known only the best. But they
were clean, as clean as her bathed skin and freshly
washed hair. The widow had also brushed the butter-
soft leather britches and polished the cordovan boots
until the well-worn leather gleamed with a dull sheen.
So Tamsyn was feeling more respectable than she'd been
in many days when she jumped energetically down the
stairs to greet the fuming and impatient Colonel, Lord
St. Simon in the street outside the cottage.

"There, milord colonel, I'm ready to go with you."
She smiled nonchalantly as if the charged moments in
the bedroom had never taken place. "And I'm hungry
as a hunter, so I trust your commander in chief keeps a
good table."

Julian didn't deign to reply, merely walked rapidly
through the cobbled streets, lit by oil lamps at strategic
intervals and still as busy as in broad daylight. The army
didn't sleep, and the siegeworkings continued in the
moonlight as busily as they did in the sunshine.

The roomful of men turned as one to the door when
St. Simon and his companion entered. "Ah, Violette."
Wellington stepped toward her. "I trust you're rested."

"Yes, thank you, I slept wonderfully." Tamsyn took
the hand he offered.

"Gentlemen, may I introduce La Violette." The
commander in chief slipped his other hand around her
waist as he presented her to his staff.

Tamsyn didn't attempt to move away from the half
embrace as she responded to the introductions with
smiling nods. She'd heard of the duke's reputation as a
flirt, and she was perfectly happy to encourage his attentions since they could only assist her purpose.

Julian stood to one side, morosely sipping sherry,

watching as the men in the room clustered around the small figure. La Violette certainly knew how to be the center of attention. Despite her masculine attire and the short, shining cap of hair, she was exuding feminine charm . . . female wiles, he amended. What the hell was she after? She'd come there to sell something, not reduce the entire high command of the English army to a state resembling Circe's fools.

A servant came in bearing a baron of beef on a wooden board. He placed it on the table set for dinner before the fire. "Sir, dinner is served."

"Good." Wellington rubbed his hands together in hearty anticipation. "Come and sit beside me, my dear." He swept Tamsyn into a chair on his right and took his place at the head. He raised his eyeglass and examined the offering on the table as servants unloaded steaming platters from their trays.

"Now, what have we here? A dish of mutton chops, I do believe. Do let me help you. . . . Tell me, must I call you Violette, or do you have another name?" He placed a chop on her plate together with several thick slices of beef.

"My given name is Tamsyn," she said, hungrily helping herself to a dish of roast potatoes. "Violette . . . Violeta—they're the names by which I'm known among the partisans."

"Do the partisans all have code names?" the brigadier asked, filling her wineglass.

Tamsyn flashed him a smile as she picked up a mutton chop with her fingers. "Maybe."

Julian watched as she tore at the flesh with her sharp white teeth, holding the chop between finger and thumb. When every last morsel of meat was off the bone, she licked her fingers, picked up her fork, and speared a potato. She ate with the natural efficiency of a hungry animal, using her fingers if they were more suitable to the task, or deftly filleting a brook trout with a couple of strokes of her knife. There was nothing distasteful about her table manners, but neither was there any formality. Food was to be enjoyed, an appetite both sensual and necessary.

He noticed that while she drank several glasses of water, she merely took occasional sips of the wine in her glass.

Casually, he turned his chair sideways to the table, resting his forearm on the white starched cloth, his fingers caressing the stem of his wineglass. "You don't care for the wine, Violette?"

She looked up swiftly, and her eyes were sharp as they met his across the table. "On the contrary, milord colonel, in the right place and time I enjoy a good rioja as much as anyone. But I have to be careful, it tends to go to my head." She smiled. "Cecile had the same difficulty."

"Cecile?" Major Carson queried, carrying a forkful of mushroom compote to his lips.

"My mother, sir. I inherited her small stature. The baron maintained we had too little height and weight to absorb much wine." She bit into an almond pastry. "It seemed as good an explanation as any."

"St. Simon tells us that your mother was English," the brigadier said, taking his nose out of his wineglass.

"Yes," Tamsyn agreed. She brushed crumbs off her fingers and played with the locket at her throat. "This belonged to my mother. It belonged to her mother, I believe."

"But how did she find herself in Spain?" Major Carson asked.

"She was paying a visit to some family friends . . . an ambassador or some such in Madrid. She disappeared into the arms of my father at some point in the journey." Tamsyn smiled as she helped herself to another sweetmeat from the basket in front of her. "And had no desire to leave them . . . until she died."

The shadow that passed across her face was gone before anyone but Julian caught it. But a hardness lingered in her face and eyes, although she continued to smile and nibble her pastry. It was as if she'd thrown up shutters to her innermost feelings, he thought. As if something too deep and too precious had come dangerously close to the surface.

The conversation became general until the covers were removed and the port decanter appeared. Chairs were pushed back from the table, cigars were lit, the decanter circulated, and it clearly didn't occur to anyone that La Violette was in the least out of place. Least of all did it occur to the bandit, Julian reflected caustically, regarding her from beneath his heavy eyelids as she joked and flirted quite openly with Wellington.

When she accepted a peeled grape from between the duke's fingers, Julian decided he'd had as much as he could take of this charade. His men were in the trenches and he had work to do. Pushing back his chair, he stood up.

"You'll excuse me, gentlemen, but I've pickets to post. I must return to my brigade."

"The men are in a filthy temper," Colonel Webster observed, suddenly somber. "They're swearing at the Spaniards in Badajos for yielding the city to the French without a fight, and they're swearing blue bloody murder at the French for holding out when they know they haven't got a chance."

"There'll be bloody work once we get into the city, you mark my words," Brigadier Cornwallis agreed in curiously detached accents as he refilled his port glass.

"Yes, we'll have the devil's own task to keep a rein on them," Julian said. "Well, I bid you good night, gentlemen." He glanced at Tamsyn and was shocked at her white set face, wiped clean of all playfulness. Again she seemed to be looking on some grim internal landscape. "Farewell, Violette," he said deliberately. "I trust your business here prospers."

Tamsyn snapped back to the present. The colonel sounded as if they were not to meet again. "I trust so, too, milord colonel. I'll see you in the morning, I daresay."

"I fear not," he said. "My work doesn't bring me into Elvas." He bowed to the commander in chief and left the cozy firelit room for the chill of his tent in the encampment and the whine of shell and thud of mortar. But he thought he would sleep well for the first time since he'd laid eyes on La Violette. Now his part in her life was done.

Tamsyn regarded the closed door with a quizzically raised eyebrow. His work didn't bring him into Elvas? He would find he was mistaken. Colonel, Lord Julian St. Simon most certainly had work to do at headquarters.

"So, Tamsyn, can we get down to business?" Wellington was suddenly all briskness, the bonhomie of a generous host vanished beneath the incisive manner of the commander in chief. "You have information to sell? What is your price?"

Tamsyn shook her head and her tone now matched

his. "I'll tell you that, sir, when you've told me exactly what you wish to buy."

Wellington listed his requirements. The code names and passwords of the partisan bands in the area. Their location and composition, so he could make contact with them without waiting to be contacted. A detailed map of the mountain passes known only to the partisans. The extent of the partisan armories and what if anything they lacked that could be supplied by the armies of the Peninsular.

Tamsyn listened intently. Then she said, "That's quite a shopping list, sir. You'll understand that I need to sleep on it."

"Of course. But I trust not too long."

"No. But I'm not going to sell you anything that might jeopardize the integrity of the partisans."

"Oh?" Wellington frowned and pulled his chin. "I hadn't thought you so nice in your dealings, Violette."

Her eyes flashed. "I don't sell my friends, sir."

"No, of course not," he said soothingly. "But you surely understand the difference between giving such information to us rather than to the French. *We* would use it to assist your friends, not to injure them."

"That may be so, sir, but my friends are jealous of their independence, and they're not always ready to accept help from anyone." She stood up, her chair scraping on the wooden floor. "Thank you for your hospitality. I'll be at your disposal in the morning."

The men rose as she left the room, and then Wellington came quickly after her, ordering the brigade-major, still at his desk, "Sanderson, see our guest safely to her lodging."

"There's no need for that," Tamsyn said. "I'll surely

meet with no insult from your soldiers." There was a venomous point to the statement that brought a dull flush to the commander's cheeks. He could think of no reason for her implicit accusation, and yet he found himself on the defensive.

"I trust not," he said stiffly. "Nevertheless, you will accept an escort."

Tamsyn inclined her head. "If you say so, sir. Good night."

She walked down the stairs, followed by the lieutenant, leaving a frowning Wellington staring after her. A strange girl, he thought. And not one to be underestimated.

Under the cold starlight Julian walked through the group of tents housing his own brigade. Two companies were at work in the trenches; the rest were off duty and sat around their fires, talking in low voices, pipe smoke drifting in a blue haze as they smoked and drank from tankards of blackstrap.

The colonel greeted them all by name, pausing to chat for a few minutes, trying to gauge their mood. Were they optimistic about the upcoming assault on the city? Eager for it? Intent on vengeance?

"Us'll be glad when we're done 'ere, sir," a burly trooper said, phlegmatically puffing on his pipe as he cobbled a hole in the sole of his boot. "This is wretched work, beggin' yer pardon, sir."

"Aye, but if old Hookey says us mun do it, then us mun do it," responded his companion with a fatalistic shrug.

Julian smiled to himself as he strolled on. The men had several affectionate nicknames for their commander in chief, most of them referring to his large hooked nose. And it was true they'd follow him into hell if he expected it of them. He glanced toward the dark shape of Badajos crouching on the plain. The walls were now breached in three places, and the attack was planned for tomorrow night, but the French garrison was efficiently repairing the breaches whenever the English bombardment permitted it. The assault was going to be a bloody business at best, and the city would pay bitterly for its intransigence.

"Sergeant Gorman's been regaling the mess with the tale of Cornichet's epaulets," a voice spoke at his shoulder out of the darkness. "I gather La Violette's something of a prankster."

"That's one way of putting it, Frank," Julian said dryly, turning toward the young captain who was his own aide-de-camp. "I'd call it something else myself."

"They're a perverse lot, the partisans," Captain Frank Frobisher observed. "Treat us more like the enemy than the enemy."

"Well, my business with La Violette is done, thank God," Julian declared. "She can play her tricks on the Peer and see where it gets her." He began to walk back toward his own tent. "Fancy a nightcap? I've a tolerable cognac in my tent, if Tim O'Connor hasn't had a go at it in my absence."

Frank laughed. "I doubt even Tim's blarney would get him past Dobbin. That man of yours is a veritable Cerberus when it comes to guarding your possessions."

They ducked into the colonel's tent, where his servant was trimming the oil lamp. A pan of water simmered on a small charcoal brazier.

"You'll be wantin' your tea, I daresay, Colonel?"

Dobbin observed comfortably, knowing the colonel's invariable nighttime routine in camp.

"Later. . . . Captain Frobisher could do with a cognac." Julian pushed forward a camp chair for his guest and bent to rummage in a wooden chest, bringing out a square bottle of *fine* cognac. "Have we glasses, Dobbin?"

"Aye, sir." The servant produced them.

"Is that cognac I smell?" A pink-cheeked face poked through the tent door. "I thought you was back, Julian. Heard you had quite a junket." Tim O'Connor brought the rest of himself into the space that seemed to shrink dramatically with his substantial bulk. He took another camp chair and beamed. "So tell us about this female bandit. Is she worth looking at?"

"Not to my taste," Julian said dismissively, and changed the subject. "The brigade's objective tomorrow during the assault is the San Vincente bastion. Any suggestion as to how we deploy the companies?"

His two friends immediately turned their attention to brigade business and the storming of Badajos, and the subject of La Violette was dropped, but St. Simon's unwillingness to discuss his dealings with the bandit, or even to satisfy the most minimal curiosity, did not go unnoticed.

After they'd left, Julian lay on his cot, sipping his tea, thinking about the following night, about the possibility of his own death, about all the inevitable deaths. He would lose friends tomorrow. In the four years of the Peninsular war, he'd lost many such, and it didn't become any easier to accept.

La Violette had seen her share of death too. It was in her eyes, in the shadow that so often passed across her face. She was a creature of wild contrasts, he thought. A deep river of dark experience flowed beneath the bright, sensual surface.

And then he remembered that he wasn't going to think of the girl again—not of her passion, her mischief, her taunts or her griefs—never again.

Chapter Seven

LIEUTENANT SANDERSON ARRIVED AT SENHORA BRA-
ganza's cottage the next morning while Tamsyn was at
breakfast in the sunny kitchen, where the door stood
open onto a vegetable and herb garden, a line of bee-
hives ranged against the warm brick wall at the rear.

"Good morning, Lieutenant." She greeted him with
a cheerful smile and waved him to a chair with a hand
holding a crust of bread dripping honey. "Coffee? The
senhora makes an excellent cup."

"No, thank you. The commander in chief sent me to
escort you to headquarters." The brigade-major shifted
from foot to foot, clearly unsure how to impress upon
this insouciantly breakfast-eating brigand the urgency of
his errand. Wellington was in one of his more irascible
moods, undoubtedly due to the impending assault on
Badajos.

"I'll finish my breakfast; then I shall be entirely at the
duke's disposal," Tamsyn said calmly, breaking another
chunk of bread from the long loaf on the table, spreading honey lavishly. "You might as well have a cup of
coffee while you're waiting."

Sanderson sat down. If he was going to be flayed, he
might as well fortify himself. Tamsyn accorded him an

approving nod, and the *senhora* immediately produced a bowl of fragrant coffee.

"Is Colonel, Lord St. Simon at headquarters this morning?" she inquired pleasantly.

"Oh, no, *señorita*. He's with his brigade. His division will be part of the assault force tonight."

"So it's to be tonight," Tamsyn said. A shudder quivered along her spine. How many men would lie dead beneath those walls by morning? Would Julian St. Simon be one of them? A little cold spot began to bloom in her stomach.

She pushed back her chair with a sudden movement that took the lieutenant by surprise. He looked up from his coffee cup and drew breath sharply at her face, which had become a mask, all light and mobility banished.

Of course, if St. Simon did fall at the storming of Badajos, she'd be back to square one. A very annoying prospect, enough to cause cold spots in anyone's belly. She stood up, wiping her sticky fingers on a checkered napkin.

"Let's go then, Lieutenant."

Her voice, incisive and commanding, brought him to his feet immediately, abandoning his half-full cup. He found he almost had to trot to keep up with her as she strode through the streets.

Wellington greeted her with brusque courtesy. He was clearly preoccupied, and Tamsyn refused the seat he offered, choosing instead to perch on the windowsill.

"So what is the price of your information, Violette?" The commander in chief came straight to the point. "Sanderson, take notes, will you?"

The aide-de-camp sat down at the desk and began to sharpen a quill.

Tamsyn said with a cool smile, "I will tell you my price in the presence of Colonel, Lord St. Simon. Not otherwise."

"What?" Wellington glared at her, remembering what Julian had said about the brigand's penchant for game playing. "What nonsense is this?"

"No, nonsense, sir." She slid off the windowsill. "That's my condition. You'll understand why when you hear my terms. You may find me at the cottage when the colonel arrives." Without further ado she left the room, offering them both a smiling nod as she did so.

"What the devil's going on between the girl and St. Simon?" Wellington mused in an undertone that Sanderson pretended he hadn't heard since it didn't seem to be directed at him. "Something's afoot there."

He paced the room from window to fireplace and back again. For whatever reason, Julian had made it clear he wanted nothing further to do with the girl. Was it fair to compel his presence just because the brigand insisted upon it?

But he wanted that information. Once Badajos had fallen, they'd be on the march again, north toward Campo Mayor, and Violette's knowledge would greatly facilitate the march. Besides, if he passed up this opportunity, he was unlikely to meet up with another such source.

"Sanderson, send someone to ask Colonel St. Simon to report to headquarters at his earliest convenience."

"Yes, sir." The aide-de-camp left at a run. It was still relatively early in the day, but in a few hours no one would have time for anything but preparations for the assault.

Julian was discussing with his company commanders the procedure for the brigade's attack on the San Vicente bastion. They would not be part of the main assault, but a flanking secondary assault made simultaneously with the main attack, intended to distract attention and divert French forces from the breaches.

The ensign, riding in great haste through the neat rows of tents, drew raised eyebrows as he approached the group of men clustered around a map spread on a rough planking table outside St. Simon's tent.

"Your pardon, Colonel, sir." The ensign leaped from his mount, offering a sketchy salute. "The commander wishes you to report to headquarters at your earliest convenience."

"Yesterday, in other words," Frank said with a grin, straightening from the map.

Julian stood, frowning. What could possibly be so important that Wellington would tear him away from his brigade on the eve of battle? The answer was a red flag waving in his brain. La Violette. Whatever this was, the half-breed brigand was behind it. And by the living God, she was going to understand once and for all that he could not be pushed around like a pawn on a chessboard!

"Dobbin! My horse!" He disappeared into his tent on the bellowed instruction, leaving his officers to exchange glances of surprise. He emerged in a minute, buckling his sword belt, thunderclouds massed on the broad forehead beneath the unruly lock of red-gold hair, his bright eyes darting around his assembled staff like fire-tipped arrows.

"I'll be no more than an hour. Major O'Connor, I want that assault plan drawn up for when I return." Impatiently, he took the reins of his horse from Dobbin and swung into the saddle.

"Yes, sir," Tim muttered. Something was awry.

Julian rarely pulled rank and was not given to taking his ill temper out on his subordinates; it was one reason his men would follow him into hell, and the competition for a place on his staff was always fierce. Lord St. Simon was one of the youngest colonels in the armies of the Peninsular, but older men were as eager to serve under him as were his peers.

"I'll lay odds that that Violette is behind this," Frank observed, stretching. "Julian don't care for her above half, and if she's pulling his string, the fur will fly, you mark my words."

"Can't see a Spanish brigand getting the better of the Peer, let alone St. Simon," Captain Deerbourne observed. "And if she's playing tricks today of all days, she's a fool."

All eyes went as one to the walls of Badajos, shrouded in the smoke from the bombardment.

Julian cantered toward Elvas, seething. The sight of La Violette sitting on a rock on the Portuguese side of the pontoon bridge did nothing to placate him. It was as clear as day she was waiting for him, and therefore that she was responsible for this summons.

Tamsyn had indeed been waiting for him. She guessed he would not be in the best of tempers and summoned up her most charming smile, rising to meet him as he walked his mount across the swaying bridge.

"Good morning, milord colonel." Hastily, Tamsyn stepped into his path when it rather looked as if he was going to ride straight past her. "I'm so happy to see you." Shielding her gaze from the sun, she squinted up at him, a smile crinkling the golden skin around her eyes, her hair almost white in the sunlight. "How nice that your work did bring you into Elvas, after all."

Julian's fingers twitched on his reins as he imagined

placing them tightly around the slender column of her throat rising out of the opened white collar of her shirt . . . and slowly squeezing. . . . And then he imagined his fingers sliding up behind her ears, those little shells lying flat against the side of her head, tickling in the tender skin behind . . .

"Get up!" he ordered curtly. "I assume we're going to the same place." Leaning down, he extended his hand. She took it without demur, put her foot on his boot, and sprang upward, with an agile twist landing on the saddle in front of him.

"Yes, I believe we are," she said cheerfully, leaning back against him so that he could feel the heat of her skin through her thin shirt. "It's certainly very convenient this way."

"And as we know, you order everything to your own convenience," he observed acidly.

"I suppose you might think that," Tamsyn said after judicious reflection. "But you don't really know me as yet."

"Oh, believe me, Violette, there's going to be no 'as yet,' " he declared with savage emphasis. "This is as familiar as we get."

"If you say so." She sounded perfectly untroubled by his statement; it was as if she were humoring a fractious child. Julian almost tipped her off his saddle at her tone.

"So the attack is to be tonight," she said in a different tone. "You won't wish to remain long away from your brigade, but my business shouldn't take long."

"Oh, I'm relieved to hear it, but you mustn't hurry yourself on my account. I'm certain the storming of Badajos can await your pleasure."

Tamsyn swiveled round to look up at him. "Don't be

petulant, milord colonel. It doesn't suit you, and it's not in the least convincing."

His jaw dropped, and inadvertently he kicked his mount's flanks. The horse broke into a startled gallop, and Tamsyn, unbalanced already by her turned position, reeled on her perch.

"Hell and the devil!" Julian grabbed at her, hauling her back with one hand as he drew on the reins with his other, bringing his horse under control. "Just hold your tongue, would you?" he gritted. "It'll be a damn sight safer all round."

"Yes, milord colonel," Tamsyn murmured with a demure smile, allowing her body to rest against him again.

Julian wondered why he wanted to laugh. It struck him as the impulse of a bedlamite in present circumstances, but there was something about her mischief that invited—no, challenged—him to a response. It was almost as if she were saying she wasn't fooled by his attitude, that she knew he was enjoying their unorthodox proximity as much as she was if he'd only allow himself to acknowledge it.

They left his horse in the stableyard at the rear of Wellington's headquarters and entered by the outside stairs again. "He's waiting for you, Colonel." Sanderson hastened to open the door onto the commander in chief's sanctum.

"Oh, good. You're both here." Wellington stood up from his desk, his expression curt. "I'm sorry for this, Julian, but La Violette insists that you must be part of these negotiations."

"So I assumed, sir." Julian regarded Tamsyn with ill-disguised resentment. "Very well, you've got what you wanted, now let's get on with it. I've more important things to do with my time this morning than humoring the mercenary spawn of a bloody brigand."

Wellington hid his astonishment at this brutal speech. A man didn't speak like that to a mere acquaintance, let alone a stranger.

Tamsyn, however, seemed unconcerned. "Yes, I understand you're both busy, but the timing of this business was not of my choice, I'll have you remember, milord colonel. I came here under your escort."

"Having delayed us by two days," he snapped. "Now, what do you want, girl?"

Tamsyn shrugged and sat down uninvited on a chair before the desk, crossing her legs, her hands clasped lightly in her lap. "Very well, to points. I will give you the information you desire, my lord, except that about the partisan armories. The condition of their weapons is not mine to reveal. They will tell you what they wish you to know. I'll also draw for you a detailed map of the mountain passes El Baron used between Spain and France. Some of them are very narrow and treacherous, but I daresay you'll discover that for yourself. They're not, to my knowledge, known to the French."

"Good . . . good," Wellington said, rubbing his hands. "This is all very good . . . very useful." He glanced at St. Simon. "Don't you agree, Julian?"

"Oh, yes," Julian agreed. "Very useful." He stood against the door, his arms folded, his eyes brightly sardonic as they rested on Tamsyn. "And what do you want of us, brigand?"

"Yes, Violette. Your price?"

Tamsyn paused before answering, her eyes on her lap, her fingers playing cat's cradle; then she looked up and met the colonel's eye before switching her gaze to Wellington. "My price, sir, is the colonel . . . Lord St. Simon."

The silence in the room was as deep and impenetrable as the grave. The two men stared at Violette, who sat back in her chair, a picture of relaxation, no sign of the ferment in her head. It was a stroke of such boldness, she was actually amazed at herself for conceiving the plan, let alone executing it.

"This is some lunatic raving," Julian declared, breaking the silence, his voice harsh as a scouring pad. "Either that or you're making game of His Majesty's army, girl, and that will cost you dear!" He crossed to her chair and leaned over her, bracing his hands on the chair back on either side of her head. She was impaled on the bright-blue ferocity of his eyes as he said very slowly and distinctly, "Cease this idle foolishness, or I'll have you thrown in irons in the stockade."

"Hear me out," she said simply, not flinching, although it cost her some effort.

"Let her speak, Julian."

"Speak!" The colonel whirled toward his commander, his eyes stark in his white face, his mouth a thin slash in a clenched jaw. "The girl's either moon mad or she's making game of us. Must I remind you, sir, that men are going to die tonight and this . . . this distempered chit is playing us for fools."

"No, I'm not," Tamsyn said swiftly. "I do assure you I'm not. Only hear me out."

"Go on," Wellington instructed, holding up a hand to silence the younger man's seething tirade. "But keep to the point. I warn you, if this *is* some kind of game, then I'll send you back to Cornichet gift wrapped and with my compliments."

The threats were flowing thick, fast, and most unpleasantly. Tamsyn swallowed the little nut of fear in her throat, reminding herself that the stakes were very high, and began to explain the plan that would require the cooperation of Lord St. Simon.

"I explained that my mother was English. Her family came from Cornwall . . . your home county, Colonel."

Julian's expression was dark. "What has that to do with me?"

"Well, I thought you could help me rediscover my mother's family," she said simply. "My mother wouldn't tell me their name. She . . . she had not been happy with them, and when she met my father, she chose to cut herself off completely from that part of her life and heritage."

Reaching behind her neck, she unfastened the locket and held it out to Wellington. "This is a picture of her. With my father. The locket is a family heirloom, and I thought perhaps with this and the portrait I might be able to locate them. My mother implied that they were quite a prominent family."

Wellington examined it and then handed it to Julian, who looked at it without really taking it in, his mind running over Cornwall's powerful families. The St. Simons and the Penhallans were the greatest landowners with the most political influence. Tregarthan, the St. Simon estate, and the Penhallan estate of Lanjerrick took up half the county. His lip curled unconsciously at the thought of the Penhallans. The viscount pursued his political ambition with utter ruthlessness, but his character was a shining example of moral rectitude compared with his nephews, the loathsome twins.

He dropped the locket onto a side table, and the

delicate filigree chain chimed as it fell. "There's no
heraldic device on this . . . no insignia to identify it."

"But there's her picture inside," Tamsyn stressed.
"Look inside."

Wellington picked it up again, snapping it open. The
woman was undoubtedly Tamsyn's mother; the likeness
was striking: the same locket hung around her neck, and
she was smiling, radiating perfect happiness. He handed
it to St. Simon, who read the signature on the back of
the woman's portrait. She'd signed herself simply Cecile, in a flowery hand, full of energy. The date was a
mere three years ago.

He glanced at Tamsyn, who sat quietly, waiting. He
examined the man's portrait, struck by the elegant features of this notorious robber baron. Black eyes like a
hawk's regarded him with a quizzical air from the delicate frame. Tamsyn had her father's mouth and that
particularly resolute set of the jaw; her mother's eyes
and coloring.

"So?" He handed back the locket. "Even if we believe your mother was English, what is that to do with
anything?"

"Why, everything," she said. They listened while she
explained that her parents had been killed six months
earlier, that her own men had either been killed in
Cornichet's ambush or had disbanded; that, with the
exception of Gabriel, she was alone in the world.

The pathos of her story was somehow accentuated by
the scarcity of detail. She said nothing as to how her
parents had met their deaths, merely stated the fact. Her
appeal when she made it was to Wellington. St. Simon
still bore the look of a man seething and impatient,
definitely not one to respond sympathetically to a sad

tale, but she thought she might be able to tug the commander's heartstrings.

"I would like to discover my mother's family," she said, twisting her hands in her lap, offering the duke a tremulous smile. "I have no one in the world to care for me or to give me a home. I thought if I could find them, they might take me under their wing. Only I see some difficulties."

The colonel made a sound between a snort and an oath and exchanged a comprehending glance with the duke. *Some* difficulties. This girl clearly didn't know the first thing about English society, how closed and prideful it was.

"And supposing you do identify them, just how do you intend to introduce yourself?" Julian demanded scornfully. "Are you going to walk up to them and say, 'I'm your long-lost cousin,' or whatever relationship you are?"

"No, I can quite see that that wouldn't do," she said in a doleful tone that caused the duke to look reproachfully at the colonel. "I don't think they'd be prepared to accept me as I am. I don't know how to go on in such society . . . indeed, I know nothing of England but what Cecile told me. And besides"—a delicate flush mantled the sun-browned cheeks—"there is one other awkwardness. . . ."

"Do go on, my dear." Wellington had quite lost his earlier harshness.

"It's somewhat embarrassing . . . but, you see, I'm not entirely sure that Cecile and the baron were ever properly married . . . in the eyes of the Church," she said in a rush, twisting her fingers into impossible knots.

"Oh," said the duke.

"Well, my mother's family might consider that I

didn't have a claim on them if they knew that, don't you think?" she said anxiously, fixing her great purple eyes on his face.

He cleared his throat. "It is possible, yes."

"Why on earth wouldn't they formalize their relationship?" Julian demanded. "If they were inseparable, as you implied last night, and they had a child."

"I don't believe they considered it in the least important," Tamsyn said truthfully. "And as for me, well, I know I was an accident—"

"Sweet heaven, what a euphemism!" Julian broke in with a harsh laugh. "Would to God the world had been spared such an accident!"

"That is unkind," Tamsyn protested, looking tremulously at Wellington.

He scratched his nose. What did Julian have against the girl? She seemed a plucky little creature. "I'm at a loss to know what this is leading to, *señorita*. How can Lord St. Simon assist you?"

"Oh, that's simple," Tamsyn said, cheering up immediately. "I don't think it should take me more than six months to learn to be an English lady. My plan is that the colonel will accompany me to England . . . to Cornwall . . . and teach me what I need to know; then I can try to discover my mother's family. Someone must have heard the story of a daughter vanishing twenty years ago on a visit to Spain. And I hope, when I'm presentable, I can effect an introduction. We could say that my mother married a Spanish grandee of true hidalgo blood and I was told of my English heritage only at her deathbed. I thought we could say that the colonel met my father in some circumstances and because of an obligation to him agreed to take me under his protection when I was orphaned.

"And perhaps," she added with a winsome smile at the duke, "perhaps it would help if we could say that your grace lent me your protection also."

"You thought we could say *what*?" exclaimed the colonel when this succinct speech had sunk in.

"That you took me—"

"All right, I heard!" he interrupted with an abrupt motion of his hand. "I've never heard such a preposterous jumble of invention in my life."

"But it will serve," Tamsyn insisted stubbornly. "I know it will. All I want is six months of your time, milord colonel. I have plenty of funds of my own, so I'll not be a charge on you in any way. I'm asking only for your attention for a limited time. You see, I don't know anyone else to ask," she added, turning once more in appeal to the duke. "And it's so convenient that you should be Cornish."

"Preposterous!" Julian repeated in disgust. "I've wasted enough of my time on you."

"Then there's nothing more to be said," Tamsyn said, and there was no sign now of the forlorn orphan in the obstinate set of her chin and the briskness of her tone. "Forgive me for wasting your time, sir." She rose and bowed to Wellington, then, without casting so much as a glance in the colonel's direction, stalked out of the room.

"Consider for a minute, Julian," Wellington said slowly. "Six months, it's not so very great a commitment."

"What?" Julian stared at the duke in disbelief. "You'd have me play schoolmaster and mentor to that . . . that . . . misbegotten devil's spawn . . . leave the Peninsula. Good God, sir, how could you consider such a thing?"

"You could do me an immeasurably valuable service while you were in England," Wellington said, sounding pensive. "I've been wondering whom to send. And six months is not so very great a time. You know how slowly things move out here. You'll be back in no time."

Julian could find no words as the incredible realization dawned that his commander in chief wanted him to take on this unbelievable assignment.

He stared in disbelief for a second, then said, "Excuse me." With a curt bow he turned on his heel and left the room. Disbelief warred with wild fury in a bewildering maelstrom of emotion that chased away all clarity of mind and purpose.

He ran down the stairs and out into the street, brushing past an orderly, his face hidden by the towering pile of the commander's freshly laundered shirts in his arms. The mountain shook and toppled to the street. The colonel didn't even notice, simply continued at a near run, leaving the orderly cursing and muttering as he picked up the laundry from the dusty cobbles.

Julian saw Tamsyn outside Senhora Braganza's cottage as he rounded the corner. She was leaning against the wall idly chatting with the senhora, who was working in her garden.

"Ah, milord colonel." Tamsyn greeted his arrival with a raised eyebrow. "I thought you'd said your piece."

"Oh, believe me, I haven't even begun," he declared, and despite her bravado, Tamsyn quailed before the livid countenance. She opened her mouth to say something she hoped was defusing, but the colonel swept an arm around her waist and bundled her ahead of him into the cottage.

On her knees before a row of cabbages, Senhora Braganza stared after them, then shook her head, muttering to herself as she dragged a weed by its roots from the thin soil.

Tamsyn reached her small room under the eaves as breathless as if she'd run up the stairs herself, although she was fairly certain her feet hadn't touched ground from the moment Julian's arm had come around her waist. The door crashed shut as she was thrust into the room, still imprisoned in the colonel's arm.

"By God!" he said in a whisper so contained it had the power of a shout. "By God, girl, you're not going to do this to me!" His free hand was at her throat, forcing her chin up so she was looking up at him, and every distinct word he spoke fell on her face almost like a slap. "I am not going to allow you to force this on me. You are a manipulative, lying little thief, and your presence in my life ends right here . . . in this room at this minute! Have you taken that into your devious head, girl?"

Tamsyn's mind raced. What she heard in his voice was akin to desperation beneath the savagery of his manner. He was afraid that somehow he'd find himself doing what she wanted against every ounce of will he possessed. What was he afraid of? Exactly what pressure could force him to help her? Wellington's orders, of course. And she was counting on the duke's pressing need for her information. But she didn't think Wellington would go beyond persuasion. It was quite another matter to compel one of his officers to do something so out of the line of duty. Which left her. . . . The colonel was afraid of her, of what she on her own could persuade him to do.

He was still holding her roughly against him, his hand

ungentle against her throat, forcing up her chin. But her own hands were free, and deliberately she slipped her arms around his body, turning herself slightly in his hold so now it would look to anyone who didn't know otherwise as if they were locked in a passionate embrace.

He jumped at her movement, his expression incredulous as he realized what she was doing. "You little whore!" he exclaimed, yanking her hands away from him, thrusting her from him with such vigor that she almost stumbled.

"No," Tamsyn protested. "Not so. You were holding me so tightly, it seemed the most natural thing to do."

He looked so astounded, she could almost have felt sympathy, but the stakes were too high, and she pressed her advantage, stepping closer to him again. "It was only a suggestion, milord colonel." Her eyes were so huge, he felt as if he were slipping into them, her smile so seductive, the ground seemed to quiver beneath his feet.

She raised a hand and lightly traced the shape of his mouth. "So stern," she murmured, her smile broadening. "Relax, I'm offering only pleasure. Remember how wonderful it was by the river, think how we could have times like that whenever we wanted them."

"Harlot! You'd sell yourself—"

"No," Tamsyn interrupted, the seductive gleam leaving her eyes. "I'm *not* selling myself. The only thing I'm selling is information that your commander in chief would dearly like to buy. I was offering you compensation, that's all."

"Compensation for dancing attendance on the bastard brat of a murdering robber!"

"Oh!" Tamsyn exclaimed, rendered momentarily speechless. "You have all the chivalry of a wood louse!

In all honesty and . . . and desirous affection, I suggest we make love and you—"

"Desirous affection!" He gave a short crack of disbelieving laughter. "Where the hell did you dredge up an expression like that? And what kind of gull do you think I am to fall for such a line?"

"It's true," she insisted fiercely.

Julian stood very still for a minute. His gaze ran slowly down the lean, tensile frame in front of him. She was thrumming with energy and indignation, and something else. That determination and purpose he'd felt the first moment he'd touched her. She was fully prepared to use her body to persuade him to do what she wanted. Well, it was time La Violette learned that not everyone could be molded to her purpose.

"Desirous affection, eh?" he mused, his hands on his belt buckle. "Prove it to me, Violette." He unfastened the buckle and swung free the heavy belt weighted with his sword, placing it on the table beneath the window. "What are you waiting for?" He glanced at Tamsyn, who still stood in the middle of the room. "Take your clothes off."

Somehow this was not going according to plan. It seemed as if it was, and yet something was amiss. However, having started on this course, Tamsyn felt compelled to continue. She kicked off her boots and undressed swiftly, tossing her clothes to the floor.

The colonel stood naked, feet apart, hands resting on his hips when she turned back to him. "I'm eager to see this demonstration of desirous affection," he drawled. "But I should warn you that I have very little time, so I hope your harlot's tricks are effective."

Tamsyn quivered and her eyes narrowed. "Oh, I believe you'll find them so, milord colonel," she said, stepping up to him.

Something warned him just in time, and he spun sideways as she brought her knee up in a vicious jab to his groin. *"Fiera!"* he bellowed, his nostrils flaring. His thigh throbbed where her knee had made savagely jarring contact, and he felt sick at the thought of what would have happened if it had met its intended target.

"You dare to insult me in such fashion!" she yelled back, rubbing her knee where it had made bruising contact with his hard-muscled thigh. "Get out of here! I wouldn't touch you if you were the last man on earth."

"Oh, wouldn't you? And just what happened to desirous affection?" He swooped on her, catching her around the waist, carrying her to the bed. "That died pretty quickly, didn't it?"

Tamsyn was aware of his vitally aroused body as he dropped her onto the coverlet. Obviously, the man liked a good fight . . . annoyingly, in the circumstances, so did she. Her body was tingling where his skin touched her, and there was a whirling excitement in the pit of her belly.

He leaned over her, pushing a knee between her thighs, and there was a predatory hunger in the bright-blue eyes. "Or did it?" he demanded, nudging her thighs apart.

"The affection part did," Tamsyn declared, moistening suddenly dry lips. His hand had found her now. His eyes never left her face as he played on her as if she were a lute string, plucking and stroking until she sang beneath his touch. When her little whimpering cries of ecstasy filled the small room, he slid his hands beneath her bottom and lifted her to meet him as he drove deep within her body while it still pulsated with her pleasure.

Satisfaction glittered in his eyes now as he moved above her, still watching her face with rapt intensity. He ran a finger over her lips, and she could taste the musky fragrance of her own body. He smiled. She smiled back, moving easily with his rhythm, as the deep, warm joy began to fill her belly and flow like honey in her veins. It was hard to imagine that a few short minutes before, they'd been fighting like a pair of mongrel curs.

His eyes glowed and he lowered his mouth to hers, the speed of his movements increasing as his tongue plunged and danced with hers and their cries of pleasure became as entangled as their bodies and the sweet liquid flow of arousal.

Tamsyn fluttered down to earth, a fragile leaf dropped finally by the airborne currents of ecstasy. She stroked Julian's back, where sweat glistened in the morning sunlight, feeling her own sweat gathering between her breasts, crushed by his weight.

Reluctantly, he moved away from her, his breathing still ragged as he dropped onto the narrow cot beside her. Then he pushed himself into a sitting position, swinging his legs over the side, turning to look at her as she lay on her back. He passed a hand over her belly in a gesture that was as much farewell as acknowledgment of shared joy, then heaved himself to his feet.

Tamsyn lay and watched him dress in silence. If that demonstration of naked desire and its delicious fulfillment had altered his determination to deny her his assistance, he gave no sign. He buckled on his sword belt and came back to the cot, bending to kiss her, a light, friendly farewell.

"Take care of yourself," he said. "Give Gabriel my regards when he comes to fetch you."

The door closed, and she heard his booted feet hurrying down the wooden stairs as if he couldn't get away fast enough.

Colonel, Lord Julian St. Simon was proving to be more resistant than she'd expected. Tamsyn got off the bed and went to the window, watching him stride up the street. Next time she saw him, the battle for Badajos would be over. It was neither reasonable nor feasible to renew her attack until then.

Always assuming he was alive in the morning.

Chapter Eight

IT BEGAN AT TEN O'CLOCK THAT NIGHT.

Tamsyn had ridden out of Elvas in the late afternoon. She rode through the army encampment, noticing the air of low-key excitement as men, fortified by an extra ration of grog, gathered in groups, checking their equipment, exchanging anecdotes of past campaigns. A few looked up as she passed, but their attention was taken more by Cesar than by the Arab's rider.

Tamsyn wondered where Julian could be in this tent city. The senior officers' tents were easily identified by their size, and she rode past several, hearing voices within raised in laughter, the sound of crockery and glass chinking as Wellington's officers dined together in the hours before the battle.

It didn't occur to her to attempt to find St. Simon; he would need all his concentration for the night to come. Her solitary reconnaissance was as much for something to do as anything else. She'd been brought up in a warrior encampment, knew the apprehension and the excitement before an engagement, and it was impossible for her to stay in Elvas, a useless spectator, watching and waiting.

With dusk came an eerie silence as the daytime gunfire and shelling tailed off. The atmosphere in the camp changed. Officers appeared from their tents, orders were given in low, crisp tones, and men began to move in groups toward the trenches. The night was dark, heavy clouds obscuring the moon.

Tamsyn rode outside the camp to a small hill, where she sat her horse and waited. Sentry lights wavered on the ramparts of Badajos, but apart from that it was still and dark across the plain, no indication of the army of men creeping through the trenches to drop their ladders into the ditches before the breaches in the city walls, or of the storming parties massed behind them.

But the French would know they were coming. Their own intelligence network would have told them to expect the assault even if they didn't know the time or the configuration. But they would be ready to defend the breaches, holding their breath in the same silence as their attackers.

The fine hairs on the back of her neck lifted, and Cesar shifted his hooves and whinnied softly.

Then the dreadful waiting silence was broken by a thundering war cry as the cheering British troops rushed through the outer ditches to reach the walls. Mortars roared in response from the ramparts, and the night was split with gunfire and exploding shells.

Tamsyn closed her eyes involuntarily as the noise became hideous, every pause in the firing filled with piercing screams, and the clarion calls of the bugles repeatedly sounding the advance. A violent light flashed across her eyelids, and she opened her eyes to see two brilliant fireballs flaming against the sky as they were shot from the ramparts to fall to the ground half a mile away, where they continued to blaze, illuminating the ghastly scene.

In the burning light Tamsyn discerned a group of men sheltered from the gunfire behind a small mound but still within range of the shells. The unmistakable figure of the Duke of Wellington stood out in the light thrown from a torch held by an officer beside him.

She urged the reluctant Cesar forward and joined the outskirts of the group, where men stood by their horses in alert readiness but at a discreet distance from the commander in chief, who was writing orders in the light of the torch. The screams of the wounded were clearer here, mingling with the long, drawn-out groans of the dying. Again and again the bugles signaled the advance, and the men hurled themselves up the ladders, to face the deadly resistance of the defenders, who hurled firebombs and barrels of gunpowder with short fuses into the ditches below, where they exploded, casting up burning bodies in a ghastly fountain of death.

Men rode up on lathered horses with information for the commander in chief from the thick of the fighting. The message was always one of failure. Every attempt was being beaten back; the troops were exhausted, decimated, their officers slaughtered like flies as the defenders hurled them back from the summit of the ladders. Wellington's face was white granite in the flickering torchlight as he received the stream of desperate communications, but he seemed to Tamsyn to be unflustered, writing more orders calmly, speaking in collected tones to his staff gathered close around him.

Then the bugle calls changed, and she recognized the note of recall. Over and over it sounded, but she could neither see nor hear any diminution in the savage conflict. The earth continued to throw up flame and burning bodies, whose hideous screams warred with the bellowing of the guns and the exploding mines. It was impossible to imagine anyone emerging alive from that inferno, and she stood by her nervous horse in a kind of numbed trance of horror, wondering why men would do this, would engage in such wholesale slaughter just to take over an insignificant heap of bricks and mortar.

But coherent reasoning wasn't possible, and her thoughts and emotions finally centered on the name of Julian St. Simon, repeating itself over and over again in her head like the refrain of a song that wouldn't be banished. He became the focus of the conflagration, the only reality her mind could grasp, but she couldn't manage to speculate where he was, whether he was alive, or whether he was lying somewhere under a heap of bodies, screaming in his agony, suffocating in the blood of others, or whether he was now only a cold, pale lump of bleeding clay.

It was half past eleven, an hour and a half after the murderous mayhem had begun, when an officer galloped *ventre à terre* through the group, his horse foam-flecked around the bit, his flanks lathered.

Wellington turned as the horse came to a heaving, panting halt beside him. The exchange was short, but it was clear to the bystanders that something had changed.

"Gentlemen, General Picton's taken the castle." Lord March turned from the duke's side to make the announcement. "He's withdrawn troops from the trenches to enable him to maintain his position. We should have the city secured shortly."

So they were in . . . or a toehold, at least. Tamsyn mounted her horse amid the murmured jubilation and rode slowly down toward the city walls. They were in, but at what horrendous cost. The bodies were piled high, the screams and groans as loud as ever. For the wounded and dying, Picton's success came too late. She rode along the walls, heedless of the firing that still continued along the ramparts. The ladders, warm and slippery with blood, still stood against the breaches, littered with severed limbs and tangled corpses.

Had Julian St. Simon survived? It seemed impossible to imagine anyone still living. But even as she thought this, a great cry of triumph went up from within the city walls, and a bugle sounded an exuberant note of victory. The city of Badajos had finally fallen to the besiegers.

Cesar threw up his head and pawed the earth frantically at the smell of blood and this new sound. Tamsyn steadied him and he stood still, obedient to his Mameluke training, but he was quivering with fright, nostrils flared, lips drawn back from the bit.

"All right," she said softly. "Let's get out of here." She turned him away from the city, intending to leave him in Elvas and return on foot, but she hadn't gone more than a few yards when a man in the green tunic of a rifleman hailed her.

Tamsyn drew rein as the man, pouring blood from a shattered jaw, stumbled over to her. He was trying to hold his jaw together with one hand, while he gestured frantically into the darkness behind him.

Tamsyn dismounted swiftly, tearing off the bandanna she wore around her neck. She was used to wounded men and didn't flinch from offering what assistance she could. The fact that she swooned dead away at the sight of her own blood was a mortifying secret that only Gabriel knew.

She bound up the man's jaw with deft, sensitive fingers. "Mount my horse and I'll take you to the rear."

The rifleman shook his head, gesturing again behind him, his eyes as eloquent as his mouth was dumb. She stepped into the darkness and almost tripped over a man groaning in the wet mud. Blood pumped from a gaping wound in his thigh, and he was using both hands to hold the severed flesh together as if it would stanch the flow.

"Me mate," he whispered. "Get 'im to the 'ospital. 'E's got a chance. I'm done fer."

"He's not going to leave you," she said softly, bending over him. "I'll use your belt as a tourniquet, and if you can get onto Cesar, we'll have you with the surgeons in no time."

She worked fast, aware even as she did so that the man's chances of survival were slim. His face was already assuming the ashen cast of a man who looked upon the grave. But his friend wouldn't leave him, and she understood the power of such loyalties.

With almost superhuman strength his friend lifted him into his arms and somehow onto Cesar's back.

"Mount behind him so you can hold him steady," Tamsyn instructed, stroking Cesar's damp neck.

The rifleman hauled himself up into the high-backed, cushioned saddle. The expression in his eyes said clearly that he didn't much relish his position atop this restless white steed, but he took a firm hold of his comrade as Tamsyn began to lead the horse toward the rear.

The way was now thronged with limbers and drays bringing the wounded off the field now that the enfilading fire from the ramparts had ceased. People glanced curiously at the small figure, androgynous in the darkness, trudging along beside the magnificent beast and its wounded riders, but everyone was too occupied to do more than stare in passing.

There was chaos at the hospital tents, where torches swung from poles casting flickering light on the bloody work below. Tamsyn grabbed the sleeve of a passing orderly.

"I've two wounded men here. Can you take them?"

He stared at her, distracted, for a minute, then said, "Put 'em down there. We'll get to 'em when we can."

"One of them needs immediate attention," Tamsyn insisted, her eyes flashing. "I didn't bring him off the field for him to die in the mud within reach of a surgeon."

"What's going on here?" A man in the blood-streaked apron of a surgeon paused beside them as he was hurrying along the stretchers, giving orders for the disposition of their occupants.

"I've two men in need of immediate attention," Tamsyn declared. "And this dolt told me to leave them to die in the mud."

The surgeon blinked and stared in astonishment. "And just who might you be?"

"The commander in chief knows who I am," she said smartly. "And I'm a friend—a close friend—of Colonel, Lord St. Simon of the Sixth. And while I'm bandying words with this village idiot, other men are dying out there because I'm not bringing them in!" She gestured to the hapless orderly with an expression of acute disgust and snapped, "Help them down."

The surgeon examined the two men as they came off Cesar. "One walking wounded," he pronounced. "Take him to the second tent."

The rifleman with the bandaged jaw shook his head, pain flaring in his eyes and indicated his comrade with the same urgency he'd shown Tamsyn before.

"All right, I'll see to him," the surgeon said with a hint of impatience. "I can't promise much, but that leg will have to come off. . . . Hey, you there, bring that stretcher." He hailed two orderlies, running past at the double.

They stopped and came over, lifting the wounded man onto the stretcher. Only when he saw his friend carried inside to the faint hope to be found in the butchery of the tents did the other rifleman go off with the orderly, sticking his hand out to Tamsyn in mute gratitude before he did so.

"Looks like we have work to do, Cesar," Tamsyn said, swinging into the saddle. "I know you'll hate it, but we can't stand around twiddling our thumbs."

She rode back toward the city, looking for wounded who could manage this awkward but speedy form of transportation.

Within the city walls Julian St. Simon, miraculously unscathed but blackened from head to toe from gunfire, stood in the central square and took stock. He'd been at the storming of Ciudad Rodrigo three months before and, horrendous though that had been, it had been nothing compared to this April night.

"Julian! Thank God, man." Frank Frobisher came running across the square. "I saw you go down at the San Jose bastion, but I couldn't get back to you in the crush." The captain had lost his hat, his tunic was ripped, and an oozing gash ran from one scorched eyebrow down to the corner of his mouth.

"I lost my footing, nothing more dramatic than that," Julian said, clapping his friend's arm in a wordless gesture. "Tim's gone to the rear. Piece of shrapnel in his eye."

"And Deerbourne's fallen," Frank said, his expression bleak. "And George Castleton and . . . oh, so many others." He looked around the deserted square.

The inhabitants of Badajos were behind locked doors, not showing their faces to the victors. Sporadic gunfire still sounded from the ramparts.

"The men are in a savage mood," he said somberly. "If the Peer allows them to fall out, there'll be a sack worse than Ciudad Rodrigo."

"He will," Julian asserted, clasping the back of his neck, arching it against his hand in a weary gesture. "They fought like tigers, they saw their comrades slaughtered, he'll give them their revenge."

Both men looked up at the sky where the evening star was fading fast. "If Wellington had hanged the garrison of Ciudad Rodrigo, he'd have saved thousands of lives today," Julian said in a deadened voice. "Philippon would never have held out here if he faced death at defeat."

Frank shrugged. "A trifle medieval, though, Julian, putting a defeated garrison to the sword."

"And you think what's going to happen here will be civilized?" Julian demanded. "The men are going to go to the devil, and we'll have the devil's own work to whip them into shape again at the end of such an orgy."

Frank made no response to this truth.

It was midmorning when the French garrison was sent under escort to Elvas and the English troops were fallen out. They poured into the city, forcing their way through the clogged breaches, exploding into the city streets, a night of bleeding informing a savage bloodlust that had been given license for unbridled satisfaction.

Two hours after dawn Tamsyn had stabled Cesar, exhausted but docile after his hours of labor, and had fallen into her bed at Senhora Braganza's cottage just as she was, muddy and bloodstained, refusing the widow's pressing offers of food and hot water.

She slept for five hours and awoke refreshed and alert, but with the unmistakable sense that something evil was afoot. She swung out of bed and went to the window. The street below was almost deserted, except for a couple of peasants standing in the shade of a wall. They weren't talking, merely leaning against the wall puffing on their pipes.

Tamsyn went downstairs. There was no sign of Senhora Braganza, and she went out into the street, still in her filthy clothes. The sounds from Badajos carried over the still morning air. It was a raucous cacophony. Shouts, crashes, screams, intermingling with odd bursts of music from pipe and drum.

She crossed her arms and shivered. She'd heard such sounds before.

Senhora Braganza came hurrying down the streets carrying a milk churn. In a voluble flood of Portuguese, she swept her lodger into the kitchen, sat her down, and prepared an omelette fragrant with crushed thyme and rosemary and a pot of strong, bitter coffee.

Tamsyn ate mechanically; then she rose to her feet, thanked her hostess with an almost absent smile, and walked back out into the street, heedless of the renewed offers of hot water and clean raiment coming from the cottage kitchen.

Her feet took her without any signals from her brain across the pontoon bridge toward Badajos.

The encampment was almost deserted except for the hospital tents where the frantic activity continued unabated, but there were fewer drays and limbers bringing in the wounded now. Once the order to fall out had been given, the men had abandoned their injured comrades for the orgiastic pleasures to be found in the sack of Badajos.

Tamsyn entered the city through one of the breaches. Someone in the ditch below was calling for water, a low, continuous supplication. She stopped, looking for the sufferer, but couldn't tell among the tangle of bodies who might be alive. Part of her knew it was madness, but something impelled her onward into the city.

A group of soldiers raced past her, their arms loaded with goods plundered from a store whose smashed door bore mute witness to the looting. The sounds of drunken singing came from an alley, where another group sat around a split casket of wine, scooping the wine into their mouths with hands or their shakos, their muskets lying disregarded at their feet. They looked up as Tamsyn came toward them, their mouths stained red, their eyes unfocused, but they were in a benign mood and only called out a few jocular gibes as she went past.

She'd left her rifle and bandolier in Elvas and carried only a knife at her belt, but it occurred to her that if her male attire didn't fool the men, her filthy, bloodstained appearance was probably sufficient protection. Her only jewelry was the locket at her neck, and that was hidden beneath her shirt.

She walked on through the cobbled streets, hearing the crack of muskets above a confused babble of screams, and shouts of laughter and rage. Somewhere a drum was beating and a pipe trilled in accompaniment. A nun in a torn black habit ran out of a church, pursued by a laughing, shouting troop of soldiers, tunics and shirts unbuttoned. One of them flourished a gold embroidered altar cloth like a flag of triumph; another carried two massive silver candlesticks.

The nun dodged sideways into a doorway, and Tam-

syn glimpsed her terrified face beneath her cowl before
the barred door behind her opened and she was dragged
inside to relative safety. The men came charging after
her, stopped when they couldn't find her, and milled
around in befuddlement, shaking their heads as if they
could solve the mystery in that way. Then someone
tossed a wineskin to his companion, and they turned in
a body as if obeying some collective instinct, surging
back toward the church.

Tamsyn shuddered, anger and hideous memory intermingling now to burn with a fierce, consuming
flame. Her hand was on her knife, and she wished she
had her rifle, not because she felt threatened herself, but
because her rage was murderous as she saw what soldiers
were doing to the inhabitants of Badajos. There were
officers here and there, trying to stop the worst of the
excesses, but the men, in the grip of wine and victory,
were beyond their control.

Tamsyn saw two officers remonstrating with a ragtag
group of infantrymen who were conducting an auction
in the street. One of the items on the block was a young
girl. A soldier fired his musket over the head of one of
the officers, another leveled his weapon at the heart of
the other. They were two against twenty drunken savages and were forced to retreat while Tamsyn watched
from a doorway.

They turned and left, and she couldn't blame them,
but she stayed herself, waiting until the girl was sold for
a ruby the size of a hen's egg and, amid gales of laughter,
tossed into the audience, into the arms of a burly rifleman with an eye patch.

The man carried off his prize, pushing through the
crowd, making for a square at the end of the alley.
Tamsyn followed, her deadly rage now focused on this

one episode. She couldn't stop the wholesale savagery, but she would stop this.

The square was an aimless tumult as soldiers wandered in and out of the stores, where doors had been smashed, the iron bars ripped from ground-floor windows, goods spilling out onto the street.

The girl was keening like a lost child, and Tamsyn increased her speed, dogging the soldier's footsteps, her eyes sweeping the ground for a weapon more substantial than her knife. Two men were playing dice, sitting on a doorstep amid the ruins of a draper's store. Their muskets were on the ground beside them. Tamsyn darted sideways, grabbed up one of the firearms, and was off and running down the street, ignoring the outraged yells behind her.

The yells ceased quickly—retrieving a musket was not a priority—and the men returned to their game.

A pump stood in the center of the square on a stone plinth reached by three broad, shallow steps. The soldier carried his prize to the steps, clearly intending to enjoy her there in the sunshine. As he set her down, Tamsyn leaped forward, swinging the butt of the musket at his head. It caught him a crack over the ear, and he bellowed, loosening his hold on his captive as he swung to face his attacker.

Tamsyn jumped back, the musket pointing steadily at his heart. "Bastard," she said with soft ferocity. "Murdering son of a bitch. Raping that little girl is going to make you very proud, isn't it? And what were you going to do with her when you'd finished? Sell her to your friends here?"

The girl was on her knees on the step, hunched over, still keening. The soldier seemed bemused, his ear ringing from the blow of the musket, blood trickling down his neck where the skin had broken. He stared at the diminutive figure confronting him, hardly hearing her words.

"Run, *niña*," Tamsyn said urgently. The girl scrambled to her feet, looking wildly around at the crowded square as if searching for safe passage. Then the soldier seemed to come to his senses, and with another bellow he lunged for the girl as she began to run. Tamsyn stuck out her foot, and he went down to the cobbles, but he was up in a second, shaking his head like an injured bull.

Colonel St. Simon and Captain Frobisher entered the square just as a group of men close to the pump became aware of the altercation on the steps. The young girl was running barefoot across the cobbles, tears of terror streaming from her eyes. She bumped into Julian, who caught her, steadying her against his body, his eyes riveted on the scene in the center of the square. The girl huddled against him, quivering like a hunted fawn, recognizing safety in the gold braid and epaulets of an officer's uniform.

"Jesus, Mary, and Joseph!" Julian murmured as a ray of sun caught the unmistakable silvery head of La Violette a second before she disappeared, engulfed by the angry crowd of jeering soldiers. He unpeeled the girl from his side and thrust her at Frank, ordering curtly, "Get her to safety"; then he was running toward the pump, drawing his sword, his pistol in his other hand.

He charged into the middle of the fracas, wielding his sword to left and right, cursing the men in the vivid language of the barracks as he cut a path through them. The vigorous cursing was more potent than his weapons at that moment and seemed to pierce the men's drunken trance, reminding them on some level of the familiar discipline of everyday life. There was a hesitation, a slight swaying of the tight circle, and Julian lunged forward to the center.

Tamsyn was struggling in the grip of the man whom she'd deprived of his prize. The musket had been wrenched from her hands, and she was fighting now to pull her knife free from her belt. Julian fired his pistol into the air at the same moment as he grabbed Tamsyn's free arm. Briefly, she was the rope in a tug of war, then Julian brought his sword slashing down, and the man let go with a roar of pain, blood spurting from a great gash in his hand.

An ugly murmur ran around the circle of men, and others began to move toward the pump from the four corners of the square. Deliberately, Julian sheathed his sword, thrust his pistol into his belt, then turned and caught Tamsyn up under one arm as if she were a sack of potatoes.

"Goddamn your black souls," he swore at them. "Let me pass. This one's mine." He pushed his way down the steps with his violently wriggling burden. Someone laughed, a drunken cackle that was taken up by the others. Their mood changed and they fell back, offering ribald suggestions to the officer, who was good fellow enough to indulge in his own sport.

"Put me down, damn you!" Tamsyn snarled, the blood pounding in her lolling head. It was ludicrous that he should be able to carry her in such a fashion, with neither her feet nor her hands touching the ground. No man had ever before taken advantage of her diminutive stature, and the murderous rage already devouring her blazed to new heights.

"No, I will not, you little fool," Julian declared, his own anger as hot as Tamsyn's. "What the devil do you think you're doing here . . . meddling in this inferno?

It's no business of yours. If I'd had a grain of sense, I should have left you to them.''

Tamsyn sunk her teeth into his calf.

Julian's yell could be heard three streets away. "Bloody savage!" He swung her upward, changing hands on her body as if she were a caber he was going to toss at the Highland games, then swung her around his neck, grasping her wrists in one hand, her ankles in another, so that she dangled like a hunter's kill.

Tamsyn's language was enough to turn the air blue as he strode out of the square with her, but Julian ignored her. He was too filled with anger and disgust at what was going on in Badajos to give a thought to Tamsyn's outrage at this cavalier treatment. He couldn't imagine what could have brought her into the city except sheer stupidity . . . unless she was intending to take advantage of chaos and do her own looting.

"God's grace, Julian, what have you got there?" Frank's startled voice arrested him as he passed a small courtyard, its metal gates hanging from their hinges.

Julian turned into the courtyard where a fountain bubbled incongruously in the midst of destruction. The girl Tamsyn had rescued was cowering behind Frank, her eyes stark with terror in her ashen face.

"This is Violette," Julian stated grimly, bending his neck and lifting Tamsyn bodily off his shoulders, setting her on her feet. The girl ran forward with a cry, flinging her arms around Tamsyn, pouring forth a voluble stream of gratitude, her tongue at last loosened.

Julian followed the gist of the tumbling words and finally understood what Tamsyn had been doing in the square. He hadn't connected the fleeing girl to Violette's presence. Thankful that he hadn't expressed his sour supposition that she'd been after her own plunder, he was about to apologize for his roughness when she turned on him.

"You . . . you're no better than that scum . . . that filthy, murdering, raping rabble!" she declared, spitting the words at him as if they were snake's venom. "How dare you treat me like that? You're a blackguard, a piece of gutter-born—"

"Hold your tongue, you!" Julian roared, forgetting all inclination to make peace under this tirade. "If I hadn't come on the scene, *mi muchacha,* you'd be lying on the cobbles offered up for whoever chose to take a turn."

"Filthy, loathsome swine," she said, her voice suddenly low and trembling. To his astonishment Julian saw a glitter of tears in the violet eyes, her face twisted into a mask of grief.

"Soldiers," she said in the same voice. "Stinking gutter sweepings, every one of them. Barbarians, worse than animals." Her hand swept around the courtyard in an all-encompassing gesture. "Animals don't behave like this. They don't treat their own kind like pieces of insensate trash to be . . ." She fell abruptly silent as tears clogged her voice. She turned away toward the broken gates, her hand pushing at the air as if she would hold off her stunned audience.

Frank stared in complete bewilderment; the girl shrank against him again. Julian, with a muttered execration, shook himself free of the mesmerizing trance of Tamsyn's violent, impassioned speech and ran after her.

"Tamsyn!"

"Leave me alone!" She turned her head aside, pushing him away as he came up to her.

A silver tear glistened on her cheek, making rills in the dirt as it trickled down to the corner of her mouth.

Her tongue darted, licked up the tear, but it was followed by another and another.

Julian forgot the accusations she'd hurled at his head. He forgot how much he disliked the brigand in her. He forgot how angry she made him almost every time they came into contact. He was aware only of the power of her distress. He noticed for the first time the blood on her clothes.

"Come," he said softly. "It's time we left this place. There's nothing anyone can do here until they're surfeited." He laid a hand on her shoulder to direct her toward the walls of the city.

"Leave me alone!" she repeated, but with less conviction.

Julian shook his head. "I'll carry you if I must, Violette."

"Espadachín," she threw at him, but the tears were flowing fast now, and she brushed her arm across her eyes, smudging the grime on her cheeks so she looked like a chimney sweep. But she didn't resist him this time when he put his hand at her waist and ushered her down the street.

"You rescued the girl," he said, trying to offer her some comfort.

"One among so many!" she shot back. "They're raping nuns, desecrating the churches, spitting men on their bayonets. I've seen it before." The last sentence was so low, he had to bend his head to hear it, but the intensity of her pain could be heard as clearly as a clarion call.

Outside the city, fatigue parties of Portuguese soldiers were digging pits for the dead, the bodies piled on carts, waiting to be consigned to the earth as soon as the pits were deep enough.

"You're all as bad as each other," Tamsyn suddenly renewed her attack. "What possible justification can there be for this? Such slaughter . . . mindless slaughter."

"Ask Napoleon," Julian said dryly. "Ask Philippon. If he'd surrendered the city when it was clear defense was no longer viable, thousands of lives would have been saved. It isn't just us, Violette."

"I didn't say it was," she retorted. "It's soldiers. Brutal, bestial——"

"It's war. It makes beasts of men," he interrupted. "But what of your father? He made war for the sake of gold . . . no principle, no——"

"Don't you dare talk of my father, Englishman!" She spun round on him, and her knife was in her hand, her eyes, still brilliant with tears, now glittered with fury. "What would you know of a man like El Baron? You puny, weak-minded English soldier!" She spat the last word as if it was the ultimate insult.

"And don't you dare threaten me, Violette." Julian grabbed her wrist, twisting until her fingers opened around the handle of the knife and it fell to the ground. "I'm sick to death of being savaged by you." He pushed her away from him so abruptly that she stumbled to her knees. "I wash my hands of you. Go where you please, just get out of my sight." He spun on his heel and marched, seething, toward the encampment. But after a few yards his pace slowed. Reluctantly, he glanced over his shoulder.

Tamsyn remained on her knees on the ground, her head bowed, tears falling into the mud where she knelt. She seemed unaware of his departure. For the first time since it had happened, she was reliving in every detail the massacre of Pueblo de St. Pedro. Always before, she'd allowed herself to remember only her father's death-defying fight, her mother lying peacefully in the shadows. But now she saw the rest of it. The murdered babies, the raped women, the tortured men as the flames of the burning village leaped into the sky. And she and Gabriel, two against several hundred, had watched it all from the hilltop, helpless to do anything. And afterward, three days later, when the savages had left the burned buildings and the massacred inhabitants, taking with them what plunder they could find, they had gone down to the village and buried Cecile and the baron and dug a pit for the others, just like the pits being dug here, because the two of them alone couldn't dig enough graves for every one of the dead.

"Come along, you can't stay here." Julian's voice was gentle as he bent over her. He lifted her up, and she turned her head into his shoulder. He felt her body shaking with her sobs. He carried her to his own tent, told Dobbin brusquely to make himself scarce, and went inside, closing and tying the tent flap behind them.

"Tell me about it," he said quietly.

Chapter Nine

JULIAN WALKED THROUGH THE ENCAMPMENT TOWARD THE hospital tents. There were many of his own men to be found there, and a visit from their colonel would do something to raise their spirits, although little for his own. Those of his men not being shoveled into the grave pits or lying mutilated in the hospitals were indulging in the depths of depravity in Badajos. Restoring them to the keen, good-hearted, spirited fighting men that he knew them to be would take the gallows and the triangles—grim work, but Wellington would order it done with the same ruthless pragmatism as he'd permitted their excesses.

"Colonel St. Simon, isn't it?"

He was startled from his morose reverie as he ducked into the first tent. A surgeon brandishing a butcher's knife looked up from the trestle table where a man lay strapped and unconscious, his right leg bared to the knee where jagged bone stuck through the skin.

"Yes." Julian paused politely. He didn't think he knew the surgeon.

"Forgive me . . . I came across a most unusual young woman last night, said she was a friend . . . a *close* friend of yours." The surgeon wiped his damp

forehead with his sleeve. "She was most insistent I give
her wounded my immediate attention . . . very per-
suasive with it. Said the Peer would know who she
was."

"La Violette," Julian said almost to himself. "What
exactly was she doing?"

"Bringing men in from the field on a magnificent
white charger . . . never seen a horse like it." The
surgeon bent again to his patient, who had stirred and
groaned. "Forgive me, he's coming round. I need to get
this leg off before he does."

Julian nodded and walked away, closing his ears to
the scrunch of knife through bone. So Tamsyn had
spent the night bringing in the wounded on that fidgety
Cesar. Offering such aid didn't quite match with her
outspoken hatred for all soldiers, but it didn't surprise
him that she'd had some part in last night's ghastly proceedings; he was beginning to wonder why she hadn't
been with Picton's men scaling the walls of the castle.

He'd learned much in the hour he'd spent with her
in his tent. She'd talked in a low voice through her tears,
but with perfect coherence. She'd told him of the horror of Pueblo de St. Pedro, and he'd had no difficulty
imagining it. He too had seen such things.

But now Colonel, Lord Julian St. Simon was troubled. La Violette had taken on different contours. He
was beginning to see complexities where before he'd
seen only the opportunistic, gloriously sensual brigand
. . . one whose seductive wiles he must resist with every fiber. Now he saw a young woman left alone in the
world by the horrific murder of her beloved parents. A
young woman who had lost all the framework of the
only existence she'd known, cast upon a world at war to
make her future as she could.

It was a disturbing picture, not least because beneath it he still saw the other Tamsyn. He still believed she'd been playing on Wellington's known susceptibilities with her pathetic story, and yet he knew in his bones that she had been manipulating no heartstrings in his tent when she'd painted the unvarnished picture for him.

He didn't know what to make of any of it. He stopped by a stretcher where a private from his brigade lay breathing raggedly through his mouth, his face smothered in bloodstained bandages.

"The surgeon says you'll be on your way to Lisbon in the morning, Carter," Julian said. "Out of it for good."

"I'll not be sorry, sir," the swathed face said. "But I've lost me nose, sir. What'll the missus say?"

"She'll be glad to have you back with two legs and two arms," Julian said, touching his shoulder and moving on, aware of how inadequate such reassurance was, and yet it was all he had.

Tamsyn, lying in a hip bath of steaming water in her room in Elvas, was trying to decide whether her emotional collapse had done her any good with Julian St. Simon. She hadn't planned it, but it had happened, and it just might be turned to good purpose.

The colonel had clearly been moved by her story. He'd been gentle and comforting, ordering his servant to make tea when her tale was told and her tears had finally dried. He'd sat with his arm around her on the narrow cot, saying nothing because there was nothing to say. She'd been more grateful for his silence than anything else. It took a sensitive man to resist the temptation to wade in with clumsy words of comfort that would only trivialize her pain.

Later he'd walked her back to Elvas and left her at her lodgings.

Thoughtfully, Tamsyn soaped her legs, grimacing at the filthy scum forming on the surface of the water. She'd need a jug of clean water to wash off the soap.

As if in answer to the thought, Senhora Braganza came puffing up the stairs with a copper jug of fresh water. Tamsyn thanked her and stood up in the tub. The senhora poured the hot stream over her hair and body, and Tamsyn shuddered with pleasure as the dirt flowed from her body.

Her own shirt and underclothes had been laundered by the senhora, but they were beginning to show serious signs of wear, and her britches were almost beyond help. She needed new clothes, and the shops in Elvas were plentifully stocked, but she had no money until Gabriel returned. Of course, once Gabriel returned, she wouldn't need to buy clothes, since he'd be bringing all her possessions as well as the treasure—her inheritance from her father that had been well hidden from his murderers.

Perhaps Colonel St. Simon could be induced to make her a small loan. It would give her an excuse to go in search of him again.

She dressed in her threadbare garments. The senhora hadn't been able to get the bloodstains out of her britches, but they blended with all the other stains accumulated in the two weeks that she'd been wearing them. At least her skin and hair were clean.

Tamsyn examined herself in the spotted glass that served as a mirror. Not too bad, considering. She felt purged in some way, as if by exposing herself to the horrors of Badajos, she'd lanced a festering boil. And somewhere inside her lurked a warm flicker of pleasure and relief that Julian St. Simon had survived the horrors of the assault.

She sniffed hungrily at the rich aromas coming from the kitchen and ran downstairs.

The senhora had prepared a hearty soup of cabbage, potatoes, and spicy sausage and watched with satisfied nods as her lodger consumed two large bowls and several thick hunks of crusty bread. Then, feeling ready for anything, Tamsyn went to fetch Cesar and rode out to the encampment in search of the colonel.

But as it happened, while Tamsyn was in the encampment, the colonel was in Wellington's headquarters, obeying an urgent summons that had taken him from his hospital visiting back into Elvas.

It was clear to Julian that the commander in chief was in a strange mood. His satisfaction in his victory was tainted by the loss of so many thousands of his best men, and his ruthless decision to give the survivors the run of Badajos did little to comfort him for that loss. Like St. Simon, he believed that if he'd made an example of the garrison at Ciudad Rodrigo in January, the garrison at Badajos would have yielded in a timely fashion and spared both sides indescribable agony. But public opinion would not have supported the uncivilized slaughter of a surrendered garrison, though it would turn a blind eye to the hideous sack and rape of the now-defenseless town.

"Julian, this business of La Violette." He came straight to the point as the colonel entered. "Have you thought any more about it?"

"There's hardly been time," Julian pointed out. "But my answer must be the same, sir. I can't possibly agree to such a thing."

Wellington frowned and began to pace the room,

hands clasped at his back. "We need her information, Julian. I'm going to drive the French out of Spain this summer and march into France by autumn. I need to know about those passes, and I need to have more freedom of movement where the partisans are concerned. Violette can make that possible."

"I don't deny it." Julian was beginning to feel he had a desperate rear-guard action on his hands. "But I also believe she'll sell the information for something other than my soul," he added caustically.

"Oh, come now, man, don't exaggerate!" the duke chided. "Six months of your time, that's all." His eyes narrowed shrewdly. "Forgive me for saying so—she must feel she has some grounds for believing you might agree to such a proposal."

"She has *no* grounds," Julian stated flatly. "No claims on me whatsoever."

"I see." Wellington scratched his nose. "Well, she is a most unusual young woman."

"A manipulative, thieving mercenary," the colonel declared as flatly as before. "I will not be a party to her games. I'll lay odds, if you offer sufficient money, she'll spill her guts without blinking an eye."

"Possibly, but I doubt it. . . . Claret?" The duke strolled to the decanters on the table.

"Thank you." Julian waited, knowing the battle was far from won. He took the glass offered him with a nod of thanks.

"I doubt it," the duke continued as if there'd been no break in the conversation. "I have the unmistakable conviction that she knows her price and won't budge. She wants only one thing . . . and, Lord in heaven, I can't fault her for it. The poor little creature's all alone in the world; she can't be more than nineteen. What kind of a future is there for her here with neither friends nor family?"

Julian sipped his wine and didn't reply, remembering the girl's anguish and desolation. Despite that, he was convinced that "poor little creature" was not an accurate description of the orphaned daughter of El Baron and his English mate.

"I'm sure she'll be able to locate her mother's family," the duke continued pensively. "But it would be better for her to present a more orthodox appearance. More convincing . . . more appealing, don't you think?"

"Perhaps," Julian agreed dryly, not giving an inch.

Wellington glanced up at him thoughtfully. "Well, if you won't, you won't. But there is something else I want to discuss with you."

Julian waited during a lengthening silence, unconvinced that his commander in chief had given up.

"I don't need to tell you how skeptical the government is about this campaign," Wellington said at last. "They say we exaggerate the importance of the victories, that we win them at too great an expense of men and money. God knows, they'll have fodder enough for plaint when the casualties from this filthy business appear in the *Gazette*."

Julian nodded. Everyone knew the opposition Wellington encountered from the English government and how near impossible it was for him to get the financial and material support he needed for the Peninsular campaign.

"I need someone to go and present our case at Westminster," the duke said. "Someone reliable, someone the government will respect, who'll give a firsthand account of the campaign. Dispatches don't present the case adequately, and civilian observers are the very devil! They haven't the faintest notion of what's going on even when it's under their noses."

"And you're fingering me for the task," Julian said without inflection. He refilled the commander's glass and then his own.

"You're the perfect emissary," Wellington said. "You're the youngest colonel in my army, you've had a brilliant career thus far and are clearly headed for a general's baton in a year or two. You've been mentioned countless times in dispatches, so your name's well-known in government circles. They'll give credence to what you say."

Julian again made no immediate response, and the commander regarded him with the same shrewd look as before. What Wellington didn't mention, because it went without saying, was that Colonel, Lord Julian St. Simon's title was one of the oldest in the land. His fortune was beyond the dreams of avarice, and his estates, not including Tregarthan, covered entire counties. Such a position and influence made him an even more powerful spokesman to the lords of Westminster.

Julian walked to the window and stood frowning down into the street. "You're asking me to leave the army just as the summer's campaigning is to begin," he said finally. "To abandon my brigade when they're going to be facing months of marching and fighting."

"I deem this mission to London to be of vital importance, St. Simon." Wellington spoke now in the clipped tones of the commander in chief, the note of intimacy vanished. "I've colonels aplenty to take over your brigade, but I've no one better suited than you to undertake this diplomatic business. If you wish, I'll give O'Connor field rank as colonel in your absence. I understand his wound isn't going to send him home." He paused, then said deliberately, "You'll have regimental rank as brigadier immediately on your return."

Julian's heart jumped. From brigadier to general was a small step, and he'd promised himself he'd carry a general's baton by the time he was thirty. But he thought he'd achieve it through fighting . . . leading his men to victory . . . not by smooth talk and careful politics in the corridors of Westminster.

"Am I to understand you're ordering me to London, sir?"

"Precisely, Colonel."

Julian turned from the window. "And this other business?"

"Oh, come now, Julian." Wellington was smiling now. "You could surely shepherd her to England, help her make contact with her mother's family. You're going there, anyway."

"Oh, escort duty would be simple enough," Julian said aridly. "But that isn't what Violette is demanding. She wants a schoolmaster, if you recall."

Wellington chuckled. "Nervy little thing, isn't she?"

Julian sighed. "I wouldn't disagree with that, sir."

"So you'll do it?"

"Supposing I arrange to hire a suitable house and a governess for her?" the colonel suggested, his back now to the wall. "I'll escort her to England and leave the tutoring to some respectable female. Then I can be back here in a couple of months."

Wellington shrugged. "We'll put it to Violette. If she accepts that price, then it's fine by me. I only want her information."

"I'll send Sanderson to fetch her." Julian went to the door and gave the order to the brigade-major, then returned to the room. The commander was standing at the open window now, listening to the confused riot of noise coming from Badajos.

"I'll give them until tomorrow; then, if we can't get them out of there, we'll erect a gallows in the square," he said evenly. "Hang a couple of looters, that should bring them to their senses."

"They'll be in bad shape, sir."

"Oh, I know. Demoralized, hung over, ashamed. Sieges are filthy work, Julian."

"None worse," Julian agreed somberly, sipping his wine.

Sanderson returned in five minutes with the information that La Violette was not in her lodgings and had taken her horse from the stables.

"Left us?" Wellington raised an eyebrow at the colonel.

Julian shook his head. "No, she doesn't give up that easily. Besides, I heard her promise that giant bodyguard that she'd wait for him in Elvas." He put down his glass. "I'll go and look for her."

He left, trying to disguise his alarm at the thought that she might have returned to Badajos. He couldn't imagine that she'd do anything so foolhardy, but Violette was a law unto herself, beyond the fathoming of any ordinary man. He couldn't understand why he was worried about her; it was the most annoying aspect of the whole business. She'd thrown his life and career into chaos, manipulated his emotions as easily as she manipulated his physical responses, and yet he needed to know she was safe.

He found her sitting amid a circle of his officers outside his tent, Cesar idly cropping the sparse grass beside her.

"Oh, there you are, milord colonel." She offered him a sunny smile as he rode up. "I have a small favor to ask, so I was looking for you and met your staff. And Dobbin very kindly made me some tea." She indicated the enamel mug in her hand.

"How pleasant," he said aridly. "Gentlemen, have we nothing better to do this morning than lounge around over the teacups?"

"We were talking of the situation in Badajos," Tamsyn said swiftly as her companions rose to their feet in one collective movement. "Captain Frobisher was telling me what he'd done with the girl I rescued this morning. And these other officers were explaining how they'd managed to secure the doors of a convent as a safe house. They've been conducting parties of women there and are just returned from the town for some rest."

Julian regretted his sarcasm as he looked at the exhausted faces of his officers. "My apologies," he said readily, with his quick, irresistible smile that had earned him pardon since childhood. "I'm out of sorts. I didn't mean to snap."

"Oh, we're all out of sorts," Frank said with a weary answering smile. "We were wondering whether we could round up our own men from the streets if we headed up a sizable party of noncommissioned officers."

"Get some rest first. We'll try this evening. They might be so insensible by then they'll come quietly." He turned back to Tamsyn. "Wellington wishes to talk to you, Violette. If you'd come with me now."

It didn't sound much like a request to Tamsyn, but she merely smiled and said mischievously, "I'd be delighted to come with you, milord colonel. As I've made clear on many occasions."

Julian's lips almost disappeared and the bright-blue eyes shot sparks as the other men suppressed their grins.

"Allow me to assist you to mount, ma'am?" Frank offered before Julian's temper could find voice. He cupped his palms for her foot, and she sprang up into the saddle with a word of thanks.

Gathering the reins together, she raised an eyebrow at the still-fulminating colonel and said, "I'm ready to accompany you, sir."

Julian turned his horse without a word and moved off down the narrow aisle between the rows of tents. Tamsyn waved a cheery hand in farewell to her companions and followed.

They rode in single file over the pontoon bridge into Elvas and into the stableyard at headquarters. Still in silence, Julian strode ahead of her up the stairs and into the building. "Is his lordship alone, Sanderson?"

"Yes, sir. Lord March left a few minutes ago."

"Good." He knocked and opened the door, gesturing brusquely to Tamsyn that she should precede him into the sanctum.

"Good afternoon, sir," she greeted the commander in chief politely. "May I congratulate you on such a splendid victory." There was no mistaking the note of bitter irony beneath the apparent courtesy, and Wellington looked at her sharply, frowning.

"My men fought like tigers," he stated. "And they died like heroes."

"I'm sure," she returned in much the same tone. "Colonel St. Simon says you wish to speak to me." She perched on the deep windowsill and regarded him with her shining head to one side, her eyes alert, like a cheeky robin, Julian thought, amused despite his irritation.

"We have a proposal to put to you. It's the colonel's suggestion, so perhaps he should explain it."

Tamsyn turned her look of bright inquiry on the colonel. "I'm all ears, milord colonel."

Julian explained his proposal, his voice expressionless, his face impassive, and Tamsyn listened with the same air of alert interest.

When he'd finished, she said simply, "Oh, no, that won't do at all."

The cool negative fell into a stunned silence. Both men stared at her; then St. Simon said, "And just why won't it?"

"Well, you must see that a mere governess couldn't give me what I need," she said reasonably. "Since I'm certain my mother's family are aristocrats, I need to know how to go on in the highest circles of Society. Governesses don't know that kind of thing. I'll need to know all sorts of things about the top families as well as all the little mannerisms and quirks and tricks of dress that only an intimate of those circles would know. And how could a governess perform the introductions when I'm ready to be presented to the family? Someone unimpeachable has to vouch for me . . . explain about the Duke of Wellington's kind protection." Another winning smile in the duke's direction.

"She has a point, Julian."

Julian met his commander's steady gaze, reading the immutable message. He swung round toward the figure on the windowsill. Tamsyn was examining her fingernails with an air of absorption.

"Damn you, Violette!" he hissed. "Damn you for a tricky, conniving witch!"

Clearly this was not a good moment to ask for a small loan. Tamsyn raised her eyes and offered a tentative smile. "I won't be a nuisance, milord colonel, I promise you. I'll be a most obedient pupil and a credit to your tutoring."

Julian's expression registered total disbelief, and Wellington gave vent to his neighing laugh.

"She has you there, Julian. Sewn up tight as a Christmas goose."

Julian walked over to Tamsyn. He leaned over her, his hands braced on the window on either side of her head, and said softly so that only she could hear, "You just might have bitten off more than you can chew, Violette. I'm going to have you jumping through hoops until you don't know whether you're in this week or the next. So be warned."

Tamsyn touched her tongue to her lips and her eyes narrowed. "I think I can handle anything you throw at me, milord colonel."

Their eyes locked. There was antagonism and challenge, but there was a perverse excitement too at the war game they were about to play.

Then Julian straightened and spoke at an ordinary pitch, but his voice was completely devoid of expression. "So we've agreed to your price, Violette. It's time to fulfill your side of the bargain."

"Certainly," she said.

Wellington called for Sanderson to take notes, and they began. St. Simon sat in a chair by the hearth, listening intently to the brigand's answers, listening for any evasion, any hint that she might be fooling them. They had only her word for the truth of the information she was providing, but he found that he trusted her to be good to that word. She was as slippery as an eel, but he thought that if she said she was playing fair, then she was.

Why he should have this faith in her, he didn't know.

It was a long and exhaustive session. At the end Tamsyn drew an elaborate map indicating the passes through the Guadarrama heights, then stretched, arching her back against her hands. "I think that's everything I agreed to."

"Yes," Wellington said with a pleased nod. "Most satisfactory. Thank you."

"I won't say it was a pleasure," Tamsyn said frankly.

"Oh, don't give me that!" Julian scoffed. "You've got precisely what you wanted for your information."

"True." *And the means now to be revenged upon the Penhallans.* "Do we begin our journey as soon as Gabriel arrives?"

"The sooner the better," he said harshly. "And I want this in writing, too." He gestured to Sanderson, still sitting at the table. "The contract is for six months, beginning this day, April seventh, 1812. It will conclude on October seventh. Whether you've achieved what you wish or no. Is that understood?"

"Perfectly."

Sanderson wrote busily, sanded the sheet, and pushed it across the table for Tamsyn's signature.

"How very formal," she murmured, affixing her signature to the document. "Anyone would think you didn't trust me, milord colonel."

"Anyone would think I had reason to trust you," he retorted, striding to the door.

"Oh," Tamsyn ran after him as he marched down the stairs. "Since our contract is to begin today, even though we haven't started our journey, I feel sure I can ask you a favor. Could you make me a small loan? Just until Gabriel returns."

He stopped at the street door and stared at her incredulously. "You want me to lend you money on top of everything?"

"Just to buy some clothes. These I have on are falling apart. I'll repay you as soon as Gabriel returns."

He regarded her in frowning silence for a moment; then slowly he nodded. "Very well. Since, as you say, our contract is to begin today, then I agree, you certainly stand in sore need of different clothes. I know just the place. Colonel Delacourt's wife was telling me all about it." Briskly, he set off up the street without looking to see if she was accompanying him.

Tamsyn hesitated. There'd been a look in his eye that made her a little uneasy, a glint of amusement that didn't strike her as particularly friendly. Then, with a shrug, she set off after him, running to catch up.

"There's no need for you to accompany me, milord colonel."

"Don't call me that."

"Why not?" she asked with an innocent smile.

"I don't care for the tone."

"Ahh. Then what should I call you?"

"Colonel will do fine. Lord St. Simon, if you prefer."

Tamsyn pulled a wry face. "That seems very formal for a six-months liaison."

"We are *not* having a liaison." He kept his voice even.

"Oh." Tamsyn followed as he turned down a narrow side street. "Why don't I call you Julian?"

"My friends call me that, and I see no reason for you to do so." He pushed open a door into the cool, dim interior of a milliner's shop, setting a bell jangling. "In here."

Tamsyn paused on the threshold. "I suppose I can

buy underclothes here. There really isn't any need for you to come in with me, my lord colonel."

The colonel didn't reply, merely planted a hand in the small of her back and pushed her ahead of him into the shop.

A woman came out from the back. She wore a gown of dark bombazine with a crisp white muslin apron and a black lace mantilla draped over her shoulders. One quick glance took in her visitor's rank, and she smiled with a hint of obsequiousness, greeting him in Spanish. "Good afternoon, sir. How may I be of service?" She cast a cursory look at the colonel's companion, seeing a somewhat undersize lad in the dimness.

"My companion here needs to be reclothed from the skin out," St. Simon said briskly, pushing Tamsyn into the ray of light falling through the window. "I think it would be simplest if she removes all her clothes and we start from there."

"Hey, just a minute," Tamsyn said. "I need a new pair of drawers, a new shirt, of lawn or silk, and a pair of stockings. Since I'm sure the senhora doesn't sell britches, I'll find them elsewhere."

The colonel ignored her, saying calmly to the astonished senhora, "She needs drawers, a chemise, petticoats, silk stockings, and a gown . . . something simple, I think. Muslin or cambric."

"What are you talking about?" Tamsyn protested, switching to English. "I cannot possibly wear women's clothes here."

"And why not? Countless other women appear to," the colonel demanded dryly.

"Because it's different . . . I'm different," she said. "I can't imagine what you're thinking of."

"When did you last wear petticoats?" he inquired, untroubled by her rising annoyance.

"I never have," she said dismissively. "Neither did Cecile . . . or at least she did occasionally," she added. "But I think that was all part of their love play. Skirts were quite impractical for the way we lived."

"Well, they're not impractical for the game *you've* chosen to play," Julian stated. "In fact they're indispensable. Permit me to remind you that at your instigation I hold the reins in that game; therefore, you'll accept my ruling. As of today you adopt women's clothes."

"But . . . but we are to ride to Lisbon presumably, to take ship. How can I do that in women's clothes?"

"The way other women do," he said. "Unless you'd rather travel in a spring wagon."

"Oh, don't be absurd." She turned back to the door with an impatient gesture. "I'll manage as I am until Gabriel arrives. He'll be bringing all my clothes."

Julian took her arm, swinging her back to face him. His eyes rested with calm certainty on her flushed face. "You wish to cancel the contract, Violette?"

Her flush deepened and her eyes flared. "You would renege, sir?"

He shook his head, still maintaining his hold, still regarding her calmly. "I warned you that we're going to play this by my rules. If you don't like those rules, you can back out anytime you wish."

Tamsyn bit her lip in chagrin, wrestling with herself. She knew he was just waiting for her to give him an excuse to end their agreement. She'd told him she could take anything he threw at her. Was she going to crumple at the first hurdle? And it was a hurdle that would have to be taken at some point, sooner rather than later. She just wasn't ready to cease to be Violette in these circumstances. Plenty of time for that transformation when they reached the peaceful, verdant English countryside that Cecile had so often described.

"Well?" Julian said, aware that the senhora was staring in unabashed curiosity, unable to understand what was clearly an acerbic exchange.

Tamsyn made up her mind. She shook her arm free of his hold, saying with icy indifference, "I see no difficulty." She began to unbutton her shirt.

"Ay . . . ay!" The *senhora* gave a squeak of dismay and hustled her unusual customer behind a worked screen.

Tamsyn stripped, tossing her garments over the top of the screen as she removed them. Shoes, stockings, drawers, shirt, and britches fell in a heap on the floor, while the senhora hastily produced a selection of undergarments, offering them with some reluctance for the colonel's inspection.

"Do you prefer silk or lawn?" Julian asked in the direction of the screen, riffling through a heap of lace-trimmed smocks.

"Silk." Tamsyn stuck her head around the corner. "But I don't want any frills or ribbons. They catch on things."

"Try this." He tossed her a cream silk chemise and turned his attention to the drawers. "Silk drawers, too, I imagine."

"No, lawn," Tamsyn said perversely. "And no frills."

"That might be difficult," he mused, shaking out delicate garments under the aghast eyes of the proprietress. "These are about as simple as I can find. They have pink ribbons."

"Ugh!" Tamsyn appeared from behind the screen,

clad in the chemise that reached the tops of her thighs.
"Let me look."

"Ay de mí," the senhora moaned as the colonel stood
aside to let the scantily clad girl examine the offered
selection.

A saint couldn't have resisted. She was leaning over
the counter, her body brushing against his. Julian's hand
slipped to her thigh. He felt her stiffen, but she affected
to be unaware, studiously searching through the filmy
pile of silk and lawn. His hand moved upward beneath
the chemise, over the bare damask curve of her bottom.
Tamsyn cut him a quick sideways up-from-under look
and grinned wickedly.

He was aware that his breathing was somewhat ragged. What had happened to his resolution to resist the
brigand's enchantment? He pinched the firm flesh of
her backside with a degree of vigor and heard her quick
indrawn breath. Then he turned with a businesslike expression to the senhora.

"Show me some gowns, senhora. I doubt you have
anything small enough. I should think something to fit a
child would be suitable."

Tamsyn lost all interest in seductive play at this patent
insult. She turned to protest but saw that they'd moved
into the rear of the shop and were deep in discussion.
She seized a pair of relatively unadorned drawers, a lawn
petticoat, silk stockings, and garters and returned behind the screen.

"This, I think." Julian held up a gown of cream
muslin with puffed sleeves, belted below the bosom
with a violet sash. Violet embroidery edged the hem
and the curving neckline.

Tamsyn emerged from the screen, her expression one

of resigned distaste. She examined the gown with wrinkled nose. "It's so flimsy. It'll tear at the first catch."

"Hopefully, you won't go around catching it on things," he declared, dropping the gown over her head, standing aside as the senhora hastened to attend to the hooks and buttons and the sash.

"It needs to be shortened about two inches," the senhora said, restored to equanimity now that her customer was decently clothed. "I can have that done in half an hour."

Tamsyn took a couple of steps, kicking the folds out in front of her as she did so. "This is ridiculous. How can one move around with all this stuff twisting around one's legs?"

"Most women seem to manage without the least difficulty," Julian said. "And it'll be better when it's shorter." He examined her with an involuntary smile. Despite the fact that Tamsyn looked thoroughly uncomfortable, the gown created the most amazing transformation. Her slight figure appeared fragile rather than wiry, accentuating the curve of her bosom and the gentle flare of her hips. The small head with its bright cap of pale silky hair sat atop a long, slender neck rising gracefully from the low, curving neckline.

"Buttercup," he said with a chuckle. "That's what you look like. No longer Violette, but a buttercup in the sun."

Tamsyn's expression showed him exactly what she thought of this revolting description. She took another turn around the room and came to a halt in front of the long cheval glass. "Santa Maria," she muttered. "I look ridiculous. I'll be the laughingstock of the town." She glared at Julian in the mirror. "I suppose that's what you want . . . revenge."

He shook his head. "Not so. Anyway, why should you imagine people will laugh at you just because you look like a woman instead of a some androgynous creature from the mountains?"

"Well, I'll laugh at me," she declared.

"Get used to it," he advised. "Because this is the way it's going to be for as long as you and I are involved in this contract."

"And you're not going to lose an opportunity to get even, are you?" She turned to face him.

"No," he agreed. "Not a single one."

Chapter Ten

TAMSYN SAT IN THE BACK ROOM OF THE MILLINER'S SHOP while a young seamstress took up the hem of the muslin gown, and Julian, armed with one of her boots for size, went off in search of shoes that would match her new image.

She'd been neatly outmaneuvered, Tamsyn reflected morosely, watching the girl's nimble fingers darting through the material. And it rather looked as if the colonel had the perfect weapon to ensure his victory in all such contentious issues. She was more interested in the arrangement's continuing than he was; therefore, she must keep him happy.

There were areas in which she wouldn't at all mind keeping him happy, and she'd rather assumed that he'd consider love play adequate compensation for inconvenience. Unfortunately, Lord St. Simon seemed determined to resist seduction. Although he hadn't been doing too well at resistance up to now.

The thought lightened her mood somewhat, and she stood up to allow the seamstress to try the dress on her. The length was pronounced satisfactory, and Tamsyn went to examine herself again in the mirror.

She didn't look in the least like herself; it was most

unsettling, rather as if her head were sitting atop some other body. But she wasn't going to give the colonel any further satisfaction. He would find her cheerfully accepting of this new costume, and if people laughed at her, then she'd laugh with them.

When Julian returned with a pair of bronze kid slippers, Tamsyn greeted him with a sunny smile and amiably extended her foot to try the shoe, commenting how pretty they were.

Julian looked at her suspiciously, meeting only that airy smile. She walked around the shop, pronounced them a perfectly comfortable fit, and asked the senhora to pack up her discarded clothes and boots.

"Keep the boots," the colonel said. "But you won't need the other things."

"Not in your company, perhaps, milord colonel," she said sweetly. "Nevertheless, I prefer to keep them."

He shrugged and pulled out a billfold from his britches pocket.

"Do keep a careful accounting, milord colonel," Tamsyn said as sweetly as before. "I should hate to be beholden to you."

"Oh, don't worry, buttercup, I'll make sure you aren't."

"Don't call me that," Tamsyn said, her amiable facade cracking.

"Then don't call me 'milord colonel,'" he returned smartly, counting out bills into the senhora's eager palm.

She seemed to have drawn a worthy opponent, Tamsyn reflected, going to the door. The evening sun cast long shadows down the narrow street, and there was a slight coolness in the air, brushing her bare arms. The thin gown fluttered against her skin, and she felt almost naked. It was most disconcerting.

"Here, you'll need this." Julian draped a silk mantilla over her shoulders. "The senhora was anxious you shouldn't catch cold."

"I've never caught cold in my life."

"No, but then you've never been so impractically clothed before."

"Oh, so you agree," she cried indignantly. "It's the most impractical, ludicrous, skimpy costume imaginable."

He chuckled, and she realized that he'd tricked her into expressing her true feelings. Crossly, she kicked the flounce of the skirt ahead of her as she strode down the street, moving with as much vigor as if she were still clad in her britches.

Julian, following a little behind, winced as the hem of the skirt caught on a loose stone and she jerked it free roughly, kicking at the stone with the dainty kid slipper.

"Tamsyn!" He caught her arm, slowing her progress. "That is not the way to walk. You must hold up the skirts of your dress and petticoat in one hand, drawing them aside . . . look, like this." He demonstrated, pinching the material of his britches at the knee between finger and thumb, taking a step. "Do you see?"

"I don't think I've quite grasped it," Tamsyn said solemnly. "Perhaps you could show me again."

"It's perfectly simple," he said impatiently. "You just draw the material aside . . . *Diablillo!*" he exploded as Tamsyn went into a peal of laughter, doubled over, convulsed with merriment. He gave her an ungentlemanly swat, annoyance warring with reluctant amusement at the absurd image he'd presented.

She straightened hastily, turning her laughing countenance toward him. Picking up her skirt in exaggerated imitation, she took a mincing step, her nose loftily tilted, eyes on the sky. "Like this, milord colonel?"

"If you don't look where you're going, buttercup, you're going to end up on your backside in the gutter," he declared.

Tamsyn grimaced and dropped the pose. She must remember not to call him that.

"Now, take my arm," he instructed, tucking her hand into the crook of his elbow. "And with your other hand, take up your skirts so they don't trail in the dirt. And watch where you put your feet."

They progressed in this fashion into the broader main street, and Tamsyn glanced around, hoping she wouldn't see any familiar faces. Since she looked ridiculous in her own eyes, she couldn't imagine anyone seeing a different picture.

"God's grace, isn't that Gabriel?" Julian said suddenly. The unmistakable giant figure astride his massive charger rounded the corner at the end of the street. He was leading two laden pack mules, and bringing up the rear of the procession was another mule with a female rider swathed in shawls and mantillas.

With a cry of joy Tamsyn dropped the colonel's arm and, forgetting her embarrassment, ran down the street, holding up her skirts with both hands so she didn't trip. "Gabriel, how quickly you got here!"

"What did you expect, little girl?" Gabriel said comfortably, dismounting. "Och, bairn, what are you wearing?"

"Oh, it's all part of my plan," she said, finally emerging from his embrace. "It makes me look silly, I know, but the colonel's insisting on it; but I'll explain later."

"Well, well," Julian drawled. "So Gabriel's not a

party to this pretty little scheme of yours. I'm astonished."

Gabriel regarded the colonel steadily. "I see you've looked after the bairn."

"Of course. Not that she's made it easy for me," he added caustically.

Gabriel nodded. "Didn't expect she would, not her way." He turned back to his pack mules, where Tamsyn was talking animatedly in Spanish to the woman still sitting on the mule. Gabriel lifted the woman down, holding her easily in his arms, although from what Julian could see beneath the mountain of shawls, the woman was no light burden.

Set on her feet on the cobbles, she shook down her shawls, revealing herself to be a short lady of substantial girth. Throwing off her mantilla, she exhibited a round face with benign features and little dark eyes like currants. She promptly flung her arms around Tamsyn, launching into a voluble cascade of loving greeting. Gabriel watched the proceedings with another satisfied nod.

"Och, woman, cease your wittering and let the little girl be," he said when he judged the greeting had gone on long enough. "I want to see these things stowed . . . don't like them out here on the open street, it's not safe."

"Oh, it's safe enough," Tamsyn said, finally turning back to him. "We are, after all, in the headquarters of Wellington's army of the Peninsular. Protected by the word of an English gentleman. Isn't that so, Lord St. Simon?"

"Most certainly," he said smoothly, refusing to rise to the bait. "I suggest you stable the animals with Cesar and see if Senhora Braganza will accommodate additional lodgers."

"That do, little girl?" Gabriel asked, not prepared to accept the word of the colonel without corroboration.

"Yes," Tamsyn said. "We can unload the pack mules and store the stuff in my room at the senhora's. It'll be quite safe there."

"Then lead on." Gabriel gathered up the reins with a careless nod. "Lead your mule, woman."

Tamsyn skipped ahead, Julian moving quickly beside her. "Who's the lady?"

"Josefa . . . Gabriel's woman," Tamsyn informed him.

"His wife?"

Tamsyn pursed her lips, considering. "Depends how you define the position, I suppose. She's been his bedmate ever since I can remember. She was my nurse. She's going to come with us to England as my attendant or duenna . . . whatever you want to call it. A hidalgo maiden would certainly have one. I thought it all out."

"I commend your foresight," Julian murmured. "So Gabriel accompanies us too?"

"Of course. He wouldn't let me go without him," she said as if it were self-evident.

"He doesn't yet know this, I gather."

"Not yet," Tamsyn said cheerfully. "I'll explain it to them tonight. At the moment he's too worried about the treasure to listen to anything else. He won't relax until he's seen it safely stowed."

"Treasure?"

"Yes, my inheritance. It'll fund this scheme of mine, Colonel. I told you I wouldn't be a charge upon you."

Julian stared. "What does it consist of . . . this treasure?"

"The fruits of a lifetime's brigandage, sir," she said dryly. "What else? Gold, silver, jewels. Doubloons, ducats, francs. Quite a fortune."

"Good God!" he muttered faintly. "Didn't that band of deserters . . ."

Her face tightened. "They were after it, of course. They'd heard of El Baron's fabulous wealth. But they didn't find it. The baron was no fool. Only he and Gabriel knew where it was. He knew, you see, that he could be sure only of himself and Gabriel if it came to torture."

"I see." There seemed no other response.

"Are you intending we should travel in an army convoy through Portugal?"

"I hadn't thought about it as yet. But with that little lot, I think the more protection we have the better." He grimaced, thinking of the responsibility of shepherding such a charge through the mountains to Lisbon. Portugal was a friendly nation, grateful to the English army for its liberation from Napoleon, but there were still brigands in the passes.

"Oh, Gabriel will pick his own men," Tamsyn said. "And they won't be soldiers. I asked about the convoy because I don't think it would be a good idea. Gabriel doesn't like soldiers . . . any more than I do . . . and he can sometimes be . . ." She paused. "Well, he can sometimes be a little unpredictable, particularly if he's been drinking."

"What do you mean, unpredictable?" Julian abruptly remembered the feel of the giant's sword on his naked back, the urgent look in Tamsyn's eyes as she'd spoken to Gabriel, desperate to convince him that she'd been a willing partner in that lusty tangle by the river.

"Hot-tempered," Tamsyn said, privately reflecting

that that was a considerable understatement, but the unvarnished truth might alarm the colonel.

"Dear God," Julian muttered. A journey escorting a baggage train of untold wealth in the infuriating and tantalizing company of La Violette was to be exacerbated by a man given to violent drinking bouts.

"It doesn't happen very often," Tamsyn reassured. "And Josefa's quite good at calming him . . . if she can catch him in time," she added as they reached Senhora Braganza's cottage.

Julian refrained from comment. "I'll leave you here. When I've made the necessary arrangements, you'll be informed."

"Oh?" Tamsyn frowned. "And when will that be?"

"You'll be informed. I suggest you occupy yourself with your wardrobe. You'll need a riding habit and a sidesaddle. I assume you'll be able to control Cesar riding sidesaddle? If not, you must procure another riding horse."

He turned aside abruptly. "Gabriel, a word with you . . . are you intending to hire a guard for that?" He gestured toward the pack mules. "On the journey to Lisbon."

"Lisbon? That where we're headed?" Gabriel shrugged phlegmatically. "Then I reckon we'll need a couple of useful men. I'll find 'em hereabouts."

"We could travel in an army convoy. They're leaving all the time, conveying the wounded to Lisbon."

Gabriel shook his head and spat in the dust. "Don't hold with soldiers, Colonel. Present company excepted, of course."

"Oh, of course," Julian concurred aridly. "Well, I'll leave it to you. You have a couple of days, maybe less."

He glanced toward the cottage where Tamsyn and

Josefa were involved in a lively exchange with the senhora, involving much hand waving and shrugging.

Gabriel followed his gaze. "Women'll be settling everything right and tight, I shouldn't wonder," he stated. "Well, I'd best be getting this stuff unloaded. Don't like it standing here in the street. Be seein' you, Colonel." He turned to unload the first pack mule, hefting an ironbound chest onto one massive shoulder.

Julian contemplated offering his assistance, then decided against it. His orders, unconventional though they were, didn't include sweating like a farm hand. He strode off to headquarters.

Tamsyn watched him go, frowning. He was very anxious to get away from her. She didn't care to be so lightly dismissed.

Leaving Josefa and the *senhora* examining the limited accommodations in the cottage, she walked back to the gate, dodging to one side as Gabriel plodded up the path with another chest.

"Hey, lad!" she hailed a small boy who was kicking a stone down the street. "Do you see that colonel?" She indicated Julian's broad retreating back. The lad nodded. "Follow him and let me know where he spends the evening. He may go back to the camp, or he may stay at headquarters. Come back and tell me, and there'll be a cruzado for you."

The lad grinned and ran off, stationing himself outside headquarters when his quarry disappeared inside.

Unaware of his young follower, Julian entered Wellington's apartment. The commander in chief was with his staff and greeted the colonel crisply.

"St. Simon, you'll join us for dinner. We're putting our heads together over what exactly you should ask Westminster for. Should we ask for the maximum and bargain down? Or make reasonable demands that won't alarm the ministry?"

Julian put thoughts of Tamsyn, treasure, and the unpredictable Gabriel aside and took a chair. Little though he relished this diplomatic mission, he understood its importance.

The lad waited until dark. The colonel didn't reappear, but a procession of servants entered the building from the kitchen in the next-door cottage, bearing trays and salvers of food, and the chink of china and glass drifted through the open window with the rich aromas of dinner and the voices of the diners.

The lad ran back to the widow's cottage, knocking on the kitchen door that stood ajar, letting in the soft spring air. He stuck his head into the candlelit kitchen where Tamsyn sat with Gabriel, Josefa, and Senhora Braganza eating a dinner much less elegant than that served to the duke and his staff. Not that such a comparison would have troubled any of the participants at this board.

"Ah, good lad." Tamsyn pushed back her chair. "Where is the colonel?"

"Eating at headquarters, *senhorita*. He went there and hasn't come out since. Didn't take my eyes off the door for a minute."

"Good." Tamsyn nodded. "Gabriel, do you have a cruzado?"

Gabriel reached into his pocket and tossed the silver coin to the boy at the door. "Now what are you up to, little girl?"

Tamsyn smiled and popped an olive into her mouth. "Just a notion I had. In about half an hour will you go to headquarters and tell the colonel I need to speak with him on a matter of the utmost urgency?"

Gabriel tore a drumstick off the chicken in front of him. "If that's what you want." He bit into the meat.

Tamsyn nodded, removed the olive pit from her mouth, and tossed it into the garden. "I have some preparations to make. In half an hour, mind. They should be circulating the port by then."

She disappeared upstairs, leaving the others to finish their meal. No one seemed to find anything in the least strange in her instructions or her disappearance, and the three of them continued eating with stolid application.

Half an hour later at headquarters, Gabriel ascended the stairs to the landing and greeted the brigade-major with a curt nod. "Colonel St. Simon in there?" He gestured to the door behind the lieutenant.

"Yes, but he's at dinner," Sanderson said haughtily, staring at the massive, ruffianly figure of his visitor, clad in leather britches and jerkin, with a rough homespun shirt, a none-too-clean bandanna at his neck, gray hair caught in a queue at its nape. "And just who might you be?"

"None of your business, laddie," Gabriel said amiably. "I'll fetch out the colonel."

"No!" Sanderson leaped to his feet as the visitor moved to the door. "You can't go in there."

"Oh, yes, I can, laddie." Gabriel caught the unfortunate lieutenant by the collar and lifted him onto his toes. "Let's not argue about it, now. Do you want to run along in there and announce me, or shall I announce myself?"

Sanderson opened his mouth on a bellow for reinforcements, and Gabriel dropped him back into his chair, saying pleasantly, "I'll announce myself, then."

By the time two infantrymen appeared, breathless,

on the stairs, Gabriel was inside the commander in chief's sanctum.

The men around the table looked up in astonishment. Julian closed his eyes briefly with a resigned sigh. Sanderson and reinforcements stumbled into the room on the giant's heels.

"I beg your pardon, sir. I couldn't stop him."

Wellington raised his eyeglass and examined the newcomer, saying caustically, "No, I can see that might be difficult. And just whom do I have the honor of addressing?"

Gabriel offered no introduction, merely saying, "Sorry to disturb your dinner, gentlemen. But I've come for Colonel St. Simon. The bairn wants him urgently."

"He's referring to La Violette," Julian drawled, leaning back in his chair, toying idly with his port glass. "What does she want now, Gabriel?"

Gabriel shrugged. "Couldn't say, Colonel. Just told me to fetch you."

Julian drained his glass and pushed back his chair. "You'll excuse me, gentlemen. Mustn't keep a lady waiting." His tone was sarcastic, and Gabriel frowned.

"You wouldn't be insulting the bairn, now, would you, Colonel?"

"That creature you persist upon calling 'little girl,' Gabriel, is a devious little devil," Julian declared roundly. "And if you want to pick a fight with me over that description, then I suggest we go outside."

There was a tense moment of silence; then Gabriel's laugh boomed through the room, setting the china shivering. "Och, I don't think I'll be quarreling with you, man. Shall we be off now?"

Julian nodded, sketched a bow to his dinner companions, and followed Gabriel out of the room, Sanderson and his cohorts falling in behind them.

"So has she explained this mad scheme to you as yet?" Julian asked as they strode through the lamplit streets of Elvas.

"Not yet," Gabriel replied placidly. "She'll tell me in her own sweet time."

"And you're not curious?"

Gabriel shook his head. "I go where she goes."

They reached the cottage, and Julian hesitated in the tiny hall, hearing the chatter of the older women from the kitchen. "So where is she?"

"Upstairs, I believe," Gabriel replied. "I'm off to smoke my pipe in the garden." He disappeared through the kitchen door, closing it firmly behind him.

Julian swore softly. Tamsyn was up to her tricks again, he was sure of it. He looked up the narrow wooden staircase, then, with an impatient shake of his head, strode up, knocking sharply on the door at the top. A low voice bade him enter, and he pushed the door open.

He stopped on the threshold, stunned and disbelieving. Milky starlight fell from the small round window onto an Aladdin's cave. Chests stood open on the floor, spilling their contents: glowing silks, rich velvets, the deep green of emeralds, the bright white of diamonds, the dark, luminous red of rubies, sea-green aquamarines, brilliant turquoises.

As he stood and stared incredulously, a low laugh came from the narrow cot. He swung his head slowly toward the bed and for a moment thought he was in the middle of some crazy dream worthy of a bedlamite.

Gold covered the cot, but not just the cot. It covered the body of La Violette. Gold coins of every currency, glittering in the moonlight, shifting against her pale skin as she breathed.

"Jesus, Mary, and Joseph," he whispered. "What in the name of grace are you doing?"

"Choose something," she said, without moving from the bed. "You're entitled to compensation for the arduous task I've inflicted upon you."

Anger flashed through him, a crimson surge. "You're offering me payment?" he demanded, unable to believe what he was hearing.

"Compensation," Tamsyn murmured. "Look around. See what takes your fancy." Her body moved slightly, and the gold coins that clothed her chinked faintly.

"You dare to offer me robber's gold?" He strode to the bed, his eyes black with anger. "Of all the insulting—"

"Don't jump to conclusions," she interrupted, smiling, her eyes as luminous as any of the jewels in the caskets. Only her face remained uncovered, and he found his eyes slowly traveling down her body, fascinated by the hillocks of gold shaped by her breasts, by the small rosy crowns peeping through their covering. Gold clustered in the concave hollow of her belly, an emerald peeped shyly from her navel, ducats lay in overlapping circles along her thighs, and each toenail carried a burnished doubloon.

"There's more than one kind of treasure on offer," she murmured. "Reject the gold and see what's below it. Maybe something there will appeal." Very delicately she moved her legs apart and the bright fire of a diamond flashed in the starlight, brilliant against the dull glister of gold.

"You . . . you . . ." There were no words. He

gazed down into the dark, rich furrow of her body where diamonds beckoned in mischievous, wicked invitation.

Slowly, he dropped to his knees beside the bed and carefully brushed coins off her breasts with a delicate fingertip, revealing the soft, pale swell. He bent his head, flicking the erect nipples with his tongue, tasting the warm sweetness of her skin mingling with the faintly metallic residue of gold.

Tamsyn lay perfectly still as, in silence, he revealed her body with slow deliberation, coin by coin, arranging them in neat piles on the floor beside him. And as he bared each circle of skin, his lips branded the flesh.

Lying still became increasingly difficult. She'd expected him to sweep the coins from her body in a surge of passion, half-angry, half-desirous. But this exquisitely slow exposure set every nerve ending atingle, brought a soft flush to her skin in the wake of his burning kisses, sent the blood racing through her veins.

He left the emerald in her navel as he continued over her belly, his tongue trailing fire over her damp skin. Slowly, he revealed her thighs, her calves, bared her feet, taking each little pink toe into his mouth in turn, stroking the soles of her feet with his tongue until finally she wriggled with a soft moan of halfhearted protest at the tickling.

Julian looked along her length, holding her feet in both hands. The diamonds winked at him from the dark, moist cleft of her body.

"Sorceress," he said softly. It was the first word that had been spoken in the small jewel-encrusted chamber for many minutes.

He rose from his knees, and she turned her head to watch him as he bent over one of the caskets, running gems through his fingers, selecting, discarding. He turned back to the bed with a handful of necklaces, bracelets, and single stones. Kneeling beside her again, he began to adorn her body, an intent expression in his eyes. He fastened bracelets at her wrists and ankles, an opalescent string of pearls around her neck. He slipped a gold chain studded with emeralds beneath her and fastened it around her waist, another to encircle her breasts.

Then he stood back and surveyed his handiwork, a tiny smile playing over his mouth. He looked down at the smooth diamond he held in his palm, and the smile spread to his eyes. "Turn over." His voice was a rich sensual throb. "But be very careful."

Tamsyn eased herself onto her stomach, and the belt of emeralds and gold pressed into the skin of her belly, cool and hard against her heated flesh.

Julian leaned over her prone form, and her skin rippled beneath the edge of the diamond as he drew it down her back, tracing the sharp lines of her shoulder blades, the delineation of her ribs, the bony column of her spine. Her toes curled into the mattress as the stone scribbled in the small of her back and then moved over her buttocks, slowly outlining their curves, before he parted the soft folds of flesh and planted the gem in the diamond garden between her thighs.

Tamsyn drew a swift, almost startled, breath, then smiled to herself. This was a lover who could meet and match any fantasy. But still she said nothing. As Julian straightened, she turned over again, careful not to disturb the garden, her eyes still rivaling the rich decorations of her body.

She watched hungrily while he undressed as if he had all the time in the world, as if he was not on fire for her as she was for him. When he stood naked, she gazed with unabashed greed at the power in his aroused body and raised her arms to him.

He leaned over her, taking her mouth with his, and there was a fierce assertion in this kiss, his tongue plundering the warm, sweet cavern of her mouth. She reached her arms around his neck, her lips parted for this driving possession, opening herself to him.

Finally he drew back, his eyes predatory, sharp-edged with needy desire. Slowly he drew his hands down her body, playing with the chains and the stones that encircled her. And finally, slowly, he drew her thighs apart, revealing the secret places of her body and the treasure they kept.

"And now, treasure trove," he said quietly.

Chapter Eleven

LONDON

"THE KING'S INSANE, PRINNY'S AN ARROGANT DUN-derhead, and the rest of 'em are clods."

This succinct, wholesale condemnation of the royal family was received in a gloomy, accepting silence. The speaker took a deep draft of his wine and glared around the table in the square chamber in the palace of Westminster as if challenging potential dissent. He was a man in his late sixties, black eyes hard and sharp as flint beneath bushy gray brows and a mane of iron-gray hair.

"And they're demmed expensive into the bargain, Penhallan," one of his three companions rumbled, leaning back in his chair, loosening a button on the striped waistcoat that strained over his ample belly. "Prinny's monstrous fantasy pavilion in Brighton! I've never seen anything like it. All those domes and dragons."

Cedric Penhallan snorted. "Hideous monstrosity. And Society nods and beams and congratulates the fool on his taste and imagination and Parliament foots the bill."

"Quite so." The agreement came from the prime minister, who sat up straight in his chair with an air of resolution, as if deciding it was time to take control of the meeting. "That is precisely the issue, gentlemen. We have Wellington demanding money on every mail ship from the Peninsula, the Admiralty needs more ships, and the palace grows greedier by the day. We cannot defeat Napoleon *and* indulge every bizarre whim of Prinny's . . . not to mention the demands of his brothers on the civil list."

Cedric Penhallan took an apple from a chased silver bowl on the table and carefully peeled it with a tiny dessert knife, frowning as he took the peel off in one perfect spiral. The conversation at this dinner with the prime minister and his few closest intimates had taken a familiar turn: how to balance the conflicting needs of a country at war, with the financial demands of an idle, autocratic regent who saw no reason why his demands shouldn't be instantly gratified by a servile Parliament.

"The Stuarts learned their lesson the hard way," he said with a cynical curl of his lip. "Maybe we should give the House of Hanover a taste of Stuart medicine."

There was a moment of stunned silence; then an awkward laugh rippled around the table. Men who dined with Lord Penhallan learned to expect the sardonic harshness of his opinions and remedies, but to hear Penhallan recommend revolution and regicide, even ironically, was a little too much even for his intimates.

"You've a dangerous sense of humor, Penhallan," the prime minister said, feeling a slight reproof was required.

"Was I jesting?" Lord Penhallan's eyebrows lifted, and a disdainful amusement sparked in his eyes. "How long does the British government intend to pander to the vulgar extravagances of a German lout?" He pushed back his chair. "You must excuse me, gentlemen. My lord." He nodded at the prime minister. "An excellent dinner. I look forward to your presence in Grosvenor Square next Thursday. I've a consignment of burgundy I'd like you to try."

Having made his farewells, Cedric Penhallan left his companions still at the table and walked out into the chilly March evening. The conversation had irked him, but he'd made his irritation felt and hopefully sowed a little seed in the corridors of power that might bear fruit. At some point someone had to put a rein on the royal family's profligacies. It was high time to remind the government that the king and his family were merely foolish mortals who could be controlled by Parliament.

He smiled to himself as he walked briskly through the streets, his step surprisingly light for such a big man. He'd enjoyed shocking them with that insouciant reference to Charles I's execution. Of course, he'd never seriously advocate such a course, and they knew it . . . or at least they thought they knew it.

His smile broadened as he climbed the steps to his own front door. He worked his own political influence behind closed doors, more with whispers and innuendo than with direct statements. In the House of Lords he was rarely seen on his feet, but Lord Penhallan's power was many-tentacled and had a long reach.

His front door swung open before he could put his hand on the knocker, and the butler bowed him into the hall.

"Good evening, my lord. You had a pleasant evening, I trust."

Cedric didn't respond. He stood frowning in the candlelit hall. A high-pitched squeal came from the library, followed by a burst of drunken male laughter. "My nephews are home for the evening," he commented acidly. It was the butler's turn not to respond.

Cedric strode to the library door and flung it open. His lip curled at the shambolic sight within. Three women, wearing little more than the paint on their faces, were standing on a table, performing a lewd dance for a group of five men, sprawled over couches and chairs, glasses in hand.

"Governor, wasn't expecting you back so soon." One of the men stumbled to his feet, a fearful note underpinning the drunken slur.

"Clearly not," his uncle declared in disgust. "I've told you before I'll not have you whoring in my house. Get those harlots out of here and conduct your business in the stews, where it belongs."

He stood to one side, watching with searing contempt as the men lurched to their feet with mumbled apologies and the women stepped off the table, hastily scrambling back into skirts and petticoats, their eyes glazed with drink yet haunted with the predatory hunger of the desperate.

One of them approached David Penhallan with a deprecating smile. "A guinea apiece, sir," she whined. "You promised, sir."

She went reeling as Cedric's nephew backhanded her. "You think I'm fool enough to pay a guinea for a drunken dance by a scrawny bag of bones?" he demanded savagely. "Get out of here, the lot of you!" He raised his hand again and the woman cowered, her hand covering the mark on her cheek.

"Oh, we should give them something for the dance, David," his twin said with a chuckle that sounded more menacing than humorous. Charles reached into his pocket and threw a handful of pennies at the women. His aim was true and vicious. A coin struck one woman in the eye and she fell back with a cry of pain, but then she bent with the others, scrabbling to pick up the coins amid the laughter from the men, who all joined in the new game, bombarding them with coins—an assault that they couldn't afford to run from.

With a disgusted exclamation Cedric turned on his heel and left the room. He despised his nephews, but he wasn't interested in their puerile little cruelties. The women they were tormenting meant nothing to Lord Penhallan; he just didn't want them in his house.

He marched up the stairs, pausing for a minute to look at the portrait of a young woman hanging above the half landing. Silvery fair hair, violet eyes, she gazed down at him with the same defiantly mischievous smile he remembered across the mists of more than twenty years. His sister. The only person he believed he had ever cared for. The only person who had dared to challenge him, to mock his ambition, to threaten his position and his power.

Cedric could still hear her voice, her chiming laugh as she told him how she'd overheard his discussion with the Duke of Cranford, how she believed that William Pitt would be most interested to know how one of his most trusted advisers was working behind the scenes to oust him. The price of her silence was her own freedom from her brother's authority. The freedom to pursue whatever little adventures she chose, and, when she was ready, the freedom to choose her own husband without thought to whether he might be useful or a liability to her brother's ambition.

Pretty, lively little Celia had made herself too dangerous.

Shaking his head, he went on upstairs, ignoring the renewed shrieks and gales of drunken laughter in the hall as the women were chased from his house followed by the revelers heading out in search of new entertainment.

Portugal

"So what's behind this journey, little girl?"

Tamsyn looked up at the sky, following the flight of an eagle as it soared above the mountain pass, its magnificent wingspan black against the brilliant, cloudless blue.

"We're going to be avenged upon Cedric Penhallan, Gabriel." Her mouth was set, her eyes suddenly hard. She looked across at him as they rode abreast, following the line of a goat track etched into the mountainside. "And we're going for the Penhallan diamonds. They were rightfully my mother's, and now they're rightfully mine."

Gabriel drew a wineskin from his belt and tilted the ruby stream down his throat. He knew the story as well as Tamsyn did. He passed her the skin, saying thoughtfully, "You think the baron would have wanted you to seek his revenge, lassie?"

"I know he would," she said with quiet certainty. "Cecile was cheated out of her inheritance by her brother. He planned her death." She tilted the skin, enjoying the cool stream as it ran down her dry throat. "The baron swore he would be avenged. I used to hear them talking at night."

She fell silent for a minute at the memory of those evenings when she lay in her own bed, the door ajar, listening to the soft voices, the baron's rich chuckle, Cecile's musical laugh, and occasionally the chilly ferocity of El Baron roused to anger by some stupidity or perceived failure of loyalty. Cecile would defuse his anger, but she never interfered in his dealings with his men, and she'd never been able to soften his icy rage at what Cedric Penhallan had paid the robber baron to do.

Gabriel frowned, his customary placid demeanor disturbed. He wasn't sure what position to take on Tamsyn's plan because he wasn't sure what position the baron would have taken. "The baron had a powerful grudge against your mother's family," he said, feeling his way. "But I don't believe he considered it your grudge, too. And Cecile always said there was nothing to avenge because her brother's plans went so far awry."

Tamsyn shook her head, screwing the top back onto the skin and passing it across to him. "And you know the baron always denied that Cedric's plans had failed. He wanted his sister out of the way, he wanted to bilk her of her rightful inheritance. He succeeded. The baron always intended to redress that wrong. He's not here to do it, so I will do it for him."

Gabriel's frown deepened. "Cecile counted that wrong as a good," he said. "There's never been a love like theirs, and she always said it was the Penhallan who put them in the way of it."

"Cedric Penhallan paid for Cecile's abduction and murder." Tamsyn's voice was almost without expression. "The fact that she found a lifetime's happiness instead with the man Cedric paid to do his dirty work is no thanks to him. It's time he paid the price."

Gabriel clicked his tongue against his teeth, considering. The baron had confided his intention to concoct an appropriate vengeance on the Penhallans. It could be said that that confidence had laid the burden now upon his old friend to do what he could no longer do. Gabriel certainly had the responsibility to protect the baron's daughter, and if she chose to exact her father's vengeance, then it seemed he had no decision to make.

For a man of action rather than decision, the conclusion came as a relief. "So how will you prove your kinship?"

"I have the locket, the portrait, and other documents. Cecile gave me all I would need to prove that I'm her daughter." Tamsyn adjusted her position in the unfamiliar sidesaddle. "She also told me that her real name was Celia. She started to call herself Cecile when she was fourteen because she thought it was prettier." A misty smile touched her lips as she heard again her mother's laughing description of her own youthful romanticism.

"She said she had some romantic notion about the name when she was a girl, and it annoyed her brother almost more than anything else when she refused to answer to anything but Cecile." She looked across at Gabriel. "She said that should I ever need to prove my identity to the Penhallans, it would be the final confirmation for Cedric if I told him that, because it was not something anyone else knew about."

Gabriel whistled through his teeth, nodding. "If she gave you all that, little girl, I'd guess she wasn't totally against the idea of vengeance, after all."

"No," Tamsyn agreed. "But she would have called it restitution." She chuckled. Cecile's delicacy of phrase had always amused her robber-baron mate. "And she also gave me a written and witnessed account of her abduction," she continued, serious again. "If that found its way into a London newspaper, vouched for by her daughter, it might cause her brother some considerable embarrassment, don't you think?"

"If her brother's still alive."

"There is that," she conceded. "If he is, I shall know what to do. If he's not . . . then what I do will depend on his successor . . . on the rest of the family, really. If they had nothing to do with Cedric's plan, then I can hardly hold them responsible. We shall see what we shall see, Gabriel."

"Is it blackmail you're talking, little girl?"

Tamsyn shook her head. "No, I intend to expose Cedric Penhallan's treachery to all the world. But for it to be credible, I must have a reputation for respectability myself. That's where the colonel comes in. Once I'm established in society as the protégée of such an eminent aristocrat, my story will carry much more weight than if it came from some unknown who just popped up out of nowhere. And once the truth is known, the diamonds will come to me without question, because they're indubitably mine by right."

"And how much of this does the colonel know?"

Tamsyn glanced down the mountainside to where the broader, more frequented, path wound its way through the pass. The tall figure of Colonel, Lord Julian St. Simon rode at the head of the baggage train, six villainous outriders bristling with weapons in escort, the pack mule carrying Josefa plodding steadily in the rear.

"None of it," she said. "He knows nothing of the Penhallans, of the diamonds, or of the plot to murder Cecile. He and Wellington know only that I'm an orphan with Cornish connections, alone in the world, desperate to find a home and family."

Gabriel threw back his head with a snort of derision. "And they fell for that story! Och, little girl, shame on you. You could make grown men weep with your tales."

"Cecile always said the chivalry of an English gentleman was a very useful weakness," she said with a complacent grin. "I need a base in Cornwall, and I need the right entrees. Under the colonel's protection, ensconced in his family home, I shall have them."

"I'd watch my step with the colonel, if I were you," Gabriel advised. "He's not one to care for being made game of . . . however chivalrous he may be."

"But I'm not making game of him," Tamsyn said judiciously. "Only use."

"He'll not care for that either."

Tamsyn was inclined to agree. "He won't be able to do anything about it. I don't intend to stay in England once I've done what I set out to do; besides, the colonel will be so relieved to get back to his beloved war, he probably won't give a damn by then anyway."

"You'd better be right, lassie."

Tamsyn merely shrugged and raised a hand in greeting as the colonel looked up toward the higher path, shading his eyes against the sun.

Julian didn't acknowledge the wave. It annoyed him that she chose to ride apart as if she and Gabriel were still riding as partisans. It left him journeying in solitary splendor with only the swathed Josefa on her pack mule as companion. One could hardly consider the outriders companions. They were the most ruffianly pack of scoundrels, led by a one-eyed villain who made no secret of his suspicion of the English colonel. However, they looked as if they'd prove effective defenders of Tamsyn's treasure if pushed to it.

He glanced up again and saw that Tamsyn had left the goat track, and Cesar was picking his way down, sure-footed, through the scrub and cactus clinging to the mountainside. They reached the main path a little ahead of the baggage train in a shower of loose gravel.

Tamsyn had no difficulty riding sidesaddle, but he hadn't really expected her to. She was as at home in the saddle as if it had formed her childhood cradle. It would be interesting, however, to see how she took to the hard, backless English saddle. She'd certainly have to abandon her exotic cushioned Spanish version for riding the tan in Hyde Park or even the quiet country lanes of England if she expected to be accepted by the highest sticklers.

"Are you lonely?" She greeted him cheerfully, turning her horse neatly on the narrow path to ride beside him.

"You and Gabriel seemed to be having a very intense discussion," he responded. A spot of color blossomed against the sun-browned cheek, and he wondered why.

"Oh, I was just filling him in on the details of the plan," she said. "I didn't really have the time to do it before."

"I see. And did he embrace your scheme with avid enthusiasm?"

"Why wouldn't he?" Tamsyn responded a shade truculently to the colonel's heavily sardonic tone.

"Oh, no reason." Julian shrugged. "I'm sure he has not the least difficulty in giving up the life and land he's called home for so many years. And even if he did have, you would still expect him to do as you wished." His voice was as dry as sere leaves.

Tamsyn's flush deepened. "I don't know what you mean."

"My dear girl, you know exactly what I mean. When you want something, you make damn sure you get it.

Gabriel's loyalty won't permit him to refuse you his support, and you'll use that without compunction."

"Oh, how horrid you are!" she exclaimed in a low voice. "What a horrid thing to say about me."

"You forget that I've been swept up by your broom as well," he replied as aridly as before. "You didn't give a thought to my position or my feelings in the matter."

Tamsyn bit her lip, startled to find tears pricking behind her eyes at the harshness of a judgment that seemed to have come out of nowhere. A judgment that deep down she recognized had some merit. Since the glorious evening in Aladdin's cave two days before, they'd hardly met at all. She'd understood that the colonel would have much to do preparing for his journey and arranging to hand over the reins of his brigade, so she'd made no further attempt to seduce him from his work. But when they'd set out from Elvas that morning, he'd been morose and uncommunicative. Hoping that quiet reflection would bring about a change in his humor, she'd chosen to ride apart with Gabriel. A forlorn hope, clearly. There was no dent in his resentment.

She blinked rapidly and urged Cesar forward, drawing away from the colonel, breaking into a trot and then a canter. Cesar threw up his head and sniffed the wind, then lengthened his stride, breaking into a gallop on the narrow, treacherous path.

"Tamsyn!" Julian yelled, his heart in his throat as horse and rider careened round a tight bend in the track where the mountainside fell steeply away; then they were gone from view.

"Said something to upset her, did you?" Gabriel's horse skittered down the mountainside onto the path beside them.

"She is the most ill-conditioned, unschooled *hel-*

lion!" Julian exclaimed. "She'll break her neck, if she doesn't break one of that animal's legs first."

"No." Gabriel shook his head. "I doubt that. They know each other too well. What did you say to upset her?"

"A couple of home truths," Julian said. "Long over-due."

"That'll do it every time," Gabriel observed placidly, offering the wineskin. "Doesn't like to be told she's wrong. It was the same with the baron . . . particularly if he *was* wrong." He chuckled, turning in his saddle to observe the progress of the mule train behind them. "I suggest we get off the road well before sundown. There's some tricky spots coming up, and I'd not relish a dusk ambush."

"Those scoundrels you picked look ready for anything." Julian handed back the skin with a nod of thanks.

"Maybe . . . but there's no point taking foolish chances."

"I agree. We'll stop at the next village with a hostelry of some kind."

"Won't be much, at best," Gabriel said. "Not in these parts."

They rode without any sign of Tamsyn for another half hour. Julian tried to conceal his anxiety since Gabriel clearly didn't seem to feel any. He told himself he had every right to lash out at her as severely as he chose. She'd forced him to leave his brigade at the most inopportune juncture. It had been one of the hardest things he'd ever done. Wellington had marched a detachment of men into Badajos and erected a gallows in the central square. Men had been tried for looting and hanged. It had brought the rest of his demoralized army straggling out of the city and back to the camp, where their officers had somehow to put them back together again. It was a dreadful time for a commanding officer to leave his brigade, even in the competent hands of the newly promoted Tim O'Connor ably assisted by the rest of his staff.

So Julian had been in a vile temper that morning when they left Elvas and he hadn't missed the opportunity to chastise the cause of his grievance. For some reason though, anger at his exploitation didn't preclude worrying about her safety, and he couldn't deny the surge of relief when she reappeared, cantering toward them.

"There's a pueblo up ahead, about three miles," she said, offering the fruits of her reconnaissance. "It's not much, but there's stabling for the animals and a stone byre where we could store the goods. It would be hard to mount a surprise attack on it, and it could probably be guarded safely with just two pickets; so if we have several watches, everyone should be able to get a few hours sleep." She addressed her remarks to Gabriel and avoided the colonel's eye.

"What kind of shelter does it have for the rest of us?" Julian asked neutrally.

Tamsyn shrugged. "The farmer offered his barn and hayloft. It'll be cleaner than his cottage, which was crawling with vermin."

The colonel nodded. They had their own provisions and needed only shelter from the cold mountain nights. He glanced at her, noting that she was still looking rather crestfallen. It surprised him that she should have taken his harshness so much to heart; it didn't seem to jibe with the manipulative brigand he knew her to be.

However, she deserved whatever treatment he chose to mete out.

"You will oblige me in future by not disappearing in that fashion," he said shortly.

"I didn't seem to be very welcome here."

"Do you expect to be?" He stared ahead down the path, his mouth hard. "Thanks to you, I've had to leave my men in the worst possible circumstances."

Tamsyn nibbled her lip unhappily, then said, "I'll try to make the journey and . . . and later . . . pleasant for you."

Julian shot her a look of total disbelief. Her anxious returning gaze was candid and ingenuous. She really didn't understand what she was doing to him? Where had she come from? How could anyone possibly reach adulthood so devoid of a sense of ordinary social responsibility? He took a deep breath and attempted a lesson that he felt was doomed to failure.

"Your compensations, my dear Tamsyn, are certainly pleasant, but that is not the point. You can't manipulate people and events to your own ends and then calmly offer your body and its admittedly manifold charms and expect that to make everything all right."

"But it's only for six months."

Total failure! He shook his head and gave up. "There's no point talking about it. I'm stuck with the situation, and I'll do what I contracted to do. If we can get through the next six months with simple civility, I'll consider it a major achievement."

Tamsyn fell in beside him and rode in thoughtful silence until they reached the village. It seemed obvious to her that six months of the colonel's time . . . a mere hiatus in his life . . . wouldn't have a far-reaching effect on his future, whereas in the scheme of her own life, those six months could mean everything. It was obvious to her, but totally lost on the colonel.

The village folk crowded out of their cottages when the procession entered the pueblo, bisected by the mountain path as its single street. Ragged children ran onto the path, shouting and waving, black-clad women stood in doorways, shawls drawn over their mouths and noses, black eyes watchful above. Men appeared in the gateways to small malodorous farmyards where scrawny chickens scratched in the dirt fighting for scraps with grubby goats.

A stream trickled down the mountainside into the middle of the pueblo where a rough dam had been built, forming a deep pool to provide the village's water supply.

Tamsyn hailed a man rather more prosperous looking than the others, standing in the doorway of a relatively substantial cottage. "He's the village elder," she explained. "It's his barn and byre we can use . . . for a consideration, of course."

Gabriel dismounted and went over to him.

"He won't negotiate with me," Tamsyn explained to the colonel, "because I'm dressed like a woman. If I'd been dressed as a partisan, he would have treated me as an equal."

Julian merely raised an eyebrow and shrugged.

"At least a riding habit is easier to wear than a dress," Tamsyn persevered, trying to elicit some conversational response. "I'm wearing britches underneath, so it feels almost normal. But it's still a disadvantage in situations like this."

"Get used to it," he advised as he'd done once before, choosing to respond to her light observations as if they were complaints. "Women don't act like men in

English society . . . or not if they wish to be accepted."

Tamsyn gave up trying to conciliate. "The baron considered Cecile to be his equal in everything," she said fiercely.

Julian looked politely incredulous. "Then he was a very unusual man." He swung to the ground and lifted Tamsyn down before she could leap with her usual agility from Cesar's great height. He closed his mind to the feel of her body in his hands, to the scent of her skin, which made his head spin with voluptuous memory.

"Women also allow men to assist them with certain actions, like mounting and dismounting, alighting from carriages, and taking their seats," he informed her with the air of a conscientious tutor, setting her firmly on her feet.

"Oh, pah!" Tamsyn said disgustedly. "There's nothing the matter with my legs."

"No, but you must learn to pretend that you go along with the myth of the gentler sex and show that you appreciate the little gentlemanly courtesies."

Tamsyn's expression was one of acute distaste, and Julian began to enjoy himself. "Unless, of course, you'd prefer to forget the whole thing," he added nonchalantly.

Tamsyn stuck her tongue out at him in a childish gesture that somehow expressed exactly how she felt. The colonel laughed, infuriating her even more, and strolled over to where Gabriel and the farmer were concluding their negotiations. He stood slapping his gloves into the palm of one hand, looking around the village, assessing its strategic advantages.

"If we post pickets at either end of the street, we

should be safe from marauders approaching convention-ally."

"Aye, but there's always the way down from above," Gabriel said, glancing up at the mountainside towering above the village. "We'll need to guard the byre itself. I'll take the first watch with three of the men. You take the second . . . if it's all right with you," he added, almost as an afterthought.

"Who's likely to know what we're carrying?"

"No one or everyone." Gabriel frowned. "Word spreads like wildfire in these passes, colonel. And there are eyes everywhere. They may not know what we've got, but they'll know by now that it's worth defending, and presumably, therefore, worth stealing."

"Well, let's make camp as we can." Julian turned back to the mule train and saw that Josefa and Tamsyn were already carrying supplies into the barnyard, Tamsyn kicking aside the skirts of her riding habit with an irritable mutter. Suddenly she stopped, dumped her burden onto the ground, and swiftly unhooked the skirt of her habit, stepping out of it with visible relief, revealing her lower limbs clad in soft leather britches. She glanced across at him with a hint of defiance as she bundled the skirt under her arm.

He chose to pretend he hadn't noticed, strolling back to the mule train.

Tamsyn and Josefa occupied themselves lighting a fire in the barnyard and preparing food. Julian, busy with the men bestowing the treasure and organizing its defense, was surprised how willingly Tamsyn assumed domestic responsibilities. He'd expected her to be working with the men, leaving the female side of the operations to Josefa. But the two women chatted cheerfully over

the fire, and soon the heady aroma of coffee rose on the
evening air.

He went over to them. "Something smells good."

"Polenta," Tamsyn said, looking up from the pot she
was stirring with a great wooden spoon. "There's a cask
of wine to be broached. Would you do it? The men'll
be thirsty. . . . Oh, it's all right, Gabriel's doing it."

Josefa muttered something as she shook a pan of
mushrooms over the fire, and Tamsyn glanced quickly at
her. "Oh, dear."

"What is it?"

"Well, Josefa's afraid Gabriel's going to enjoy himself
this evening. She says it's been at least a month since he
let himself go with a cask of wine, and he's got good
company for it."

"He wouldn't drink himself stupid with that treasure
to guard, surely?"

"Oh, he doesn't ever drink himself stupid," Tamsyn
said. "Just aggressive. If you get on the wrong side of
him. The treasure will be as safe with Gabriel drunk as
sober, I assure you."

"He wants to take the first watch."

"Then he is intending to get soused," Tamsyn said
with conviction. "He plans it so that he'll be able to
sleep it off and be good as new in the morning. Stir this,
will you? It mustn't stick. I have to find the outhouse."

Julian found the spoon thrust unceremoniously into
his hand as Tamsyn skipped hastily over the cobbles in
the direction of the pueblo's communal outhouse on
the outskirts of the village.

Gabriel came over with two tankards of red wine.
"Drink, Colonel? Santa Maria, but I've a thirst on me
tonight."

"Thanks." Julian took the tankard. "And I gather you intend to slake it."

Gabriel looked over to where Josefa, still muttering, was slicing onions. "The old woman's been talking, eh? Well, it does a man good once in a while. I'd invite you to join me, Colonel, but you'll need your sleep in the first watch, and I'll need mine in the second." He chuckled hugely and drained his tankard with one interminable swallow.

"It's not really my style," Julian said. "If those villains of yours pass out, we'll be in poor shape to defend ourselves."

"Oh, I'll not be drinking with them," Gabriel said. "They'll have a glass or two with supper, but they'll keep themselves sober or feel my whip at their backs, and they know it. No," he said happily, "I've discovered some friends in the village. A little dice, a little card play . . . relaxes a man."

Julian raised an eyebrow but offered no contradiction to this. The evening would bring what it would bring.

After supper a group of men drifted in from the village, rolling another cask of wine between them. They greeted Gabriel with much backslapping and shoulder punching before they settled down in a corner of the barnyard to play dice on an upturned rain barrel.

Tamsyn came back from the stream with Josefa, where they'd been cleaning the supper bowls and trenchers. "He's well away," she commented, stowing the dishes in a saddlebag with a deft domestic efficiency that again surprised Julian. Josefa was still muttering, casting black looks at the men in the corner of the yard. Then she shook out a blanket and spread it on the cobbles, hauled a saddlebag onto the blanket as a pillow, and promptly lay down, drawing her various shawls, mantillas, and cloak around her.

Tamsyn chuckled, whispering, "She'll not let him out of her sight when he's started on this road. Not that he appreciates it. He'll curse her up hill and down dale if she interferes."

Julian glanced up at the velvet-black sky with its dazzling panorama of stars. The air was chill now, a fresh breeze coming down from the mountain peaks. "You'd better get some sleep in the hayloft."

"What about you?" Tamsyn hefted a roll of blankets onto her shoulder. It dwarfed her diminutive figure, yet she carried it with ease.

"I'll bed down somewhere," he said dismissively.

"But I could make up a bed for both of us in the loft," she said, her teeth flashing in the darkness as she smiled invitingly. "It'll be cozy in the hay."

"For God's sake, girl, what does it take to get through to you?" he demanded in a fierce undertone. "Get up into the loft and get some sleep. I'm going to have a word with Gabriel."

He turned away from her hurt gaze, which reminded him absurdly of a kicked puppy, and strolled over to the now noisy group. Gabriel looked up, his eyes bleary but his expression jovial. "Anything I can do for you, Colonel?"

Julian shook his head and pulled out his watch. "I'll relieve you at two."

"Och, aye, that'll be grand," the giant said serenely, attempting a wink but managing a squint instead. "I'll be a rich man long afore then." He rolled the dice and chuckled at the three sixes they gave him. "Can't do a thing wrong tonight." There was a guffaw from the men surrounding him, and the village elder refreshed

Gabriel's tankard of wine from a stone jar he held between his feet. Fortifying it with the rough, stomach-burning brandy of the region, Julian assumed. A mixture that would put an ordinary man under the table after a couple of swigs.

He cast a glance around the yard. Gabriel had positioned his sentries sensibly enough. One of them was stationed at the rear, commanding the foot of the goat track that wound down from the heights. He had a pitch torch at his feet, a rifle between his knees, and was smoking a noxious pipe. The other two were stationed at either end of the village, guarding the main path. Gabriel had seated himself so that he faced both the entrance to the yard and the byre where the treasure was stored.

But the man couldn't see straight!

Julian decided he'd keep his own watch during Gabriel's tour. He'd had many a sleepless night during the four years of the Peninsular campaign—one more wouldn't hurt him. He turned toward the barn.

"Keep the bairn close to you," Gabriel called after him, and his voice was less thick than it had been.

Julian glanced back. Gabriel nodded significantly at him. Drunk or sober, his little girl's safety was clearly still uppermost in his mind.

Julian raised a hand in acknowledgment and went into the barn. The other three outriders were sleeping on the floor, snoring in the straw until it was time to take their watch. He sat in a corner of the barn, close to the ladder to the hayloft, drew his cloak tight around him, and prepared to wait until Tamsyn was safely asleep.

After half an hour he judged it safe to go up to the loft. Temptation should by now be deeply asleep. He climbed the ladder softly. Tamsyn had spread the blankets and was curled in a comfortable nest of hay. Moonlight fell through the round window, silvering her pale hair, and her deep, even breathing filled the small fragrant chamber.

Julian tiptoed to the window. It looked down on the yard, and he could clearly see Gabriel and his fellow drinkers. It looked a peaceful, convivial scene.

He glanced back at the sleeper. Only her silvery hair was visible in the straw and blanket nest. How could such a wild and unusual girl expect to make her way in English society; expect to persuade some stiff-necked Cornish family, overly conscious of lineage and position, to take her to their bosom? It was always possible she was mistaken about her mother's social position, and her family were simply landed gentry or country squires. If so, she might have a better chance of winning them over. But to turn this bastard brigand into an English aristocrat was the stuff of a lunatic dream. It would take a damn sight longer than six months to achieve such a miracle. And it would need more of a miracle worker than he believed himself to be. But he hadn't guaranteed success, he reminded himself. Then again, he couldn't tolerate failure. He never had been able to.

Grimly, he turned back to his observation of the yard. He didn't know how long he'd been staring down at the glowing embers of the fire and the flickering torchlight around the dice players when he caught sight of the dark shadow flitting behind the byre. He blinked, wondering if it was a trick of the shifting light, and then Gabriel bellowed, leaping to his feet, sending the rainbutt crashing and rolling onto the cobbles. A cudgel appeared in his hand from nowhere, swinging in a deadly arc.

Julian was already sliding down the ladder, his pistol in his hand, when Tamsyn sat bolt upright, wide-awake, listening intently to the confusion below.

The three outriders still slept in the hay at the foot of the ladder, and Julian kicked at them impatiently, trying to rouse them. The only result was a deeper snore and a muttered protest. His foot caught on something, and a stone jar like the one he'd seen in the yard rolled along the floor. He picked it up and sniffed. The jar had contained brandy and something else; a white, powdery residue coated the bottom. Gabriel had forbidden them to drink after supper, but obviously someone had provided them with liquor, carefully spiked.

He raced into the yard. Gabriel was surrounded by the men he'd been drinking with, wielding his cudgel and bellowing some bloodthirsty Highland war cry as they came at him, moonlight glinting on steel.

Julian drew his curved cavalry sword and leaped into the fray. Clearly the threat they'd had to worry about came from within the village. He could see the dark shape of the other sentry on the ground, presumably dispatched by the black shadow he'd noticed from the loft, and he guessed the two at the entrances of the village had been taken from the rear as well. But if they'd been intending to put Gabriel out of commission with the same draft they'd given the outriders, they'd miscalculated.

The man was a lion, still roaring his war cry. His eyes shone red in the light of the torches they'd been playing by, and he greeted Julian's arrival with a ferocious snarl that Julian correctly interpreted as "Welcome to the fight."

The men began to fall back as the two wielded cudgel and sword; then suddenly Tamsyn was in their midst. She grabbed one of the flaming-pitch torches and drove it into the face of a man flourishing a wicked serrated knife. He covered his face with a shriek and the knife clattered to the cobbles. She dived to the ground, snatching up the knife. And then the men were running from the courtyard, pursued by Gabriel and Julian and an irate Josefa, who, Julian realized incredulously, was wielding a broomstick to painful effect.

"Madre de Dios," Gabriel said as they slammed shut the gates to the yard. He wiped sweat from his brow with his forearm and grinned. "I do believe they thought to get me drunk." He laughed uproariously, his massive shoulders shaking with mirth.

"They were spiking the wine with more than brandy," Julian said. "Those three"—he gestured with his head toward the barn—"are out for the count."

"Pedro's got a bump on his head the size of an apple, but he's alive." Tamsyn had run with Josefa to examine the stricken sentry. "What about the two in the village?"

"Let's hope they'll be no worse," Julian said, frowning at her. "That was a foolhardy trick with the torch. You could have set fire to the barn."

"I was careful," she retorted. "And it worked."

"Yes, I grant you that. But it was still foolhardy."

Tamsyn shrugged. "In an emergency you use what tools are available."

Julian couldn't fault this logic. He knew he'd have done the same himself. He turned to Gabriel with an abrupt change of subject. "We'd better hole up here until dawn and then make a break for it."

"Aye." Gabriel nodded. "We'll pick up the other

two as we leave. Let's get these others sobered up. We'd do well to show all the force we can on the way out, although I doubt they'll be too anxious for a repeat engagement. Woman, make more coffee."

Josefa, without a word, dropped her broomstick and went to the still-glowing embers of the fire.

"Help me load up the mules." Julian beckoned Tamsyn, who came over with alacrity, her eyes sparkling in the firelight, her body thrumming with energy in the aftermath of excitement. "I want to be ready to go the minute the sky starts to lighten."

"They won't give us any more trouble," Tamsyn said confidently. "A tribe of shameful incompetents." She grinned. "The baron would never have taken them into his band. His raids never failed."

Julian chose to refrain from comment.

Two hours later they stormed out of the yard, Julian with drawn sword at the head of the column, Gabriel bringing up the rear on his charger, waving his broadsword and bellowing his war cry. Tamsyn drove the laden mules between them, cracking a mule whip with gleeful ferocity, the three less than fully conscious outriders swaying in their saddles but still brandishing weapons.

The village stayed behind its shutters, however, recognizing it had met its match. They found the other two outriders sitting beside the road, nursing bleeding heads but able to mount their horses, and the procession continued its way to Lisbon.

Chapter Twelve

"I DON'T KNOW THAT I CAN LET YOU HAVE THREE FOUR-pounders, Captain Lattimer," the ordnance master said with lugubrious satisfaction. "The *Isolde* took six yesterday."

Captain Hugo Lattimer, R.N., controlled his irritation with difficulty. He ran a hand through his thick chestnut-brown hair and glanced around the ordnance wharf. He'd been third in line that morning, and there were six other captains, as desperate as he to fit out their commands, waiting their turn to wheedle and cajole the ordnance master.

"If you could see your way to letting me have two, then I'll stand in your debt," he said, smiling with what he hoped was sufficient obsequiousness. "How's Mrs. Huston? She was a bit under the weather last time I was in Lisbon."

The other man's face softened slightly. "Oh, she's well enough, thank you, Captain. In an interesting condition."

"Well, congratulations." Captain Lattimer beamed as broadly as if it were his own lady about to present him with an heir. "Do give her my best regards."

"Yes, yes indeed, I'll do that, thank you kindly. Now, it was three four-pounders you were wanting?"

"Exactly so," Hugo said, allowing not a flicker of triumph to show in his green eyes. "And I'll be most grateful to you, sir."

The ordnance master scribbled in his ledger, his face as pained as if he were losing blood, and handed over the precious requisition order. Hugo touched his gold-laced hat and left the ordnance wharf, exulting in his success.

The Lisbon morning was hot, but there was still a breath of spring in the air to soften the burning quality of a Portuguese summer that scorched even the coastal areas. The harbor seethed with life, feluccas, longboats, and fishing boats darting among the more ponderous merchant craft. Four British men-of-war lay in the outer roads, three ships of the line, and a dainty, thirty-six-gun frigate.

Captain Lattimer's eyes rested with pride on the *Isabelle*'s elegant lines as she swung at anchor. He raised his glass, examining his command. The Blue Peter was furled against her fore-topmasthead, ready to be broken out when she sailed, and her decks were a bustle of activity. He nodded his satisfaction. Tomorrow morning they'd be under way, leaving the frustrating politics of harbor life behind.

"I beg your pardon, but do I have the honor of addressing Captain Lattimer?"

"You do, sir." The captain turned and found himself facing a tall man of about his own age in the uniform of a cavalry colonel.

"Colonel St. Simon." Julian extended his hand in greeting. "Admiral Moreton told me where I might find you."

The harbor admiral was an infernal nuisance, always

interfering in his captains' best-laid plans. "Indeed." Hugo kept his expression impassive as he shook the colonel's hand. "How may I be of service, Colonel?"

"By giving me passage on your ship." Julian came straight to the point. "I understand you're sailing for Portsmouth tomorrow."

It was standard practice for a naval ship to carry diplomatic and army passengers. "I see no difficulty," Hugo said, smiling with relief at this simple request.

Colonel St. Simon scratched his head a little uncomfortably and said, "Well, it's rather more complicated than that, Captain. Do you have time to take a glass of wine with me, and I'll explain."

"Tell me something," Hugo said conversationally. "Am I going to have a choice, or do you have written orders for me from Admiral Moreton?"

"The admiral agreed to accommodate the wishes of the Duke of Wellington," Julian said delicately. Traditionally, the navy was the senior service and even the commander in chief of the army would request rather than order a senior naval officer.

"I see. In that case perhaps you had better give me a glass of wine to soften the blow," Hugo said wryly.

"I'm . . ." Julian cleared his throat. "We are putting up at the Rose. The taproom's pleasant enough."

"By all means." Hugo had not missed the change of pronoun.

They turned together away from the quay just as a figure came barreling toward them in the broad-striped trousers and red waistcoat of a seaman, two hooped earrings swinging, a spotted handkerchief tied over his long tarred sailor's queue.

"Eh, Cap'n, sir. I've found us a brace of pigs, bonny

as you please, and three nanny goats, burstin' with milk." He beamed with pride.

"Good, Samuel. Listen, take this requisition and get it filled. Three four-pounders and as much round shot as you can squeeze out of 'em."

"Aye, sir." The sailor took the parchment, cast an incurious glance at the captain's companion, and rolled away with his swaying seaman's gait.

"Samuel could find a filled scuttlebutt in a desert," Hugo Lattimer commented as they turned into the cool dimness of the Rose. "Invaluable man."

"I know the type," Julian said, indicating a table in the window, instructing the waiter, "Lad, bring a bottle of port."

The captain sat down, sweeping aside the skirts of his blue coat to free his sword. A dusty bottle and two glasses appeared; the wine was poured. The captain downed his first glass almost without tasting it.

"First one fast, second one slow," he said without apparent humor, refilling his glass. "So let's hear the worst, Colonel."

"Four passengers, three horses, and a mountain of baggage," Colonel St. Simon stated bluntly.

"Dear God!" Captain Lattimer stared at him. "How am I to find room in a frigate? The *Isabelle* is not a ship of the line, sir."

Julian moved his hands in a gesture combining both comprehension and powerlessness. "The admiral seemed to think . . ."

"The admiral is an interfering old busybody who doesn't understand the first bloody thing about commanding a man-of-war. He's sailed a desk throughout his entire career," Hugo said furiously. He refilled his glass and tossed the contents down his throat with a flick of his wrist.

Julian was accustomed to men who drank deeply, and refilled the captain's glass without giving it a second thought.

"Oh, there you are, I've been looking all over for you. You'll be pleased to know that we'll be two chests lighter. . . . Oh, I beg your pardon?" Tamsyn stopped in midspeech and looked inquiringly at the gentleman in his white-lapeled blue coat with its deep white cuffs and gold-buttoned sleeves.

"This is Captain Lattimer. And a taproom is no place for a lady." Julian made no attempt to conceal his annoyance. He'd hoped to have everything settled with the captain before exposing him to the full effects of Tamsyn's presence.

"Well, I'm no lady, as you never tire of telling me," Tamsyn said cheerfully, putting one booted foot on a spare chair, resting her arm on her knee. "Good morning, Captain. Are we to voyage in your ship?"

Hugo blinked at the diminutive figure with her vibrant violet eyes and the short shining cap of silvery hair. She was wearing a riding habit, the skirt hiked up by her inelegant stance to reveal leather britches. *Not if I can avoid it, lass.* It was a silent declaration as he thought of the havoc such an astonishingly unconventional creature could cause among the crew.

"In the name of grace, take your foot off there," Julian said, sharply pulling the chair out from under her foot. "Sit down, if you must."

Tamsyn put her bottom where her foot had been and smiled warmly at the captain. "Don't mind the colonel. He's as cross as two sticks this morning. I expect it's the heat. My name's Tamsyn." She held out her hand in a friendly manner.

Bemused, Hugo took it. *Tamsyn what? Doesn't she have a surname?* "Delighted, Miss Tamsyn," he murmured.

"I promise we won't be in the least a nuisance on your ship," Tamsyn continued blithely. "Josefa and I can share a sleeping space. We're perfectly accustomed to discomfort and cramped spaces, you should know. And you'll find Gabriel a very useful person to have around . . . won't he, Colonel?"

"Quite possibly," Julian snapped, still recovering from the implication that he was suffering from heat stroke. "Where is he?"

"Concluding the deals we made with the merchants," she said. "I told you we'll be two chests lighter for the rest of the journey. We've sold all the bolts of cloth and the smaller casket of jewels. That leaves just the gold and the two bigger caskets. You'll have room to store such things, Captain?"

"Hell and the devil," Hugo muttered, developing the unshakable conviction that he was as firmly caught as a fish on a hook. "You'd better show me what you've got."

"Come upstairs, then." Tamsyn pushed back her chair, getting energetically to her feet. "You can meet Josefa at the same time. She's standing guard at the moment."

Hugo sent a glance of despairing incomprehension toward the colonel, who was looking grimmer than ever. "I had hoped to ease you into this more gently," he said. "But there's no such thing as gentle, with Violette around. She has about as much finesse as a stampeding herd of elephants."

"Violette?" Captain Lattimer's bemusement was running amok. "I understood the lass to say her name was Tamsyn."

"Yes," Julian said. "I'll explain the situation to you in full." He turned to Tamsyn. "Would you make yourself scarce for half an hour . . . if it isn't too much to ask? When Gabriel returns, ask him to join us here."

"Are you going to tell the captain everything? Because if so, I'm sure I ought to be here." Tamsyn's brows drew together in a somewhat aggrieved frown. "It is my plan, after all, and I could surely explain better how—"

"No," Julian said flatly. "I will apprise Captain Lattimer of the facts in my own words. He and I speak a language that you do not. Now, be off."

Tamsyn, very put out, nibbled her lip. This was her enterprise; surely she should be present at strategy discussions. Then it occurred to her that while the cross-country journey had been conducted according to her wishes, from now on she would be a guest of His Majesty's navy, under the escort of the army. She didn't know anything about such travel, and she certainly didn't have the right to make decisions or even offer an opinion. And Colonel, Lord Julian St. Simon wasn't going to lose the opportunity to let her know it, however public the arena.

It was a galling thought. Without saying anything else, she turned and trailed forlornly from the taproom.

Julian watched her crestfallen departure. It was surprising that such a fiery individual could be cast down by a sharp snub. Well, she'd better get used to it. He turned back to his visibly confused companion. "Let me fill you in, Lattimer."

•   •   •

Tamsyn lay listening to the rhythmic scrape of a holy-stone on the quarterdeck a few inches above her face. Judging by the heavy rasping, they were also using one of the massive lumps of granite studded with nails that they called bears. It was close to dawn, a faint graying light seeping through the small window in the captain's sleeping quarters.

She stretched and turned onto her side, the hanging box bed swinging with her movements. It was like being in a permanently rocking cradle, very soothing combined with the gentle motion of the frigate on the presently smooth Atlantic waters. Josefa, in her own box across the small space, muttered as she came out of sleep.

Then the peace of early morning was shattered by a loud shrilling of whistles as the bosuns woke the watch presently sleeping belowdecks. Feet pounded on the decks, voices bellowed down the companionways, "Tumble up . . . tumble up!" And the racing feet sounded like roll after roll of thunder as the men scrambled on deck with their rolled hammocks to stow them in the nets along the frigate's sides.

After three days at sea Tamsyn had become accustomed to the noise of this morning ritual. Josefa, however, continued to grumble at being awoken with such violence. Now she sat up, grabbing the wooden sides of her cradle as it swung wildly with her movements.

"Ay de mí," she sighed as she did every morning, contemplating maneuvering her ample frame out of the cot and onto the shifting timbers of the cabin floor.

"Buenos días, Josefa." Tamsyn sat up, her own slight body barely creating a stir in the supporting ropes.

There was a loud bang at the door, and the man Samuel's voice came through the oak. "Hot water, missus."

"Gracias, señor." Josefa shuffled to the door, drawing her shawls modestly around her. She opened it a crack, met Samuel's grinning face, seized the copper jug, and dragged it inside. Josefa didn't hold with sea travel, and she didn't trust sailors.

Tamsyn was sitting up, hugging her knees, a slight frown drawing her delicate arched eyebrows together. "It's Monday, isn't it, Josefa?"

"So I believe," Josefa said, pouring water into a bowl.

"The last Monday in April." A little sinking feeling settled in her belly. Cornichet's ambush had been on March 28. Her monthly bleeding had almost ended; she remembered how she'd sat huddled in his cabin with the rope around her neck ironically thanking heaven for small mercies.

But in that case it should have started again five days ago. She touched her breasts, feeling for telltale soreness. Nothing. It had been a risk, those three glorious encounters. The first occasion there'd been no time in the swirling conflagration of ecstasy to think of consequences. The other times she hadn't wanted to spoil the rhythm and spontaneity to consider practicalities. She'd never had that problem before, but Lord St. Simon was no ordinary lover.

She'd persuaded herself that the time in her cycle was relatively safe. The village women held to the lore that pregnancy tended to coincide with coupling in the middle of the woman's cycle. It sounded a haphazard lore to Tamsyn, but she'd chosen to believe it.

"Damnation!" she muttered under her breath.

Grimly, she swung herself out of the box and disappeared into the quarter-gallery opening off the sleeping cabin, in the faint hope that a visit to the privy would reveal what she knew hadn't happened.

It was a forlorn hope, as she'd known it would be, and she returned to the cabin, pulling her nightgown over her head. Maybe it would start today. She wasn't always reliably regular, and five days wasn't that late. She sponged her body vigorously, as if she could bully it into behaving properly, then dressed in the britches and riding habit that allowed her some freedom of movement without breaking the colonel's sartorial rules.

She could hear Captain Lattimer talking with St. Simon next door, in the captain's day cabin in the stern of the ship. Lattimer had given up his sleeping quarters to the women and had slung two hammocks in his day cabin that he now shared with the colonel. Gabriel had placidly slung his own hammock in the gun room and spent much of his time in the company of the master gunner and Samuel, with whom he'd developed an easy rapport.

The smell of breakfast took Tamsyn into the cabin. It was filled with early sunshine coming from the sweep of handsomely mounted inward-sloping windows in the stern. Cushioned lockers stretched beneath them to provide seating, and the paneled bulwarks were lined with bookshelves. The captain and his passenger were seated at a laden table in the middle of the room. If it weren't for the two guns mounted at either end of the stern windows, it could have been a pleasant breakfast parlor in a country house.

"Good morning, Miss Tamsyn." Captain Lattimer greeted her arrival with a wave to a chair. He had a tankard of grog in his hand and was addressing a mutton chop and fried eggs.

The colonel looked up from his own breakfast and

accorded her a brief nod—a curt acknowledgment suitable for a slight and not very well-liked acquaintance. He pushed back his chair and rose to his feet. "I'll take a turn around the deck. If you'll excuse me."

Tamsyn frowned. He always found something else to do the moment she appeared. Except at dinner, when they both dined with the captain . . . and then he barely addressed two words to her. She sat down at the table, and Samuel put a boiled egg in front of her.

"I'll take a tray into your woman now, miss, if'n she's ready."

"Yes, thank you, Samuel." Tamsyn gave him a quick smile. Josefa insisted on taking her meals apart in their sleeping quarters. Gabriel took his in the gun room with the warrant officers.

"How soon before we cross the Bay of Biscay, Captain?" She sliced the top off her egg and to his amusement dipped a slice of toast into the yolk.

"This evening, with any luck. How are you in a rough sea, lass?"

"Lord, I don't know," Tamsyn said, dipping another slice of toast into her egg. "I've never sailed before, but I'm not an invalidish sort of person."

"No, I should imagine you're not." Hugo grinned. St. Simon had given him a brief description of the girl's antecedents, but he'd filled in the details for himself with little difficulty. He understood the colonel was escorting her to her mother's family in Cornwall, but he had the sense that there was more to it than that. Colonel St. Simon clearly wasn't happy with his mission, but Hugo was convinced the tension between the colonel and the girl had its roots in something much deeper.

"Well, if we're in for a Biscay widowmaker, you'll discover what kind of a sailor you are," he said cheerfully, pushing back his chair. "The bay's notoriously rough even without a full-blown storm."

"I stand warned, Captain." She smiled and drank her coffee with relish. Pregnancy was supposed to put one off one's food . . . or at least in the morning. So far, she was as hungry as ever.

The captain left the cabin, returning to his quarterdeck, and Tamsyn finished her own breakfast while Samuel cleared up around her. "Do you know where Gabriel is this morning, Samuel?"

"Watchin' 'is treasure, like as not," Samuel opined, sweeping crumbs into the palm of his hand. "Doesn't like to let it out of 'is sight, though it's stowed right and tight in the 'old."

"Perhaps he's afraid someone might make off with a ducat or two," Tamsyn said laughingly, although she knew that was exactly what Gabriel was afraid of.

"Not on this ship, they won't," Samuel declared, a touch of passion enlivening his customarily stolid countenance. "There's no thieves in Cap'n Lattimer's ship. Every man jack of 'em knows the cap'n turns thieves over to their shipmates, powerful 'ard on a man 'is own mates are. Damn sight 'arder than the cap'n."

Tamsyn had already decided that life before the mast on one of His Majesty's men-of-war was about as grim as life could be, so she merely nodded her comprehension, finished her coffee, and went up to the quarterdeck.

She'd learned in her first hour that the starboard side of the quarterdeck was holy ground, the captain's preserve, to be entered only on invitation. Lord St. Simon, however, seemed to have a standing invitation. In the orderly quiet of midmorning at sea, the two men were talking together at the starboard rail; the marine sentry turned the hourglass at the half hour and struck three bells to signal the third half hour of the watch. A bosun's whistle shrilled, and a trio of midshipmen jumped for the rigging, scrambling up into the shrouds and racing each other along the ratlines to the masthead some hundred feet above.

Tamsyn's toes curled in her boots as she craned her neck to watch them enviously. The view must be spectacular from the top, and it didn't look that hard. If she took off her skirt . . .

"Don't even consider it."

"Oh!" She spun round to find Julian regarding her, his heavy-lidded eyes shrewd and for once amused. It wasn't the first time he'd second-guessed her. "How could you possibly know what I was thinking?"

He gave her a lazy smile. "Believe me, buttercup, there are times when I can read you like a book."

"Oh, don't call me that," she said crossly.

He laughed. There was something about the beauty of the morning that for the moment eroded his bitterness. He didn't attempt to examine whether Tamsyn's own brand of beauty on this gorgeous day could have contributed to his general sense of well-being. "It's hard to resist when the sun's shining on your hair." He ran a flat palm over the top of her head. "When I was a boy, the village girls used to hold buttercups under their chins on May Day. And if the golden glow was reflected, it was said they'd find a lover before the day was out."

Tamsyn wondered why he had so suddenly lost his stiffness. He leaned on the port rail beside her, gazing out to sea, his demeanor relaxed and friendly. Tamsyn continued to watch the boys in the rigging, swinging like monkeys from shroud to shroud, but her mind was on her uncooperative body. She didn't feel any different, but that didn't mean anything. And what in the name of grace was she going to do if she *was* pregnant?

Julian glanced sideways at her, feeling the tension in the slight frame. "What's troubling you?" He told himself he couldn't care less, but he asked the question anyway.

Tamsyn met his eye for a second before turning back to watch the game in the rigging. "I'm just tired of twiddling my thumbs when I could be up there, or doing something useful."

The fib convinced him, as she'd expected it would. It was only half a fib, anyway. "You put one little toe on that rigging, my friend, and our contract is broken . . . finished, permanently. Understand?"

"You are, as always, perfectly lucid," she said, for once glad that they were quarreling.

"I do my best," he said acidly. He was about to return to the captain's side when a voice bellowed from the masthead.

"Sail ahead, sir. Three points on the starboard bow."

Hugo raised his glass, gazing across the flat expanse of ocean. He could just make out her royals on the horizon. "Send the signal midshipman up to the topmast, Mr. Connaught." His voice was quiet and without a hint of the exhilaration ripping through him. "I want an identification."

"Aye, sir."

The ferment on the ship was palpable, and yet it evinced itself in no sudden sounds or movements, only in a watchful silence. The hands on deck had moved to the rails, the bosuns stood with their pipes ready, every eye was on the horizon, every ear waiting for the midshipman to identify the ship's flags.

The lad's voice drifted down, shaky with nervous excitement. "It's flying the Frenchie flag, sir. I'll lay odds."

"I don't want a wager, Mr. Grantly, I want facts." The captain's voice cut like a diamond through glass. "Crowd sail, Mr. Connaught. Let's see if we can help the young gentleman by getting closer."

The bosuns' pipes shrilled and the ship was abruptly galvanized. Tamsyn watched, fascinated, as men swarmed like flies over the rigging, and sail after sail was unfurled until the *Isabelle* surged forward under full canvas.

"It is, sir. It's flying French colors," the young gentleman at the topmast yelled, almost falling off his perch in his excitement.

"Good. Break out the American flag, Mr. Connaught. We'll confuse 'em a bit." He turned to Julian, standing discreetly at his side. "Fancy the prospect of a fight, St. Simon?"

Julian's smile was answer enough. He watched as they pulled down the English flag and ran up the American colors in its place. It was a standard deception; only the distress flag was sacrosanct. They would break out their true colors at the last possible minute as a declaration of battle.

"Beat to quarters, Mr. Harris."

The bosun's pipe shrilled and the call resounded, "All hands on deck."

Tamsyn's blood stirred with excitement as the watch below came thundering on deck, rubbing sleep from their eyes in some cases. The mass of men—too many, it sometimes seemed, for such a small space—surged in a tidal wave of what to an observer looked like confusion, but which quickly came clear as an orderly swoop to their fixed places. Then a great silence fell over the ship, every man at his place, only the creak of the rigging as the *Isabelle* sped across the water.

Gabriel appeared beside Tamsyn, his face grim. "Those Froggies take one look at that treasure, little girl, and that's the last we'll see of it."

"They'd have to win first, Gabriel, and somehow I don't think Captain Lattimer intends to lose this battle prize," Tamsyn said, unable to hide her own thrill.

Gabriel grunted and drew his broadsword, holding it up to the light. He spat on the blade and polished it with his kerchief before thrusting it back into its sheath.

"Clear for action, Mr. Connaught." Captain Lattimer's voice was as quiet and controlled as ever, but there was a gleeful light in the bright-green eyes, a light reflected in the colonel's equally bright-blue orbs. "But keep the marines out of sight for the time being. Their scarlet coats are a giveaway." He glanced sideways at the colonel, who with a grin shrugged out of his own scarlet tunic.

The decks were swabbed and scattered thick with sand. The guns were run out in a silence as smooth as silk. Cannon balls, chain shot, and canister shot were assembled. The six-man gun crews stood to their guns, the surgeon and his mates retreated to the cockpit, setting out their instruments on the midshipmen's trunks that served as a makeshift operating table.

"The lass had better go below," Hugo said to the colonel, indicating Tamsyn, still standing rapt at the port rail.

"I'll leave you to give the order, then," Julian said with a dour smile. "She's a warrior; she won't go easily."

Hugo frowned, staring at the figure standing against

the far rail, her feet apart, braced comfortably against the pitch of the deck, her head held high, the wind lifting her short hair. Currents of energy seemed to flow from her.

Tamsyn felt his eyes upon her and boldly crossed the small space. "You wanted to speak to me, Captain."

"I was contemplating sending you below. The deck of a frigate in the midst of battle is no place for a lass."

"Maybe not, sir." She returned his gaze steadily, knowing that the captain's word was law on this ship. If he ordered her below, she'd have no choice but to obey. At least initially. Once the action began, she'd be able to return and no one would notice.

"But I doubt you'd stay there," he said pensively, and then laughed at the shock in her eyes. "That was what you were thinking?"

"Yes," she agreed in chagrin.

"I suppose I could have you battened down in the hold for the duration," he mused. "What's you opinion, Colonel?"

"It's your command, Captain," Julian said formally. "I wouldn't presume to offer an opinion."

Tamsyn had the unmistakable feeling that the two men were making game of her, yet they both looked as solemn as deacons.

"Well, on your own head be it," Captain Lattimer said. "But if you get in the way, lass, I'll have you carried below bodily by a marine."

"You don't have to worry about that," Tamsyn said with as much dignity as she could muster, and returned to her post.

The French ship grew on the horizon, taking shape as a square-rigged frigate. Hugo knew the *Isabelle* would be under scrutiny from the French quarterdeck. They'd see the American colors, which would confuse them for a while. America was on the verge of declaring war with England and was no enemy of the French. But they'd also see she was cleared for action. It would puzzle them, but for how long? Long enough to allow the *Isabelle* to draw close enough to fire the first broadside?

They were about a mile apart now. "Bring her round six points to starboard, Mr. Harris," he instructed the master navigator at the helm, his voice sounding loud in the expectant silence. The *Isabelle* swung round slowly so that her starboard side faced the French ship.

And then the French seemed to understand. Wild activity erupted on her decks as she cleared for action, the snub-nosed guns appearing in the gunports.

"All right, Mr. Connaught," Hugo said softly.

The English flag broke out at the *Isabelle*'s masthead.

"Fire, Mr. Connaught."

Chapter Thirteen

THE MASSIVE POWER OF THE *ISABELLE*'S STARBOARD GUNS exploded in a noise more terrifying than Tamsyn could ever have imagined. The broadside raked the length of the French ship, and she saw rigging flung loose and a great hole appearing above the waterline as the smoke cleared. Screams filled the air, and then there was another massive bellow as the French returned the broadside. Tamsyn stared in horror down into the waist of the ship, where a cannon ball had exploded, sending up a shower of deadly splinters into the nearby gun crews. Then she was running down the gangway, unhooking her skirt as she did so, leaping into the confusion.

The lieutenants at the guns were bellowing their orders to the gun crews, struggling to make themselves heard above the screams of the wounded. The *Isabelle*'s starboard guns fired again, and she swung slowly round to bring her port guns into play while the starboard rushed to reload.

A powder monkey hurtled past Tamsyn, his arms full of the lethal cartridges of gunpowder that had to be brought from the handling chambers, where they were kept well away from the guns until needed. A flying splinter lodged into his cheek, and he dropped his precarious load to the deck.

A bosun's mate raced for him, swinging his rope's end, screaming like a banshee. The lad curled, sobbing, on the deck, blood pouring from his eye. Tamsyn bent, gathered up his cartridges, and ran for the nearest gun, handing the gunpowder to the fifth crewman, whose face was already blackened with smoke. The lieutenant in charge of the gun cast her one astonished glance and then forgot all about the unorthodox powder monkey, giving the order to tilt the gun so they could fire a round of chain shot into the enemy rigging.

Tamsyn, grimly recognizing that she had a useful part to play, ran back, down into the bowels of the ship, along the narrow gangways, scrambling down the steep companionways leading from deck to deck, into the handling chamber, where she loaded up with more cartridges and repeated her journey.

The noise was so deafening now, it was as if it lived in her head. She couldn't separate its different components, but sometimes the screams became discrete sounds. One minute a man was standing upright beside her; the next he was writhing at her feet, both legs vanished in a crushed tangle of flesh and sinew, and the sounds of his agony pierced her through and through.

She dropped to her knees beside him, helpless and yet unable to abandon him in such hideous pain, but someone said roughly, "For God's sake, get that bleedin' shot to number-six gun," and she was up and running, closing her nose to the nauseating stench of burning pitch from the surgeon's cockpit as he amputated with the speed of a butcher, cauterizing each stump with the pitch before moving on to the next victim.

Her foot slipped in a pool of blood as she delivered her load, and she grabbed wildly, catching the skirt of the lieutenant's coat. He stared at her, then clipped, "Sand!"

She understood and ran for the barrel of sand in the corner, flinging it over the deck in great handfuls to soak up the blood. Again and again the guns spoke, and she dodged and whirled and ducked as she ran. Whenever she had a chance to look over at the French ship, it seemed to have lost more spars and rigging, and yet they fought on, her guns bringing a devastating sweep of death and ghastly injury to the *Isabelle*'s crew.

Hugo Lattimer closed his mind to the destructive havoc in the waist of his ship. "Mr. Connaught, boarding nets." He looked for the colonel and saw him with the marines, now ranged along the rail. He'd armed himself with a musket and was picking men off the French ship's rigging, the giant Gabriel at his side.

"Colonel, are you coming aboard her?" Hugo called.

Julian saw the boarding nets swinging across the narrowing space between the two hulls and drew his sword with a flourish. "My pleasure, Captain." He leaped down to the quarterdeck, Gabriel still beside him. In the press of battle he hadn't given a thought to Tamsyn. Now he glanced around the shambles of the quarterdeck.

"Are you looking for me?" Tamsyn spoke, breathless, behind him.

He whirled round, then stared at her. Her clothes were bloody, she was black from head to toe, her eyes huge violet pools in the filth, her teeth startling as she offered a weary smile. "They've stopped firing the guns, so I'm not needed down there anymore."

"What in the devil's name have you been doing?" he demanded.

"Running gunpowder for the gun crews," she said matter-of-factly. "What did you think I was doing?"

Julian shook his head. "I don't know what I thought, but I should have known you'd be in the thick of it." Of course Tamsyn would be where she could be most useful. She'd give not a thought for her personal safety in such a situation. He had a sudden urge to brush the matted hair from her brow, to wipe away a streak of someone's blood from her cheek. To share with her the satisfaction of a battle well fought.

"The surgeon could use your help," Captain Lattimer said brusquely to Tamsyn, breaking the intensity of the moment, allowing Julian to step back from the precipice. As far as Hugo was concerned, his passenger was behaving like a member of his crew; it seemed only logical to treat her as one.

He drew his sword. "Come, gentlemen."

Tamsyn watched a little enviously as the boarding party surged across the netting, swords in their hands. She understood hand-to-hand fighting much better than this mass slaughter by cannon. It wasn't as wholesale as the storming of Badajos, but it was a dreadful business, nevertheless.

And there was work to be done among the wounded now that the fires of destruction had ceased. Resolutely, she returned to the waist of the ship.

Julian leaped onto the deck of the *Delphine*. The *Isabelle*'s men were engaged in fierce hand-to-hand fighting amidships, and he could see Hugo Lattimer cutting a swath through them, heading for the quarterdeck, where the French officers were to be found.

Some angel's hand was on the colonel's shoulder, and

he spun around just as a wild-eyed officer leaped at him from the forecastle. He parried, danced backward, lunged, but his opponent was a skilled swordsman, and he realized with a mixture of exultation and dread that he had a fight on his hands.

Gabriel, meanwhile, was beating back a group of sailors armed with knives and spars. The giant's broadsword flashed in the sunlight as he sliced and slashed, bellowing his terrifying war cry, driving his opponents into a corner of the deck, where they cast down their weapons and surrendered on the wise assumption that the battle was lost anyway and there was no point inviting further injury.

Gabriel, having secured his section of the fight, glanced around and saw the colonel still engaged with the French lieutenant. Julian was hard-pressed, but his mouth was twisted in a grimace of determination, and then his opponent slipped in a pool of blood and went down on one knee.

Julian dropped his point and stood aside as the man came to his feet again. The two men looked at each other; then the lieutenant shrugged and bowed, handing his sword, hilt first, to the English colonel.

Julian touched the sword in ceremonial ritual, then gestured courteously that his opponent should keep it. The man bowed and sheathed his weapon, and the two looked around, no longer enemies, simply battle-weary warriors.

On the quarterdeck Hugo Lattimer was accepting the surrender of the *Delphine*'s captain with the same courtesy, insisting that he keep his sword. One didn't humiliate an enemy who'd fought bravely, and one could never be sure in the fluctuating fortunes of war when the situation would be reversed.

Julian made his way to the quarterdeck. Hugo greeted him with a tired smile. "Colonel St. Simon, may I make you known to Monsieur le Capitaine Delors?"

The two shook hands, and the captain introduced the rest of his officers. It was all very courteous and civilized, as if the murderous mayhem of the last hour had never taken place. Except for the smell of blood and the continuing groans and screams of the wounded, and the broken spars and ripped rigging littering the blood-stained decks.

"I'll put a prize crew aboard her under Will Connaught," Hugo said. "Together with our wounded. He can sail her back to Lisbon with a bit of make and mend." He couldn't conceal his satisfaction as he looked around the captured vessel. It had been a good day's work. The French frigate was a fat prize and would bring him a much-needed injection of funds, and the *Isabelle*'s crew would have their share, which would ensure a jubilant ship for the rest of the voyage.

Julian left him making these dispositions and returned to the *Isabelle,* swinging himself across the boarding nets. "Knows what he's doing, that Captain Lattimer," Gabriel observed, landing beside him on the deck. "Where's the bairn?"

"Still in the thick of something, I imagine." They made their way to the waist of the ship, where order miraculously was emerging out of chaos. Tamsyn was kneeling beside a wounded man waiting his turn for the surgeon's attentions. He'd lost a finger and seemed relatively unperturbed, his chief lament being that the wound wasn't enough to send him home.

"Is it over?" Tamsyn looked up as Julian and Gabriel crossed the deck.

"So it would seem." Julian scrutinized her blackened countenance. "Are you all right?"

"Yes." She stood up, stretching wearily. "I don't know how, though. I don't know how anyone could survive in that inferno. It was horrible. Worse than anything I've ever been in."

Julian made no reply. There was no disputing her statement, but they were both soldiers, and battle horrors were intrinsic to the life.

"Josefa's helping the surgeon," Tamsyn said to Gabriel. "He says she's a lot more skilled than his assistants." She turned toward the cockpit, caught her foot in a coil of rope, and fell headlong on the deck.

She must be exhausted, Julian thought, reaching down a hand to help her to her feet. When she didn't immediately take it, he bent over her and lifted her to her feet, hiding his concern, stating briskly, "You're done in, girl."

Tamsyn didn't seem to hear him. She was staring down at her thigh, where a jagged splinter stuck out through a rent in her britches. Blood was seeping out of her flesh where the splinter was lodged. "Look! I'm cut. It's bleeding." She raised her eyes, and he saw they were filled with a sick horror, her face suddenly deathly white beneath the grime.

"Colonel, catch her!" The sharp, urgent command came from Gabriel, standing behind him.

Tamsyn swayed, her knees buckling. Just in time Julian moved, catching the slight figure as she crumpled to the deck. "What the hell . . . ?" He stared down at her, unconscious in his arms, then looked incredulously at Gabriel. "She must have fallen on a splinter, but it doesn't look bad."

"It's the blood," Gabriel said matter-of-factly. "Always sends her off like that."

"But she's already covered in blood," Julian said in disbelief.

"Aye, but it's not hers," Gabriel explained. "The bairn can't abide being cut. As a babby she'd scream the house down for a pinprick . . . anything more than that, she'd be beside herself. The baron tried everything to get her out of it, but he gave up in the end."

"Dear God," Julian muttered. Of all the absurdities. She rode like a cossack, fought like a mountain lion, didn't flinch from discomfort and deprivation, but she fainted dead away at a pinprick. He thought of Cornichet's knife and wondered in amazement what it must have cost her to face up to the mere prospect without breaking.

"We'd best get this splinter out quickly," he said. "It's going to bleed a lot more then than it is now."

"I'll get Josefa."

Julian carried Tamsyn into the day cabin, and her eyelids fluttered open as he laid her down on one of the cushioned lockers.

"What happened? Oh, God, my leg. It's got that thing in it!" Her voice rose on a frantic note.

"We're going to take it out," he said calmly. "It's just a splinter. You must have fallen on it when you tripped."

"But it's sticking out of me! All my blood's coming out!"

"Tamsyn, don't be absurd!" It was so ridiculous he wanted to laugh, but her distress was acute and definitely not feigned. He pulled his dirk from his belt and cut the leather of her britches away from the wound. "Now, don't look," he instructed when she wailed in horror at the sight of the splinter and the blood that was now flowing strongly.

"I hear you need my services." The surgeon sounded amazingly cheerful as he came into the cabin, still in his bloodstained apron, accompanied by Josefa and Gabriel. "Oh, my, that's a big one," he said with the same cheeriness. "Soon have it out."

"No!" Tamsyn screeched. "I'll do it." She struggled to sit up, reaching for her thigh.

"No, you won't! Now, stop being so silly!" Julian sat down behind her, lifting her head onto his lap, holding her shoulders steadily. "Keep still. It'll be over in a minute."

Josefa bustled over, taking her nurseling's hands, chafing them, crooning softly to her, as the surgeon deftly pulled the splinter clear. Blood spurted; Tamsyn groaned and fainted again.

"Good God, what's going on?" Captain Lattimer entered his cabin to find it filled with people not generally welcomed into his private quarters.

"We're having a little trouble," Julian said, a chuckle in his voice. He shook his head in renewed disbelief, maintaining his hold on Tamsyn's shoulders. "This absurd girl is behaving like a milk-and-water miss because she has a splinter in her leg."

"Good God!" Hugo said again. "After what she was doing during the battle! According to Lieutenant Godfrey nothing slowed her down."

"There's none so strange as folks," Samuel declared in his Yorkshire burr, bringing a bowl of hot water to the surgeon. "I'll fetch ye a roll of bandage."

Tamsyn came round again as the surgeon was washing the wound. She gazed up into Julian's face. "Has it stopped?"

Her face was deathly pale, her expression as fearful and vulnerable as a terrified child's. All the resilience, the dominance of her personality, had vanished as she looked to him for reassurance and comfort with a trustfulness that he couldn't possibly have destroyed.

He smiled and brushed her hair away from her forehead as he'd wanted to do earlier. "It's almost stopped. The surgeon's going to bind it up, and you'll be as good as new in a day or two."

"It wasn't too deep, Miss Tamsyn," the surgeon said, shaking a dusting of basilicon powder over the wound. "There should be no danger of infection." He wound gauze and bandages around her thigh, and the patient lay very still, her color returning slowly. "It'll probably ache, though. Would you like some laudanum?"

"I don't mind it hurting," Tamsyn said. "I just don't like it bleeding."

"Well, it'll stop soon enough." The surgeon dusted off his hands and stood up. "I recommend you don't do too much running around for a day or two, though. Let it heal up first."

"I am sorry," Tamsyn said in a small voice. "Did I behave very badly?" She asked the question of Julian, her embarrassment and anxiety clear in her eyes.

If he'd wanted revenge, now was the perfect opportunity. But he couldn't take it. She was trusting him to help her with the same simplicity with which she offered him her body, invited him to join in her love games.

" 'Unexpectedly,' is the word I would have chosen." He hitched her up until she was sitting on his lap, leaning against his chest. "But we're all entitled to our foibles."

"I feel very peculiar," Tamsyn declared, settling naturally against him. "All weak and shaky."

"You could do with a bath, like as not," Samuel suggested. "And some 'ot milk and rum."

"See to the hot water, then, Samuel," Hugo said. "Set it up in here, there's more room. And take what you need from my supplies. We'll leave the lass and her woman to themselves." Having nobly relinquished his sanctum, he turned to go back to work, and it was only when he reached the quarterdeck that he realized that while everyone else had followed him, the colonel had remained behind.

He raised an eyebrow, regarding the closed door to his cabin, where a marine sentry had taken up his customary post now that the ship's routine was in a fair way to being restored. *Interesting,* he thought, *but for some reason not surprising.* He turned to his second lieutenant, who'd taken over from Will Connaught, now commanding the prize crew on the *Delphine.*

"We'll splice the mainbrace, Mr. Denny. The crew have earned it."

A ragged cheer went up when the order was given, and Hugo nodded to himself, well satisfied. At the moment he had a happy ship.

In the day cabin Tamsyn remained in Julian's comforting embrace, while Samuel heated up rainwater from a scuttlebutt on deck and filled a hip bath. The baron used to hold her in much the same way on similar occasions, and it felt both natural and reassuring. She was still embarrassed by what she knew must have been a ridiculous display, although she couldn't remember much of what she'd said—only the horrible panic that overwhelmed her at the thought of her flesh tearing.

She knew it was irrational, but she could no more control it than she could part the waters of the Atlantic.

Josefa bustled around the cabin, ordering Samuel about in voluble Spanish, commands that he basically ignored, going about his business in his own way.

Once he'd left them, Julian heard himself instructing the Spanish woman, "Bring a nightgown and robe, Josefa, and then you may leave us." He hadn't intended to say anything of the sort. He'd intended to deposit his burden on the cushions and leave her in the competent hands of her nurse. Nevertheless, that was what he said.

Josefa looked as if she didn't care for this instruction, but the colonel's air of authority was intimidating, and her nurseling offered no objection. In fact, Tamsyn's eyes were closed, and it looked as if she was dozing.

"Ay de mí," Josefa muttered in customary fashion, and hurried next door to fetch the required items, placing them carefully over a chair. Then she stood irresolute for a minute before hurrying out with an expressive shrug.

"I'm going to cut these britches off you," Julian said matter-of-factly. Rational thought told him he was mad to continue along this path, but Tamsyn had so completely relinquished control over herself to him that it seemed natural to complete the task. Both natural, enjoyable, and utterly compelling.

She was as light and fragile as a leaf in the circle of his arms. The vibrant sexuality he found impossible to resist had vanished, but it was replaced with this soft vulnerability that he found equally irresistible.

He eased her onto the cushion beside him and pulled off her boots.

"I can undress myself," Tamsyn said, sounding stronger. "I've stopped being silly."

"Good. But you might as well let me do it now I've started. You don't want to jolt the wound."

A little shudder rippled through her, and she immediately lay still as he stripped off her stockings and sliced through the britches with his dirk, peeling them away from her. She felt very sleepy, on the brink of some warm, dark, beckoning chasm, and his hands on her body were infinitely soothing as he removed the last of her clothes. In the back of her mind swam the half-formed thought that she was wasting an opportunity here. For some reason, St. Simon had softened toward her, but she couldn't seem to do anything about it except yield to his ministrations. The dark thought of pregnancy writhed to the forefront of her mind, but she couldn't concentrate on it, and it slithered away.

She lay back in the hot water, her injured thigh propped on the side of the hip bath, while his hands moved over her with a matter-of-fact familiarity more suited to a nursemaid than a lover. She smiled dreamily at the thought, wished again that she could summon the willpower to pursue greater intimacies, then decided she was enjoying this too much to change it even if she could.

"What are you smiling at?" Julian reached for the towel, aware that he'd been fooling himself. There was nothing platonic about what he'd been doing to her body, and his own as a result was on fire.

"No reason." Tamsyn regarded him through half-closed eyes, seeing the tension on his face, the tautness of his mouth. She could think of only one reason, and some of her languor dissipated. "I feel very weak," she said. "I don't think I can stand."

Julian swore under his breath, but he'd started this and he had to finish it. He lifted her out of the bath, holding her wet body against him, and she nestled her head into his shoulder with a little murmur of pleasure. Was she doing it deliberately? The suspicion grew.

Firmly, he sat her on the locker again and wrapped the towel around her. "You can dry yourself sitting down. I'll do your legs and feet."

Oh, well, Tamsyn thought, it had been a good try. She rubbed herself dry as best she could, and Julian handed her the nightgown, hiding his relief as her body disappeared under the folds of lawn. He handed her the wrapper.

"Put this on too; then you can put your legs up and rest against the cushions," he directed, in what he hoped was the neutral and efficient tone of a nurse. "I'll see how Samuel's doing with that hot milk."

Tamsyn made herself comfortable. She felt a lot better, but still rather shaky and slightly queasy. She closed her eyes and suddenly opened them again, holding her breath as she listened to her body. The dull cramping ache in the base of her belly was faint but unmistakable. Had the bad bleeding set off the good? Please don't let the cramp go away! The prayer went round and round in her head, blocking out everything else. *Please let it get worse.*

Samuel came in with a tray bearing a glass of steaming hot milk. He set it down on the table and laced it liberally with rum from one of the array of bottles the captain kept in a locker. "That'll settle ye, lass," he declared.

Julian had helped himself to a glass of Hugo's claret and now sat down at the table, watching Tamsyn as she sipped her milk in preoccupied silence. She looked as soft and innocent as a kitten in her white nightgown and wrapper and that silky silver hair. But he knew a damn sight better. He'd allowed himself to be fooled, and his body was letting him know it in no uncertain fashion.

Tamsyn put down her glass and said suddenly, "I need the quarter gallery." She swung her legs off the locker with a vigor that belied her earlier weakness, then grabbed the side of the table with a muttered, "Ouch," as her leg throbbed painfully.

With a grim set to his mouth Julian lifted her and carried her into the next-door cabin, setting her down at the door to the privy.

"Thank you. You don't need to wait, Josefa will help me back." She smiled sweetly.

"I'm going on deck," he said abruptly. "Stay off that leg." He left her, going swiftly up to the quarterdeck, hoping the air would cool his brain and his overheated blood.

Tamsyn, when she emerged from the quarter gallery, realized she'd never fully understood what relief was before. Her heart sang with it as she asked Josefa to find the required items in her baggage. Never again . . . never, ever again would she tempt providence.

Wrapping the robe securely around her, she hobbled back to the captain's cabin and ensconced herself under the windows again, looking out at the sweeping expanse of sea, stretching to a gray horizon. She allowed her body to relax, welcoming the fierce cramping, honeyed relief dancing in her veins.

Julian came into the cabin after half an hour to fetch his boat cloak. The wind was getting up, and they seemed to have left the warmth of Portugal far behind. "How are you?" It was a distant, politely neutral inquiry.

"Wonderful," she said with a fervency that startled

him. "I have my monthly terms," she said. "I was late and I was afraid . . ."

"I've been waiting for you to say something," he said flatly.

"Well it's all right," Tamsyn responded with a rueful smile, pushing her hair away from her forehead. "And we won't take any risks in future."

The colonel's mouth tightened, and his eyes were steel-bright, sword-sharp as he came over to her. "Understand this, Tamsyn. There will be no future. I'll fulfill this damn contract because I must, but that's as far as it goes. Is that clear?"

Tamsyn turned her head away from the piercing blue glare, gazing out of the window at the now gray and heaving sea. "If you say so, milord colonel."

Chapter Fourteen

"THE CARRIER JUST DELIVERED A LETTER, MY DEAR. IT looks like St. Simon's hand?" Sir Gareth Fortescue strolled into the breakfast parlor examining the letter in his hand with unusual interest. "Franked in London, by God! I thought your brother was in the Peninsula for the duration."

He dropped the letter beside his wife's plate and stared with a jaundiced air at the dishes arrayed on the sideboard. "I don't know how many times I've told that damn cook I like my bacon crisp. Look at this." He picked up a rasher on the serving fork. "It's as white and soggy as a pig's underbelly."

Lucy Fortescue flushed and pushed back her chair with a little murmur of dismay. "I'm so sorry, Gareth, I didn't notice. Shall I ring for Webster and tell him to bring some more?"

"No, don't bother." Her husband flung himself into his chair at the head of the table with an irritable grimace. "I'll make do with the sirloin."

Lucy hesitated, anxious to read her brother's letter but equally anxious not to neglect her husband at this critical morning juncture. It was clear from his heavy eyes and less than glowing complexion that Gareth was suffering this morning. She wasn't sure where he'd passed the previous evening, or even the night. It hadn't been in his own bed and certainly not in hers. She didn't enjoy what went on in the marriage bed, but it was essential to a marriage, and it couldn't be right that her husband was so often content to leave her to sleep alone.

She sighed and then flushed again, afraid that he would have heard the little sound. Gareth detested it when she moped. He read into her unhappiness unspoken criticism and dissatisfaction with her lot.

Both of which were true. But Lucy swiftly buried that rebellious acknowledgment; her mother had told her more times than she could remember that a wife's duty was to show her husband only unquestioning support and obedience and to accept cheerfully the life he chose to give her. And Julian, after her father's death the only man whose opinions she'd been aware of, obviously shared her mother's viewpoint. Besides, he'd been so much against the match in the first place, she couldn't possibly expect his sympathy because marriage to Sir Gareth Fortescue wasn't all that she'd dreamed it would be.

But it was very hard. Another little sigh escaped her. It was very hard, at eighteen and after only ten months of marriage, to be left alone day and night after day and night while her husband pursued all his old activities and relationships as if he'd never stood at the altar with her.

"Well?"

She looked up guiltily at this sharp interrogatory. Gareth was scowling, his hand circling a tankard of ale.

"I beg your pardon, Gareth?"

"Well, what does your brother have to say?" he demanded impatiently.

"Oh, I haven't read it yet." She offered a timid little smile and slit the wafer sealing the missive.

"Oh," she said again. The letter was as brief and succinct as all her brother's communications, and it took but half a minute to make herself mistress of the contents.

"Well?"

"Julian says he's going to be in England for a few months. He has some work to do at Horseguards and at Westminster for the Duke of Wellington, and then he's going to Tregarthan for the summer."

"Good God! Whatever for? Has he bought himself out of the army or something?"

"No, I don't think so," Lucy said, frowning. "But he says he has someone with him . . . a . . . a Spanish lady." She looked up in clear bewilderment. "He says he owed her father a favor, and when he was dying, he asked Julian to take his daughter under his protection and arrange for her introduction into English society. Apparently she has some Cornish connections that she hopes will acknowledge her."

Her china-blue eyes widened as her bewilderment increased. "It doesn't sound at all like Julian, does it?"

Gareth gave a snort of laughter. "If it were anyone but St. Simon, I'd say he'd brought himself a light skirt back from the wars, but he's such a stickler for the proprieties, he'd never sully the precious turf of Tregarthan with an irregular liaison."

Lucy blushed crimson and took a hasty gulp of her tea, choking as the liquid scalded her throat.

"Don't be such a ninny, Lucy," Gareth said, not unkindly. "You know something of the facts of life, my dear. You're a married woman now, not a virginal chit. St. Simon's as red-blooded as the next man, he's just deuced straitlaced about where and when he indulges a man's natural urges."

"Yes . . . yes, I suppose so." Lucy pushed back her chair and stood up hastily. "If you'll excuse me, Gareth, I must talk with cook about the menus."

She hastened from the room, leaving her husband to reflect that if St. Simon had been less straitlaced, Lucy might have been a more lively partner, both in bed and out of it. Her brother, ten years older than herself, had been her guardian for the seven years before her marriage, and his notions of propriety when it came to the behavior of a St. Simon were devilish strict.

It was a pity, really. Gareth refilled his ale tankard, noting with relief that his hangover was dissipating with each gulp. Lucy was a pretty little thing, and he found her soft, feminine roundness quite appealing, but she didn't know the first thing about pleasing a man. It was no wonder he continued to take his pleasures where he'd always taken them.

His scowl returned abruptly as some memory of the previous evening dimly surfaced through the brandy haze in which he'd spent the majority of the night. Marjorie had been nagging him again. She was always wanting something more. The diamond bracelet he'd given her hadn't been of the first water . . . the new dressmaker didn't know what she was doing, it was absolutely imperative she patronize Lutece instead. The money was nothing . . . nothing . . . not if he truly cared for her . . . and didn't she make him happy? Happier than a man deserved to be?

Gareth shifted in his chair, remembering with the familiar ache how very happy Marjorie could make a man. But her price was too damn high—and getting higher by the day.

He looked around the elegant parlor of the gracious Sussex mansion, out through the windows to the smooth expanse of lush green lawn. His family home had been going to rack and ruin when he'd married Lucy St. Simon. Her dowry had put it to rights, and it was her dowry that was financing Marjorie's expensive tastes . . . or, rather, his own expensive habits.

A faint waft of distaste disturbed the normally unruffled surface of his self-assurance, and the astonishing thought presented itself that he might try to break some of those habits. He *was* a married man, when all was said and done.

And the pile of bills from his creditors was growing ever larger . . . tailors and wine merchants and shoemakers and hatters. Tattersall's had to be settled, of course, on settlement day, and his debts of honor couldn't wait either. Fortunately, the tradesmen weren't pressing too hard for payment as yet; his marriage was recent enough to give him fairly extended credit, but he didn't care for the idea of having to apply to his brother-in-law for a loan to settle his debts. St. Simon had already cleared a mountain as part of the marriage settlements.

Not that St. Simon would refuse him, or even pass comment on his brother-in-law's profligacy, but he'd raise one of those bushy red-gold eyebrows and look as mildly incredulous as good breeding permitted.

No, it wasn't to be countenanced, if it could be avoided. Gareth pushed back his chair and stretched, frowning as an idea percolated through the gradually clearing fog of his hangover. Why not pay St. Simon a visit in the ancestral home? Rustication would be tedious, of course, but it would take him away from the temptations of Marjorie and the racetrack and the gaming tables, not to mention provide respite from his creditors' billets-doux. And maybe it wouldn't be *that* tedious. It might be amusing to see this Spanish lady St. Simon had under his wing. There was something rum there . . . very rum.

And besides, a little Cornish air would do Lucy the world of good. Quite peaky she'd been looking just recently. She loved Cornwall and all her childhood haunts and would be overjoyed at the prospect of spending a few weeks of the summer there with all her old girlhood friends.

Firmly convinced that he was acting entirely in his wife's best interests, Gareth Fortescue strolled out of the breakfast parlor to inform Lucy of his brilliant and noble decision.

"But, Gareth, Julian hasn't invited us." Lucy turned from the secretaire in her parlor, dropping her pen to the carpet in her dismay. "We can't arrive uninvited."

"Oh, nonsense!" Gareth dismissed this with an airy wave. "He's your brother, he'll be delighted to see you. Why, you haven't seen him since the wedding, and even that was only a fleeting visit, he was in such a hurry to get back to his regiment."

"Yes . . . but . . . but, Gareth, what of this Spanish lady? If he'd wished me to come, he'd have asked me."

"He didn't like to ask you to give up your summer to help him with this obligation, depend upon it," Gareth declared comfortably. "After all, we're still barely home from our honeymoon."

He smiled and chucked her beneath the chin. "Depend upon it, Lucy, he'll be grateful to have your help in entertaining this guest. Besides, he should have a hostess if he's entertaining a single lady, even if he is in some fashion her guardian. Your arrival will make everything all right and tight."

Bending, he kissed her lightly. "Now, be a good girl and arrange everything, so we may leave by the end of next week. We'll journey by slow stages, so you won't become fatigued."

"Oh, dear," Lucy murmured as the door closed on her husband's confident departure. While it was wonderful to have Gareth so cheerful and attentive, she knew her brother and knew that an unheralded arrival would not be appreciated. He didn't approve of Gareth, and sometimes Lucy had the sneaking suspicion that he didn't particularly like him, either. Her brother's bright-blue eyes would go cool and flat when he was talking to Gareth or even mentioning him in conversation. And he was always impeccably polite to him, as if to some very distant acquaintance.

Lucy had seen and heard her brother with his friends, and she knew how he despised what he called Society's fribbles—men who wasted their time and energies in the clubs of St. James's and dancing attendance on the Season's belles and heiresses. Even from her own prejudiced viewpoint, Gareth came into that category. Unlike Julian, he was not a man of action and fierce opinion. But he was hardly unusual in that. It was Julian who was the strange one, according to Society's lights.

She sighed and turned back to her secretaire, drawing toward her a piece of hot-pressed paper in her favorite pale blue, nibbling the end of her quill as she tried to think of a tactful way of announcing to her brother their imminent arrival at Tregarthan.

And what of this Spanish lady? What could she be

like? Was she young? Presumably, if her father had left
her to Julian's protection. It was not at all like Julian to
take on such a task, but, then, he did have a very honed
sense of duty and obligation. Perhaps the lady's father
had saved his life, or something equally desperate.

Was she beautiful?

And what in the world would Cornish society make
of someone sounding so exotic? They were plain, insu-
lar folk who had little truck with the world outside their
own Cornish land. Maybe the Spanish orphan didn't
even speak English.

It was all most extraordinary. Fired by curiosity now,
Lucy began to write rapidly, following Gareth's suggestion that her brother might wish for a hostess if he was
entertaining guests. She'd be happy to take on the duty
for her dear brother and was looking forward to seeing
him again after such a long time. She trusted he was well
and sent her . . .

Here she paused. What did she send him? Her love?
No, that sounded contrived. Julian was always pleasant
to her, but he'd always been somewhat distant and
hadn't hesitated to exercise his authority as brother and
guardian on the rare occasions when she'd been
tempted to balk at the restrictions he and her mother
considered necessary for a daughter of the house of St.
Simon.

She settled for warm regards, sanded the sheet, folded
and sealed it, then went in search of Gareth to frank it
for her. Julian should be almost in Cornwall by now,
since his letter had been dated a week previously, so this
missive should arrive at Tregarthan a few days after his
own arrival. Too late for him to write back and tell
them not to come, and he was far too courteous to send
them away once they arrived.

He could be very chilly, though. Lucy pushed this aside, finding herself eager for the change the journey promised. And Gareth would be with her for the next few weeks. There'd be no more nights spent with . . . with whomever he spent them. And maybe she could learn to please him a little . . . or at least to appear as if she didn't find that unpleasant tangling of bodies completely distasteful.

Feeling much more cheerful, she went into her bedchamber to examine her wardrobe and decide what she should take with her for a summer in Cornwall.

Did it ever stop raining in this ghastly gray country? Tamsyn leaned out of the window of the inn at Launceston, gazing across the jumble of slate roofs glistening and slippery with rain. It hadn't stopped since they'd landed at Portsmouth two weeks previously. It wasn't fierce and tumultuous, like Spanish rain; it was just a continuous wet mizzle, and the cold was so damp, it seemed to seep into the marrow of her bones.

Behind her in the small bedchamber, Josefa muttered to herself as she repacked the belongings they'd used overnight. She was not enjoying this sojourn in the cold, gray land where the sun never shone, but El Baron's daughter had said it had to be, a decree that for Josefa was as powerful as if it had come from the baron's own lips.

There was a brisk rap at the door, and Gabriel entered, ducking beneath the low lintel. Rain dripped off his heavy cloak. "You ready with that portmanteau, woman?"

"*Ay de mí,*" Josefa muttered, struggling with the stiff straps and buckles. "I'll be glad when we get where we're going."

"Won't we all?" Gabriel said dourly. His big hand rested for a moment on her arm in a rare gesture of sympathy. At least he'd been born in this land, but it was an alien shore for a peasant woman from the barren mountains of northern Spain. She gave him a rather shy smile, then bobbed her head, basking in the surprising gentleness of his sudden smile. Gabriel was her man, the sun to her earth; she always walked two steps behind him, and his word was law.

Gabriel hefted the portmanteau. "Little girl, you're to travel inside the carriage today. Colonel's orders."

"Since when has he been giving orders?" Tamsyn snapped irritably to Gabriel's retreating back. It seemed the last straw on this dismal morning. "I've no intention of being swayed and jolted in that chaise. It makes me feel sick."

She followed Gabriel down the creaky wooden staircase, across the lamplit stone-flagged hall, and out into the gloomy inn yard, where stood the postchaise that had brought them from London, ostlers putting the horses to, one of them tethering Cesar behind.

Colonel, Lord St. Simon stood watching. His cloak was black with the drizzle, and a steady stream ran from the brim of his beaver hat, but he seemed oblivious of the weather.

"Good morning." He greeted Tamsyn briskly. "I trust you slept well?"

"I always do," she replied. "Even when the sheets are damp. Will it ever stop raining?"

He laughed shortly. "Yes, one day it will. One morning you'll wake up to bright-blue sky and sunshine and birdsong, and you'll forget all about the rain. It's one of England's tricks."

Tamsyn grimaced, disbelieving, and huddled into her cloak, her hair already plastered to her head.

It was no weather for a buttercup, Julian caught himself thinking with a ripple of amusement. She looked shrunken and doleful, her bright hair rain-dark, her small body hunched into the heavy cloak, all her challenging, impudent sparkle vanquished by the dreary climate. Then he began to wonder what his brigade was doing, and his amusement died. If she didn't like the weather in her adopted country, she had only herself to blame.

How long had it had taken Tim to whip the men into shape after the excesses of Badajos? Where were they on the long march to Campo Mayor? Who was still alive? The questions as always roiled in his brain, and he had to force himself to come back to the rain-soaked yard of the inn at Launceston and his present preoccupations.

"I want you to travel inside the chaise with Josefa this morning," he said curtly.

"So Gabriel said, but I don't wish to. I'd rather be wet than nauseated in that smelly, jolting box." She turned to release her horse from the rear of the chaise.

Julian caught her arm. "I need you inside, Tamsyn."

"Why?"

"We're crossing Bodmin Moor," he stated as if that were answer enough.

Tamsyn frowned. They'd arrived at Launceston early the previous afternoon, and the colonel had insisted they go no farther that day, citing in much the same tone as now the crossing of Bodmin Moor. "So, milord colonel?" She dashed rain from her face as she regarded him with raised eyebrows.

"So, buttercup," he replied deliberately, "I need you

to ride with your damned treasure. Gabriel and I will be outside as a first defense, and you will be armed and ready within."

"Oh. Are there bandits on this Bodmin Moor, then?" Her expression livened considerably.

"We call them highwaymen," he said with an arid smile. "But they're as savage and ruthless a breed as any mountain brigand or robber baron."

Tamsyn decided to let that pass. "Gabriel has my weapons. I'll fetch them." She went off immediately, her step much crisper at the prospect of a little excitement to enliven this dreary journey.

Julian stamped his feet on the cobbles and turned up the collar of his cloak, running a mental check over his own weapons. "Into Bodmin and out of this world" was what the locals said when preparing to cross the bleak, windswept moor. Apart from his school years he'd grown up at Tregarthan, the St. Simon family estate overlooking the River Fowey, and considered himself as much a Cornishman as the landlord of this Launceston inn, steeped in the lores and customs of the county. And he loved every blade of grass, every flower of the hedgerow. He took pleasure in the thought of getting his hands on the reins of his estate again, of walking around his house, riding over his lands. If he was truly honest, there would be some compensations for this enforced rustication.

He'd made some progress on Wellington's account in London, presenting to the lords of Westminster the duke's urgent need for more men and money. They'd listened to him with flattering attention and suggested he return in a month to answer further questions once they'd had a chance to mull over the duke's request. The wheels of government turned very slowly, and

Julian had not expected any immediate decisions. He'd
written to Wellington with what news he had and was
resigned to returning to London in July, when he hoped
there'd be more concrete results to impart. He knew
this politicking was vital work, but it was dull work,
nevertheless, for a man who thrived on the smell and
sound of gunfire, the challenges and privations of forced
marches, and the quirks and vulgarities, the courage and
the foolishness, of the common soldier. Not even the
prospect of his own house and land could truly com-
pensate for that loss.

And if it weren't for the bastard spawn of a Spanish
robber, he would still be with the army. Wellington
would never have sent him on this diplomatic mission if
the opportunity hadn't presented itself so forcefully.

Tamsyn was blithely unaware of his reflections as she
installed herself in the coach with the shivering Josefa
and ran her eye over the chests of gold and jewelry
stashed beneath the seats. Their presence made the
inside of the vehicle very cramped. Normally this
wouldn't trouble anyone, since until today only Josefa
had been traveling inside. But Tamsyn couldn't fault the
colonel's defensive measures if they were really about to
cross wild and dangerous country, so she curled herself
into a corner, leaving as much room for the larger figure
of Josefa as she could, and checked that her two pistols
were primed. Josefa would reload for her if they were
attacked.

Gabriel stuck his head through the window. "We'll
be off now. You all right in here?"

"How far is it across this moor?" Tamsyn asked.

"Don't know." He withdrew his head. "Colonel,
the bairn wants to know how far she needs to travel in
the coach."

"It's twenty-one miles to Bodmin," Julian said, swinging onto his horse. "After that she can ride if she wishes. It's but twelve miles to Tregarthan from there."

Tamsyn nodded, satisfied. It was only just past dawn, and they should accomplish thirty-three miles easily by nightfall; they'd been managing forty a day from London along the paved stagecoach roads with frequent changes.

However, as they left the ruined keep and tower of Launceston Castle behind, it became clear that the narrow, rutted track across Bodmin Moor was no stage road. It was an ancient road, known as the Tinners Way, used to carry tin and clay from the mines from Fowey through Bodmin and across the moor into southern England. On either side the dark, rainy land stretched to the horizon, scrawny trees bent double with the force of the gusting wind, stumpy clumps of broom and gorse clinging to the peaty earth. The coachman kept his horses at an easy trot as the track crested steep hills and plunged down again into the flat moorland. The iron wheels churned the wet earth into a sea of mud, and every now and again the chaise would lurch almost to a halt as the wheels became enmired.

When that happened, the coachman cursed and whipped up his horses, glancing anxiously around, his blunderbuss across his knees. On either side of the coach rode Gabriel and Julian, muskets across their saddlebows, pistols at their belts, hat brims down and collars turned up as they faced into the stinging, wind-hurled rain.

They rode in grim silence, ever watchful, but finally came off the moor after a tense five hours, having seen neither hide nor hair of a potential highwayman, or, indeed, of any fellow travelers on this raw day of early summer.

The horses trotted wearily down the steep hill into the center of Bodmin. Tamsyn leaped from the coach with a sigh of relief as they came to a halt in the inn yard. She was feeling queasy from the motion, and there was an ominous tightening around her temples. She looked around through the continuing drizzle at the town, a patchwork of slate-gray roofs and gray stone-work climbing up the steep hillside.

The colonel dismounted and came over to her. His eyes were sharp as they rested on her face, noticing the pallor beneath the suntan and the shadows below the almond-shaped eyes.

"Tired?"

"Not really. I feel as if I'm going to puke. It's that coach—I can't abide traveling in that fashion."

"It was necessary."

She shrugged. "I didn't see any of your highway robbers, Colonel."

"The precaution was necessary," he responded indifferently. "Go into the inn and bespeak a private parlor for us and a nuncheon. I'll see about fresh horses."

"Yes, milord colonel." She touched her forelock in mock salute.

"You must learn to curtsy, buttercup," he responded with the nonchalance of before. "Tugging forelocks is appropriate only for grooms, ostlers, and farm laborers. Serving maids curtsy."

"I am *not* a maid."

"No," he agreed. "Not in any sense of the word." He turned from her, ignoring the dangerous flash in her eyes.

Tamsyn chewed her lip in frustration, staring at his

departing back, before she turned into the welcome warmth and lamplight of the inn.

The innkeeper made no attempt to hide his astonishment at these new arrivals. The rotund Spanish lady huddled in her shawls and mantillas poured forth a stream of incomprehensible laments that were as incomprehensibly responded to by the giant oak of a man who carried a massive broadsword thrust into the crimson sash at his waist. The diminutive figure of their companion, to his relief, spoke in the king's English with a perfectly ordinary request for a parlor and refreshment. But there was something exotic about her, too. He didn't know whether it was the short hair or the way she walked with an easy, swinging stride quite unlike a woman's walk. Her riding habit seemed conventional enough, but there was something about the way she wore it that was not ordinary, although he couldn't for the life of him pinpoint what it was.

Then Lord St. Simon entered the inn, and the landlord immediately ceased his speculation. He hurried to greet one of the largest landowners in the county, bowing and offering an effusive welcome.

Julian stripped off his gloves, responding to the landlord's greeting with patient courtesy.

"Show us to a parlor, Sawyer," he interrupted finally. "It's been the devil of a drive across the moor, and we're famished."

"Yes, of course, my lord." The landlord bustled ahead. "And I'll have a bottle of burgundy brought up straightway. I've a fine Aloxe Corton from the Gentlemen's last run. Would the . . . the ladies . . . ," he said resolutely, "care for a dish of tea, perhaps?"

"I'll have a tankard of rum," Gabriel declared before Julian could reply. "And the woman, too. I've a hole in my gullet the size of a cannon ball. What of you, little girl?"

"Tea," Tamsyn said. "And perhaps I'll take a glass of the colonel's wine, if he has no objection." She offered the bewildered landlord a sweet smile as he opened the door onto a cheerful parlor overlooking the street. "It might settle my stomach, I feel as sick as a dog. That's a poxy road across your godforsaken moor."

The landlord's jaw dropped to his knees, and his eyes slid, scandalized, toward Lord St. Simon, who said brusquely, "We're sharp set, Sawyer. Bring us a dish of pasties with the drink."

"Yes, my lord. Right away, my lord." The landlord bowed himself out of the parlor, his eyes round as buttons in the rosy folds of his face.

"Congratulations, Tamsyn. You've certainly managed to set Sawyer on his heels," Julian said with a sardonic twist of his lips. "If you intended to make yourself conspicuous and give rise to a firestorm of gossip, you've succeeded beyond your wildest dreams."

"I suppose English ladies don't say things like that," Tamsyn admitted in clear chagrin.

"On the whole, they do not," Julian agreed, tossing his gloves onto a wooden settle beside the fire and shrugging out of his cloak. "But, then, as my mother always said, you can't make a silk purse out of a sow's ear."

"Oh!" Tamsyn exclaimed, indignation chasing away her chagrin. "I am *not* a sow's ear."

Gabriel was warming his backside before the fire, listening to this exchange with an expression of mild interest. He'd decided many days ago that he had no need to jump to the bairn's defense when it came to the colonel's frequently acid tongue. Besides, he could see the colonel's point of view. If one wasn't bound body and soul to the family of El Baron, one might legitimately object to being compelled to partake in this venture.

"You're a long way from being a silk purse," Julian responded coolly.

"Well, that's your job, isn't it?" she fired back.

He responded with a careless nod. "It's my job to *try*. I've never guaranteed success, if you recall."

The landlord came back at this juncture, saving Tamsyn from the need to reply. She retreated to the window seat and sat glaring through the befogged mullioned windowpane, watching the people in the narrow street below. They seemed unaffected by the rain, but then, she supposed one would learn to be so, since it appeared to be a constant fact of life.

While she watched, a horseman rode up before the inn's front door, a large man wrapped in a heavy cloak. He was obviously well-known at the inn, because two liveried footmen ran out into the rain to hold his horse even before he had time to dismount. He stood for a moment in the rain, glancing up and down the street, and Tamsyn felt a curious prickle on the back of her neck. An unmistakable aura of power and authority clung to the man. Then he turned and strode into the inn, pulling off his dripping beaver hat to reveal a luxuriant mane of iron-gray hair the minute before he disappeared from sight.

The strange prickling sensation increased, and Tamsyn decided that she was cold. Instinctively she turned back to the cozy room, away from the wet, dark day outside. Mr. Sawyer drew the cork on the wine bottle while a maidservant hurried to set the round table before the fire. Gabriel buried his nose in his tankard of rum with a grunt of satisfaction. It wasn't as good as the grog he'd become accustomed to on the *Isabelle,* but it still did a man good as it warmed his belly. He glanced at Josefa, sitting on the settle, her hands clasped around her own tankard. She looked a little less unhappy now she was out of the rain, and her eyes rested with eager anticipation on the platter of golden Cornish pasties keeping warm on the hob before the fire.

It was a generally silent meal. Tamsyn's one attempt to initiate a conversation met with a monosyllabic response, and she lapsed into her own thoughts. Somehow she had to soften the colonel's anger. It seemed to have deepened since they'd landed on English soil, as if their arrival in his homeland had finally convinced him that he had no way out of a detestable situation. But surely it didn't have to be detestable? Surely she could find a way to make it palatable for him? Her eyes rested on his face across the table. Firelight flickered over the strong features but did nothing to soften the harsh line of his mouth, the grim set of his jaw. She thought of how he was when he laughed with genuine amusement instead of that sardonic crack that was all she heard these days. She remembered his surprising tenderness when he'd looked after her on the *Isabelle.* There had to be something there that she could work with.

"If you're finished, I'd like to get on the road again." The colonel's voice broke hard and abrupt into the silence, and Tamsyn jumped, wondering if he'd been aware of her scrutiny. "I'll order the horses put to." He pushed back his chair and stood up. "Come down as soon as you're ready."

The door banged on his departure, and they heard his booted feet pounding the stairs with the surging energy that characterized all his movements. Gabriel and Josefa followed him while Tamsyn went in search of the privy. As she descended the stairs to the hall five minutes later, Julian's voice rose from below.

Tamsyn stopped on the stairs, listening. There was a quality to his voice that she hadn't heard before. An icy politeness that made her think of the frozen tundra. She took another step down, realizing that for some reason she was walking on tiptoe, almost holding her breath, although she had no idea why. She stopped again at the turn of the stair, where she had a clear view into the hall below. It was dark, heavily paneled, the gloom relieved only by an oil lamp hanging from the low-beamed ceiling.

Julian was talking to the man she'd seen from the window. Without his cloak he seemed even more massive. His belly pushed against his waistcoat, his thighs strained the buckskin britches, the shoulders in his riding coat bulged. And yet, she thought, he didn't strike one as a fat man, merely a massive bulk exuding power. Even St. Simon seemed diminished by him, and Julian was no lightweight. But he was lean and muscular, not an ounce of spare flesh. . . .

She squashed the images thrown up by such a reflection and leaned forward to catch what they were saying. As she did so, the gray-haired man looked up and saw her.

His black eyes seemed to shrink to pinpricks, and Tamsyn felt that same prickle on the back of her neck. She stood immobile, a fly in the spider's web as the spider stared at her.

Cedric Penhallan saw Celia on the stairs in the shadows. Silvery hair, huge dark eyes, the full, sensuous mouth, lips slightly parted, the graceful slenderness. But

Celia was dead. Celia had been dead these past twenty years.

Julian turned to the stairs, his eyes involuntarily following his companion's rapt gaze. Tamsyn stood in the shadows at the turn, one hand on the banister, the other holding her skirt clear of the step, foot poised as if to continue her descent. The air crackled, and he had the absurd fantasy that a lightning bolt had flown between Tamsyn and the man he was talking to.

It was, of course, absurd. Tamsyn, with her short hair and strangely exotic air was an unusual sight in such a country backwater, which must explain Lord Penhallan's interest. Julian decided that an introduction was not necessary.

"Your servant, Penhallan," he said curtly with a cold bow before turning to the door standing open to the inn yard.

"St. Simon." Cedric tore his gaze from the apparition on the stairs. His face had lost some of its ruddiness. "I daresay we'll run across each other again if you're making an extended stay at Tregarthan."

"I daresay," Julian said with the same ice. He paused and said softly over his shoulder, "Keep your nephews off my land, Penhallan. One straying toe, and I'll not answer for the consequences." And he was gone, without waiting for a response.

Indeed, Cedric hardly heard him. His gaze returned to the figure on the stairs. Then she moved, springing lightly to the hall, jumping the last two steps. She brushed past him, following St. Simon into the yard.

Cedric went to the door. He watched as St. Simon tossed her onto the back of a magnificent cream-white Arabian steed. Then he turned and went back into the inn.

Celia had returned to Cornwall. Or Celia's ghost.

Tamsyn turned her head to look back at the inn as they rode out of the yard. There was no sign of her uncle, but her blood surged. Cedric Penhallan was still alive, and the battle lines were drawn.

Chapter Fifteen

TAMSYN AWOKE EARLY THE NEXT MORNING AND LAY UNDER her mound of quilts, for a moment bewildered. Her eyes were still closed, her body still half in sleep, but every sense told her that the world had changed. There was a buttery warmth against her eyelids, and almost afraid to believe what her senses were telling her, she opened her eyes.

The sun was shining. And not just a reluctant ray or two—the bedchamber was filled with a golden light. Dust motes danced in the beams pouring through the mullioned windows, and the cut-glass jars on the dressing table sparked blue and red diamonds.

Tamsyn kicked off the covers and jumped to the floor. She threw off her nightgown and stretched, reveling in the warmth of her naked body. Her skin was opening up to the fingering rays, and she felt as if she'd been hibernating in some dank, cold cave for months.

She ran to the window and flung it wide, gazing in breathless wonder at the panorama spread below her. They'd arrived in the dark the previous night, and she'd seen nothing of the outside of the house. They'd hurried in out of the rain, and she'd been aware of candlelight throwing shadows on dark paneling and beamed and plastered ceilings; of fires in massive fireplaces; of a graceful double staircase rising out of the vast Great Hall.

St. Simon had excused himself immediately after presenting his guest and her attendants to the housekeeper, and Tamsyn had found herself ensconced in a large corner apartment with a big canopied bed, tapestry-hung walls, embroidered carpets on the shining oak floor. She'd been brought hot water and a supper tray by clearly curious but uncommunicative servants while Josefa had bustled around unpacking the clothes they'd acquired in London. And she'd sought her bed early and with relief, enjoying, after nights in ill-kempt hostelries, the clean, crisp sheets smelling of dried lavender, the flicker of the fire on the molded ceiling, the deep comfort of the feather mattress.

Now she looked upon another world. Ahead of her stretched rolling green lawns, separated by parterres studded with flower beds, and beyond was the sea, sparkling blue under the early sun. The deeply indented coastline stretched to either side, the chalky headlands shining white against the brilliance of the sea and the sky.

She ran to the east window, flinging that wide too, and leaned out with her elbows resting on the deep stone sill. The view was as spectacular from this angle, the rising sun setting the waters of the River Fowey alight, glittering on the fleet of boats swinging gently at anchor in the estuary, glowing on the roofs of the little fishing village of Polruan on the far bank.

"How beautiful," Tamsyn murmured in delight, breathing deeply as the scent of roses wafted up to her, mingling with the rich fragrance of golden wallflowers planted in a wide bed below the window. This was her mother's land, the soft, verdant countryside she'd described so lovingly to her daughter under the harsh glare of the Spanish sun.

She pulled on her britches and a shirt and ran barefoot from the room. The house was very quiet, although, from the light pouring in through the many mullioned, transomed windows, she guessed it was about five o'clock. But, then, it was Sunday, so perhaps the household slept late.

The bolts were heavy on the massive front door, and she hauled them back with an effort. The door swung open, and she stood blinking in the brilliant morning, her spirit unfurling to the warmth and the light. The forecourt faced east, toward Fowey, and Tamsyn made her way through a small arched gateway in the stone wall surrounding the court and into the main garden that swept down to the sea. She glanced up at her own window, realizing for the first time that it was set into a square ivy-covered tower.

Colonel, Lord St. Simon's house was magnificent, she thought appreciatively. It must represent a fair degree of wealth and power. Wealth and power in the wandering life of a mountain brigand had not been evinced by the ownership of bricks, mortar, and land, but Cecile had told her about how Englishmen viewed the importance of such acquisitions.

Cedric Penhallan was a kingmaker, a power broker, and Cecile had explained that his vast, landed wealth made it possible for him to wield his far-reaching political influence. Without that, not even a man of Lord Penhallan's merciless ambition could have achieved his covert pinnacle of power. And pride of lineage informed the personal power he wielded over every individual who could claim Penhallan blood, however diluted. A power that had rolled over his rebellious sister like a juggernaut.

But it wouldn't roll over this Penhallan, Tamsyn thought with a grim little smile as she set off across the lawn toward the beckoning sea, disdaining the neat gravel path, choosing instead to curl her toes in the still rain-wet grass. This Penhallan was going to bring down the kingmaker, hoist him with his own petard. Yet even as she thought this, the image of her uncle rose in her mind's eye. The extraordinary force she'd felt emanating from him, a menacing avalanchine energy that would cut down all in its path. He'd seen her on the stairs. And what he'd seen had brought him up short. Astounded, disbelieving recognition had flashed across his eyes . . . recognition and for the briefest instant something she would have sworn was fear.

But he didn't know who she was. And he wouldn't know the truth until she chose to announce herself—a public announcement—Cecile's ghost come for restitution and vengeance, her advent swift and sure as a dagger thrust. And until then he'd be tormented with a half-formed familiarity whenever he saw her, apparently no more than an innocent young visitor to a strange land.

But how much contact would she have with the Penhallans while she was under St. Simon's roof? Tamsyn paused in her dancing progress across the rolling lawns. She'd sensed animosity between St. Simon and Cedric Penhallan. A deep animosity, if the ice in Julian's voice had been any indication. And what had he meant with that warning about Cedric's nephews? *Keep your nephews off my land, Penhallan, or I'll not answer for the consequences.* And who were these nephews? Her cousins, presumably.

There were puzzles here, but they could be solved. Gabriel could do some investigating in the local taverns. He was always at home in such places and was a skilled spy, as skilled at planting information as he was at gleaning it. The important thing was: the game had begun.

With a little nod of satisfaction Tamsyn pranced lightly over the grass toward a low stone wall at the edge of the lawn. Then she stopped, her mouth opening on an O of delight. The ground fell away, a long, curving sweep cut into the cliffs rising on either side, dropping to a small sandy cove; but what stunned Tamsyn was the brilliant mass of color filling her eyes as she gazed down. She paused for a second, then with a little cry of pleasure plunged into the glorious swaying field.

From the sweeping windows of his own apartments Julian watched her dancing progress across the wet grass. He'd been in the process of dressing when he'd been drawn to the window by some unarticulated urge and now stood shirtless, thumbs hitched into the waistband of his britches, regarding the sprite below with a frown of annoyance. She'd broken the rules, going abroad in those clothes. It was one thing to discard female attire on the deck of a man-of-war in the midst of battle, but in the peaceful and conventional Cornish countryside it was quite different.

There was going to be enough gossip about her presence as it was, without giving the servants fuel for the bonfires. She certainly wouldn't achieve acceptance in local society, let alone in the upper echelons of the ton, if she made herself notorious in such a shameless costume.

But, then, if she didn't choose to cooperate, he was well within his rights to call a halt to the exercise.

He strode from the room, passing a sleepy-eyed

maidservant hurrying from her attic bed to rake the kitchen fires before cook and the upper servants appeared. She bobbed a curtsy, blushing at his lordship's bare chest. Julian accorded her a brief nod. She was unknown to him, and he made a mental note to discuss with the housekeeper the servants who'd been taken on in his absence.

He let himself out of a side door and made his way across the lawns, following in Tamsyn's footprints, still visible in the wet grass. His irritation lifted somewhat in the soft air of the new morning, the carpet of raindrops glittering in the sun, the fresh-washed fragrances rising from the parterres as he stepped down toward the stone wall.

Reaching it, he stopped, gazing down toward the cove. For the moment he couldn't see Tamsyn anywhere, and yet she had to be there, unless she'd climbed one of the steep cliffs on either side of the narrow valley. Then he caught a glimpse of silvery hair halfway down the slope, the rest of her lost in a rioting mass of purple-red foxgloves and lilac rhododendron.

He jumped lightly over the wall and made his way down toward the bobbing head. "Tamsyn!"

She turned and waved, her face alight with pleasure, her violet eyes blending with the armful of blooms she held.

"Aren't they so beautiful? I've never seen such an incredible sight," she called, beginning to wade through the waist-high field of color toward him.

"Judging by your clothes, I assume you're no longer interested in this contract you insisted upon," he declared, his mouth close-gripped, as she reached him.

If Tamsyn heard, she chose to ignore it. She buried her nose in the flowers she held. "What are they called?

I've never seen anything like them, just growing wild like this."

"Foxgloves," Julian said.

"And the sun's shining, and the sea's sparkling. It's all so lovely, I would never have believed England could look like this," Tamsyn continued, her head thrown back to catch the sunlight, her neck curving gracefully from the open collar of her shirt, her eyelashes thick half-moons on her sun-tipped cheekbones. "Cecile used to describe Cornish summers, but after the last few days, I'd decided absence must have distorted her memory." She laughed, a happy, chiming chuckle.

She was radiating a deep, sensual delight and Julian was moved despite every effort he made to resist—a buttercup lifting its golden head to the sun. Vigorously, he dismissed such whimsy and said sharply, "Have you any idea the talk you're going to cause in those clothes? Give me one good reason why I should persist with my side of this ridiculous scheme of yours when you won't even follow the most elementary rules."

"Oh." Her eyelashes swept up, and her almond-shaped eyes gazed at him with their habitually quizzical air. "I don't mind not wearing them in the least, milord colonel."

Before he could react, she flung her arms wide, tossing the red and purple armful over him so he dripped foxgloves, and with a deft movement stripped away her shirt, kicked off her britches, and stood naked in the purple sea, grinning wickedly at him. "This better, sir?"

"Sweet heaven," he murmured, his disordered senses tumbling in a maelstrom, all reason and resistance slipping from him like a boat loosed from its mooring at high tide.

She was a creature of the sun and the sea breeze and

the rich wildflower fragrances, and her hands were on his waist, nimble with the buttons, her tongue peeping from between her lips, her eyes intent as she bared his belly, traced the thin dark line of hair running from his navel, down over the muscled concavity to disappear into the shadows of his body. Slowly she pushed his britches down over his hips, releasing the erect shaft of flesh. She stepped closer, pressing her belly against the hard, pulsing warmth, sliding a hand between his thighs; then she raised her eyes and laughed up at him, reaching up to brush a broken velvety purple glove from his chest.

"Better, milord colonel?"

He didn't understand why he couldn't stop this. Why he couldn't put her away from him, drag his britches up again, subdue his errant flesh, and walk away from her, back to the house. She'd broken the rules, he could legitimately refuse to be manipulated for another moment.

Instead, he stood looking down at her, lost in her eyes, his loins heavy with longing at the press of her smooth, bare belly against him. His hands moved to span her waist and her breasts trembled, her nipples rising hard against his chest.

Slowly, she sank down into the purple mattress, her hands sliding over his hips, down his thighs, as she slipped to her knees. She bent her head to take his aching stem into her mouth, teeth grazing lightly, tongue caressing in long, sweeping movements that brought a groan of joy to his lips. His fingers twisted in the silky cap of her hair; he gazed down at her bent head, the exposed nape of her neck, the sharp shoulder blades, the curve of her spine, the flare of her backside, the grass-stained soles of her feet, as she knelt to pleasure him.

He hauled himself back from the brink with a shuddering breath and came down on his knees beside her, cupping her face, taking her warm, busy mouth with his; the salty taste of his flesh was on her tongue, her skin was infused with the scents of her own arousal.

He pressed her back into the purple waves around her, and her body was pink and cream against the flower mattress. Her thighs parted for his own grazing exploration, and little murmuring cries of pleasure bubbled from her, her fingers tangling in his hair, her hips lifting in ecstasy as his breath was hot and then cool on her petaled flesh and his tongue burned within her.

Smiling, his eyes hooded, molten with passion, he came up her body, drawing his tongue upward between her breasts, darting into the hollow of her throat, licking a little bead of sweat from her skin, his mouth once more fastening upon her lips as his hands moved beneath her to cup her buttocks, lifting her now to meet his surging entry into the silken sheath that tightened and closed around him, sending ripples of delight along his flesh so that he was moving in an exquisite world of sensation, bounded by the sweet flesh beneath him and around him.

He heard as if from a great distance her softly jubilant cries as she neared the pool of glorious extinction where she would lose herself, the shape of herself dissolved into the cool void of pure sensation. And with a supreme effort he clung to reality just long enough to withdraw from her body the instant he joined her, sinking into the ever-expanding space of eternal pleasure.

He came to himself with the sensation of the sun hot on his back. He was still clasping the small body tightly against him, and with a groan he rolled over, bringing her with him, so she lay beached on his length, her head drooping into the curve of his shoulder. She felt formless and weightless, her skin damply melding with his, and he was filled with a euphoria he'd never known before. None of his sexual adventuring had brought him this glorious satiation, this sense of fusion and peace.

Gently he patted her bottom, and Tamsyn raised her head with visible effort. "How did that happen . . . whatever it was?" She smiled dreamily, kissing the corner of his mouth.

"I don't know," he said, kneading the curve of her backside. "You aren't real."

Tamsyn chuckled weakly. "Oh, yes, I am, milord colonel. I'm flesh and blood to the very tips of my toes." She pushed upward on his chest and sat astride his thighs. "And just to show you how real I am, I'm going to swim."

"It's freezing," he protested. "But, then, it's probably not as cold as the Guadiana in March."

"Precisely." She swung off him with an agility that belied her earlier dissolution. "Are you coming?"

"Maybe . . . in a minute."

Tamsyn ran off and Julian remained on his back, one arm over his forehead shielding his eyes from the sun, facing facts. He'd succumbed again. And for as long as this brigand sprite was in his vicinity, he was going to continue to succumb—particularly if she continued this habit of stripping naked in the most unlikely places and without so much as a word of warning. Maybe he *should* simply accept the pleasures of her body as just and well-deserved recompense. She was using him, so he might as well exact a price. It was one she was more than willing to pay.

He stood up, watching as Tamsyn ran into the gently lapping surf on the small sandy beach. She didn't pause, simply plunged headlong into the waves that he knew must be frigid, coming up for air, then striking out with a strong overarm stroke across the cove, presumably testing the strength of the undercurrent.

She seemed as at home in the water as she was on horseback, but that was hardly surprising, given her rugged upbringing. He strode down to the cove and walked into the water, shivering as the cold water crept up his thighs. A wave curled toward him and he dived into it, the icy cold a cleansing knife along his sweat-slick skin. When he broke the surface, he saw Tamsyn's sleek head to his right. She raised a hand and waved, then rolled onto her back, floating on the waves as they swelled beneath her.

The sun warmed the surface of her body, and the gentle rocking motion insinuated itself into her bodily currents, reminding her of the earlier moments of ecstasy. She barely noticed the cold water now; her eyes were closed and the sun was hot and growing hotter by the minute, creating a warm red glow behind her eyelids.

Julian swam strongly toward her, then trod water beside her. "Come in now, Tamsyn, it's colder than you think."

She murmured assent but didn't immediately move. He turned and swam in, running up the beach, shaking water off his skin, clapping his arms around his chest as he jumped on the sand, watching her. She had rolled over now and was stroking inward, using the waves to carry her to shore.

Yes, love play was certainly some compensation for the months of inaction lying ahead, Julian reflected, finding his britches and stepping into them. Not that inaction was precisely the right word for the task that lay ahead of him. He couldn't begin to imagine how local society was going to react to this extraordinary newcomer. She was bound to have to make some social forays before he'd managed to smooth her rough edges, and the prospect of Tamsyn drinking tea at the vicarage under the eagle eye of Mrs. Thornton made him shudder. Unfortunately, it also made him laugh. Of course, the sooner they could discover her Cornish antecedents, the clearer his path would be, but the fact remained that she couldn't be presented to her long-lost family until she was presentable.

He sighed. He had his work cut out for him, and his charge was going to have to cooperate. He didn't think she understood quite what a large mouthful she'd bitten off, but she was going to have to swallow it.

Tamsyn ran up the beach toward him, shivering but laughing. "Wonderful. I love swimming in salt water." She grabbed up her shirt and used it to dry herself, rubbing herself vigorously, her teeth chattering, her lips blue, but her eyes shining.

Julian watched her, hands resting lightly on his hips. His voice was deliberately cool and clipped, disguising the pleasure he was taking in the sight of her body and her uninhibited movements as she dried between her legs. "One thing you need to understand. If you wish to continue with this charade, this is the last time you'll behave in this fashion while you're under my roof. Do I make myself clear?"

"I'm not sure," Tamsyn said thoughtfully, pulling on her britches. "What behavior are you talking about, exactly, milord colonel?" She shrugged into her now soaked shirt, shivering as the material clung to her skin.

"Wearing these clothes; swimming; or what we've just been doing amid the flowers?"

She buttoned the shirt, regarding him with her head to one side, a slightly sardonic gleam in her eye as she posed the question that would force him to admit that he wanted their love play to continue.

"Public indiscretion, buttercup," he said deliberately. "That's what I'm talking about." He turned and walked back up the slope toward the garden, whistling carelessly, hands thrust into his pockets.

Tamsyn grinned appreciatively. He'd managed to wriggle out of that one without admitting anything, while leaving private indiscretion wide-open for further interpretation. She scrambled up the valley after him.

Julian paused as he reached the wall, waiting for her to catch up with him. The small, firm swell of her breasts was clearly outlined beneath the wet shirt, the nipples dark points.

"You'd better stay here while I fetch you a cloak," he said. "You can't enter the house looking like that, it'll be all over the countryside within the hour. But be warned, this is the last time I shall cover up your . . . your . . ." His eyes rested in leisurely fashion on her breasts; then he put a hand on the top of her head and turned her like a spinning top. His free hand moved in a pointed caress over the indentation of her waist and the curve of her backside. "You understand me, I'm sure."

"It would be hard to misunderstand you, sir." There had been something faintly insulting about the strokes, something a little vengeful. Tamsyn twitched away from him, crossed her arms over her chest, and sat on the wall. "I will await you here."

She sat facing the sea, kicking her feet against the stone. She may have overcome his resistance to lovemaking this morning, but she hadn't won over his attitude.

She shrugged, trying to convince herself that his attitude didn't matter so long as she had his cooperation. But she didn't want to be at odds with him. They were too alike; they had shared so many experiences, the brutality and the triumphs of war; they enjoyed each other too much, and not just in love play. Tamsyn had the sense of a whole country of pleasure, of talk and laughter and shared opinions, just around the corner, but the border was patrolled by his resentment and her own purpose.

She glanced idly up at the cliff top toward Fowey and frowned, squinting against the sun. Two figures on horseback were outlined against the cloudless blue sky. They were too far away to see anything clearly, except that they were men, their horses had the elegant lines of good pedigree, and she thought she could see shotguns across their saddles. Tamsyn wondered without much concern how long they'd been there and how much they could have seen of the goings-on in the cove. They wouldn't have witnessed that lusty tumble in the foxgloves—the flowers had formed a perfect privacy screen —but two naked figures running into and out of the sea would have been hard to miss.

As she watched, they turned their horses and galloped out of sight over the cliff, and when Julian returned with her cloak, she didn't mention their possible audience, reasoning that it would only add fuel to his annoyance.

"Wrap this around you and don't talk to anyone as you go to your room," Julian directed crisply. He was wearing shirt and boots now and looked perfectly respectable. "The household is barely awake, so with luck

you won't meet anyone anyway. After breakfast come to
the library, and we'll get started. Wear one of the morning gowns you bought in London—I want to work on
your posture."

"My posture?" Tamsyn demanded with more than a
touch of indignation, but he'd already started back to
the house, striding swiftly, making it clear he didn't
wish for her company.

Posture? What on earth could he mean? Tamsyn
scrambled after him, following him through the side
door into the house, but he turned aside into the breakfast parlor, leaving her to make her own way upstairs in
disgruntled puzzlement.

The door to Tamsyn's bedchamber stood ajar, and
she could hear Josefa engaged in a somewhat one-sided
exchange with a maidservant, who had brought a
morning tray of chocolate and sweet biscuits for his
lordship's guest.

Tamsyn wrapped the cloak securely around her so
her unorthodox costume was fully hidden and entered
the room with a cheerful, "*Buenos días,* Josefa."

"Oh, miss." The girl turned with visible relief before
Josefa could return the greeting. "I was trying to explain
to your maid here that breakfast is served in the small
parlor behind the library, but she doesn't seem to understand."

"No, I'm afraid she won't," Tamsyn said, smiling.
"But I can translate, and if there's a problem belowstairs,
Gabriel will translate."

"That's that big bloke, is it, miss?" The girl's eyes
were very round in a very round face.

"An accurate description," Tamsyn agreed with a
grin. "He's her husband." It seemed simplest to tell the
conventional fib.

"Right. Then I'll tell Mr. and Mrs. Hibbert—they're the butler and housekeeper," she added. "We wasn't sure about how things stood, miss. You arriving so sudden like, and his lordship not being a great one for explanations." She blushed in sudden confusion, clearly feeling she might have spoken out of turn, and bobbed a swift curtsy, backing out of the room muttering about fetching hot water.

"*Ay . . . ay,* I'll never understand my man's tongue," Josefa declared. "Such a jabber. I told that girl three times that you'd be wanting hot water, and she just stared at me like an idiot."

"She doesn't understand you, *querida,* any more than you understand her," Tamsyn said, chuckling, as she threw off her cloak and the britches and shirt beneath. "But Gabriel or the colonel or myself will translate for you. Now, which of those stupid dresses shall I wear?"

Naked, she wandered to the armoire, taking the cup of chocolate on the way. She stood frowning in front of the wardrobe's contents, sipping chocolate, nibbling on a biscuit.

They'd spent five days in London, putting up at Grillon's hotel. The colonel had vanished once he'd seen them installed and hadn't reappeared until it was time to begin the journey to Cornwall. He'd given her a list of dressmakers and milliners, together with what he considered minimum requirements for a would-be debutante's wardrobe, and left her to make shift as she could.

Tamsyn had found it tedious work putting together such a wardrobe, but she'd tackled the task with the grim determination she would have brought to any piece of necessary preparation for some serious venture. The colonel had inspected the fruits of her shopping the night before they'd begun their journey and had pronounced himself satisfied. Any other necessities or forgotten accessories could be purchased in St. Austell or Lostwithiel.

She heard the bustle behind her as Mary reappeared with a heavy copper jug of steaming water but didn't turn around, idly flicking through the garments. She disliked them all, reserving her greatest distaste for a sprig muslin that the colonel had particularly approved. She drew the dress out and held it up to the light. It was very pretty, pale lilac with a pattern of darker flowers and a cream sash.

"Ugh!" she muttered, tossing the despised gown onto the bed. "It had best be this."

"Such a pretty dress, miss," Mary said, fingering the material admiringly. "It'll suit your coloring."

"I suppose so," Tamsyn agreed halfheartedly, turning to the washstand where Josefa was filling the basin with hot water.

She scrubbed the salt from her skin with a soapy washcloth, enjoying the glow that her rough attentions left in their wake, then set about the tedious task of donning stockings, drawers, and chemise. So many clothes, and so unnecessary when the sun was as warm as it was today. She scrambled into a lawn petticoat, kicking at the folds with a grimace.

Josefa dropped the gown over her head, and she thrust her arms into the little puff sleeves with a roughly impatient movement that caused the other woman to tut reproachfully at the possible damage to the delicate material. The gown was hooked, the sash tied beneath her bosom, and she examined herself in the mirror. She really didn't look like herself.

"My hair's getting long, Josefa, you must cut it for me." She brushed her fingers through the smooth, fair cap. "It's straggling on my neck and the fringe is getting in my eyes."

As satisfied as she was likely to be in such a costume, Tamsyn went downstairs to the breakfast parlor. The colonel had clearly been and gone, and only one place was laid at the round table in the bay window overlooking a side garden. The morning's activities had given her a good appetite, and she greeted with enthusiasm a footman's arrival with a dish of eggs, bacon, and mushrooms.

"Coffee or tea, miss?"

"Coffee, please."

"Your manservant wishes a word with you, miss. Should I tell him to wait until you've breakfasted?"

"Ye'll no be telling me anything, laddie." Gabriel spoke from the doorway. "And I'll thank ye to bring me another dish of the same. Good morning, little girl."

Ignoring the footman's indignantly indrawn breath, he pulled out a chair and sat down. The footman was puffing up like a rooster, and Tamsyn said swiftly, "Gabriel isn't my manservant. He's more of a bodyguard. I'm sure Lord St. Simon will explain the situation to you."

"Yes, miss." The man sniffed and shot Gabriel a fulminating glance.

Gabriel's benign expression didn't change, but he pushed back his chair a fraction, his massive hands resting on the edge of the table. "And I'll have a tankard of ale with my breakfast, if you please."

The footman paused, then beat a hasty retreat with as much dignity as he could muster. Gabriel's booming chuckle filled the small room as he reached for a crusty roll and slathered it with rich golden butter.

"I'll be needing to set a few things straight," he observed. "Don't seem to know what to make of me in this house. I'd best have a word with the colonel."

"Yes," Tamsyn agreed absently. "I saw Cedric Penhallan yesterday."

Gabriel's eyes sharpened. "Where?"

"In the inn at Bodmin. I couldn't say anything to you on the ride back because of the colonel."

"Aye," Gabriel agreed, falling silent as the footman returned with a tankard of ale that he placed beside him with an emphatic thump before turning to take a laden platter from the kitchen boy who'd followed him in.

"My thanks, laddie," Gabriel said blandly, burying his nose in the tankard. The footman looked as if he would burst, and the boy stifled a grin, scuttling from the room before Tom took his fury out on him with a clout around the ear.

"You didn't speak with him?" Gabriel speared a mushroom and dipped it in his egg yolk.

"No, but the colonel did. They seem to know each other."

"Most folks do in these parts."

"I daresay, but they don't like each other, Gabriel. In fact I suspect that's an understatement." She gave him her impressions, relating the snatch of conversation she'd heard.

"I'd best look into it, then," Gabriel said comfortably. "Ask around in the taverns. They'll be cousins of yours, then, these nephews?"

"So it would seem. The children of Cecile's younger brother, I suppose. I can't remember his name—she did tell me once, but I've forgotten. She didn't consider him to be important in the family setup."

"Seems like only Cedric's important in that setup," Gabriel observed, burying his nose in his tankard.

"Up to now, Gabriel," Tamsyn said with a small smile. "Up to now."

"Well, well, I'll be damned. Did we really see St. Simon sporting in the waves with a doxy?" Charles Penhallan sighted, aimed, and his gun cracked. A crow plunged to the cliff top.

David grinned at his brother as he took aim himself. Scaring crows was dull work but better than taking pot-shots at rabbits, and it was all the legitimate sport available at this time of year.

"I'd recognize that red head anywhere," he said. "And he doesn't get any smaller does he?"

"No, but clearly less of a prude these days." Charles rested his shotgun on his saddle bow. "Either that or he's a hypocrite. Didn't think much of the whore, though. Scrawny little thing."

"Looked more like a lad to me," David observed, bringing his own gun down. "Perhaps the army's given him different tastes."

They both laughed. Two men with lean, pointed faces, mouths a mere slash, small, deep-set brown eyes, hard as pebbles. They were thin, sharp-shouldered, narrow-chested, but what they lacked in physique they made up for in the general air of malevolence that surrounded them like an aura. Men tended to cross the street when the Penhallan twins approached. They rarely appeared singly, and conversed together in oblique sentences, presenting an intimidating front to the world, with which not even their few intimates were comfortable.

"I wonder if the governor knows St. Simon's at Tregarthan?" David said, frowning now. "He's probably back from Bodmin by now."

"If he doesn't know now, he'll know soon enough. We'd best get off St. Simon land," Charles said reluctantly. "We don't want anyone seeing us here and carrying tales."

"Can't think why St. Simon made such a fuss," David declared with a curl of his lip. "The girl was nothing, just some whore's daughter."

"She was his tenant and it was on his land."

Charles spurred his horse, turning him to the boundary of Tregarthan land, and his brother followed, his expression sullen.

"He's a prude and a hypocrite," he declared. "One of these days I'll see that damnable St. Simon pride in the dust."

"Oh, yes," Charles promised softly. "One of these days we both shall."

Chapter Sixteen

"SO WHAT IS IT YOU WANT TO SAY ABOUT MY POSTURE?"
Tamsyn strode into the library. Hitching her skirts up,
she sat astride the arm of a leather sofa and regarded the
colonel with an air of intelligent inquiry.

Julian looked up from the *Gazette* and stared at her.
"Don't sit like that! Quite apart from the fact that it's
disgracefully inelegant, you'll split the seams of your
gown."

Tamsyn swung both legs to the same side of the arm
and perched there, her head to one side, her eyes bright,
reminding him yet again of a cheeky robin. "Is this
better?"

"Only marginally." He tossed the newspaper onto a
side table. "Ladies sit on chairs, with their legs together,
their hands in their laps. Go and sit on that chair by the
window, the straight-backed one."

Tamsyn marched over to the window and sat down
in the required chair, looking at him expectantly.

"Sit up straight. You're always slouching."

"But why should that be important?" She was genuinely puzzled, never having given a moment's thought
to something as irrelevant as how she held herself.

"Because it is." Julian stood up and came over to her,

going behind the chair. Taking her shoulders, he pulled them back sharply. "Feel the difference?"

"But it's ridiculous," Tamsyn said. "I can't sit like this, I feel like a stuffed dummy."

"You must sit like this, stand like this, walk like this, and ride like this," he declared firmly, keeping his hands on her shoulders. "You ride like a sack of potatoes. It's all the fault of that Spanish saddle. It's more like an armchair than a proper saddle. It encourages you to hunch over."

Tamsyn did not consider wholesale criticism of her riding to be part of the contract. What could it possibly have to do with learning to be ladylike? "You can't ride a hundred miles over rough terrain sitting up like a stuffed dummy," she retorted. "And I can ride without tiring all day and all night, as you well know."

"You won't be required to ride all day and all night as an English society lady," he informed her. "The hardest riding you're likely to be doing is to hounds, and that won't start until October. You must learn to ride elegantly before then. But an English saddle should put that right."

"You relieve my mind," Tamsyn muttered, but Julian chose not to hear.

Releasing her, he walked round to the front of her chair and examined her. "Put your feet together, so your anklebones are touching, and let your hands rest lightly in your lap."

Tamsyn followed these instructions with exaggerated care, then sat staring fixedly in front of her.

"Relax."

"How can I possibly relax sitting like this?" she asked, barely opening her mouth so her expression remained as rigid as her posture.

Julian refused to be amused. "If you're going to insist on making a game of this, then I'm washing my hands of the whole ridiculous business. Believe it or not, I have better things to do with my life than playing governess and dancing master to an uncivilized brigand. Stand up."

Tamsyn obeyed. The colonel was clearly not in the mood to be diverted. She stood with her hands hanging loosely at her sides, gazing straight ahead of her, awaiting further instruction, trying to keep her expression impassive.

"For heaven's sake, you're as round-shouldered as a hunchback." Impatiently, he pulled her shoulders back again. "Tuck your bottom in." His palm tapped emphatically against the curve in question.

"Anyone would think I was made of wire," Tamsyn grumbled. "My body doesn't bend like this."

"Oh, you forget, buttercup. I've seen you perform some amazing gymnastic feats," Julian stated, stepping back and examining her critically. "Now smile."

Tamsyn offered him a simpering smile, elongating her neck, pushing back her shoulders and clenching her backside. "Like this?"

"Sweet Jesus," he muttered, losing the battle with his laughter. He turned away abruptly, struggling to regain his critical demeanor. He swung back to her just in time to catch her satisfied grin before she wiped it off her face and tried to look once more suitably solemn.

"This is not a laughing matter!"

"No," she agreed. "Of course not, sir." But her lips twitched.

"If you can't do it on your own, then you'll have to have some help," Julian stated. "A backboard should do the trick."

"A what?" All desire to laugh vanished.

"A backboard," he said, explaining with great gravity. "It's used in most schoolrooms. Girls wear it strapped to their backs to correct posture. Of course, they're usually a lot younger than you, but it might do some good, nevertheless."

"That's barbaric!" Tamsyn exclaimed.

"Not at all. My sister wore one for several hours a day for a year or two," he responded with a bland smile. "I'll go into town and procure one. We'll see how you improve by wearing it every morning. If that doesn't have the desired effect, then you must wear it all day."

Tamsyn regarded him in fulminating silence, recognizing that he'd fired the opening shots in a war that she had hoped would become a game, even if for her it was a deadly serious one.

"But until I can procure a board, we'll try something else," Julian continued with the same suave insouciance. Going over to the bookshelves, he selected two heavy leather-bound volumes. "Come over here."

Tamsyn approached him warily.

"Stand very still." Delicately, he balanced the books on top of her head. "Now, walk around the room without dislodging them. You'll have to keep your head up and absolutely immobile. It'll also ensure you have to take small steps instead of galloping along like some unruly puppy."

Tamsyn drew in her breath sharply but closed her lips and refused to rise to the bait. Her neck wobbled under the weight of the books. Grimly, she fixed her gaze on a knot in the paneling and balanced herself. If Colonel, Lord St. Simon was trying to drive her to give up her scheme, he'd discover she was a lot tougher than he bargained for. She took a hesitant step, and the books shivered but stayed put.

Julian grinned and flung himself down on the sofa, casually picking up his discarded newspaper. "An hour of that exercise should prove beneficial," he said. "And when you've learned to keep your back straight, I'll teach you how to curtsy, as you'll have to if you're intending to be presented at court."

That didn't figure in Tamsyn's plans, but she could hardly admit that. Julian returned to his reading as if he considered his morning's task accomplished.

Tamsyn swore silently, allowing her mental tongue free reign as she cursed him for a self-satisfied, odious, vindictive, gloating cur. She walked up and down the room, trying to keep the books from falling. Several times they did so, crashing to the carpet with a loud thump. The colonel raised his head, waited until she'd replaced them and begun her walk again, then returned to the *Gazette*.

Her neck was aching, her shoulders cramping, and her head began to feel as if the books were wearing a hole through her scalp. She glanced at the clock and saw a bare fifteen minutes had passed. It was a torture to beat anything, even riding through the broiling midday heat of a Spanish summer with an empty water flask, flies feeding on her sweaty face, every muscle in her body aching.

Don't be silly! Of course it isn't as bad as that. She'd endured much worse, although she didn't think she'd ever looked more ridiculous. But the damned English colonel wanted her to throw in the towel, and she couldn't afford to do that, even if she was prepared at this point to give him that satisfaction.

Julian could guess her thoughts; they were clearly

written on the mobile countenance where disgust warred with determination. He leaned back, linking his hands behind his head, watching her through half-closed eyes, contemplating what other diabolical little training methods he could devise. She did have a very dainty figure in that dress, he thought dreamily; it somehow softened the athletic lines of her body without in any way diminishing her compact grace.

There was a knock at the door. Tamsyn immediately ceased her promenading, reaching up to lift the books from her head.

Hibbert, the butler, entered. "Visitors, my lord. Mrs. and Miss Marshall, Lord and Lady Pendragon, the Vicar and Mrs. Thornton."

He cast a swift covert glance in the direction of his lordship's guest. The household was in a ferment of speculation about the young lady and her foreign maid and the giant Scotsman who was a law unto himself. Lord St. Simon had offered only the information that the young lady was in his care and would be spending the summer at Tregarthan before making her debut in London the following October.

Julian grimaced. Presumably every kitchen in the vicinity had been buzzing since early morning with the interesting news from Tregarthan. And what was told in the kitchens was taken abovestairs with the morning chocolate. The local gossips hadn't waited long before coming to see for themselves.

"You've shown them into the drawing room, Hibbert?"

"Yes, of course, my lord."

"I'll join them directly. You'd best bring up a bottle of the ninety-eight burgundy for Lord Pendragon and the Reverend Thornton. Tea for the ladies, unless they'd prefer ratafia. Do we have any ratafia?" he asked in afterthought.

"Yes, my lord. Miss Lucy is partial to it, if you recall, so we always keep a few bottles in the cellar."

"What's ratafia?" Tamsyn asked when the butler had departed.

Julian's expression of distaste grew more pronounced. "A disgusting sweet cordial."

"Who's Miss Lucy?"

"My sister." He stood for a minute staring at her, frowning. "You're going to have to be introduced, since that's what they've come for . . . unless I say that you're unwell after the journey." He shook his head. "That won't wash for more than a couple of days. We'd best get it over with."

"I'm not a complete social pariah," Tamsyn protested, rather hurt at his obvious dismay.

"My dear girl, you're impossible. In this society you'll stick out like a sore thumb," he said shortly. "You can't even sit properly." He glanced up at the clock, his frown deepening. "I'll go and greet them and explain who you're supposed to be, and you may join us in about ten minutes. When you're introduced, you must bow, just a slight bend from the waist, like this." He demonstrated while Tamsyn nodded solemnly.

"Now show me," he demanded, watching critically as she imitated his movement. "Not perfect, but it'll have to do," he said. "From my description they'll expect you to be shy and retiring as befits the convent-reared daughter of a hidalgo grandee."

He strode to the door, then stopped, remembering something that had somehow never come up. "You'll have to have a surname. Miss Tamsyn is fine for the staff, but not for the rest of the world. What *is* your last name?"

Tamsyn shrugged, still struggling with her chagrin. She hadn't believed she was impossible. "I don't have one. My father was only ever known as El Baron."

"Then you'll have to be the daughter of Señor Baron," he said crisply. He came back to her, one hand catching her chin, his expression menacing in its gravity. "One indiscreet word or gesture in front of these people, *muchacha,* and that's the end of it. You'll be out of this house so fast you won't know what hit you. Is that clear?"

"Why would I be indiscreet?" she demanded. "It's hardly in my interests."

"No, but just you remember that, because believe me, I have never been more serious. One slip of the tongue, however accidental, and you're on the road. I have my own reputation to consider in the county, and I'm not jeopardizing it for *you.*" His eyes held hers in a ferocious glare; then abruptly he released her chin and left the library.

Tamsyn dropped the books onto the desk. What did he think she was going to do, fling her arms around him and engage him in a lascivious embrace? Or was he simply afraid she would say something indiscreet, something overly familiar? Of course it was possible she might, since she didn't know what these strangers in this strange land might consider out of order. Her lessons hadn't reached that stage yet.

She stood on tiptoe to examine her reflection in the mirror above the mantel, combing her hair with her fingers, flicking at the wispy fringe. It really was getting too long. How would a convent-reared hidalgo maiden conduct herself? She tried a shy smile but somehow it didn't look convincing. Perhaps she should pretend she didn't speak English very well. That would ensure she made no accidental errors. She would sit in meek silence, smiling and nodding, willing to be agreeable but suffering from blank incomprehension.

It would have to do, for safety's sake. The colonel had meant every word he'd said, and she couldn't risk an accidental slip at this stage of the game. She marched out of the library and across the Great Hall to the drawing room on the far side. Just in time she remembered to correct her stride. Shoulders back, bottom in, head up, neck straight . . . *Por Dios!* but how could one remember all these things?

She opened the drawing-room door softly and stood hesitantly on the threshold, waiting for someone to notice her. Her heart began to beat fast as she realized that this was the beginning, and for the first time, as she absorbed the group of people gathered in a circle at the far end of the room, she understood what a daunting task she'd set herself. She'd never faced such a group of people before. Indeed, she'd never stood on the threshold of a drawing room before. What would they see when they finally noticed her? One thing she knew with absolute, instinctive certainty: despite her conventional gown, they wouldn't see a woman who looked like one of them. It was not so much her physical appearance that set her apart, as something indefinable she felt in herself . . . something that grew from the way she'd lived her life and what she expected from that life. It marked her like a brand.

Three of the women were matrons in their middle years, clad in dark satins with severe lace caps. The younger one wore a driving dress of soft beige cambric and a chip-straw hat. For all her youth, it was clear in every line of her body, in the way she wore her clothes, that she would look exactly like the other women when she reached matronhood. Tamsyn knew she would never ever resemble any of the women in the room. She felt as alien as if she'd descended from the stars.

Lord Pendragon and the vicar stood in front of the empty hearth, sniffing appreciatively at the wine in their glasses. They were both corpulent gentlemen, with the self-satisfied air of those who knew their place in the world. The Reverend Thornton saw Tamsyn first.

"Ah," he boomed genially. "Our little foreigner has come among us."

The colonel rose from a spindle-legged chair that looked too fragile for his large frame. "Tamsyn, come and be introduced." He came toward her, his expression grave. "I've been explaining to my guests your unfortunate circumstances."

"Perdón?" Tamsyn said, smiling anxiously. *"No comprendo, Señor St. Simon."*

Julian's expression was so astounded, she forgot her moment of apprehension and nearly gave herself away with a peal of laughter, but resolutely she maintained her composure, peeping around him to the visitors, offering them her nervous little smile.

Julian's hand closed over her bare elbow. "I think you will find that you do understand if you listen carefully," he stated deliberately, his fingers hard on her flesh. "Ladies and gentlemen, may I introduce Señorita Tamsyn Baron?"

Tamsyn maintained her fatuous smile during the introductions, offering a series of creditable bows that nevertheless made her feel absurdly like a bird pecking in the dust. She was aware of the sharply assessing eyes of the elder women, who all offered noncommittal nods as she bowed and smiled. Lord Pendragon's scrutiny, however, was of a very different kind. She might be under the auspices of Lord St. Simon, but she was still a young woman, and he was appraising her as such. The vicar took her hand in both of his and said unctuously that although he assumed she practiced the Catholic faith, he hoped she would find his church not too strange. They were very High Church in the parish of Tregarthan, and he would be happy to hear her confession if that would comfort her.

Tamsyn took refuge in incomprehension, with lowered eyes and an inaudible murmur, before turning with relief to Miss Marshall, whose smile was warm and uncritical.

"You poor dear, it must be so strange for you, and so sad to have to leave your own country."

"Perdón?" Tamsyn looked up inquiringly at Julian, who through gritted teeth translated.

"Ah, muy amable," Tamsyn gushed, taking the offered hand and shaking it heartily. Too heartily, judging by the recipient's startled look as her fingers were gripped with unusual firmness by this diminutive creature.

"Tamsyn has made a remarkable recovery," Julian said. "Sit down, *niña.*" He pushed her into a chair, hearing her swift indrawn breath with silent satisfaction. "She actually speaks and understands English perfectly well, but she's afraid to make mistakes." He smiled at her with his mouth, but his eyes promised retribution.

Tamsyn looked suitably flustered. "The . . . the *señor* is . . . is . . . *muy amable.*"

"Oh, I believe you overstate the case," Julian said smoothly. He turned to his visitors. "If you speak slowly, she has no difficulty following you."

Hester Marshall nodded her comprehension and articulated slowly and loudly, "Do you ride, *señorita*?"

"Ride?" Tamsyn frowned. "*A caballo?* Oh, *sí* . . . I like it much . . . very much, but the Señor St. Simon, he say I don't do it well." She cast a doleful look at the colonel.

"Oh, I'm certain Lord St. Simon will be able to find you a quiet horse to practice on," Hester said warmly. "We must ride together. I don't care to do more than trot gently around the lanes myself, so you needn't be afraid we'll do anything you're not ready for."

Tamsyn gulped and Julian said, "That would be very nice for you, *niña*. I'm sure you'd enjoy that, now the weather has become so much pleasanter."

"Yes, it has been so dreary," Mrs. Marshall agreed. "The farmers are at their wits' end about the harvest. How long is your leave from the Peninsula, Lord St. Simon?"

"I have some negotiations to conduct on Wellington's behalf at Westminster," Julian said. "And the duke is also anxious that Tamsyn is well settled in her new country before I return. He was also acquainted with her father. I'm hoping that when the Season begins, I can prevail upon Lucy to sponsor Tamsyn."

This was news to Tamsyn. "*Perdón?*" she said. "Please . . . *no comprendo.*"

By the time I've finished with you, buttercup, you're not going to understand the time of day, Julian swore silently. "My sister," he reminded her, without a trace of emotion.

"*Ah, sí.*" She leaned back in her chair and crossed her legs, smiling sunnily.

Lady Pendragon stared in shocked disbelief, but Julian moved swiftly, crossing in front of Tamsyn to refill the vicar's glass. As he did so, he kicked her ankle sharply, and Tamsyn hastily sat up straight, clasping her hands in her lap.

"Where were you educated, Señorita Baron?" Lady Pendragon asked slowly.

Tamsyn blinked and frowned, as if trying to understand. Then she nodded and beamed as if finally comprehending the question. She rattled off a stream of Spanish, nodding and smiling, gesturing eloquently while her audience stared uncomprehendingly until she'd fallen silent, when six heads turned as one to the colonel, who was now leaning against the mantelshelf, arms folded, an expression of sardonic resignation in the bright-blue eyes.

"In a mountain convent, ma'am," he said. "A very strict order in a convent perched on a mountain peak. It could only be reached by mule, so the pupils saw very few people other than the sisters. Tamsyn's mother died when she was ten, and she was sent there after her death. Then, when she was eighteen, her father sent for her to Madrid. She was to be presented at court."

Tamsyn nodded, twisting her hands in her lap, her violet eyes brimming with emotion throughout this translation.

"Unfortunately, Señor Baron died very suddenly and consigned his daughter to the care of his good friends the Duke of Wellington and myself."

"*Sí . . . sí,*" Tamsyn said, now smiling radiantly at Julian before rattling off another stream of Spanish.

"It was thought best she should come to England, at least until the war in Spain is over," Julian translated without a flicker of emotion. Despite his annoyance with this playacting, he had to admit that Tamsyn was providing an immaculate background cover.

"Quite so," Lady Pendragon said faintly. "How very unfortunate for you, Miss Baron."

"Forgive me, my dear, but have you been ill?" Mrs. Thornton asked, leaning forward to pat Tamsyn's knee with her mittened hand.

Tamsyn looked blank for a minute, then responded cheerfully, nodding at Julian to provide translation.

"She says she is never ill, ma'am," he responded obediently.

"I just wondered . . . her hair . . . most unusual."

Now, how was she going to explain that one? He threw her the question.

"Oh, that was the convent," Tamsyn invented without missing a beat. "The sisters insisted we have our hair cut very short . . . to prevent the sin of vanity, you understand."

"Very commendable," Mrs. Thornton said with a nod at her husband as Lord St. Simon finished translating, his voice devoid of expression, his face a mask. "We have often commented at the vicarage how young girls these days think too much of their appearances. Not Hester, of course." She smiled at Mrs. Marshall and her daughter. "Hester is a paragon . . . so helpful around the parish."

"Lady Fortescue will sponsor Señorita Baron at court, Lord St. Simon?" Mrs. Marshall inquired, accepting the compliment for her daughter with a complacent nod.

"I trust so," he said dryly, sipping his wine. "I'm anxious to return to the Peninsula, as you might imagine."

"What's your feeling about the way it's going, St.

Simon?" Lord Pendragon asked, and the men drew apart, becoming involved in war talk.

Tamsyn sat demurely in her chair while the ladies chatted among themselves, nodding at her occasionally so she shouldn't feel completely excluded from a conversation that was as incomprehensible to her as if she really didn't speak English. They talked about recipes for calf's-foot jelly, blonde lace for trimming a gown, and the intransigence of parlor maids, while Tamsyn strained to hear the men's conversation, constantly biting her tongue to keep from contributing to a discussion that touched her much more nearly.

"I trust your . . . your ward . . . will accompany you to church on Sunday." Mrs. Thornton drew on her gloves as the visitors finally rose to leave.

"Tamsyn will worship in our church for want of her own," Julian said coolly. "Won't you, *niña?*"

"Perdón?" Tamsyn said sweetly, fluttering her luxuriant eyelashes as she gazed up at him in innocent inquiry. His responding glare scorched a warning, and she fell back discreetly as he escorted his visitors to their various carriages.

"Does the child have a duenna?" Mrs. Marshall asked as Julian handed her into her barouche.

"Oh, yes, a most fearsome Spanish lady," Julian assured her solemnly. "And if she isn't enough, Tamsyn's also accompanied by a bodyguard—a veritable giant of a Scotsman, whose task, it seems, is to keep all strangers at bay until they've been duly vetted. I'm sure the village will be talking about him soon enough. Gabriel's a hard man to miss."

Mrs. Marshall considered this for a minute, then nodded as if satisfied. Her daughter stepped up and took her place beside her.

"Good-bye, *señorita*." Hester leaned over, holding her hand out to Tamsyn. "We must have that ride soon."

"Yes," Tamsyn said bravely, taking her hand rather more gently this time. "And please . . . please call me Tamsyn. It is *muy bien*, more pleasant, *sí*?"

"Tamsyn," Hester said, smiling. "Such a pretty Cornish name. Lord St. Simon said your mother's family came from these parts many, many years ago. You must call me Hester. I know we shall be good friends."

The carriages rolled down the driveway, with Tamsyn waving energetically at Lord St. Simon's side.

"All right, you, inside!" Julian turned on Tamsyn once the carriages were out of earshot. His arm went around her waist, and he swept her into the house. "Just what the devil was all that about?"

"It seemed the perfect solution," Tamsyn protested in wide-eyed innocence as he propelled her back to the library and the door shivered on its hinges under his vigorous slam. "I was afraid I would say something accidentally indiscreet or perhaps offend them, because I don't know anything about English society, so I thought if I didn't say anything very much, then it would be safe, and you wouldn't have cause to be vexed." She laid a hand on his sleeve. "You were so ferociously threatening, Colonel."

"Don't give me that mock innocence," he said. "You were making game of them . . . and of me!"

"No, I wasn't," Tamsyn declared. "If you think for a minute, you'll see what a perfect solution it is, so long as I can remember to keep it up. If I don't speak, I can't say the wrong thing, and everyone will expect me to be different, so no one will look askance at any strange behavior. While you're teaching me not to make mistakes, I can be pretending to learn English properly, so when I make my debut . . . or whatever you want to call it . . . when it's safe to let me loose, then I can speak English without its seeming peculiar."

"Safe to let you loose?" Julian murmured. "Dear God!" He ran a distracted hand through the burnished lock of hair flopping on his forehead. "You're about as safe as a cobra in a mouse's nest."

"Oh!" exclaimed Tamsyn. "What a horrible image! And what's wrong with my plan? It's a perfect cover."

Julian shook his head in defeat. He was obliged to admit that she was right, but he couldn't bring himself to say so. He went over to the sideboard and poured himself another glass of wine, regarding her in fulminating silence for a minute.

"I'll tell you something else," Tamsyn said with sudden trenchancy. "If you ever call me *niña* again, St. Simon, I'll cut your tongue out!"

"My dear girl, for the role you insist on playing, it's the most suitable form of address," Julian said airily. "A mute little girl, struggling to accustom herself to the customs of a strange land, trying to adapt to the terrors of the wide world after all those years sequestered in a mountaintop convent, fighting the sin of vanity."

"I thought it was a piece of very fast thinking," Tamsyn said defensively.

"Oh, you are nothing if not inventive, *niña*," he said. Laughter trembled on his lips as, infuriated, she bared her little white teeth at him.

He caught her round the waist as she leaped toward him, and lifted her off her feet. "An inventive, fast-thinking brigand who's now going to have to trot decorously along the lanes on a fat pony because she says that the Señor St. Simon says she doesn't ride very well."

"Oh, no!" Tamsyn wailed, kicking her legs.

"Oh, yes," he said with a grin. "Inventive little lies come home to roost, *muchacha*. You can't possibly show yourself atop Cesar."

"Then I'll ride only at night," she declared disgustedly. "Put me down."

He let her slide slowly through his hands, his mocking smile fading as his fingers brushed the swell of her breast. The indignation died out of the violet eyes at the touch. Her feet reached the carpet, and he moved his hands to run his knuckles over her breasts beneath the delicate sprig muslin. The nipples rose instantly, supremely sensitive as always, and her lips parted on an eager, expectant breath.

"Here?" she whispered, a catch of excitement in her voice. "Now?"

It was the middle of the morning, in the middle of his house. Domestic sounds reached them through the closed door. Julian glanced through the window to where a gardener was weeding the parterres in direct line of sight.

He looked down into Tamsyn's upturned face, glowing with desire and reckless invitation. She moved against him, a lascivious wriggle of her hips sending a jolt through his loins that took his breath away.

"Against the door," he directed, his voice clipped and stern in its urgency. "Quickly." He pushed her backward until she was pressed up against the door, his body hard against hers. Roughly he pulled her skirt up to her waist.

"Is this what you want, Violette?"

"Yes," she whispered.

"And this?" His hand slipped between her thighs, pressing the dampening material of her drawers into the moist furrow, his touch burning into the soft petaled flesh beneath.

"Yes," she whispered, her eyes luminous, her skin translucent as she stood still for him, for once making no moves of her own.

It was lunacy. He was swept up on the crazy tide of this foolhardy passion. Her drawers fell to her ankles, her legs parted under the pressure of his impatient palms. His fingers moved within her, on her, until she was lost in a swirling crimson fog, her head thrown back against the paneled door, her hips thrust forward for his probing, questing hand.

His mouth brushed against the soft curve where her neck met her shoulder, and his teeth nipped where his mouth had been. She cried out, a soft female sound in the back of her throat, and then his flesh was within hers and she braced herself against the door, gripping his hips as he drove deep within her and her blood roared in her ears and he stopped her mouth with his own, suffocating the wild cry of delight before it could leave her lips.

And then it was over, and she stood trembling, her knees week, her gown clinging to her sweat-slick skin. Julian smiled a long, slow smile of sensual satisfaction. Lightly he ran his fingers over her mouth so she could taste the scents of her own arousal.

"What would they say in that convent of yours?" he murmured. "That strict order in the mountains?"

Tamsyn merely shook her head. For once Colonel, Lord Julian St. Simon had defeated her, rendered her speechless.

Chapter Seventeen

"St. Simon's back at Tregarthan," Cedric Penhallan announced, sniffing the claret in his glass. He took a considered sip, then nodded to the butler, who proceeded to fill up the glasses of the Penhallan twins sitting opposite each other at the oval table. The last rays of the setting sun caught the sapphire signet ring as the viscount raised his glass.

"We saw him this morning, sir." David helped himself to a dish of squab.

"Stark naked, playing in the sea with a doxy," Charles expanded with a throaty chuckle.

"You were on Tregarthan land?" Cedric's black eyes were agate, a white shade appearing around his fleshy mouth.

Charles turned scarlet. "Just on the cliff top above the cove. We were shooting crows and accidentally strayed—"

"You did not accidentally stray, sir," his uncle pronounced with deadly calm.

"We didn't know St. Simon was at home, Governor," David put in, a sulky note in his voice. "He's been out of the country for two years . . . except for his sister's wedding."

"And two years ago you were warned off St. Simon land," Cedric stated with the same venomous calm. "And why were you so warned?" He looked between the two, his black eyes seething with contempt.

There was no response. The two young men bent their heads to their plates. The butler moved discreetly into the shadows.

"Well?" Cedric demanded softly. "One of you must remember, surely."

The twins squirmed; then David said with the same sulkiness, "She was a whore. We played with her, that's all."

"Oh, is that all?" His uncle's eyebrows lifted. He regarded a platter of brook trout swimming in butter, selected the largest, and slid it onto his plate. He ate for a few minutes in a charged silence where no one but himself moved, and the squab on David's plate congealed in its gravy.

"Is that all?" he said again in a musing tone. "You waylaid a child . . . how old was she? Fourteen, I believe?" He looked between the two again, politely waiting for a response.

"She was ripe for it," Charles said. "Her mother was a whore. Everyone knew it."

"Oh, I thought her mother had died the year before," Cedric said questioningly. "I was under the impression that the child lived alone with her father . . . a man much respected by St. Simon people. One of St. Simon's favored tenants. But perhaps I'm mistaken." He gestured to the butler to refill his glass.

"Am I mistaken, sir?" His black glare arrowed into David, who stared down at the table, concealing the naked hatred in his eyes.

"No," he muttered finally. "But we weren't to know that."

"No, of course you weren't." Cedric sounded almost soothing. "When you raped and beat her and left her naked on the beach, barely alive, you weren't to know that you had interfered with one of St. Simon's tenants on Tregarthan land."

The viscount took another deep draft of his wine and with seeming placidity allowed the silence to build around them. He cut into the pigeon pie, and if he was aware that only he had any appetite for dinner, he gave no sign of it.

"Of course you weren't to know that," he reiterated in the same tone. "Just as of course it wouldn't occur to you that the girl might tell someone . . . might even know who it was who had assaulted her throughout one long summer afternoon. It wouldn't occur to you, of course, that everyone knows you in these parts. You've only lived here since you were infants." His voice was suddenly sharp, spitting his angry derision.

"I don't give a tinker's damn what you do, you pair of bumbling idiots. You can rape a regiment of women if you wish. But not even dogs soil their own turf!"

The two inhaled sharply, flushed, and then paled in unison. Cedric smiled. Their anger at this public humil-iation pleased him, and the fear that made them swallow their anger pleased him even more, although it increased his contempt.

Only Celia, of all the Penhallans, had stood up to him.

Suddenly he lost interest in tormenting his nephews. The image of Celia filled his head. And the girl he'd seen yesterday. The girl who for a minute he'd mistaken for Celia. It was absurd, of course. His memory was hardly accurate after all these years. He'd been fooled by the fair hair and the slight frame. Nevertheless, it had been an extraordinary resemblance. The girl was probably about the same age Celia had been when he'd sent her away. That was what had given him such a start.

She'd been traveling with St. Simon. He looked up again at his nephews, an arrested light in the piercing black eyes. "What did you say about seeing St. Simon with some doxy this morning?"

Charles and David visibly relaxed, knowing that their uncle had lost interest in his malign castigation. "They were in the sea in the cove, sir," David said hurriedly. "We couldn't see very clearly from the cliff top, but they were naked. The girl was so scrawny, she could have been a boy, we thought." He chuckled, looking at his twin for corroboration.

"We thought perhaps St. Simon had developed new tastes in the Peninsula," Charles said with a curl of his thin mouth.

"Don't be a fool," his uncle said wearily. "What was she like?"

"Small, very fair hair." Charles made haste to repair his error. "That was all we could see."

Cedric frowned, stroking his chin thoughtfully. It fitted with the girl he'd seen in Bodmin. "St. Simon bringing his mistress to Tregarthan?" He shook his head. "That's not his style. Who the hell could she be?"

He didn't realize he'd spoken out loud, and he didn't notice the quick look that flew between the twins. He helped himself from a platter of roast potatoes and chewed steadily. Silence returned to the dining room, but the twins now felt safe enough to resume their own dinner.

Cedric found his mind returning yet again to his

sister. He rarely thought about her these days, but the
girl in Bodmin had triggered a host of involuntary
memories. Celia had been clever, very quick-witted.
She could have been very useful to him if she'd agreed
to follow his direction and mingle with the right people. He could have used her as a conduit for his influence. She would have been a worthy partner in his
ambition if she'd agreed to be molded.

He wiped a dribble of gravy from his chin. But Celia
had been so devilishly unpredictable, with no sense of
family duty. And she'd threatened to ruin him. He'd
had no choice but to take drastic measures to deal with
her. A pity, really . . . it might have been amusing to
have her companionship at this stage in life, when he
was surrounded by people who wouldn't even look him
in the eye. As for his brother's two sons . . .

Nasty pair they were . . . had been from the moment they'd passed into his guardianship at the age of
seven. But they'd surpassed themselves over that business with the girl and St. Simon. If he hadn't opened his
purse generously to the wench's father, it could have
been very ugly. St. Simon had been insisting on hauling
them before the justices, but the girl's father had settled
for the equivalent of a handsome pension to keep his
daughter quiet, and St. Simon hadn't been able to persuade him to change his mind. But St. Simon had sworn
his own retribution if the Penhallan twins set foot on his
land again, and Cedric had no doubt he meant it.

In fact, he thought, looking at their thin, pointed
faces, he might almost enjoy watching St. Simon exact
that retribution. Their reputation preceded them wherever they went. It was no wonder no respectable family
would countenance a match with either of them, despite the Penhallan name.

"Bring cognac to the library," he ordered, pushing back his chair with a harsh rasp on the oak floor. His voice and the sound of the chair were like a thunderclap after the long silence.

The twins half rose politely as their uncle stalked from the dining room without a further word to them, the butler following him with the brandy decanter.

A footmen placed a decanter of port at Charles's elbow, bowed, and left them to themselves.

"What say we answer his question for him?" Charles filled his glass and pushed the decanter across the table to his brother.

"What question?" David squinted in the candlelight that now lit the room. His eyes, like his brother's, were glazed. While they'd had little appetite for dinner at the beginning of the meal, they'd had no such problem with the wine.

"About St. Simon's doxy," his brother explained carefully, draining his glass and reaching for the decanter again. "Governor wants to know who she is, we'll find out. He'll be glad to know, stands to reason."

"Maybe even grateful," David said, tapping the side of his nose suggestively. "But how do we find out?"

"Ask her . . . politely, of course."

"Ah, yes, ask the whore politely," his brother agreed, winking. "But how can we ask her if we're barred from St. Simon land?"

Charles thought about this, staring into his glass as if the answer would be contained in its ruby depths. "She's got to venture out sometime. Can't stay there forever. People to see, errands to run, shopping to do."

"Unless St. Simon keeps her naked in the house," David suggested with a lewd chuckle. For a minute they contemplated the exciting prospect of a woman kept naked to await their pleasure.

"Not St. Simon's style, though," Charles said finally on an almost regretful note. "Household would be bound to know. Be all round the county in no time."

"She'll have to leave the house at some point. So we'll ask her nicely when we come up with her," David pronounced. "If we ask her nicely enough, she'll tell us what the governor wants to know."

"Best she doesn't know who we are, though," Charles said wisely. "Governor wouldn't like it . . . not after the other one."

"Loo masks," David said. "Loo masks and maybe even dominoes . . . that'll do it."

"Not dominoes," his brother said earnestly. "Can't carry a domino in your pocket, not like a loo mask. Carry that everywhere and no one knows you've got it."

"True," his brother agreed, seeing the wisdom of this practicality. "We'll carry 'em with us everywhere, and when we see her, we pop 'em on and ask some questions."

Well satisfied, the brothers turned their attention more seriously to the port.

"The mail carrier brought you a letter." Tamsyn entered the library the next morning flourishing a wafer-sealed paper. "It's from a woman, judging by the handwriting. Do all society ladies write with these flowery curls? Should I learn to do it too?" She examined the missive with a critical air. "Very fancy . . . and on pale-blue paper too. Is she your mistress?"

Wordlessly, Julian extended his hand for the letter. Tamsyn passed it over and perched on the edge of his desk. "Do you have another mistress? But, then, I don't think 'mistress' is the right word to describe me, do you?"

"I don't believe the language contains a suitable description for you," he observed dryly. "You beggar description. Get off the desk. It's most unladylike."

"Why, certainly, milord colonel." She slipped off her perch and essayed a demure curtsy, sweeping her muslin skirts to one side, one foot delicately pointed, her rear sinking onto her other heel. "Is this deep enough for the king, or will it only do for the queen?"

Julian regarded her with a gleam, certain she hadn't realized the dangers of her exaggerated position. "Now try to get up."

Tamsyn realized immediately that it was impossible. She overbalanced in a heap on the carpet and sat there with such an expression of aggrieved mortification he couldn't help laughing as he returned his attention to the letter.

His amusement died rapidly. "I suppose I should be grateful she doesn't scent her writing paper," he muttered, breaking the wafer.

"Who doesn't?" Tamsyn scrambled to her feet, dusting off her skirts.

"My sister," he said shortly, scanning the crossed and scrawled lines of the epistle. "Hell and the devil! Gareth put her up to this—it has that ramshackle idler's mark all over it."

"Over what?" Tamsyn resumed her perch on the edge of the desk.

"My sister and her husband are paying me a visit. I imagine Gareth wishes to remove himself from his creditors' orbit for a while, and enjoy some free hospitality while he's doing so."

He looked up at her, and deep frown lines creased his brow, the humor of a few minutes earlier completely vanished. "I just told you not to sit like that!" He slapped her hip in emphasis.

Tamsyn stood up and regarded him thoughtfully. "Why are you so annoyed that your sister is coming?"

"Why do you think?"

"Because of me?"

"Precisely."

Tamsyn frowned. "Why will it be a problem? Won't I like her? Or is it that she won't like me?"

He stared at her for a minute, wondering if she was being disingenuous. But she was returning his gaze with her usual candor, and as he took in the small nose and determined, pointed chin, the flutter of her luxuriant eyelashes on her smooth brown cheeks, a rapid, unbidden surge of desire startled him. In achingly vivid memory he felt her body moving against his, heard her exultant little chuckle as she drew close to her own mountaintop.

How could he possibly house this extraordinary creature under the same roof as his sister? Lucy was such an innocent, so well schooled, so demure, a perfect lady. Everything that a St. Simon woman should be. And this misbegotten brigand, his mistress, was her antithesis in every respect.

But it was too late to do anything about it. Judging by the date on the letter, Lucy and Gareth would be arriving any day. They could be crossing Bodmin Moor at this moment.

"Let's get one thing clear," he said, his voice as flat as the Dead Sea. "My sister is to know only the story that everyone else knows. You are an orphan, a protégée of the Duke of Wellington who has consigned you to my unofficial guardianship. You will at no time give any indication that that is less than the truth. Is that clear?"

Tamsyn shrugged and nodded. "I've no desire to upset your sister."

"Make sure that you don't, because one word out of place and you leave my roof."

Tamsyn chewed her lip. "But if your sister's married, she can't be a total innocent."

Julian's eyes flashed blue fire. "You are not qualified to make any kind of judgment on my sister. You couldn't begin to understand women like her . . . the way they've been educated, the way they look at life. You don't know the meaning of the word 'virtue,' you couldn't begin to understand the sanctity of the marriage vows. For God's sake, your own parents didn't see the point of marriage—"

"Don't you criticize my parents," Tamsyn said with deadly ferocity. "Let me tell you, Lord St. Simon, that *you*, with your prating about convention and form and sanctity and virtue, that *you* couldn't begin to understand the depths of a love that doesn't need society's sanction to validate it."

She was pale with anger, but there was more than anger in her eyes, as huge and depthless as a violet sea. She turned from him with an inarticulate gesture, and there was more than bitterness in her voice now. "You couldn't imagine loving someone just for her own sake, could you? You couldn't imagine loving someone who didn't fit your perception of the right mold."

Before he could respond, she had left the room, the door banging closed on the whirl of her skirts. He stared at the closed door. Where had it come from? Why had she attacked him like that? Perhaps he had been a bit harsh about her parents, but the personal edge to her attack had come from nowhere. This talk of love. What business was it of hers whom and how he loved?

But there had been tears in her voice beneath the bitterness. Hurt in her eyes beneath the liquid anger, and he knew he'd crossed some invisible line. He'd had no right to attack her parents.

He ran a hand through his hair, understanding now that he'd reacted from fear, the fear of his own weakness when he was with her. He wouldn't be able to resist her, even with his sister in the house.

He caught a glimpse of Tamsyn through the window running across the lawns toward the cove. She was barefoot, holding up her skirt to keep from tripping on it. Her hair glittered in the sunlight. He'd never meet another woman like her. Not if he lived to be as old as Methuselah. There couldn't be another woman like her. Not anywhere in the four corners of the globe.

Tamsyn plunged down the flower-banked slope toward the cove. She felt she was running from something, something she didn't want to acknowledge, but as she reached the small sandy shore and her toes curled into the smooth white sand and there was nowhere else to run, she drew breath and walked slowly into the rippling shallows at the edge of the beach. The tide-ridged sand rubbed the soles of her feet, and the water was sunwarm.

She let her skirt fall, and the little wavelets soaked the hem as she walked along the shore. What had happened? The words had poured from her as if a lid had been lifted from a bubbling cauldron. She had defended her parents. That was not strange. That was inevitable. But all that about love? Why did it matter to her, the daughter of Cecile and El Baron, that a stuffy, prideful

English lord could only see a future with a woman of his own kind?

She was going back to Spain as soon as Cedric Penhallan was ruined. Julian, Lord St. Simon was useful to her. She needed him. And when it was all over, and he realized how she'd used him, he'd probably want to tear her limb from limb. And she wouldn't blame him one bit.

Gloomily, she stopped paddling in the shallows and looked around her, trying to cheer herself with the beauty of the gently curving bay, the sweep of the sea and the headland, the brilliant blue sky. She glanced up at the cliff top, and her stomach lurched. The two horsemen she'd seen the other morning were there again, outlined against the sky.

They were watching her. The strangest sense of menace crept up her back, and her scalp contracted. She turned, splashed out of the water, and headed back toward the house, the hem of her skirt and her bare feet now coated with damp sand.

Gabriel came around the side of the house as she trudged across the lawn. He raised his eyebrows at her grubby appearance, saying with a laugh, "Och, little girl, it's to be hoped no visitors turn up to see you like that."

Her confused unhappiness resurfaced. "I'm going in to change," she said listlessly.

Gabriel looked at her sharply. "What is it, bairn?" He put a large arm around her.

"Nothing really," she said, smiling effortfully. "I was thinking of Cecile and the baron." Which was perfectly true, although only half the story.

"Ah." He nodded, for the moment satisfied. He hugged her tightly, then said briskly, "Well, I've some information that might interest you. Heard a story down at the quay from a couple of crabbers."

"About the Penhallans?" She was immediately diverted as he'd known she would be, and her eyes quickened with interest.

He nodded. "Those nephews . . . your cousins. Twins they are, apparently. Let's take a walk."

They strolled into the orchard on the far side of the house. Tamsyn had been intrigued by the traditional seventeenth-century design that dictated the fruit trees be planted in a pattern that offered a straight line to the eye from whichever angle one looked. It struck her as an amusing quirk for something as functional as an orchard.

"So?" she said eagerly, when they were deep among the trees. Gabriel's information related to the issue that had brought her to this place. A simple and straightforward issue, with no confusing emotions to muddy the waters. She would focus only on that, and these nonsensical and irrelevant feelings she was harboring for Julian St. Simon would fade into insignificance.

"It seems that a couple of years ago your cousins did a bit of trespassing . . . on rather more than the colonel's land."

Tamsyn listened as Gabriel told her the story. She kicked her feet through the grass, rubbing the sand off, her stomach churning at the thought that she shared close kinship with such gutter sweepings.

Gabriel reached up to an overhead branch and tested a pear between finger and thumb. "They've a few weeks to go yet," he observed dispassionately, as if he were completely unaffected by the story he was telling. But Tamsyn knew better.

"Nearly killed the girl, I gather," he continued in his leisurely fashion.

Tamsyn plucked a crab apple. She bit into it, relishing its puckering sourness; it took her mind off the thought of some innocent little girl in the vicious, defiling hands of these as yet unknown cousins.

"You'll get the bellyache if you eat too many of those," Gabriel observed. "Anyway, from that day the colonel banned the Penhallans from his land. He's on speaking terms with the viscount, I gather. But only in public. They can't help but meet occasionally around the neighborhood. But the twins keep out of his way."

"What do they say in the countryside about my cou—about the twins?"

"No one has any truck with 'em. They're cowards; they think they can do whatever they like. They're Penhallans and that's all that counts."

"Cecile said that was exactly what Cedric believed," Tamsyn said thoughtfully. "No one could touch a Penhallan except himself."

"Well, we'll be changing that, little girl," Gabriel said, deceptively mild.

Tamsyn looked up at him and her eyes were almost black. "Yes," she said. "We'll bring them down, Gabriel. For Cecile, and for that girl."

She shivered suddenly, despite the sultry warmth in the orchard, as she thought of the two horsemen on the cliff. Two horsemen. Twins? Cousins? Watching her?

Cedric had seen her once. Had that one brief glimpse been sufficient to arouse his curiosity?

Chapter Eighteen

"I DO HOPE JULIAN WON'T CONSIDER OUR VISIT AN imposition," Lucy said, unable to hide her renewed agitation as the chaise turned into the gates of Tregarthan.

"Why should he?" Gareth asked with a touch of impatience. "Tregarthan is big enough to house a regiment." He shifted his long legs in the cramped space. "By God, I'll be glad to be done with this infernal coach travel. I should have brought my riding horse."

Before they'd left, he'd said that as he didn't have a horse in his string to match any one of his brother-in-law's, he'd let Julian mount him during their stay. But Lucy didn't remind him of this. She let down the window, closed to keep the dust from filling the coach, and leaned out, ready to catch her first glimpse of her beloved Tregarthan as they bowled around the corner at the head of the drive.

"Good God! What an incredible animal!" Gareth exclaimed, looking out of his own window. He banged on the roof and the coachman drew rein. Gareth leaned out of the window, mouth agape, at the two riders emerging from the trees onto the drive just ahead of them.

Tamsyn shaded her eyes from the sun as she ex-

amined the coach standing in the middle of the driveway. "It must be the colonel's sister," she declared after
a brief and puzzled contemplation. "I wonder why
they've stopped." Leaving Gabriel on the drive, she
cantered back toward the coach. "Good afternoon. Is
something the matter?"

"That horse," Gareth declared. "I beg your pardon,
but I've never seen such an animal."

"No, Cesar is magnificent, isn't he?" Tamsyn
beamed, forgetting for the moment her disgruntlement
that she could only ride him around the estate, thanks to
her own overly clever invention. "Are you Sir Gareth
Fortescue?"

"Yes." Gareth blinked, bemused by the combination
of the milk-white Arabian steed and the diminutive
rider, her silvery cap of hair shining in the sun, astonishingly violet almond-shaped eyes regarding him with
frank but friendly curiosity.

"We've been expecting you," Tamsyn said, leaning
down to extend her hand. "I'm Tamsyn."

"Oh," he said. "Yes . . . yes, of course." He took
her hand. Julian had made no mention of his protégée's
name, but Gareth was positive Tamsyn wasn't a Spanish
name. In fact, there didn't seem to be anything Spanish
at all about this girl. "My wife . . ." He gestured behind him into the dimness of the chaise and leaned back
slightly so Lucy could take his place at the window.

Lucy's startled face appeared in the aperture. "I understood you were Spanish," she said, speaking her husband's thoughts and quite forgetting the niceties in her
astonishment.

"Half-Spanish," Tamsyn said cheerfully, leaning
down to shake her hand. "My English is very good
when I'm not nervous, but when I go out into com-

pany, I seem to forget it all." She smiled, continuing expansively, "My mother was Cornish, which is why I'm staying with Lord St. Simon. We hope to discover her family, and in the meantime I'm learning to be English so I can make my debut. My parents are both dead, you see, and the Duke of Wellington agreed to be responsible for me."

"Oh," Lucy said faintly, as confused as ever by this explanation. "I'm so sorry about your parents."

A shadow flitted across Tamsyn's countenance, showing Lucy for a minute a disturbingly different side to the brown-faced, bright-eyed, smiling girl. Then Tamsyn said, "Introductions in the middle of the driveway are a little uncomfortable. Shall we return to the house? Your brother should be home by now. He's been paying calls."

She turned her horse to ride beside the chaise as it continued up the drive. Gabriel had disappeared, presumably already returned to the stables.

Julian, hearing the bustle in the Great Hall, came out of the library, a frown in his eyes, a smile on his lips. "Lucy, this is a pleasure." He lightly kissed his sister's cheek and turned to his brother-in-law. "Fortescue. What a delightful surprise."

Gareth shook the proffered hand and told himself he'd imagined the slightly ironic note in St. Simon's voice. "Thought we'd pay a family visit," he said obviously. "Lucy thought she could be of help since you're entertaining visitors. . . . We met Miss . . . Miss—"

"Tamsyn," Julian supplied calmly. "Tamsyn Baron. But Tamsyn will do fine."

"Ah, yes, of course . . . of course." Gareth turned with a hearty laugh toward the subject of the conversation, standing quietly behind them, waiting for the family greetings to be concluded. "Staggering piece of horseflesh, St. Simon."

"Tamsyn?" The colonel's eyebrows disappeared into his scalp.

"No . . . no," Gareth blustered, his ruddy complexion taking on a slightly mottled hue. "You know what I mean, St. Simon."

Lucy was looking uncomfortable. For some reason Julian always managed to make Gareth look stupid. He was never rude, but somehow in his presence Gareth became clumsy and tongue-tied.

Tamsyn stepped forward. "Milord colonel is fond of teasing, Sir Gareth. But you may compliment Cesar to your heart's content, it will only endear you to me." She turned to Lucy. "Lady Fortescue, you must be tired after your journey."

"Oh, please call me Lucy." Lucy's mind was racing. She'd expected either some pathetic, mute orphan or an exotic dark lady, swathed in lace mantillas, fluttering a fan. This boyish, self-assured young woman who spoke English with only the trace of a foreign accent was a total surprise.

"Why, Miss Lucy, you must be exhausted." Mrs. Hibbert, wreathed in smiles, came bustling from the kitchen. "Now, you come along upstairs and I'll have a bath and tea brought up to you directly. You'll be wanting your dinner on a tray, I'll be bound."

"Oh, yes, thank you, Mrs. Hibbert." Lucy visibly relaxed into the comforting care of the housekeeper, who immediately hustled her toward the stairs. But Lucy paused, her foot on the bottom stair, turning back to the hall. "Tamsyn, would you perhaps come and drink some tea with me while I have my bath?"

Tamsyn glanced quickly at the colonel. They had not

referred to his sister's arrival since the argument the
previous day; in fact, they had barely talked at all the
harsh words still lying like stones between them. Now
his bright-blue eyes held hers for a minute in clear
warning, and a fresh surge of unhappiness washed over
her, swiftly chased by annoyance. He ought to know she
wasn't stupid, whatever else he thought her.

She turned away from him and back to his sister.
"Yes, of course I will, Lucy. But I'm sure you'll feel able
to come downstairs for dinner, once you've rested." She
was quite unable to imagine preferring a solitary dinner
on a tray in one's room.

Lucy considered this and realized that she'd only
thought she'd prefer to dine alone because Gareth and
Julian would expect it of her. As it happened, she didn't
wish to in the least. "Yes," she said. "I'm certain I will."

"Good." Tamsyn accompanied her upstairs, leaving
Gareth and Julian in the hall. If the colonel thought she
was going to be stupid enough to throw the cat among
the pigeons, then more fool him. She had no intention
of denting his sister's precious innocence.

"So what's the story, St. Simon?" Gareth asked
heartily as the women disappeared up the stairs. "Lucy's
consumed with curiosity about the gal. Little thing, isn't
she?"

"So I owe the pleasure of your company to Lucy's
curiosity," Julian observed coolly. "Funny, but I'd have
laid odds you were in debt, Fortescue, and needed a
short respite from the duns." He turned to the library.
"A glass of wine?"

"Thank you." Gareth followed his host, wishing the
older man weren't quite so cool and quite so perceptive.
"I'll have to ask you to mount me, St. Simon. My horse
strained a fetlock just before we left."

Julian smiled. "Of course," he said smoothly, handing his guest a glass. "I didn't expect anything else."

Gareth's wine went down the wrong way. "Lucy will be a companion for the chit," he said when he'd recovered somewhat. "She'll be glad of a little feminine company, I'll be bound. You know what women are like."

"Yes, on the whole I believe I do," Julian responded, gesturing to a sofa as he took a seat himself. "Tamsyn, however, is rather out of the common way." He sipped his wine, then asked, "And how is my sister? I trust marriage suits her."

It was a pointed question, and Gareth didn't miss the point. St. Simon had agreed very reluctantly to the marriage, citing Fortescue's libertine propensities and his runaway extravagance, but his sister had begged and pleaded and threatened to go into a decline if she couldn't have the one man she could ever love.

"Oh, Lucy's well enough," Gareth said. "Gets the megrims occasionally . . . like most women. You know how they are."

"Yes, I think we've established that I do." Julian regarded him thoughtfully. "Keeping to the straight and narrow, are you, Gareth?"

Gareth flushed. "Of course. . . . I'm a married man now. What kind of a question is that?"

"Oh, just the question of a concerned brother," Julian said casually, reaching for the decanter to refill their glasses.

Upstairs in Lucy's apartments Tamsyn installed herself on the window seat and prepared to get to know Julian's sister.

"These are nice rooms," Lucy said a little wistfully as her maid unbuttoned her gown. "But I always feel strange not sleeping in my old bedchamber when I'm here." She pulled her shift over her head. "Of course, it's not big enough for a married couple. And Gareth needs his dressing room." She dipped a toe into the hip bath of steaming water. "You may leave us now, Maggie. I'll ring when I need you to dress me."

The maid curtsied, gathered up the discarded clothes, and hurried out with them.

"Gareth sleeps in his dressing room when he comes in late so he won't disturb me. He's very considerate that way."

"Comes in late from where?" Tamsyn sipped tea, watching as Lucy lowered herself into the water. She had a pretty round figure, with a tiny waist, swelling bosom, and curvy hips. Very pretty, Tamsyn thought a mite enviously, wondering for the first time in her life if she was perhaps rather underendowed.

"Oh, from his clubs, or wherever. Men are never at home. I'd thought perhaps married men might be, but it doesn't seem to be the case."

There was a touch of constraint in her voice, and she began to soap her legs busily. "Tell me how you come to be here, Tamsyn. My brother didn't really say in his letter. He's not very communicative at the best of times," she added.

Tamsyn gave a word-perfect rendition of the approved version of her tale. "I think your brother is hoping to persuade you to sponsor me when I make my debut in October," she added.

"Oh, I should be delighted," Lucy said with genuine pleasure. "It will be such fun to have someone to go about with. And have dinner with. Gareth doesn't often dine at home." She slipped down into the water and switched the subject. "I'll help you learn how to go on in society while I'm here. . . . I'm sure it's very different from Spanish society. . . . We should have a little party for you. I'm sure Julian would approve. It's been ages since Tregarthan had a proper party . . . not since my wedding."

Lucy was chattering as if they'd known each other all their lives. Tamsyn had never spent much time with other girls; her position as El Baron's daughter had set her apart in the encampments, but she'd seen and often envied the easy camaraderie of the village girls. In the same way, Lucy's confidential chatter seemed to assume some kind of shared female experience and viewpoint.

Lucy stood up in a shower of water and reached for the towel. "How do you get on with Julian?" she asked somewhat diffidently. "He's not easy to talk to, is he?"

"Oh, I think he is," Tamsyn said, surprised. "I never have any difficulty talking to him." *At least, not when we're in charity with each other.*

"Is he very strict?" Lucy stepped out of the bath. "He always was with me."

Yes, Tamsyn thought, *I'm sure he was. He sets very high standards of behavior for a St. Simon.*

"I'm not his sister," she said neutrally. "He's merely repaying a favor to my father and following the Duke of Wellington's orders. He doesn't like being away from his regiment, and it makes him annoyed on occasion."

"It's not comfortable when Julian's annoyed," Lucy confided.

"No," Tamsyn agreed. "It's not." Abruptly, she stood up. "I must go and change for dinner."

"Oh, what are you going to wear?" Lucy was immediately diverted. Swathed in a towel, she bounced over to the bed, where her clothes lay waiting to be hung in the armoire. "We should coordinate our gowns so we don't clash."

Tamsyn blinked. "Clash?"

"Yes . . . you know. If I wear a pink gown and you wear puce, we'll look awful."

"I don't have a puce gown," Tamsyn said with relief.

"No, it's a horrid color. It was just an example." Lucy riffled through the pile of material. "Now, which do you think?"

Tamsyn pretended to devote her attention to this clearly important question. Lucy's china-blue eyes were not as sharp or as piercing as her brother's, but they were a lovely color. Her skin was fair, and her brown hair had chestnut glints in it, much less startling than her brother's thick red-gold thatch.

"The dark blue," she said at random. "How long have you been married?"

"Ten months." Lucy held the gown up and examined it in the mirror. "Yes, I'll wear this."

"And your husband sleeps in his dressing room?" Tamsyn was not known for her tact.

Lucy flushed. "When he comes in late, he's usually foxed. Men are like that."

Tamsyn looked doubtful. "Are they?"

"Oh, well, you wouldn't know because you're not married, dear," Lucy said, adopting a slightly patronizing air. "When one's married, one learns a great deal about men."

Tamsyn scratched her head. Lucy was a year younger than Tamsyn, and it didn't seem that she knew anything at all about anything very much. But that, of course, was only to be expected. She was a virtuous, sheltered English lady. Heaven forbid she should come face-to-face with some of life's grittier realities. "I daresay Spanish men are different," she said neutrally. "I'll see you downstairs."

"Oh, no, I must come and see your wardrobe," Lucy said, dropping the towel and shrugging into a wrapper. "I do so love shopping, don't you? Perhaps Julian will let us borrow the landaulet and we could go into Bodmin, or maybe even down to Truro. We could buy matching outfits." Linking her arm through Tamsyn's, she ushered her out of the room. "Which bedroom do you have?"

"The corner room in the east tower."

"Oh, yes, that's such a lovely room." Chattering gaily, Lucy pranced down the corridor, arm firmly linked in Tamsyn's.

Julian, appearing at the head of the stairs, caught sight of the two disappearing into Tamsyn's apartments, the sound of Lucy's bright prattle hanging in the air.

Tamsyn wouldn't be fool enough to defy him, he reflected, entering his own apartments. They hadn't made up their quarrel, but he couldn't believe she would ruin her own plans just to get back at him.

She was a damnable, manipulative, seductive hellion. But she was neither a fool nor vindictive. Untying his cravat, he strolled to the window, looking out across the lawns to the sea. Why did he find her so impossible to resist? He wanted to go back to Spain, go back to his men and his friends, fighting and dying in the broiling summer heat. He wanted to forget all about this bloody-minded brigand . . . didn't he?

He tossed the cravat to the floor and shrugged out of his coat. He'd spent the afternoon riding around the estate, visiting his tenants, asking questions of the older ones, the men and women who'd been on Tregarthan land for the last fifty years or so. He'd been asking if anyone remembered the disappearance of a young girl from one of the families of the landed gentry. No one had anything to offer. There'd been a Penhallan daughter who had died in Scotland. An elaborate funeral, the family in mourning for a year. Everyone remembered that. But no disappearances on trips to Spain.

He stepped out of his britches and went to the washstand, splashing cold water on his face. Perhaps Tamsyn was the daughter of some minor landowner from farther south, beyond Truro, toward Penzance.

He buried his face in a towel, scrubbing briskly. He had until October to find them. And if they couldn't be found, then that was Tamsyn's problem. He'd have fulfilled his end of the bargain.

Tamsyn, having finally persuaded Lucy to return to her own apartments, thoughtfully flicked through her own selection of gowns, brushing her hair while Josefa fussed around her.

Her mind was racing as she realized just how Lucy's arrival could be turned to good account. The idea for a party at Tregarthan was ideal for her purposes. It was essential that Tamsyn be accepted in society when she exposed Cedric Penhallan. It was essential that she be seen to be respectable, to be under the protection of a powerful family; otherwise, no one would give credence to her story. But people would listen in horror to the friend and confidante of Lady Fortescue, the protégée of the Duke of Wellington, the unofficial ward of Lord St. Simon.

And once she'd told her story, it would be over. She'd have to flee the colonel's wrath with all dispatch, abandon this burgeoning love, and return to her old life that now offered only a barren landscape.

"*Por Dios!*" she muttered, absently walking away from Josefa's fingers busily hooking her gown.

"Ay . . . ay . . . ay!" Josefa cried, following her. "Stand still, *niña.*"

Tamsyn stood still, staring down at the carpet. If only there was a way she could do what she had come there to do and keep the colonel in ignorance. If she could do that, then just possibly she might be able to change his view of her. Show him another side to the unscrupulous adventuress that he believed her to be. It didn't seem possible that she could feel for him the way she did without there being some reciprocation. Perhaps he just needed to look into his heart, and then all his preconceived prejudices would vanish.

But first they had to make up their quarrel. She examined her reflection in the mirror, putting her head to one side, trying to see herself as the colonel would see her. She saw an insignificant figure in a green muslin gown. He'd teased her about her height often enough, but usually only when he was annoyed. Perhaps she should wear some of the jewels. Maybe the emeralds would give her more stature. Then she shook her head. She was as she was, and she'd never given it a second thought before. But later tonight, when they were at peace with each other again, she would ask Julian exactly what he did see when he looked at her.

Sir Gareth was the only occupant of the drawing room when she entered. He turned from the sideboard where he was pouring himself sherry. "Ah. Good evening, Miss . . . uh, Tamsyn." He smiled. "We're ahead of the others. But Lucy always takes hours over her toilette." His eyes ran over her, automatically appraising. "May I offer you a glass of sherry, or madeira, perhaps."

"Sherry, please." Tamsyn was aware of the appraisal. She'd come across Gareth Fortescue's type before. Lord

Pendragon had been a case in point. Such men habitually examined all women who might be considered even vaguely eligible to receive male attentions. It was second nature.

She took the glass he offered. "I understand from the colonel that your family home is in Sussex. I've never been there. Is it as pretty as Cornwall?"

"Softer," he said. "We have a quieter sea and the South Downs instead of the blasted moors. Bodmin, Exmoor . . . and of course Dartmoor; that's in Devon, but it's close enough."

"We crossed Bodmin Moor on our way here. It was certainly a bleak, unfriendly spot." She sat down, returning his scrutiny. He had a large, sensuous face with fleshy lips topped by a bushy curled mustache, gray eyes under drooping lids, curly dark hair. Attractive in his way . . . . and he knew it.

The frankness of her gaze startled Gareth. He was accustomed to covert assessments of his charms; women didn't in general make their interest quite so blatant. He stroked his mustache in a habitual gesture and smiled, his eyes narrowing.

Tamsyn supposed he couldn't help this performance. Kindly, she changed the subject. "You're something of a judge of horseflesh, I gather."

"I pride myself on being so," he said, taking a seat opposite her, his inviting lethargy banished by enthusiasm for the topic. "But I've never seen an animal like that beast of yours. You must be a capital rider."

"The colonel has his reservations on that subject," she said demurely, taking another sip of sherry.

"On what subject?" Julian inquired from the doorway.

Tamsyn looked up quickly, seeing him now with the

eyes of acknowledged love. He was in morning dress, gleaming tasseled Hessians, coat of gray superfine, plain waistcoat, and cream pantaloons, his cravat simply tied. She was so accustomed to seeing him in uniform that it always took her a minute to adjust to his civilian dress. She glanced at Gareth, also informally dressed, but his cravat fell in elaborate folds, and he wore several gold and diamond fobs in his striped waistcoat. His coat didn't sit as well on his shoulders, Tamsyn thought critically, suspecting pads. And his thighs in the skintight pantaloons were a mite pudgy.

"My horsemanship, milord colonel," she replied. "I was about to explain to Sir Gareth that I was permitted to ride Cesar only around the grounds."

Her smile was both complicit and appealing, and it stunned him. There was a quality to it he didn't remember seeing before. Something beyond the sensuous, inviting mischief her smiles usually implied. She took another sip of her sherry, draining her glass, as she waited for a response to what she hoped he would accept as an overture.

"There's nothing wrong with your horsemanship, Tamsyn," he stated, keeping his voice light, hiding his response to that smile. He turned aside to pour himself sherry. "Not when it comes to mountain passes. It's just a trifle unorthodox for the English countryside."

"May I have some more?" She extended her empty glass.

He refilled her glass and offered Gareth the decanter. "I imagine Lucy's still fussing with her dressing."

"Women," Gareth said largely. "You know what they're like."

It seemed a frequent refrain of his brother-in-law's, Julian reflected acidly. He glanced again at Tamsyn; she was trying to hide her laughter, and his own sprang unbidden into his eyes.

"Not all women, Sir Gareth," she said sweetly. "Convent-reared Spanish girls are taught to eschew all the vanities. Hence my short hair. It makes one's toilette very simple."

"Ah . . . ah, yes, of course," Gareth agreed, somewhat nonplussed. He examined her again over the lip of his glass. A most unusual-looking girl, he concluded. But there was something devilishly appealing about her . . . devilishly inviting . . . despite the short hair and the slight figure in the unadorned gown.

"Am I late?" Lucy came tripping into the room, a vision in her dark-blue silk gown over a half slip of cream lace, a diamond comb in her soft hair, that had been coaxed into ringlets drifting over her bare shoulders.

"It was worth waiting for, my dear," Gareth said gallantly, taking her hand and raising it to his lips.

Lucy blushed, unaccustomed to compliments from her husband. Suddenly she became aware of a curiously charged atmosphere in the drawing room, a pulsating tension as if something forbidden and dangerous lurked below the surface. She looked at the other three and could detect nothing in their expressions to explain such an odd sensation.

"Shall we go in to dinner?" Julian put down his glass, offering his sister his arm.

Gareth, with alacrity, offered Tamsyn his, and they went into the dining room. Julian drew out the chair at the foot of the table for Lucy, and she looked startled, then laughed. "I've never sat here before. But I suppose I must . . . just until you get a wife, Julian." She gave him a shy smile as she took her place. His eyes were unreadable and he made no response, merely taking his own place at the head of the table.

Lucy was flustered, wondering if she'd said something indiscreet, but she couldn't imagine how such a self-evident truth could be construed as tactless or inappropriate. She glanced at Tamsyn, who was helping herself to a dish of deviled chicken legs with hungry enthusiasm. Gareth, busily approving the claret in his glass, also didn't appear to notice anything untoward in her statement, so she decided it was just her brother's manner. He'd never welcomed personal comments.

Tamsyn, however, had heard both the remark and the conspicuous silence it generated. Perhaps Julian found the subject uncomfortable in her presence. Maybe he thought it would be indelicate to refer to the possibility of marriage in front of his mistress. It was probably just one of those gentlemanly conventions Cecile had told her about. Thrusting the melancholy conclusion to the back of her mind, she picked up a succulent chicken leg and took a delicate bite.

Julian noticed Gareth's eyes fixed on Tamsyn across the table as she deftly stripped the meat from the bone with her teeth. His brother-in-law was fascinated by her, and Julian could understand why. There was something astonishingly sexy about Tamsyn gnawing on a bone.

"Tamsyn, in polite English society we don't eat with our fingers," he corrected, before Gareth's fixed stare became too obvious. "I know I've mentioned it before."

"Oh, yes, I forgot," she said hastily, putting the bone down and licking her fingers. "It seems silly to use a knife and fork, though, when fingers and teeth are so much more efficient."

Gareth's laugh resounded around the room, bouncing off the paneled walls. "Very silly," he agreed. "There's far too much nonsense about such things. Why shouldn't one eat with one's fingers if one wishes?"

"I imagine Spanish customs are very different from English," Lucy said with a rather rigid smile. "It must be hard for you to remember everything."

"It is," Tamsyn said frankly. "I'm hoping you won't mind helping me, Lucy. I'm sure your brother would be glad to be relieved of some of the burden. I know he finds it onerous."

Her smile deepened as she looked at Julian, and two dimples appeared beside her mouth. He wondered why he hadn't noticed them before. Her cheeks were a trifle flushed, her eyes very bright. The footman refilled her wineglass, and Julian found himself counting. It was her third glass of wine, after two glasses of sherry.

She continued in this unusual fashion throughout dinner. The only effect it seemed to have was to make her sparkle. Julian knew from experience that Tamsyn rarely did anything without purpose. Clearly she wanted to make up their quarrel.

Gareth was obviously fascinated with Tamsyn, his eyes following her every move, his rumbling laugh greeting her every sally, and Lucy became increasingly silent. Tamsyn was not encouraging him in the least, but then that wasn't necessary to get Gareth Fortescue's attention.

When the ladies withdrew to the drawing room, Gareth sniffed his port appreciatively. "Lively little thing, isn't she? I'd always thought Spaniards were devilish straitlaced with their women . . . convents and duennas and so forth. But that chit's as lively a piece as I've come across."

"You always did have a delicate turn of phrase, Fortescue," Julian said with a touch of ice. His brother-in-law had imbibed heavily and was looking very flushed, his eyes a trifle unfocused.

"Oh, beg your pardon, St. Simon." Gareth smiled expansively. "No offense meant, of course. Dear little innocent, of course. Father was some Spanish grandee, didn't you say?"

"And a close acquaintance of Wellington's," Julian stated.

"Wealthy, I should imagine? These grandees tend to be, I gather." Gareth hiccuped and selected a grape from the bowl in front of him.

"So I understand."

The subject was not proving promising, and even Gareth finally got the message and lapsed into a doleful silence. The prospect of the long summer months in the company of his unforthcoming and straitlaced brother-in-law, with no Marjorie to spice the mixture, began to seem less attractive than it had.

In the drawing room Lucy was struggling to recover her equanimity as she took the hostess's place behind the teacups. "Do you drink tea after dinner in Spain?"

"Not in general." Tamsyn regarded Lucy thoughtfully. It seemed to her that Julian's sister was in need of a little sisterly guidance. The question was: how to dispense it without giving too much away?

Lucy poured tea. "We always put the milk in afterward," she offered a shade stiffly.

"Why is that?"

"So that one can adjust the strength," Lucy said. "You can't tell if you put the milk in first."

"No, I suppose not," Tamsyn agreed, taking a seat on the sofa beside Lucy. "I must remember that. Tell me about your husband."

"Why would you want to know about him?" Two spots of color burned on Lucy's cheeks as she handed Tamsyn a cup.

Tamsyn took a sip and decided that now was not the moment for tea. "Because I think you need some help," she said candidly, discarding her teacup. "After only ten months of marriage a man should still be sleeping in his wife's bed. And if you're not careful, that husband of yours is going to start some serious wandering."

"Oh, how could you say such a scandalous thing?" Lucy clapped her hands to her flaming cheeks. "What could you possibly know about such things?"

"I'm Spanish," Tamsyn said vaguely. "We're perhaps a little more open about these matters." She rose to her feet and went to the decanters on the sideboard. She'd have to slide carefully around her cover if she was to help Lucy, but their earlier conversation combined with an evening in the company of Gareth Fortescue had made it very clear to her that young Lucy needed some help.

She poured herself a glass of wine, sympathetically regarding the girl's flushed and bemused indignation. "Do you care for your husband, Lucy?"

"Of course I do!" Tears sparked in the china-blue eyes. "And he cares for me."

"Yes, of course he does." Tamsyn sat down again, cradling her wineglass. "But he's older than you, and a deal more experienced. Do you enjoy being in bed with him?"

Lucy stared at her, dumbfounded.

Tamsyn nodded. "You were a virgin, of course. And

I don't suppose he thought to discover what pleased you. Men like that often don't."

"Whatever do you mean?" Lucy was struggling for words, unable to believe she was really hearing this. "I don't want to talk about this . . . it's horrible . . . it's not decent."

"Oh, for heaven's sake, Lucy. If you don't talk about it, how will you ever learn to make love? And if you don't learn, then you won't learn to enjoy it, and neither will your husband. And then you really will be in a pretty pickle." She drank her wine with a matter-of-fact nod. "Cecile was always telling me about the prudishness of the English and how women weren't expected to know anything about pleasuring. . . . In fact, when she was a girl, it was considered quite shocking for a woman to enjoy coupling."

"Cecile?" Lucy said faintly.

"My mother. She would have talked to you just as I am, Lucy, so please don't be offended."

Lucy stared at this extraordinary girl who was regarding her with an air of confident authority that made her feel like a patient with a physician.

Before she could gather her wits, however, Julian and Gareth strolled into the drawing room.

"Lucy has been explaining to me the correct way to pour tea in the drawing room," Tamsyn said. "May I pour for the gentlemen, Lucy?"

Lucy moved away from the tea tray, aware that Tamsyn had noticed her hands were not quite steady. When Julian suggested she play, she went to the pianoforte reluctantly. Her head was so full of what she'd heard that her fingers were all thumbs, and after two muddled and discordant attempts at a folk song, Gareth said with a degree of brutality, "Oh, for God's sake, Lucy. Spare our ears. It sounds like a tribe of cats on the prowl."

Lucy dropped the lid of the instrument with a bang. "I beg your pardon." She got up and returned to the sofa. "I'm sure you'd prefer to hear Tamsyn play. I'm sure she counts it among her many accomplishments."

"I don't play the pianoforte, only the guitar," Tamsyn said readily, ignoring Lucy's petulant tone. She'd shocked the girl and would renew her tutorial in the morning, when Lucy had had a chance to absorb what she'd heard.

"How exotic," Lucy murmured.

"Not where I come from," Tamsyn responded. "It's considered a minor accomplishment."

"Like other things, I imagine."

"Possibly."

Julian frowned as Lucy's barbed comments flew and Tamsyn batted them gently back without any sign of hostility. But Lucy was radiating antagonism.

Gareth cleared his throat. "Think I'll take a stroll down to the village before bed. I daresay I'll see you all in the morning." He bent over Lucy and pecked her cheek. "Good night, my dear. Don't stay up late, now. You've had a long journey."

Lucy's cheeks paled, and then the pallor was driven away by a crimson tide. Her eyes darted involuntarily toward Tamsyn, who studiously avoided meeting her gaze.

The door closed behind Gareth, and Lucy stood up hastily. "I do find that I'm very tired. If you'll both excuse me, I think I'll go to bed." Tears were heavy in her voice, and she dashed an arm across her eyes as she went to the door.

"Bastard!" Julian swore as she left. "I'm damned if I'll permit him to go whoring in the village while my sister lies weeping upstairs."

"Yes, very insensitive of him," Tamsyn agreed. "But if you drag him back, he'll sulk. He's that type."

Julian regarded her with a frown, noticing the wine-glass she still held. "Why have you been dipping deep this evening? I thought it didn't agree with you."

"Oh, it agrees with me, all right," she said lazily, running a hand through her hair, her eyes narrowing seductively as she drew her knees beneath her in the big armchair. "But it tends to make me rather uninhibited, and it stimulates my imagination. Shall we go upstairs, since your guests have disappeared?"

The prospect of a more than usually uninhibited and imaginative Tamsyn was heady indeed. Her violet eyes were luring him, the slight body curled in the chair radiated sensual invitation. A wicked, exotic invitation. And there would never be another woman like her.

"Forgive me," he said abruptly. "I've some work to do in my book room."

The rejection was so unexpected that Tamsyn stared stunned as the door closed behind him. Tears burned behind her eyes and she blinked them away angrily. She'd been offering an overture all evening, and he'd seemed to accept the end of their quarrel. But now to turn from her so coldly . . .

But she wouldn't be defeated. Her mouth took a stubborn turn.

Chapter Nineteen

GARETH STROLLED BACK TO TREGARTHAN UNDER THE moon, dolefully contemplating the lack of entertainment to be found in a small Cornish fishing village. The taverns in Fowey offered a sad dearth of eager young wenches ready to dally with a well-heeled member of the Quality, although the landlady at the Ship had winked at him and allowed him a discreet fondle of her ripe bosom, leaning over his table as she served his tankard of gin and water. Unfortunately, her husband had appeared on the scene, genial enough on the surface but with a pair of massive forearms that rivaled the giant Gabriel's, with whom he'd been drinking in a dark corner of the taproom.

Extraordinary-looking man, the Scotsman. Some kind of bodyguard apparently, all very rum. In fact, Gareth decided with a discreet belch, it was a rum business whichever way you looked at it: Julian, far from his beloved battlefields, playing guardian to an unknown Spanish chit. Of course, if the Duke of Wellington had commanded it, that would explain it. A great stickler for his duty, was Julian.

Deciding to take the cross-country route, Gareth swung himself over a stile, catching the toe of his boot in the top rung and almost plummeting headlong. Cursing under his breath, he regained his balance and continued across the field.

The Penhallan twins had been in the tavern, drinking by themselves in a corner. He'd exchanged a nod with them, but they didn't move in his circles in London, so he hadn't felt a need to do more than that. There was something deuced smoky about those two . . . always had been. There was bad blood in the Penhallans, everyone said.

Gareth lurched through a gap in a bramble hedge and paused. Behind and below him the lights of Fowey were all but extinguished, just a lantern swinging on the quay in case anyone decided to row across the river from Polruan at dead of night. Ahead, there seemed only an expanse of field and cliff top. He could hear the breakers on the shore way below at the base of the cliff. Damnation, surely he wasn't lost? He should have stuck to the lanes. He looked up at the star-filled sky, peered into the distance, caught a glimmer of light through a stand of trees ahead, and decided it must be the gatehouse of Tregarthan.

With renewed energy he strode on and was immensely relieved when he identified the stone gatehouse at the bottom of the drive. His fob watch told him it was barely eleven o'clock. In London the night would just be starting, and all he had to look forward to here was an early night listening to the sea and the owls.

As he approached the house, a massive shadow fell across his path. His heart jumped into his throat, and he whirled to see the giant Gabriel behind him, holding a lantern. Gabriel grinned amiably. "I hope you enjoyed your evening. Good company these Cornish folk, I find."

Gareth was dumbfounded at being spoken to with such familiarity by a servant. "My good man—"

"Och, aye, laddie, I'm no' your man . . . good or otherwise," Gabriel said with no diminution in his affability. "I'm no' a servant, either. My job's to look after the bairn as I see fit . . . just that. So to avoid any unpleasantness, I suggest you bear that in mind. I'll be bidding you good night, now." Gabriel turned toward the side of the house, then paused, glancing over his shoulder. "By the by, laddie. I'd not be paying too much attention to Jebediah's woman, either, if I were you." And he walked off around the house, whistling to himself, leaving Gareth staring in mute and indignant astonishment.

Gabriel turned up his nose in the darkness. The colonel's brother-in-law was a blockhead. Put a pistol in his hand, and he'd probably shoot his foot. Couldn't hold his liquor, either. He turned into the stableyard and climbed the outside stairs at the side of the stable block to the whitewashed room he shared with Josefa. He preferred the privacy out here away from the house, and the room above the stables much more closely resembled the simple cottage rooms that he and Josefa were accustomed to.

She greeted him softly as he ducked beneath the low lintel and entered the cheerful, tidy room. His woman had a talent for creating domestic comfort wherever they happened to fetch up, even in the most unlikely places. In fact, Gabriel often said she could make a home under a cactus. He flung himself onto a low chair, and Josefa bustled over to pull off his boots.

"I came across those cousins of the bairn's tonight," he said, unbuttoning his shirt as Josefa poured him his nightly tankard of rum. The woman nodded, her eyes bright with understanding as she took his shirt and carefully folded it.

"Right nasty-looking pair," he went on, kicking off his britches, standing on one leg to pull off his sock. "They'll bear watching." He stood on the other leg to remove his other sock before pushing off his woolen drawers.

Josefa gathered up his garments as they fell to the floor, folding them with loving care and placing them in a cedar chest. She didn't say anything while he mused, imparting little snippets of information, more to clarify things in his own mind then to share his thoughts. But she heard and nodded, and he knew she was storing it all away, and if he ever needed advice or an opinion, she would give it sensibly, so long as it was solicited.

He drained his tankard and with a groan of contentment fell onto the bed, the bed ropes creaking mightily under his weight. Josefa clambered in beside him, and he reached for her warm, soft, accommodating roundness, burying his head in the pillowy bosom. She made a little clucking sound of pleasure and wrapped her short arms around him as far as they would go, opening herself readily as he burrowed into her.

"You're a pearl, woman," Gabriel muttered, and she smiled and stroked his back. "But those twins will definitely bear watching."

Gareth's indignation was only exacerbated when he entered the house and saw that his new Hessians were caked with mud and gave off a pungent farmyard aroma. The hall was dimly lit with a thick wax candle on a table at the foot of the stairs, two carrying candles beside it. A light showed beneath the library door. Presumably St. Simon was still up and would claim the second candle.

Presumably someone would also lock up. Or perhaps they didn't bother in this neck of the woods.

Gareth lit his candle and stomped up the stairs. Two candles in wall sconces lit the long corridor, and the house was very quiet. He found his way to the bed-chamber at the end of the corridor and opened the door softly. The curtains were drawn around the bed, moon-light filtering through the thin summer curtains at the window.

"Is that you, Gareth?" Lucy's voice spoke nervously from the tented bed.

"And who else would it be?" He realized he sounded ungracious, but the reek from his boots was almost overpowering. He yanked them off against the andirons, picked them up, and deposited them gingerly outside the door for the boot boy.

He undressed, put on his nightshirt, and took a step toward his dressing room. Then he paused. He was damned if he was going to be deprived of a decent bed when he didn't have anything to feel guilty about . . . nothing to send him to the narrow daybed next door. He blew out his candle and pulled back the bed cur-tains. Lucy was curled on the far edge of the bed, a lace cap on her brown hair. He slid in beside her. Her sweet-smelling warmth filled the dark cavern of the bed. He reached out to touch her and felt her immediate recoil.

Sighing, he rolled onto his side, facing away from her. He was no brute, and he hated it when she wept and shivered beneath him and he knew he was hurting her. Every now and again he forced both of them to go through the motions, because there must be a child of the union. Once he had an heir or two, then they could both let the whole miserable business slide.

He closed his eyes and conjured up the image of

Marjorie, her knowing hands, her lascivious little wriggles.

Lucy lay wide-eyed in the darkness, trying not to weep, thinking of the shocking things Tamsyn had said. How dared she talk in that fashion? And how in the world did she know about such things . . . an unmarried girl?

Julian heard Gareth's return and waited until his footsteps had receded on the stairs; then he snuffed the candles and left the library. He locked and barred the front door, lit his own candle, extinguished the wax taper, and made his way up to bed, leaving the candles alight in the sconces in case anyone wandered abroad at night.

His own apartments, consisting of bedchamber, dressing room, and private parlor, occupied the center of the house with a sweep of mullioned windows facing the lawns and the sea. On either side were the tower rooms. Opposite were a string of guest apartments, the largest being occupied by his sister and her husband.

He let himself into his bedchamber, feeling restless and yet jaded. His sister's marital problems depressed him, but that was not at the root of his dissatisfaction. Part of it was the acute discomfort of his own need aroused by the liquid light of inviting arousal in Tamsyn's eyes, the catlike sensuality of her body in the chair. That was part of it, but it was also caused by distaste at his own roughness. He'd hurt her without a word of explanation and certainly without justification. She had done everything she could that evening to repair the breach between them, and then she had offered herself in her customary open, trusting fashion with no expectation of rejection. He'd seen the flash of shock, the glitter of tears in her eyes, before he'd turned from her, and he couldn't rid himself of the image.

He closed the door of his bedchamber and then turned back to the room, holding his carrying candle high. For a crazy moment he thought he was seeing simply the figment of his imagination, and then he knew that of course he should have expected it. Tamsyn was not one to accept rejection, however hurt and vulnerable she might have looked.

She sat naked on the window seat in the moonlight, chin cupped in her palm as she looked out over the silver-washed lawns to the horizon where black velvet sky met the midnight-blue line of the sea.

And his pulse raced . . . his blood sang.

"There you are," she said cheerfully, as if they'd never had a cross word. "I was beginning to think you'd stay up over your work—if that's what it was—all night."

"What the hell are you doing in here?" he demanded in a fierce whisper, fighting himself, fighting yet again the knowledge that there would never be another woman in his life like this one. He set his candle on the table. "I told you that for as long as my sister's in the house, you may not come in here."

"You weren't that specific," Tamsyn said, uncurling herself from the window seat. "Besides, your sister's tucked up in bed." She slipped from the seat and came toward him. "Everyone's asleep, milord colonel. Who could possibly know what goes on behind these doors?"

"That is not the point," he declared, shrugging out of his coat. "My sister is an innocent young girl. We know that doesn't mean anything to you, but—"

"Oh, please don't start that again," Tamsyn pleaded, so close to him now he could sense the warmth of her bare skin even through his shirt and the fine knit of his pantaloons. "Must we quarrel about it again?"

Julian looked down at her helplessly. The liquescent eyes, the slight quiver of her soft mouth, the imploring voice, were totally unexpected. He thought he knew how to handle the fiery brigand, but he didn't have the faintest idea how to deal with this manifestation.

"Look, Tamsyn," he tried. "I realize it's hard for you to understand. Lucy must seem like some precious flower to you. A rare orchid in a hothouse, she's such a tender—"

"Oh, *estúpido!*" Tamsyn exclaimed, forgetting all her resolutions to be conciliatory and feminine and loving under this disgustingly sugary misrepresentation of the facts. "For your information, your precious, tender little sister has been so violently shocked by the marriage bed and that insensitive lout of a husband you allowed her to marry that she's unlikely ever to recover if someone doesn't do her a kindness and open her eyes to the realities."

Julian tore off his cravat with a rush of relief. He glared at her, his eyes points of blue fire. This Tamsyn he could deal with. "When it comes to my sister, I'm not in the least interested in the opinion of an unschooled, misbegotten hellion who's never learned to obey convention."

"Oh, pah!" Tamsyn declared in disgust. "Convention!" she mocked. "Convention as applied to women. It doesn't apply to Gareth, does it? He can go spreading his favors around to all and sundry, and that's considered perfectly acceptable."

"No, it's not!" Julian snapped, pulling his shirt out of his britches and tossing it to the floor. In the passion of the moment it didn't occur to him that stripping off his clothes in front of the naked Tamsyn might be offering a mixed message. "As it happens, I hold no brief whatsoever for Gareth's indiscretions . . . any more than I do for yours."

"And what of yours?" she retorted. "These indiscretions, as you so delicately phrase them, take two. I haven't noticed you being a particularly unwilling partner hitherto, milord colonel."

Her eyes flashed, and her small body was rigid with angry conviction. "If there's one thing I cannot abide, it's a hypocrite."

"I am not in the least hypocritical where my sister is concerned," he snapped, kicking off his boots. "I will not have her innocence sullied by your experience!"

"Sullied!" Tamsyn exclaimed. "You dare to accuse me of sullying your sister as if I were some loathsome piece of scum! The only person who's sullied Lucy is her damned husband. And so I tell you."

Bending in one fluid movement, she grabbed up his discarded shirt. "If you'd done the decent thing by your sister, if you'd really cared for her, you would have given her a few of the facts of life and she wouldn't be in this position now. I bid you good night, Colonel, I've no time for blind hypocrites." And she pushed past him to the door, shoving her arms into the sleeves of his shirt as she did so.

"Don't you walk off like that! Come back here." Forgetting that the one thing he'd wanted was Tamsyn's absence from his room, Julian grabbed her arm. "Explain yourself!"

She twitched free and darted sideways out of his reach. "You work it out for yourself, sir."

He sprang forward, and in the same moment Tamsyn

grabbed the water jug off the washstand. Her eyes were living coals.

"Oh, no," he said softly. "Don't you dare."

"I dare," she said, and hurled the contents at him.

In the room across the hall, Lucy shot up in bed at the roaring bellow of an outraged bull. "Whatever's going on?"

"God knows." Gareth pulled himself up sleepily. He'd been about to sink into the blissful world of alcoholic slumber and now sat blinking in the dark, trying to decipher the thumps and bangs. "Sounds like a fight of some kind."

"A fight?" Lucy pushed aside the bedclothes. "Who could be fighting in the house at this hour . . . at any hour?"

Gareth listened, his head to one side. There was another shivering crash, a bellow that definitely came from his brother-in-law, followed by a squeal of rage in a much higher range.

"Good God," he said again. "It's coming from your brother's room." He swung out of bed, shoving aside the curtains. "It couldn't be an intruder, surely."

He'd reached the door, Lucy on his heels, when the sound of St. Simon's door opening and then violently slamming made them both jump. The door opened again immediately on the slam.

A finger to his lips, Gareth gently eased their door ajar, and they peered into the dimly lit corridor, eyes stretched at the extraordinary sight before them.

Julian, wearing only his britches, water dripping from his hair, leaped after the slight figure of Tamsyn, clad only in his discarded shirt.

"Come back here!" Julian's fierce whisper echoed in the deserted corridor.

"Go to hell!" Tamsyn hissed over her shoulder, losing speed for a fatal instant as she did so.

Julian grabbed the collar of his shirt. "You're not getting away with it, *mi muchacha!*"

With a deft wriggle Tamsyn shrugged out of the shirt and raced on, leaving him holding the empty garment.

"Fiera!" Julian's voice was still a whisper, but now the stunned audience, cowering in the shadows, heard both laughter and powerful determination.

He sprang forward and tackled Tamsyn, diving for her waist, sweeping her off her feet. For a moment her body arced through the air; then she came to rest across his shoulder with a low wail of indignation.

"Espadachín! Miserable cur!" She reared up against his shoulder, pummeling with her fists, forgetting the need for quiet in her outrage.

"I should settle down, buttercup," Julian said, his voice soft, his tone affable, as he turned back to his room. "You're presenting rather a tempting target at the moment."

"Oh, I'll kill you," Tamsyn declared, dropping forward again. "Gabriel will cut out your black, hypocritical heart and I'll catch your blood in my hat."

Julian's low laugh lingered in the corridor as he went back into his room with his burden, closing the door quietly behind him.

"Well, I'll be damned!" Gareth murmured, looking down at Lucy. "I'll be damned!" He became aware of his own powerful arousal and the swift surge of blood in his loins. The sight of Tamsyn's naked body curved over Julian's shoulder, glowing under the candlelight, had excited him almost beyond bearing.

"So that's what she meant," Lucy whispered, gazing up at her husband. "She said she knew things . . ."

Her voice faded as she saw Gareth's expression. She was aware of a strange tingling sensation in her body, little prickles of excitement in her belly, and she wondered what it could be.

"Lucy," Gareth said huskily. His palm cupped her cheek as he read the almost bewildered thrill in her eyes, the flush on her cheeks. Could she also be affected by that scene? She didn't move away from him, and he lifted her against him, feeling her skin soft and warm, the rich curve of her bottom beneath her nightgown. Her nightcap fell off as she moved her head against his shoulder. He bent and laid her gently on the bed.

For the first time she allowed him to remove her nightgown, and when he touched her, she was moist and open, although her limbs became abruptly rigid, her expression taut with apprehension.

"It'll be all right," he said softly, hardly able to contain himself, but somehow managing to control the vigorous surge of his entry so that she didn't tighten against him as she had always done in the past. It was over very quickly, but when he rolled away from her, he knew that for once he hadn't hurt her, and his own explosion of pleasure had seared him to his toes.

Lucy lay thoughtfully in the darkness, listening to Gareth's gradually deepening snores. She felt most peculiar, but also quite pleasantly relaxed. But she had the unshakable conviction that what she had just experienced was as nothing to what Tamsyn was experiencing in Julian's bed.

She was Julian's mistress. How exotic, and how shocking. No wonder she seemed so different, and no wonder she'd offered her opinion so freely. Well, in the morning Lucy would seek more of those opinions. She certainly had a new perspective on her straitlaced

brother, though. An involuntary giggle escaped her, and
she turned her face into her pillow. She'd take his stric-
tures a little less to heart in future.

Gareth wasn't sure how to greet his brother-in-law the
following morning, but Julian's "Good morning" over
the breakfast table was accompanied by an imperturb-
able smile and the civil invitation to look over his stud
and take any horse that met his fancy, with the exception of Soult.

"I rode Soult from Badajos to Lisbon," Julian explained. "But the rest of my campaigning string is in the
charge of my groom in Spain."

"When do you expect to return?" Gareth piled ked-
geree onto his plate and sat down, filling his tankard
from the jug of ale.

"By October at the latest. I have to be in London
again next month." He wiped his mouth and tossed his
napkin to the table. "Well, if you'll excuse me, Gareth,
I've work to do."

He strode to the door just as it opened to admit
Tamsyn, in a high-necked, long-sleeved dress of
sprigged muslin. "Good morning, milord colonel."

"Good morning, Tamsyn." His voice was cool, his
eye amused, as he noticed that she had chosen a costume
that covered every inch of her skin. They'd both acquired a few bruises in the night's rough-and-tumble.

"Don't let me keep you, sir."

"I won't. Termagant!" he added in a soft whisper. He
flicked her cheek carelessly; the residue of passion still
lurked in his eyes . . . that and laughter. He'd woken
up laughing, convinced he'd been laughing in his sleep.

"Bully!" she mouthed, her own gaze sparkling.

"Virago!" He left on the whisper, and Tamsyn

turned her attention to Gareth, who tried to pretend he hadn't been straining his ears to catch the whispered colloquy.

"Good morning, Gareth. Is Lucy still abed?" She sat down and took a piece of toast from the rack. "Could you pass the coffee, please?"

Gareth obliged. "Lucy usually takes her breakfast abovestairs." He found himself examining her covertly, his memory alive with the image of her body beneath her clothes. He wondered if she'd be open to a proposition from himself. He ought to be able to match whatever Julian was offering her. Unfortunately, he didn't see how he could make such a proposal while they were both under St. Simon's roof. A man didn't poach on another man's territory while he was enjoying his hospitality. But maybe while Julian was in London, he might sound her out.

The prospect brought a smile to his lips, and unconsciously he touched his mustache, smoothing it with a fingertip.

Tamsyn buttered her toast, wondering what could have brought that irritating smirk to his face. She fervently hoped it was nothing to do with her. Could he have heard anything last night? No, their voices in the corridor hadn't risen above a whisper, and everyone had been asleep.

She left the breakfast parlor while Gareth was just settling into his second plate of sirloin. Those pudgy thighs weren't going to get any the less so, she reflected, but one woman's meat was another's poison.

"Tamsyn, good morning."

Lucy's voice aptly broke into Tamsyn's charitably philosophic reflection. Lucy was coming down the stairs, her expression both excited and a little shy.

"Good morning." Tamsyn greeted her pleasantly, relieved to see that she seemed to have recovered her good humor over night. "I'm going for a walk. Do you care to accompany me?"

"Oh, yes, I should love to. I'll just fetch my parasol and pelisse."

"Oh, you won't need those. It's very warm out, and I intend to go to St. Catherine's Point. It's quite a scramble over the cliffs, so you won't want to carry clutter."

Lucy, expecting a gentle, chatty stroll through the shrubbery, was aghast at such a prospect; however, she said stoically, "No, of course I won't. Are you leaving now?"

"If you're ready," Tamsyn said politely.

They were halfway down the drive when Gabriel appeared through the trees, on foot, a gun over one shoulder, a game bag over the other. "Where are you going, little girl?"

"To St. Catherine's Point. Then into Fowey to buy some needle and thread for Josefa."

He nodded, smiled amiably at Lucy, and continued on his way.

"Your servant is very familiar."

"Gabriel is no servant, and don't ever treat him as one," Tamsyn said. "He becomes very upset. He was my father's most trusted friend, and he looks after me."

"You must do things very differently in Spain," Lucy observed, feeling for a way to start the conversation she had in mind.

"You could say that." Tamsyn struck out toward the steeply rising cliff path, her stride long and easy. Lucy puffed behind her, waving at flies that swarmed around her as the sweat started to break out on her forehead.

"You talk about things differently." They reached the crest of the path and Lucy stopped, gasping in the cool breeze now blowing fresh from the sea stretched out below them. "I mean the things you said your mother had told you." Her cheeks were hot, and she knew it wasn't just the result of exertion.

Tamsyn's laugh lilted on the wind. "Your mother didn't tell you such things, I imagine?" She started off again, running down the path toward a ledge that hung out over the Fowey estuary, just above the ruined walls of St. Catherine's fort, which once had commanded the entrance to the river as part of Henry VIII's coastal defense system.

By the time Lucy had reached her, Tamsyn had kicked off her sandals and was stretched on her stomach, gazing down at the fort, and across the wide mouth of the estuary. A clipper, laden with china clay, was tacking out of the estuary to the sea.

"No, she didn't," Lucy said, dropping to the grass beside her, wondering if she would get grass stains on her pale cambric gown. "The only thing she ever said to me about marriage was that there were some aspects that were not pleasant, but it was one's duty to endure them."

"Lie back and think of England!" Tamsyn said in disgust, chewing on a strand of grass. "And I don't suppose your brother mentioned anything either?"

"Julian!" Lucy stared at her in horror. "He couldn't talk about things like that to *me*!"

"Oh." Tamsyn decided it would be dangerous to discuss Julian in such a context in case she inadvertently gave something away.

"I know it's not at all respectable of me to want to talk about such things," Lucy ventured.

Tamsyn laughed and rolled onto her back, squinting against the sun. "Respectability can make life very dull. I'll wager you anything that Gareth would much prefer an unrespectable woman in his bed."

"He has plenty of those," Lucy said tartly, and then gasped, amazed at herself for saying such a shocking thing.

Tamsyn merely grinned. "But if he had one at home, then he probably wouldn't need to wander off quite so often."

"So what do I have to do to be unrespectable?" Lucy demanded. "Since you seem to know so much about it." It was on the tip of her tongue to say what she and Gareth had seen in the night, but she was too embarrassed to admit to having watched in secret . . . and far too embarrassed to admit that they'd both found the watching curiously exciting.

"I'll tell you, if you promise not to say a word to your brother. If he thinks I've been corrupting you, he'll throw me out of the house."

"Would he?" Lucy breathed. She found her brother thoroughly intimidating, but after what she'd seen last night, she couldn't imagine Tamsyn accepting such a decree without a murmur.

"Probably," Tamsyn said. "So you must promise."

"I promise."

Tamsyn smiled into the sunshine and began to impart to the wide-eyed innocent beside her some of the joys of love.

It was a very thoughtful Lucy who walked alone back to Tregarthan an hour later at a much slower pace than the one set by Tamsyn on the way to the point.

Tamsyn took the steep, winding path down to the town, deep in thought. It was gratifying to put someone else's life in order, even if she couldn't understand what Lucy could possibly see in Gareth Fortescue. He didn't strike her as seriously unpleasant so much as lazy, conceited, and self-indulgent. Quite usual characteristics of the English male aristocrat, if Cecile was to be believed. He wasn't a man to be solely contented with the marriage bed, however satisfying that bed might be, but presumably Lucy would find it easier to accommodate her husband's wanderings if she was herself no longer dissatisfied. They'd certainly seem less threatening to the stability of her marriage.

She made her purchases in the draper's and strolled in the sunshine along the quay. David and Charles Penhallan saw her from the steps of the white Customs House, where they were talking with the Revenue Officer, a portly gentlemen who struggled daily with the paradox of having to do a job that went against his own interests. For a man who loved his wine and cognac as Lieutenant Barker did, preventing the Gentlemen from making their runs was the devil's own work. He was an expert at turning a blind eye, and the smugglers generally let him know when it would be expedient for him to do so.

"Lord Penhallan was remarking only the other day that since he started using mantraps at Lanjerrick, his gamekeepers have noticed much less poaching." He stroked his rotund belly and belched softly. Kippers for breakfast always sat heavily, but he couldn't resist them. "I was thinking of mentioning it to Lord St. Simon. His bailiff was lamenting how many pheasants they were losing. . . ." His voice faded as he realized that he was talking to thin air. The Penhallan twins had moved away and were sauntering down the street.

Tamsyn walked back up the narrow, steep streets of

the little town, pausing now and again to look over the jumbled roofs below her, looking down into small walled cottage gardens fragrant with roses, fishing nets drying in the sun, crab pots piled in corners.

Could she live here? Leave the wild passes and the soaring eagles, the smell of crushed thyme beneath her feet, the ice-capped mountain peaks, the clear, frigid mountain rivers? Leave the punishing summer sun for this gentle cousin; leave the air so sharp it pierced your lungs for this soft air, as gentle as spring rain?

But the question was academic. She knew there was no way to expose Cedric Penhallan as she intended and keep Julian in ignorance. And if she couldn't do that, then she couldn't persuade the colonel to look into his heart and see what she believed was there. So she was going back to Spain as soon as she'd done what she had come here to do, and she'd take with her memories of a man and a love that would have to last a lifetime.

She turned out of the town as she reached the top street, and took the high-hedged lane that wound its way to Tregarthan. Firmly, she forced herself to dwell on the glories of her homeland, to think how wonderful it would be to be back with the partisans, to have a clean, clear-cut purpose in life again. To put this emotional quagmire behind her.

She was so deep in her musing that she didn't notice the two men keeping their distance behind her.

David and Charles had kept to the side of the narrow, climbing streets in the village, pausing casually in doorways, taking little alleys between cottages that would bring them up onto the next street without its looking as if they were following her. Now, as they dogged her steps along the deserted lane, they both had their hands in their pockets, fingers twisting around the black silk loo masks, and they both wore the same expression—an eager, predatory glimmer in their eyes, their mouths twisted into the same grim quirk.

Tamsyn left the lane, slipped through a kissing gate beside a stone cattle grid, and turned along the edge of the field in the shade of the hedge. David and Charles silently drew out their masks and as silently tied them on.

Tamsyn heard the gentle buzz of a bumblebee in the honeysuckle, the frantic crackle as a startled pheasant took wing from the ripening corn. The sun was hot, the earth dry; a frog hopped out of the ditch beside the hedge. It was quiet, almost somnolent, and the hairs on the back of her neck lifted and her scalp crawled.

She stopped and very slowly turned around. Two masked men stepped toward her, malevolent intent wreathing around them. Tamsyn stood stone still. There was no one in the field but herself and the two men. A herd of cows raised their heads and stared with bovine curiosity through sleepy brown eyes, their jaws rhythmically working as they chewed the cud.

"Well, well," Charles said, approaching her. "If it isn't St. Simon's doxy of the seashore."

The men of the cliff top. Were they her cousins? She said nothing.

David chuckled. "Fancy St. Simon housing his harlot under the precious roofs of Tregarthan . . . with his sister, no less." He reached out and touched her cheek. Charles stepped up beside him, and she was backed against the hedge. No chance to outrun them. Still she said nothing.

"So how about you tell us something about yourself?" David invited, pinching her cheek so the flesh whitened as the blood fled.

Tamsyn shook her head. *"Perdón?"* she whispered.

"Your name, whore." He pinched her other cheek, bringing her face very close to his. "Your name and where you come from."

"No comprendo," Tamsyn whispered, praying that her fear wasn't showing in her eyes. If these two smelled her fear, there would be no stopping them.

"Oh, don't play dumb with me, whore!" David released her cheeks, took a swift, darting step, and moved behind her, grabbing her arms, pulling them hard behind her, pushing them up her back.

Tamsyn knew that she couldn't hope to defend herself physically. There were two of them and they were twice her size, for all their willowy stature. If she'd had a weapon, a knife, anything, maybe she would have had a chance. But she had nothing.

Except for the needle and thread she'd bought for Josefa. Her mind raced as she continued to stand immobile. She had the absolute sense that if she was not to be badly hurt, she must offer no resistance unless she was certain it would work. There was something about them that sent ice down her spine. Worse than Cornichet, she thought distantly. At least Cornichet had a reason for what he did, a reason she understood.

Charles's eyes laughed at her, and yet they were as cold and deadly as a viper's. David released her arms and she breathed again but it was a false respite. Charles took her chin between finger and thumb in a hurtful grip, and his other hand grabbed a handful of her hair, jerking her head toward him. Then he brought his mouth to hers in a violent assault that made her want to vomit. His tongue pushed into her mouth and battered against her throat; her head swam as she gagged, fighting for breath. Her hand closed over the packet of needles.

Somehow she extricated them from her pocket, and in desperation, as she felt her senses swimming, she stabbed upward into the soft skin beneath her assailant's chin.

Charles bellowed and pulled his mouth from hers. He hit her with his open palm. "Vicious little whore. By God, you'll pay for that." Disbelieving, he touched his chin where a ruby bead blossomed; then he caught her wrist, bending it back until she cried out and the packet of needles fell to the ground. He put a hand on her breast, rubbing his palm against the nipple; then he pinched the soft mound, watching the tears spring into her eyes, squeezing until she could no longer keep back the cry of pain.

"Let's get her to sing first," David said, seeing the intent in his brother's eye. "Let's get what we want out of her first; then you can have your revenge."

"All right, whore!" Charles's fingers closed viciously over her nipple. "What's your name? Where did St. Simon find you?"

"Bastardo!" She spat in his eye. They forced her to her knees, yanking her hands so high up her back that she knew one more jerk would break her arm. Even through her tears she cursed them in Spanish, struggling to control the pain and the surging nausea as she knelt on the hard ground, her head drooping to her chest.

And then the tableau was shattered by a roar, so wild with savage fury that even Tamsyn shuddered. Her arms were abruptly released, and the masked men were suddenly gone. Dully she raised her head and saw them, through the tears coursing down her cheeks, running as if pursued by hell's furies.

Gabriel charged past her, still bellowing his war cry, and then suddenly he stopped. With a vile oath he abandoned the pursuit and ran to the huddled figure now lying on the grass. He dropped to his knees beside her. "Och, little girl . . . I'll get them later."

He lifted her up and held her, cradling her against his massive chest, rocking her as if she were a baby. Her face was white, her eyes violet stones, and for a few minutes she lay shivering in his arms. Then she pushed away from him with an inarticulate mumble. The taste of the man was in her mouth, and she retched into the ditch.

"Oh, I'll kill them inch by inch," Gabriel swore softly, rubbing her back as she crouched on the ground. "I'll hunt them down like the curs they are, and when I have them, I'll flay them with an oyster shell." It was no idle threat, as Tamsyn knew.

"They wanted to know who I was, Gabriel." She found to her surprise that her voice was perfectly steady as she straightened. "Who I was and where I came from. I'm sure they were my cousins." She stood up, thoughtfully massaging her bruised and aching wrists.

"Do you think your uncle set them up to it?"

She shook her head. "From what Cecile said, I doubt Cedric would be so indiscreet. He's a subtle man, and he wouldn't want such a filthy assault to be laid anywhere near his door. But I've obviously aroused his curiosity."

Calmly now, she smoothed back her hair, flicked grass and dried mud from her skirt. "What brought you so fast, Gabriel?"

He shrugged. "Just a feeling. I was uneasy after I left you with that Miss Lucy, I don't know why. I thought I'd stroll to the village and escort you home."

"Thank God you did." She took his large hand in both hers. "We'll get even with them, Gabriel, but please wait. It'll spoil everything if you end up on the scaffold in Bodmin jail for murder." She tried to smile, but her face ached from the slap and the violent pinching. "When we go after Cedric, we'll get them too."

"Just you remember they're mine," he said with low-voiced savagery.

"They'll be yours," the daughter of El Baron promised, well aware of what she was promising and feeling not a twinge of compassion for her cousins.

"And until then, little girl, you go nowhere alone. Maybe your uncle didn't set those scum on you, but if he's on the scent, there's no knowing what he might decide to do."

"No," Tamsyn agreed flatly. "A man who could dispose of his sister so ingeniously could probably manage to arrange for a stranger's disappearance without too much difficulty."

Chapter Twenty

"She doesn't speak a word of English, Governor."

"Who doesn't?" The viscount looked up irritably at this interruption. He glowered at David, who stood somewhat hesitantly in the doorway of the library, unwilling to come farther without an invitation.

"St. Simon's doxy, sir," Charles put in from behind his brother. "We thought you'd like to know."

Cedric carefully folded his newspaper and put it on the sofa beside him. "You thought what?" His black eyes had narrowed. "I trust you haven't been meddling in my affairs, sir."

David shuffled his feet but responded with his habitual note of sulkiness. "You said the other evening at dinner that you'd like to know who she was. We thought you'd like us to find out for you."

"And just what could have given you that idea, you bungling clod!" Cedric exploded with a soft ferocity that was all the more alarming for its quietness. The two young men took an involuntary step backward. "Since when have I ever asked you to involve yourself in my business? Just what have you been doing?"

"We asked the girl a few questions," David said

lamely. "But she doesn't speak English . . . rattled on in some foreign language."

"Not Froggie, though," his brother put in helpfully. "We'd have known if it was that."

Cedric stared at them in disbelief, wondering how it was that they could still surprise him with their idiocy. "She's Spanish," he said deliberately. "As I've known for the last two days."

"Oh." Charles scratched his head. "Only trying to help, Governor."

"Oh, spare me," Cedric said in disgust. "Where was the girl when you had this illuminating discussion?" His eyes sharpened. "Not on St. Simon land?"

"Oh, no, sir," they said hastily. "She was in Fowey, so we followed her and . . . and just asked her her name."

Cedric leaned back against the sofa and regarded them steadily and with a powerful revulsion. "Did you hurt her?" he asked gently. "Did you hurt a woman under St. Simon's protection? A woman living as a guest in his house? Of course you didn't. Of course you wouldn't do anything so asinine. . . . *Would you?*" he shouted suddenly.

"No, sir . . . no, of course we didn't," they said almost in unison. "We just asked her a few questions."

Cedric closed his eyes with a sigh of weary disgust. He knew them too well to believe them. It seemed they could derive sexual pleasure only from causing a woman pain. Their father had had the same quirk, and his wife, a pathetic little mouse, had cowered and hidden her bruises until she'd died from a fall down the stairs when she was six months pregnant. No one who knew Thomas Penhallan had believed Mary had fallen down the stairs. But the twins had inherited his twisted appetites. At least in general they devoted their malign attentions to women of the streets and left their own class alone. It was to be hoped no woman was ever fool enough to marry one of them.

Presumably in this instance they'd concluded that the girl was St. Simon's whore and therefore fair game.

"Besides, she wouldn't know who we were," Charles said on a note of pride. "We wore loo masks—"

"You wore *what*?"

"She won't be able to identify us . . . not like the other girl," David explained. "Not that we did hurt her," he added hurriedly. "It wasn't like that other time at all." They looked at their uncle hopefully, still expecting some congratulation on their foresight, at least. There was clearly to be no gratitude for their impulse to assist him.

Congratulations were not forthcoming. *"Get out of here!"*

They fled, and Cedric stared into the empty fireplace, wondering how much damage they'd done. He'd set his own inquiries in motion and had discovered easily that the woman at Tregarthan was Spanish, that she'd come from Spain ostensibly under the protection of Colonel, Lord St. Simon at Wellington's behest. That was common knowledge in the neighborhood now. Thanks to his nephews' spying, he knew rather more about the relationship than the neighborhood did. He wasn't particularly interested in whether St. Simon was sleeping with the girl or not, but he was intrigued as to what had brought them together, and why in the world St. Simon would trouble to bring his mistress from Spain and house her at Tregarthan.

Who was she and why was she there?

Whichever way he looked at it, he couldn't ignore

two facts: the girl bore an uncanny resemblance to Celia; and she was Spanish.

Pure coincidence? No, Cedric didn't believe in coincidence. He believed in planning and minds as devious as his own.

The abduction had gone according to plan, except for that fool Marianne, who had lived to tell the tale. However, he'd dealt with her easily enough—fear, a generous pension, and a secluded cottage in the Highlands had ensured her silence. She'd been dead these last ten years, carrying the secret to her grave. But had Celia escaped from her abductor? Escaped . . . married some Spaniard . . . fathered a child?

It didn't make sense. If she'd escaped, she would have come home. It wouldn't occur to her that her brother could have had anything to do with some robber on a mountain pass. And if the girl was legitimately Celia's daughter, why didn't she come out and say so?

If she *did* have anything to do with Celia, then he had to deal with her. A matter somewhat complicated by St. Simon's protection. And further complicated by the fact that she now knew that someone was unusually interested in her. It was, of course, possible that she wouldn't be able to identify her masked attackers. She was a stranger, she'd certainly never seen the twins before. There was no reason why she should connect them with himself . . . unless she told St. Simon of the attack. He would have little difficulty naming those louts. But there was no reason why he should link their behavior with Cedric. He would be most likely to assume that they were up to their old tricks again.

He got up and poured himself a cognac, rolling the amber liquid on his tongue, frowning. If the girl did have anything to do with Celia, what could she possibly want? She had to want something. Everyone wanted something. Was it money she was after?

Well, whatever it was, he would discover soon enough. Perhaps he could encourage her to reveal her hand.

"It wouldn't be a big party, Julian," Lucy said, her china-blue eyes glowing with enthusiasm. "Just ten couples or so, and the usual families. No formal dancing, although perhaps we could roll up the carpet after supper. Not an elaborate supper—"

"My dear Lucy," Julian interrupted, raising a hand to halt the flow. "If you wish to give a small party, I have no objection. The only question is whether Tamsyn wishes to try her society wings so soon."

"Oh, of course she does," Lucy said warmly. "It won't be in the least alarming. Everyone is so kind and they're all so interested in her and want to get to know her. You do wish to, don't you, Tamsyn?"

Tamsyn, who'd been listening to Lucy's bubbling excitement with some amusement, said obligingly, "If you say so, Lucy."

"But you know how you become quite overcome with shyness and forget all your English," Julian pointed out casually, leaning back in his chair, regarding her from beneath drooping eyelids. "Do you think you're really ready to burst upon the social scene without becoming completely incomprehensible?"

"But Tamsyn speaks perfectly good English," Gareth protested, frowning as he flicked with his handkerchief at a spot of dust on his glistening Hessians. "Native, I would have said."

"Ah, that may seem to be the case," Julian said

gently. "But, unfortunately, under pressure she forgets all her English and lapses into streams of Spanish."

"I believe I've conquered my shyness," Tamsyn declared with dignity. "I believe I'll be able to conduct myself without disgracing you, milord colonel."

"Do you, now?" He stroked his chin, still regarding her with lazy amusement.

Lucy glanced quickly between them. Most of the time Julian treated Tamsyn with a careful, almost distant, politeness, and it was very difficult to believe what she and Gareth had seen in the corridor. Sometimes, though, as now, there would be something about their conversation or the way they looked at each other that hinted at some shared secret.

"Tamsyn couldn't possibly disgrace you," she said a little awkwardly. "And I will stay beside her the whole evening and show her how to go on if she has any difficulties."

"Then it seems the matter is settled," her brother said, his voice once more cool and matter-of-fact. "Just don't expect me to make any of the arrangements. You may tell Hibbert to provide the wine and champagne from the cellars."

"We must have an iced punch," Lucy declared, leaping to her feet. "It was all the rage in London last Season. Amabel Featherstone has a wonderful recipe— I'm sure I wrote it in my pocketbook. I'm certain Mrs. Hibbert will be able to make it up."

She headed for the door, her usual indolence vanished. "Tamsyn, come and help me decide on the supper menu. And you could help me with the invitations, if you don't mind. It's tedious work writing them all out, but if we can do them all this evening, then Judson shall deliver them in the morning."

"When are we to have this party?" Tamsyn inquired, reluctantly abandoning her plan for an evening gallop on Cesar.

Lucy paused to consider. "Next Saturday. Would that be all right, Julian?"

"Oh, perfectly," he said. "With any luck I should be able to wangle an invitation somewhere else."

"Oh, no!" Lucy exclaimed, horrified. "We cannot have a party at Tregarthan if you're not here to host it."

"I believe St. Simon was jesting, my dear," Gareth said, standing to peer into the mirror to make a minor adjustment to his cravat.

Lucy looked a little bewildered. "Come, Lucy," Tamsyn said, taking her arm firmly. "You can show me exactly how one organizes a Society party. The only parties I have ever attended have been—"

"You attended parties in that convent of yours?" Julian interrupted in swift warning.

Tamsyn kicked herself. She'd been about to describe the glorious almost tribal affairs in the mountain villages, where they roasted whole sheep and goats and the festivities could continue for three days.

"No," she said. "But before I went to the convent, before my mother died, I did once attend a birthday party."

"Oh, you poor dear," Lucy exclaimed, shocked to her core at such a pathetic memory. "And you haven't been to a party since?"

"No," Tamsyn said soulfully, glancing at the colonel.

"Pobrecita," he murmured, eyelids drooping over the mocking glint in the bright-blue orbs.

"Will you wish to examine the guest list, Julian, when I've made it out?" Lucy asked, still intent on the matter in hand.

"No, I leave it entirely in your more than capable hands," he responded, pointedly picking up the newspaper.

Lucy nodded complacently. "I have a talent for organizing social events. We gave a very grand reception last Season, do you remember, Gareth?"

"Oh, yes, my dear," he agreed, remembering also that he'd pronounced it a great bore and had taken his leave at the earliest opportunity, fleeing to Marjorie's cozy little house. Lucy had wept bitterly for most of the next day, but not a word of reproach had passed her lips. Guilt, as a result, had made him storm out of the house, saying he couldn't be expected to spend time with a watering pot.

The recollections were uncomfortable, and he resumed his seat as Tamsyn and Lucy left the room. Restlessly, he picked up his wineglass. It was empty. He peered into it for a moment, trying to recover his usual composure. He'd make it up to the pretty little thing, he decided. She was such a sweet innocent, and he hadn't taken that into account when they'd married. Couldn't expect her to perform like Marjorie . . . stupid of him to have thought she could. In fact, now that he gave the matter some thought, he didn't want his wife behaving with Marjorie's knowing ways. Quite shocking, it would be.

"I doubt your glass will fill just by looking at it, Fortescue."

His brother-in-law's cool tones broke into his musing, and he looked up, startled. Julian stood over him with the decanter, one eyebrow raised. "Deep thoughts, Gareth?"

Gareth's countenance took on a ruddy hue. "Nice

for Lucy to have something to plan," he said. "Makes her happy when she's got something to do."

Julian merely raised an eyebrow and returned to his newspaper. Presenting Tamsyn formally to local society under his sister's auspices would be more convenient and more conventional than doing it himself. Lucy knew all the intricacies of the local family networks, and he could trust her not to step on any toes with her invitations. She would ensure that the old tabbies like the Honorable Mrs. Anslow and Miss Gretchen Dolby would be included, as well as the younger set. And it was always possible that someone of that generation might remember a disappearance over twenty years ago.

Tamsyn was still an exotic flower in this country backwater, but if she didn't talk too much and kept herself in the background, she should be able to muddle through an evening with Lucy and himself to steer her.

It was interesting that she and Lucy had become such good friends, the constraint of that first evening vanished. Gareth still attempted some heavy-handed flirtation, but Tamsyn skillfully turned it aside and Lucy no longer seemed troubled by it. In fact, she seemed happier altogether. It was one less thing to worry about. But it wasn't enough to lift his depression.

He knew perfectly well that he was depressed because he was stuck here while his friends and his men were enduring the broiling heat of the summer campaign. Unless some miracle happened, he would stay stuck until October, when he would leave Tamsyn to whatever life she'd made for herself here and sail back to Lisbon, hopefully rejoining the army before they went into winter quarters.

But dwelling on that prospect didn't lift his spirits either, and he knew why. He was not looking forward to bringing his liaison with the brigand to a close. In the dark reaches of the night, when she slept beside him, curled like an exhausted puppy against his chest, he had allowed himself to imagine going back to Spain with her. Setting her up as his established mistress. She would have no trouble following the drum; campaigning was in her blood. But he'd have to persuade her to give up this plan to find her mother's family, and what would he be offering in its place? A liaison for an indeterminate length of time, trailing after the army over a country ravaged by war. And when the war was over, he'd have to come back here, take himself a wife, and set about building a dynasty.

It wasn't fair to ask her, and Tamsyn showed no signs of suggesting such a thing herself.

In a small parlor at the rear of the house, Lucy drew a sheet of paper toward her. "I'll make a list of all the people we should invite. I'll explain who they are to you as I do it, so you'll learn who are the really important families."

Tamsyn sat down beside her. "How many are you going to invite?"

Lucy tapped her teeth with her quill. "We really have to invite everyone," she said. "Unless it's to be a very small, intimate gathering."

"Which it isn't going to be."

"No," Lucy said with a chuckle. "What's the point of going to all this trouble just for twenty people? Julian won't mind so long as we don't trouble him with any of the arrangements." She began to scribble a list of names, rattling through a description and tidbits of gossip attached to various people as she compiled the list.

"There, now." She sat back, shaking her wrist at the

end of fifteen minutes of busy scribbling. "I think that's everyone who is anyone, from as far away as Truro. A few of them won't come, of course, but they'd be bitterly offended if they didn't receive an invitation."

Tamsyn scanned the list of over a hundred names. She'd been waiting for Lucy to mention the Penhallans, but the name didn't appear anywhere.

"Gabriel mentioned a very prominent family called Penhallan," she said with an air of mild curiosity. "He'd heard talk of them in the taverns in Fowey."

"Viscount Penhallan," Lucy said. "He's very important, but he doesn't go into local society. He's very powerful in the government, I think. I've only met him twice, in London." She frowned down at the list, saying absently, "I didn't like him. He's very intimidating."

"Does your brother know him?"

"Oh, yes, of course," Lucy said, still distracted. "But there was some scandal about his nephews, and no one receives them anymore. . . . I don't know what it was, and don't say anything to Julian, because he'll accuse me of gossiping and then he'll be very toplofty and uncomfortable."

"Shouldn't you invite Viscount Penhallan if everyone else is invited?" Tamsyn asked carelessly, helping herself to an apple from the fruit bowl on the table and polishing it busily against her skirt.

"Oh, he won't care to come," Lucy said confidently.

"But you said other people wouldn't come, but they had to be invited nevertheless."

"Oh, yes, but they're different. Lord Penhallan is a *very* important person, and he wouldn't expect to be invited to a little reception like this."

"A hundred guests isn't that little." She scrunched into her apple. "It seems like half the county to me. At least if you invite him, he can't possibly be offended. Better to be safe than sorry, I always say."

Lucy contemplated the list with a frown. "I suppose it might be considered a slight to leave him out."

"I will write the invitation," Tamsyn said, drawing a sheet of paper toward her with a businesslike air. "Shall I do the second half of the list and you do the top?"

Would he come? If he was curious about her, then he would come. She was convinced he hadn't set the twins to attack her—it was too clumsy an act for someone as clever and devious as she knew her uncle to be. But neither had it been random. The twins had taken their uncle's business into their own vile, clumsy hands.

Cedric Penhallan was definitely curious about her, and he would come.

The invitation arrived with Cedric's breakfast the next morning. He read it twice, a slight smile curving the fleshy mouth. The handwriting was bold, the strokes heavily inked—not an overtly feminine hand. Certainly not the hand of Lucy Fortescue. Somehow he knew it had been written by the girl he'd seen on the stairs, the girl with the violet eyes who rode that milk-white Arabian. He scrutinized the missive, looking for some link to Celia. There was nothing, and yet he could scent the challenge rising from the heavy vellum. The invitation was an opening move.

But where in the name of grace did Julian St. Simon fit into all this?

Chapter Twenty-one

"I SHALL WEAR THE RUBIES TO THIS PARTY," TAMSYN announced, sitting cross-legged in the middle of Julian's bed. She was as usual naked, and she was watching him undress with close attention.

"No, you won't," the colonel said, bending to splash water on his face from the ewer.

Tamsyn hungrily absorbed the clean lines of his back, the lovely, taut buttocks, the long, muscular length of thigh. "Why not?"

He turned and she lost interest in the answer to the question, jumping off the bed with a little predatory whoop like a huntsman on the track of the fox. . . .

"Why won't I wear the rubies?" she asked some considerable time later. "They will go beautifully with the gown that Josefa is making for me. It's silver lace, opening over a half slip of cream silk, with a demitrain. I haven't the faintest idea how I'm to manage the train—it catches in one's feet most dreadfully. I shall probably trip down the stairs, or fall flat on my backside in the middle of a dance."

Julian blew away a tickling strand of silver hair from his nose. "I doubt that, buttercup. You seem to be a natural dancer."

"It's my Spanish blood," she said. "You should see me dance at fiesta, all swirling skirts and castanets and a lot of bare leg."

"Very appropriate for a small reception in a sleepy Cornish village," he observed.

Tamsyn wondered if he knew just how big this small party was going to be. He'd evinced no interest in the details at all.

"Anyway," he said, reverting to the original topic. "You may not wear the rubies because young unmarried girls wear only pearls, turquoise, garnets, or topaz. Anything more serious would be considered vulgar."

"How stuffy!"

"Very," he agreed. "And the other thing you must remember is that ingenues do not put themselves forward in any way. You may not dance unless a partner has been properly introduced to you, and you may dance only once with each partner. When you're not dancing, you must sit by the wall with the chaperons."

"You are not being serious?" Tamsyn pushed herself up against his chest and stared down at him in the dim light behind the bed curtains.

"Never more so," he said, grinning at her dismayed expression. "But this is the part you wish to play, remember."

"And you really enjoy rubbing it in, don't you?" She glared at him, but her eyes were still glowing from their loving.

"Maybe," he said, still grinning. "However, you may dance more than once with me, since I'm your guardian . . . oh, and it would be perfectly acceptable for you to dance several times with Gareth."

"Thank you. What an entrancing prospect." She flopped down beside him again. "Oh, I meant to

say . . ." She bounced upright again. "I don't know
how much this is all costing you, but since it's all part of
my plan to make my debut, of course I expect to pay for
it. So if you would give me an accounting . . ."

"Oh, a ruby will probably cover it," he said carelessly. His throat suddenly tightened as he remembered
the Aladdin's cave in Elvas, when she'd offered him her
treasure and he'd misunderstood and been wild with
fury at the thought that she would pay him as if he were
some hired lackey. But what she was offering him were
the glorious treasures of her body and her wonderfully
inventive imagination.

"What is it?" Tamsyn saw the tautness of his features,
the grim set of his jaw when a minute before he'd been
laughing, his eyes heavy with sensual pleasure, his expression soft and amused in the way she loved.

He didn't answer, merely pulled her down to him
again, rolling her beneath him. Tamsyn was still puzzled
by the strange change in him, by the roughness of his
body on hers, the urgency of this suddenly rekindled
hunger. But she allowed herself to be swept up in his
passion, to adapt the contours of her body to the hard
one above her, to take him within herself, to lose herself
in the rhythm of his body because the weeks were galloping by and Cedric Penhallan was approaching her net
. . . and it would all too soon be over.

"Goodness me," Tamsyn murmured, examining herself
in the cheval glass the following Saturday. She'd become
accustomed to seeing herself in gowns, but the light
cambrics and muslins she'd worn hitherto hadn't prepared her for this image. The gown left her shoulders
and arms bare, and was cut low across her bosom, re-

vealing both the upper swell of her breasts and the deep valley between them.

She rarely gave her body more than a passing thought and was as comfortable in her skin as she was clothed, but drawing attention to parts of her anatomy in this way struck her as almost indecent. She remembered Cecile describing some of the gowns she'd worn as a debutante, cut so low that her nipples were barely covered. And she remembered how Cecile had laughed, her violet eyes mischievous as she'd demonstrated with her fan how she used to draw attention to her bosom while seeming modestly to hide it.

Tamsyn swallowed the lump in her throat and turned to Josefa. "So what do you think, Josefa? Do I look at all like Cecile?"

Josefa's bright black eyes darted up and down the slender figure. "To the life, *queridita,*" she pronounced, and her own eyes misted; then she smiled and bustled over, bending to smooth down the skirt and adjust the train.

There was a tap at the door. "May I come in?" Lucy popped her head around. "Oh, Tamsyn," she said, coming fully into the room. "How beautiful you are."

"Nonsense," Tamsyn said, blushing slightly. "I'm thin and brown-skinned, and my hair's unfashionably short."

"No," Lucy said, shaking her head. "You're quite wrong. You look wonderful. Different . . . but lovely." She turned to examine herself critically in the mirror. "I quite liked this gown a minute ago, but now it seems dull and boring compared with yours."

"Nonsense," Tamsyn said, laughing. "You're fishing for compliments. Shame on you, Lucy."

Lucy laughed self-consciously and patted a ringlet

into place. She knew she looked both pretty and elegant. However, she thought, examining Tamsyn's image
in the mirror, Tamsyn's appearance took one's breath
away . . . perhaps because she was so unusual.

"Well, if you're ready, let us go down. I'm sure
Julian and Gareth are already downstairs."

"You go on," Tamsyn said, suddenly needing to
gather her thoughts. "I'll follow in a few minutes."

Lucy hesitated, then went off with an equable shrug
of her creamy round shoulders.

Tamsyn went to the window, drawing aside the curtain, gazing out across the lawn to the sea. It was a
delightful summer evening, a crescent moon swinging
low on the horizon, the first pale glimmer of starlight
against the darkening sky.

Cecile had once described her favorite gown. It had
been of silver lace and cream silk. Tonight her daughter
would appear to Cedric Penhallan in the same colors. A
vastly different style of dress, of course. Where Cecile
had worn swaying side panniers and a tightly corseted
bodice, her daughter wore a slip of a gown that glided
like gossamer over her figure. But her violet eyes were as
deep and luminous as her mother's, and they glowed
against the pale shimmer of her gown. Her hair was the
same burnished silver, and her frame was as slight and
slender.

Would Cedric Penhallan see his sister?

She touched the locket at her throat, drawing
strength and determination from the images of Cecile
and the baron smiling beneath the delicate filigree silver.
Then she went to the door, her step vigorous, the energy of purpose coursing through her veins.

Julian was in the hall, waiting for her at the bottom of
the staircase with a degree of impatience. The first

guests could arrive at any minute, and he wanted to be certain Tamsyn hadn't committed any serious solecisms, like smothering herself in rubies and diamonds.

He saw her in the shadows at the top of the stairs and called up to her. "Hurry, Tamsyn, people will be arriving at any minute."

She came running down the stairs toward him with her usual impetuous vitality, one hand carelessly holding up her skirt, her half train swishing behind her. "I'm sorry. I didn't mean to keep you waiting." She jumped the last step and flashed him a smile, tilting her head to one side in her robin imitation. "So what do you think, milord colonel? Will I pass muster?"

"Good God," he said softly.

"Is something wrong?" Her smile faltered.

"Yes," he said. "Ladies don't hurtle down the stairs as if all the devils in hell were on their heels. Go back and come down properly."

"Oh, very well." With an exaggerated sigh Tamsyn gathered up her skirts again and scampered back up the stairs. At the top she stopped, turned, laid one hand on the banister, and floated gracefully down the curving sweep to the hall.

Julian stood, one hand on the newel, one foot on the bottom step, watching, his critical expression masking his whirling senses. The exquisite gown did nothing to disguise the deep currents of sensuality that flowed through her, glowing in her eyes and in the translucent depths of her skin. The pale colors and delicate material merely accentuated her thrumming vibrancy. And he wanted to catch her up in his arms, bury his lips in the delicate curve where her neck met her shoulder, inhale the mingled honeyed scents of her skin, run his fingers through the shining cap that clung to the small, well-shaped head.

He wanted to claim her. Hold her in his arms, secure in the knowledge and rights of possession. He wanted to proclaim his possession to the world.

He took her hand as she reached him, raising it to his lips in a formal salute. "Try to remember for the rest of the evening not to gambol like a colt." Then he released her hand and turned back to the drawing room.

Tamsyn bit her lip. She hadn't expected fulsome compliments, but something other than a schoolmasterly castigation would have been nice.

Over the next two hours, as the house filled with a laughing, chattering crowd, Julian watched her. She stood beside Lucy at the head of the stairs as Lucy welcomed the stream of guests and introduced Tamsyn. He noted with wry appreciation how, while she spoke English fluently, she adopted an exaggerated Spanish accent that made her seem even more exotic and foreign than she appeared. And he saw how the young men gathered around her, laughing uproariously at her every conversational sally, gazing with rapt admiration into her glowing face. And the older men, taking advantage of the license of age, touched her arm and patted her hand, and she smiled up at them and flirted with an innocent charm that clearly entranced them.

It was an amazing performance, Julian thought. No one looking at her now would credit the fierce, lean warrior that he'd first met; or the indomitable fury of Badajos; or the weary, blackened powder monkey on the decks of the *Isabelle*. All those characters were his, he thought, with an overpowering surge of longing in the maelstrom of his confusion. This consummate performer belonged to the room. She was acting a part and only he knew it.

But the essential Tamsyn belonged only to him. And he wanted to leap forward, sweep her out of that circle of besotted, spotty youths, and proclaim his possession to the world.

Madness. Utter madness. He was as seduced by her performance as the rest of the room. He knew what she was. An illegitimate, half-breed brigand without a scruple to her soul or an ethical bone in her body.

"Amazing likeness, isn't it?" a voice quavered at his elbow.

He snapped out of his reverie and turned with a polite smile to the ancient lady beside him, bent double over a silver-topped cane. "Lady Gunston, how are you?"

"At ninety-six, young man, one doesn't answer such a question," she said with a cackle of laughter. "Help me to a chair and procure me a glass of negus; I can't think where that ninny has disappeared to."

Julian obeyed with a smile. Letitia Gunston was a local institution. She never refused an invitation, and her long-suffering companion, almost as old as she was, bore the social round with almost as much fortitude as she endured her employer's acerbic and continual complaints.

"Here you are, ma'am." He handed her the negus and sat down beside her. "I added a little extra wine, knowing how you like to taste it."

Lady Gunston cackled again and took a critical sip of the sweetened flavored wine and hot water. "I've had worse." She nodded and allowed her rheumy eyes to wander around the room again. "Quite an astonishing resemblance, don't you think?"

"Who, ma'am?" He leaned closer to catch the thin voice.

"That gal." She gestured with her stick across the room. "Haven't seen her before. But she's the spitting image of Celia."

"I don't follow you, ma'am." Julian's blood seemed to slow.

She turned to look at him. "No, of course not. Celia died when you were still in short coats, I should imagine. Lovely gal, she was, but a mite too lively for propriety. Never knew what she'd be up to next." She laughed, coughed vigorously, and took another hearty swallow of negus.

"Celia who, ma'am?" He was very cold, his entire body suspended, waiting for the information he knew was coming . . . the information that would bring his adventure with a brigand to a close.

"Why, Penhallan, of course. Celia Penhallan, she was. Died of some fever in Scotland." Lady Gunston nodded her head again, peering across the room to where Tamsyn was dancing with some young scion of local nobility. "The hair's the thing," she mused, her voice dropping so Julian had to lean even closer to catch her words. "Never seen hair that color before. Can't see her eyes, though."

"Violet," Julian said, his voice seeming to come from a great distance.

"Ah, yes, they would be." The old woman smiled, toothless and smug. "Celia had violet eyes." Her head jerked suddenly, and she said, "Fetch that ninny of mine, young man. It's time I went home."

Julian went in search of Miss Winston. He was moving through a void, his mind numb. He saw the old lady to her old-fashioned berlin. The liveried footman half lifted her inside, little Miss Winston weighed down with an armful of cloaks and spare reticules struggling up behind her. The driver touched his cocked hat, cracked his whip, and the cumbersome vehicle lurched down the driveway.

Julian stood in the doorway, listening to the strains of music, the muted voices, an occasional burst of laughter wafting from the rooms behind him. Lucy had surpassed herself, he thought distantly. If this was her idea of a small reception, he dreaded to think what she'd do with a proper ball.

Celia Penhallan. Cecile. But how did Celia Penhallan become Cecile, the mate of a Spanish robber baron? How did a death in Scotland square with an abduction in the Pyrenees?

Cedric Penhallan presumably would know the answer.

He walked out on the driveway and turned to the side of the house, heading for the dark seclusion of the orchard. His absence wouldn't be noticed for a while in the crush inside, and he couldn't face returning to the social inanities, the fatuous smiles, the mindless chatter. Not until he'd cleared his head.

Penhallan blood ran in her veins. The blue blood of one of the greatest families in the land. But it was bad blood. Tainted with the ruthless ambition of the viscount and the vile and vicious antics of the twins.

God in heaven! In those delicate blue veins so clearly visible beneath the white skin of her wrists, the blood of an outlaw mingled with the blood of a tyrant. He thought of the way she stood, the arrogant tilt of her chin, the way her eyes flared if she was challenged, the set of her mouth if it looked as if she wasn't going to get her way. Penhallan traits, every one. And the ruthless determination, the blind pushing for her own goals, the way she swept all obstacles from her path.

But Cedric Penhallan would never acknowledge her, even if her claim was cast iron. Not only would his personal pride never permit him to acknowledge a relationship with such a creature from such a wildly impossible background, but if he accepted her claim of kinship, he'd have to explain publicly that the death and the burial and the ceremonious mourning for his sister had all been a sham. And why, in the name of grace, had he perpetrated that hoax? Knowing Cedric, to avoid some scandal. Perhaps Cecile . . . Celia . . . had run away from home. Had fled to Spain to escape her brother's long reach, and Cedric had simply concocted an explanation for the public domain. It made perfect sense.

Julian's head felt as if it were going to burst. He loathed the Penhallans and everything associated with them. Twenty years ago Cedric had manipulated the lives of those around him for his own purposes, and Tamsyn was the unforeseen product.

And that unforeseen product was beginning to raise Cain with his own view of his world and all his preconceived ideas of the future of Lord St. Simon of Tregarthan. In some perverse fashion he was caught up in a web of Penhallan spinning, and that old manipulation was now at work on his own life.

He faced it clearly, but it did nothing to clarify his present turmoil. It was inconceivable that he should make a life with Tamsyn, and yet he found he couldn't formulate the thought of leaving her. He couldn't imagine what it would be like now to live his life without her.

And should he tell her what he'd discovered? Would

it do her any good to know? Cedric Penhallan would laugh in her face, destroying that eager dream to discover a family who would make up for the loss of her own.

While Julian was walking through the orchard, Cedric Penhallan drove up to Tregarthan. He was deliberately late, and his hostess had left her post at the head of the stairs long before he strolled up them.

He paused at the double doors standing open onto the main salon thronged with brightly clad women like so many butterflies and their more somberly dressed escorts. The musicians were playing a waltz, and he saw Celia's daughter immediately, twirling gracefully in the hold of a young man in scarlet regimentals.

Cedric remained standing in the door, fixing his gaze on the slight figure. Celia had worn those colors, he remembered. And she too had danced with that lively grace.

"Lord Penhallan, we're honored." Lucy hurried across the room toward him, sounding breathless and startled. Her eyes darted in search of Julian, who surely should be there to greet this important guest, but there was no sign of her brother. She bowed and shook hands with the viscount.

"May I procure you a glass of wine . . . Oh, Gareth." With relief she saw her husband a few paces away. "Gareth, here is Lord Penhallan."

Gareth too looked for his brother-in-law. He didn't feel in the least competent to deal with a man who moved in lofty circles far out of his own orbit, and who was gazing at him with a look of derision from beneath his bushy gray eyebrows. But he searched manfully for a suitable topic of conversation and asked his lordship about his stud.

Tamsyn had felt her uncle's arrival, just as she'd felt his eyes on her. As the music died, she smiled at her partner and excused herself, refusing his eager offer to accompany her into the supper room.

She walked steadily across the floor. Cedric's eyes met hers as she approached.

"Oh," Lucy said, relieved at the diversion. "Permit me to introduce Lord Penhallan, Tamsyn. Viscount, this is my brother's ward, Señorita Baron. She's come to us from Spain, the Duke—"

"Yes, I have heard the story," Cedric interrupted rudely. "It's common knowledge in the neighborhood."

"Of course, how stupid of me," Lucy murmured, flushing.

Cedric made a briefly dismissive gesture and said, "How do you do, Miss Baron?"

"Well, I thank you, *señor.*" She smiled sweetly as she bowed. "It is an honor to meet you." Her hand fluttered toward the locket at her neck before she said, "Please excuse me, I have promised this dance, and I see my partner waiting."

She walked off without a backward glance, but the hairs on the nape of her neck stood up as she felt his eyes on her back and the force of that speculative, menacing gaze swept over her.

Lord Penhallan watched her for a minute; then he said shortly, breaking into Gareth's elaborate recitation of a race he'd seen at Newmarket, "Good night, Lady Fortescue." His massive bulk spun with extraordinary agility, and he was gone.

"Well!" Lucy said, outraged. "What a horrible man! How could he be so rude? What did he come for if he was going to leave the minute he arrived?"

"No telling," Gareth said. "But the Penhallans are all toplofty . . . think they're too good for everyone else."

"Not a St. Simon," Lucy said, drawing herself up to her full height. "St. Simons are as good as Penhallans in anyone's book."

"Yes, I daresay," Gareth said soothingly. "But Lord Penhallan is mighty powerful in the government. It's said the prime minister never makes a move without his approval."

"Well, I think he's detestable. Thank goodness he's gone." On which note Lucy went off to ensure that the tables in the supper room were being replenished.

Julian reentered the house through a side door and thus missed Viscount Penhallan's brief visit. He glanced into the salon. The company was thinning, but Tamsyn was still dancing. He crossed the floor and lightly tapped her partner on the shoulder. "Forgive me, but I'd like to claim a guardian's privilege, Jamie."

The young man relinquished his lady with a jerky bow and went to lean disconsolately against the wall.

"Are you enjoying yourself?"

"Oh, yes," Tamsyn said, but she sounded distracted, and he could feel the tension in her body as he turned her on the floor. There was an almost febrile glitter to her eyes, and her skin was flushed.

"How much wine have you had?" he asked, steering her off the floor.

"A glass, no more."

"It must be excitement, then." Smiling, he took his handkerchief and wiped her damp brow.

"It is my first party since I was seven," she said with an answering smile, but the attempt at mocking humor lacked conviction.

"I'm going to London in the morning," he said abruptly, realizing as he said it that he'd only just decided what to do.

"Oh?" She looked at him, and her dismay was a clarion call. "Why?"

"I have Wellington's business to see to."

"But you weren't going for another two weeks." She nibbled her bottom lip, frowning. "Why so sudden, Julian?" There was a look in his eye that filled her with a deep apprehension. He looked like a man steeling himself to jump off a cliff.

He didn't immediately reply but drew her backward into a deep window embrasure. His voice was low and grave. "Come back to Spain with me, Tamsyn."

Whatever she'd been expecting, it hadn't been that. "Now?"

"Yes." He brushed a wisp of hair from her brow. "Come back with me and we'll go campaigning together. And we'll stay together and enjoy each other until it's over."

Until it's over. Her heart wept at the finality of the words and the closed mind of the man who couldn't embrace a future with the woman who loved him because she didn't fit the right mold.

"But I haven't done what I came here to do," she said quietly.

"Does it really mean that much to you, Tamsyn? What kind of life would you have in England, even supposing you found your mother's family and persuaded them to accept you? This isn't right for you, you know it isn't." He gestured to the emptying room, where the musicians still played, though desultorily now. "Let's go back to Spain. We can be together there in a way we can't here."

"Do you care for me?" Her voice was small, her face as pale now as it had been flushed before.

"You know I do," he said, touching a finger to her lips. "That's why I'm asking you to do this."

"But we have no future together? No *real* future?"

His silence was answer enough.

"I suppose not," she said dully, answering her own question. "A St. Simon could never have a future with an illegitimate brigand. I know that." She tried to smile but her lip quivered.

"That sounds so harsh," he said helplessly.

"The truth often is." She stepped backward and her eyes focused, the sheen of tears vanishing as anger and pride abruptly came to her aid. She would not permit this man to look down upon her, to decide she was not good enough for him. The daughter of El Baron and Cecile Penhallan had no need to stoop to placate and beg a St. Simon. "No, I can't come back with you. I will do what I came here to do. But I absolve you from the contract, milord colonel, since you can no longer see your way to honoring it."

She was pure Penhallan now, cold and arrogant, and he fought his own surge of anger at her insolence.

He bowed stiffly. "Of course, you may stay at Tregarthan for as long as you wish. Lucy will continue to sponsor you, I'm sure. I believe you'll find her a more appropriate sponsor than myself, anyway."

Appropriate! What had that to do with anything? She turned from him with a curt gesture of farewell, her mouth hard, her jaw set. "I bid you Godspeed, Colonel, and a safe journey."

He stood there in the embrasure as she walked away, across the nearly deserted salon, and out of the room. Silently, he cursed his own stupidity in making the offer that he'd known she wouldn't accept. He had made it partly for himself, but also partly for her, a desperate attempt to prevent her from discovering who she was and the inevitable hurt that would follow when Cedric Penhallan laughed her from his door.

But it was done now, and he wouldn't wait until the morning to set off for London. If he left just before daybreak, he would reach Bodmin in time to break his fast, and he could cross the moor in daylight.

Tamsyn went up to her tower room without a word to anyone. Josefa was waiting for her, dozing in a low chair by the fireplace. She sprang up full of eager inquiry as her nurseling entered, but her eagerness changed to a cry of distress as she saw the girl's face.

"I don't wish to talk of it tonight," Tamsyn said. "Go to bed now, and in the morning we'll talk, the three of us."

Josefa left reluctantly, but she knew the tone—she'd heard it often enough from the baron, and one didn't argue with it.

Tamsyn shivered as a sudden gust of wind blew through the open window. She could hear the surf pounding on the beach as the wind rose. Hugging her breasts, she went to the window. Clouds scudded across the moon in an ever-thickening band, and the soft sea breeze had suddenly changed into a cold, damp wind. The glorious spell of summer weather seemed to be breaking.

She could hear the voices from the driveway as carriages were called for and the last of the guests left, hurrying now to get home before the weather turned.

Tamsyn didn't know how long she stood at the window, watching the storm clouds gather, feeling the increasing sharpness of the wind as it rattled the panes of the open window and set the curtains swirling about her immobile figure. The first drops of rain woke her from her reverie. She closed the window, drew the curtains to shut out the now unfriendly night, and undressed, her mind working furiously, finally overcoming the paralysis of shock.

She hadn't expected Julian to bring everything to a close so abruptly. If only it hadn't come on the heels of her encounter with Cedric, she knew she would have responded differently. But she'd been too absorbed in the encounter that had opened the game of vengeance to think clearly, to respond intelligently to anything outside her immediate preoccupation. Cedric had known who she was—the recognition had been clear in his gaze as he had picked up the glove she'd thrown at his feet. She had wanted to play with him a little, let him see her moving comfortably in this society, let him wonder what she intended, wonder about her history. And Julian had blundered into her excitement, dropping a bombshell into her carefully constructed scheme, throwing all her plans awry. So instead of analyzing his proposal, working out how it could bring them closer together, she'd heard only the words and reacted with blind emotion. And blind emotion was an indulgence she could not afford. Not in her schemes of vengeance, and not in her schemes of love.

She climbed into bed, pulling the bedclothes up to her chin.

If Julian was going back to Spain, then she would go with him. Half a loaf was better than none, and half a loaf could grow.

Rolling over, she blew out her candle and lay in the darkness, listening to the rain now beating heavily on the window. The crash of the surf could be heard clearly above the rain, and the night grew ever wilder.

She loved him, loved him as Cecile had loved the baron. The only love of her life . . . a love for all life. And if he could only offer her half of himself, then for now she would take that. But she had to tell him so. And then she had to deal with Cedric. But in the light of this new scheme, how was she to do that?

An answer would come to her in the morning. As soon as she'd rested and was calm again, she would tell Julian that she'd changed her mind.

The storm abated just before daybreak, and in the damp chill Julian swung onto Soult, his portmanteau strapped to the saddle behind him. The sky was gunmetal-gray, the sea dark, the lawns sodden, the gravel of the par-terres studded with puddles. He glanced upward at the east tower, at the ivy-garlanded window overlooking the drive. Then he turned his face north and cantered down the drive.

Tamsyn, hollow-eyed after a sleepless night, stood at the window and stared into the rain-dark morning as Julian rode away. Had he gone so soon? How could he be so perverse as not to know that she would change her mind once her temper had died down?

She moved in a whirlwind, racing out of her room, down the back stairs, out into the stableyard, and up the stairs to Josefa and Gabriel.

"Och, little girl, steady now," Gabriel said, leaping from his bed as she came in, her eyes wild. "Tell me, now." He wrapped his arms around her and held her tightly against his barrel chest so that she couldn't have spoken if she'd wished to.

But at last she was able to tell them what had happened. "I have to go after him," she said simply, sitting on the end of their bed, her hands twisting in her lap. "I love him . . . it's like Cecile and the baron, it's something I can't do anything about. It *hurts*." She looked between them. Josefa's eyes were bright and sharp and Gabriel pulled at his chin.

Slowly, he nodded. "Then we'd best be on our way. Josefa will stay here. She'll no' relish charging around the countryside riding pillion behind me." He glanced at the woman, who nodded phlegmatically. It wouldn't be the first time she'd waited behind while they'd gone off on some campaign or another.

"I'll tell Lucy that we have some vital business in Penzance and we'll be back in a week or two."

"You're coming back for the Penhallan, then?"

Tamsyn looked at him in helpless uncertainty. "Yes, I must. I promised the baron . . . and Cecile . . . in my mind, I did. But I don't know anymore, Gabriel. I don't know what will happen."

"Och, aye, dinna fash yourself, bairn. What will be will be," he said comfortably. "I should go and ask Miss Lucy for the direction to the colonel's house in London. Best we know where to find him."

Tamsyn flung her arms around his neck. "What would I do without you . . . without you both?" Tearfully, she hugged Josefa, who had been calmly dressing herself all the while.

"We should pack some clothes," the woman said, patting her back. "It's not seemly to make such a journey without clean drawers."

"No, Josefa," Tamsyn said meekly, allowing herself to be hustled out of the loft room and into the dank morning, hearing Gabriel's low, reassuring chuckle behind her.

Chapter Twenty-two

THE HOUSE ON AUDLEY SQUARE HAD A SMALL GARDEN AT the back, reached through a gate from the mews. Lucy had said that her brother's book room opened onto the garden.

Tamsyn sat in the railed garden in the center of Audley Square as dusk fell, waiting for Gabriel to return from his reconnaissance. She was pleasantly weary after five days of riding close to fifty miles a day. Their horses were now stabled in a coaching inn near Charing Cross, where Gabriel would also stay that night, while Tamsyn sprang her surprise on the colonel.

She hoped a pleasant surprise.

She could, of course, walk up to the front door and bang the knocker, but she had a taste for something a little more dramatic, something in keeping with the shocking abruptness of Julian's departure.

The click of the gate made her jump, and she realized how very nervous she was—as apprehensive as if the man she was intending to suprise was a stranger—someone whose reactions she couldn't predict—instead of a man whose life and bed she had been sharing for the last four months.

Gabriel's boots scrunched on the gravel path winding

through privet hedges to the middle of the garden where Tamsyn sat on a stone bench.

"Well, it seems simple enough," he said without preamble, sitting beside her. "The gate from the mews is locked, but I can put you over it without difficulty. The colonel's book room has two windows, both low, easy for you to hitch yourself up without my help."

"Not open, I suppose."

"They might be. If they're not, you'll have to break one of the panes. You can do it easy enough with a stone wrapped in cloth. It shouldn't make too much racket."

"Unless the colonel's in the room," she mused. "If he is, then I can simply knock on the window."

"You wouldn't consider the door, I suppose," Gabriel remarked mildly. "Seems so much simpler."

Tamsyn smiled. "Simpler but a lot less amusing."

"Aye, I daresay. And I suppose it'll be less amusing in broad daylight, too."

"Yes," she agreed. "So let's get some supper and come back when it's full dark . . . about ten o'clock."

They ate in a dingy chop house in Piccadilly, and Tamsyn drank several glasses of porter, trying to quiet the little devils of anxious excitement dancing in her belly. She couldn't understand why she should be so nervous. She knew the man; she knew his body almost as well as she knew her own; she knew his moods and the way the light changed in his eyes; she knew what it meant when he held his body in a certain fashion, when his mouth quirked, when those mobile red-gold eyebrows twitched and his eyelids drooped lazily, half concealing the bright-blue eyes.

And she knew his anger. But why would he be angry? She was simply here to tell him she'd changed her mind, and she was ready to go back to Spain with him . . . ready to accept the limited liaison that was all he thought he could offer.

Gabriel said little, concentrating on his mutton chops and wine, but his mild gray eyes were sharply assessing. He wasn't at all sure about the wisdom of this enterprise, and if the truth were told, he wished Colonel, Lord St. Simon to the devil. Tamsyn may have decided she'd found the love of her life, but he could wish she'd settled on someone easier to handle and more conveniently situated than this uncompromising English lord.

If the English lord hadn't turned up, Tamsyn would have found some man like the baron, and they'd all be living contentedly in the mountains, doing what they were good at.

And pigs might fly, Gabriel thought with a dour smile.

"Let's get on with it, lassie." He pushed back his chair. "You're fretting yourself into a frazzle."

"No, I'm not," Tamsyn denied, but she couldn't hide her relief that the waiting was over. "You'll wait in the mews until I'm in the house?"

"I'll wait until you let me know I can seek my bed," he asserted.

They walked briskly and in silence back to Audley Square. St. Simon's house was lit up, and a lantern hung over the front door. "Perhaps he has visitors," Tamsyn said, the possibility occurring for the first time.

"Once you're in the house, you can wait until they leave," Gabriel said calmly. "If there's only a skeleton staff, you should be able to dodge them, and you've a decent plan of the house."

"Yes." Tamsyn slipped her hand into the pocket of her britches. Lucy had said that Julian kept a very small caretaking staff in the London house because it was used so rarely. It had been very easy to engage her in a casual discussion of the house, and with very little prompting she'd sketched a floor plan to illustrate her description. The paper now crackled reassuringly against Tamsyn's fingers. If Julian was not alone, or wasn't in the house, then she could make her way upstairs and into his bed-chamber.

The mews was quiet, only the soft shufflings and whickers from the horses bedded down for the night. The night was overcast, but a lamp glowing in a round window above the stable block where the head groom lived threw a puddle of golden light on the clean-swept cobbles. Tamsyn and Gabriel slipped soundlessly through the shadows, Tamsyn's bright head covered by the hood of her dark cloak pulled tight around her.

The gate into the garden was locked as Gabriel had expected. "Up you go." He lifted Tamsyn easily, setting her atop the gate.

She dropped from sight immediately, then whispered from the other side, "There are lamps lit in the book room."

"Buena suerte," Gabriel whispered back, and stepped into the shadows.

Tamsyn crept around the edge of the walled garden, once catching her cloak on a thorn from an espaliered climbing rose. She stopped and painstakingly pulled out the thorn, flattening herself against the wall beside the rose. Light poured from the windows of the book room, illuminating neat flower beds and a square of lawn, and she prayed the shadow of the wall was sufficient con-cealment if anyone was looking from an upstairs win-dow.

Free again, she flitted forward until she was pressed against the wall beside the lighted window. It was closed but the curtains were open. She sidled sideways until she could peer into the room. Her heart was thudding and her palms were slippery, but she couldn't decide whether it was nerves or excitement.

Julian was sitting at a desk with his back to the window. He was writing, his pen flowing over the parchment. As she watched, her heart in her throat, he paused, leaned back in the chair, and stretched, arching his neck; then he dipped his quill into the inkwell again and resumed writing. Her blood seemed to speed through her veins as she watched him in his absorption, imagining his face when he turned and saw her. He *would* be delighted . . . of course he would.

Tamsyn scratched on the window, then stepped back into the shadows.

Julian was preparing a report to present to the prime minister in the morning. Lord Liverpool had asked for yet more information on the action and casualties of Ciudad Rodrigo and Badajos to bolster the Peer's request for more men and more money.

At the first scratching sound he glanced over his shoulder at the window. A branch tapping against the pane, presumably. Wearily, he rubbed his eyes. He was finding it difficult to concentrate, and he couldn't seem to connect with the words he was writing. He kept hearing Tamsyn's sensual chuckle in his head, and her smile, mischievously inviting, hung disembodied in his mind's eye. He supposed the images would fade in time. Once he got back to Spain, he wouldn't have time to think about her. But even as he told himself that, he knew that in Spain it would be even harder to forget her. The memories would be even more achingly vivid in the land that had produced that extraordinary, impossible creature, with her Penhallan blood and . . .

Frowning, he squeezed the back of his neck, trying to massage a crick; then resolutely he returned to his report.

The scratching came again, more insistent this time. He ignored it. Then it changed to a drumming, a rhythmic tap-tap-tap. He spun round in his chair. There was nothing at the window. Impatiently, he pushed back his chair and went over to the window, flinging it wide. There were no bushes or trees near enough for an errant twig to be scratching the pane. He stared into the garden but could see nothing.

Then an unmistakable voice said from somewhere below him, "Good evening, milord colonel."

He dropped his gaze to below the level of the windowsill. Her eyes gleamed purple in her pale face, the hood of her cloak had fallen back, and her silver hair was a beacon in the shadow of the wall.

"I was beginning to think you'd never come to the window," she said when he seemed dumbstruck. Turning her back, she reached up to rest her hands on the broad sill, then jumped her backside up. Turning in the window, she smiled, and if he'd been less stunned, he would have read the anxiety behind the smile. "Aren't you going to say anything?"

"You . . . you imp of *Satan*!" He found his voice. "How the *hell* did you get here?" Catching her around the waist beneath the cloak, he lifted her off the windowsill into the room, but instead of setting her on her feet, he held her up as easily as if she were a rag doll, his large hands spanning her waist, her face on a level with his. Her cloak fell to the floor, revealing the britches and shirt of the brigand.

"On Cesar, of course," she said, smiling.

"Don't play games, girl!" He shook her as he held

her off the ground, but she couldn't tell whether he was really annoyed or still just surprised. Either way, though, he didn't seem overjoyed to see her.

"I had to come," she said. "You went off without a word and—"

"I was under the impression we'd had all the words necessary," he interrupted flatly. "You'd made it very clear—"

"Yes, but you took me by surprise," Tamsyn protested, still dangling from his hands. "How was I to know you would just waltz off into the night without a backward glance?" She tried an experimental kick to encourage him to put her down, but it didn't seem to have any effect.

"Oh?" A red-gold eyebrow lifted. "So that little exchange in the salon was merely an opening skirmish? You tell me with that goddamned arrogance of yours that you want no more to do with me, and I'm supposed to interpret that as an invitation?"

"It wasn't quite like that," she said, her voice low. "You were the one bringing everything to a close, not me."

"I thought I was suggesting the opposite," he replied quietly, his gaze fixed steadily on her face.

This wasn't getting them anywhere. He was still holding her as if she were a scarecrow stuffed with straw, and she was damned if he was going to put her in the wrong when it was as plain as day to anyone with eyes open that *he* was the one causing the difficulties. He was the one who couldn't see straight.

"You talk about *my* arrogance. Well I tell you, Colonel, that you're stubborn and stiff-necked and twice as arrogant as I am!" she snapped.

To her fury tears suddenly clogged her voice and

filled her eyes. She wanted to say she loved him, but the words wouldn't come. She wanted to tell him that he loved her, he had to love her, because she couldn't feel the way she did if he didn't feel the same.

"You," Julian said deliberately, "are a stubborn, spoiled, manipulative siren." He thought he'd accepted that the adventure was over, that she would leave his life as decisively as she'd entered it, but now he knew that he hadn't accepted anything of the kind.

"Well, I'm sorry I came, then," Tamsyn declared, sniffing crossly. "And if you'll put me down, I'll go away again."

"No, you will not, you lawless hellion!" The wonderful, familiar urgency of passion was sweeping through him as he held her, feeling the lissome slenderness in his hands, inhaling the honeysuckle fragrance of her skin, losing himself in the great drowned pools of her eyes. And now as he held her and the silence became charged, he felt that seductive energy pulsing from her, and he realized that, as always, she'd caught his arousal and without volition was responding with her own. Her eyes were luminous, the long lashes dark and sticky with unshed tears, her lips now slightly parted as she acknowledged what was happening and waited for him to move.

"Never let it be said I looked a gift horse in the mouth." With a deft twist he tucked her under his arm, as he'd done in Badajos, and strode out of the room with her.

He marched up the stairs, and Tamsyn, keeping very still, could only be thankful that they met no member of the household. Julian opened the door of his bedroom, stalked in, and dropped his bundle onto the bed.

He stood looking down at her, his hands resting

lightly on his hips, a smile playing over the well-shaped mouth.

"Irresistible," he said in a musing tone. "I don't understand why such a scrawny, ill-schooled, unprincipled little manipulator should be irresistible. But it seems to be the case."

Tamsyn's eyes narrowed seductively, but she said nothing. She'd done enough pushing and plotting and arranging for the moment. Maybe the time would come when he would no longer resist what was happening between them, would no longer believe that the currents flowing between them were only and ephemerally sexual . . . would look into his own heart. But until then she'd settle for what she had, and "irresistible" was a good start.

She heeled and toed her boots, and they fell with a soft thud on the Aubusson carpet.

Her hands went to the buttons of her britches. With a deft wriggle she pushed them off her hips, then eased them down her legs with her heels.

Julian bent and helpfully yanked them over her feet. While he was there, he pulled off her stockings, then straightened to resume the voyeur role.

"Must I do this all on my own?" She offered a mock plaintive smile.

"Yes." His eyelids drooped, lazily seductive, and he remained immobile, hands back on his hips, looking down at her.

Tamsyn squiggled out of her drawers, unbuttoned her shirt, and stripped it off; then she lay naked on the coverlet and regarded him quizzically.

"And now you may help me," Julian directed, his cool voice quite at odds with the fire in his eyes.

Tamsyn sat up on the bed, placed her hands on his

hips, and drew him close to her. She unbuckled his belt with deft efficiency, letting it drop to the floor. "You don't mind if I start here?" she said conversationally as she unbuttoned his britches.

"Not in the least."

She eased his britches over his hips with a slow delicacy that Julian found as arousing as Tamsyn did. Her fingers stroked over his hipbones, her palm flattened against his belly, and his muscles jumped involuntarily. Slowly, her hand slid over his stomach and between his thighs as she bent and kissed his belly, drawing her tongue upward in a moist, searing stroke, darting into his navel as her fingers stroked and kneaded, until he groaned softly. Reaching behind, her fingertips dug into the taut muscles of his buttocks as she reached against him so that the hard shaft of flesh lay between her breasts.

Softly she brought her hands round to cup her breasts, squeezing them as they cradled his throbbing stem. Julian's breath quickened; the exquisite rhythmic friction increased, and he threw his head back with a low groan of pleasure. "Stop," he whispered. "For pity's sake, stop now."

Tamsyn merely smiled, her eyelashes fluttering wickedly against his chest as she brought him closer and closer to the brink until he shuddered and ecstasy bubbled hot in his veins as the world dissolved.

"Diablillo," he chided as his breathing slowed, his eyes, hooded and languorous with fulfillment, gazed down at her upturned face. "You have only yourself to blame."

"I've noticed you have a quick recovery time, milord colonel," she said with an impudent grin, falling back on the bed, pulling him with her.

He kissed her with rough satisfaction, pinching her jaw between finger and thumb. "I don't know what you deserve."

"Neither do I, but I don't mind just so long as I get it."

"Oh, you will," he promised, taking her mouth again, but this time with a long, slow exploration, his tongue flickering over her lips.

"Oh! Oh, I forgot. How could I have forgotten!" With shocking suddenness Tamsyn pulled her face away from him and pushed at his chest, struggling to get off the bed. "This room's at the back of the house, isn't it?"

Julian rolled over onto his back, unsure whether he wanted to laugh or scream. "Gabriel, I suppose?"

"Yes, he's waiting outside in the mews." She flew to the window, throwing it wide.

"Tell him to come in," Julian said with a sigh.

"No, he has to go back to Charing Cross to look after the horses." She leaned out of the window, cupped her hands around her mouth, and produced a perfect imitation of a barn owl, waited a few seconds, and then repeated the sound. It was answered immediately. Tamsyn produced another series of birdcalls, pausing for a response.

Charing Cross? Why Charing Cross? But then again, why not? There was no point examining the finer points of Tamsyn's convoluted schemes. Gabriel's participation, of course, was inevitable.

Amused and impressed by the unusual colloquy at the window, Julian hitched himself onto his elbows. He gazed at her naked back curved in the open window and lost interest in the conversation. She did have the most entrancing backside, he thought dreamily.

"There." Tamsyn straightened. "That's all settled, then."

"Good. Then perhaps you'd like to get back here," he requested in a tone of ironic courtesy.

"Oh, have you recovered?" She turned with a grin.

"I anticipate a full recovery in about two minutes. Now, *get the hell over here!*"

Tamsyn hopped across the room and leaped onto the bed beside him. "Yes, milord colonel. Anything you say, milord colonel."

Chapter Twenty-three

Tamsyn was still asleep when Julian awoke in the morning. It was raining outside, and the room was dark, the general gloom exacerbated by the massive oak furniture and the heavy velvet hangings. The house was badly in need of redecorating, but he'd always assumed that it could wait until he married. A wife would enjoy putting her own mark on the place, much easier to do than at Tregarthan, which bore the unmistakable imprint of four generations of St. Simons.

He'd spent so little time in London in the last few years that the general air of neglect in Audley Square hadn't troubled him unduly, but now it occurred to him that he probably ought to tackle the issue before the deterioration became too bad. The prospect of his marriage was way in the future, something he couldn't contemplate until Napoleon was finally defeated.

He turned his head on the pillow to look at the sleeping face beside him. At some point he was going to have to find himself a wife, but he could not get away from the rueful knowledge that drifting in this diminutive bandit's anarchic, sensual wonderland was in a fair way to spoiling him for the kind of woman who would make an exemplary Lady St. Simon of Tregarthan.

His memories of the night remained sharply vivid both in his body and in his mind. It was one of Tamsyn's talents that every lovemaking with her was somehow unique, had something special that lived on in delicious memory.

He sat up to look at the time. It was six, and he was to meet with Lord Liverpool at eight.

Tamsyn groaned and turned onto her stomach, burying her face in the pillows. "What are you doing?"

"Getting up." Bending, he kissed the back of her neck, and she wriggled at the tickling warmth of his breath. "Are you coming back to Spain with me, Tamsyn?"

"Why else do you think I'm here?" she mumbled into the pillow.

"And you'll give up the idea of finding your mother's family?" He stroked a finger down her spine.

Tamsyn lifted her head out of the pillow. "Why did you say it wasn't right for me to stay in Cornwall? I thought I was doing very well. People at the party seemed to think I fitted in all right."

"But you were playing a part. We both know that the person you really are doesn't have a place in that kind of life, Tamsyn. You would be bored to tears in a few weeks once the novelty had worn off."

"But I played the part well," she insisted.

"Yes, I grant you that."

Tamsyn dropped her head back into the pillow. He was right that it wasn't the ideal life for her, and she'd certainly never intended that it would be permanent. But she could learn to adapt in the right circumstances. At least Julian had admitted that she could fit in if she put her mind to it. It was a step in the right direction.

"And you've abandoned the idea of finding your mother's family?" he repeated.

"Yes," she said, reflecting that since she'd already found them, it was hardly a lie.

Relief was sweet. He ran his hand in a slow, stroking caress down her back beneath the covers. "Go back to sleep, buttercup." She moaned into the pillow but made no attempt to stop him when he slipped from the bed. He pulled the bed curtains tightly around her before ringing for shaving water.

Julian dressed rapidly in the scarlet tunic and fur pelisse of the cavalry officer, buckling on his sword belt, his curved sword snug against his hip. He was on army business, and his reflection in the mirror brought him deep satisfaction. It was good to be dressed again in this familiar way on an enterprise that was vital to the business that informed his life. He'd rather be on the battlefield, but soon he would be. They would go back together, and there would be no resentment, no anger, no sense of being used, to spoil the pleasure they took in and of each other.

Before he left, he drew aside the bed curtains. Tamsyn was asleep again, turned away from him, her cheek pillowed on her hand, her complexion delicately flushed with sleep. He stood for a minute looking down at her, unaware that he was smiling but aware that he was stirred by her yet again. But it wasn't the usual hot, racing blood of arousal he felt, it was something much softer.

He let the curtain fall again and left the room, closing the door quietly. Before leaving the house, he told the old retainer who managed the skeleton staff in the house that there was a young lady in his apartments who should be provided with whatever she asked for.

"Yes, my lord." The man bowed as he held open the front door. It wasn't the first time his lordship had entertained a bit of muslin in the London house, and doubtless it wouldn't be the last.

As soon as the door closed on Julian, Tamsyn sat up, not a sign of sleep in her eyes. She hadn't wanted to continue that conversation, and feigning sleep had seemed the easiest way to avoid it. If it could possibly be managed, her mother's family would never be mentioned between them again. If it was at all possible, the colonel should forget that her mother had had a family.

Tamsyn knew exactly what she had to do now. If Julian discovered the truth about the Penhallans and what had really brought her to England, then everything would be over. He would not be able to tolerate the thought of being a tool in such a deception, so he mustn't find out. But since she'd begun the game with Cedric, then she had to finish it in some way. She could no longer afford to expose his treachery, since that would mean revealing her own identity in public—but Cedric didn't know that, and the threat of it gave her a powerful weapon. If she played her cards right, she could come away with the Penhallan diamonds.

It would be a fitting restitution, one that Cecile and the baron would find pleasing. And once that was settled, she could return to Spain with the colonel and work to weave her future into his.

She sprang energetically out of bed, splashed her face with the rapidly cooling water in the ewer, borrowed Julian's tooth powder, used his comb, and dressed. Then she ran downstairs. Before she went back to Cornwall to tidy up the loose ends, she had a little plan for the colonel's entertainment, one that would throb and glow in his memory until she returned.

An elderly man was crossing the hall. He looked up and blinked rheumy eyes in astonishment as Tamsyn jumped from the bottom stair.

"Good morning, you must be Belton," she said with a cheerful smile. "Lady Fortescue told me how wonderfully well you manage this household."

Lady Fortescue! The old man stared, and Tamsyn could almost see the cogs turning in his brain as he tried to fit this astonishing britches-clad figure who'd spent the night in his lordship's bed with Lord St. Simon's sister.

"If Lord St. Simon returns before I do, will you tell him that I'll be back this afternoon?" she said blithely, going to the door.

"Yes, miss," he muttered, belatedly moving to open the door.

"That's all right, I can manage, thank you, Belton." Tamsyn pulled open the door. "Oh, it's raining again! What a poxy miserable climate this is." She pulled up the hood of her cloak, raised a hand in farewell to the dumbstruck servant. "Until this afternoon!" And she was gone, jumping down the three steps to the pavement and racing up the street, head down against the persistent drizzle.

Belton shook his head in bemusement, wondering if he was getting too old for his job. Had she really been dressed in britches? His lordship must have developed some strange tastes in Spain—a heathen land it was, or so they said. Closing the door, he tottered off to his pantry and the bottle of medicinal brandy he kept there for moments of stress.

Tamsyn hailed a hackney, directed him to the King's Head at Charing Cross, and sat back going over her plan. The rain was a damned nuisance with so many errands to run.

Gabriel was stolidly consuming a platter of eggs and sirloin in the taproom as she entered. "You're early," he observed.

"Yes, and I haven't had breakfast." She hitched a chair over with her toe and sat down. "Landlord, I'll have a plate just like this, please."

The landlord grunted. In the dim light he could see a lad sitting beside the giant Scotsman. He went into the kitchen, and a few minutes later a serving girl brought a second plate.

" 'Ere y'are, sir." She bobbed a curtsy, shooting Tamsyn an appraising look from beneath her eyelashes, clearly wondering whether the young man was worth cultivating.

Tamsyn grinned. She was accustomed to such mistakes when the light was bad. She leaned over and chucked the girl beneath the chin. "Here's a pretty lass. What's your name, then?"

"Annie, sir." The girl blushed and turned her head aside.

"Well, fetch me some coffee will you, Annie?"

"Aye, sir." She bobbed another curtsy and hurried off.

"Och, little girl, you ought to be ashamed of yourself," Gabriel said mildly, taking a draft of ale. "Teasing the child like that."

Tamsyn merely chuckled and attacked her breakfast with a voracious hunger.

"Things went all right, then," Gabriel observed. "Looks like you had a night to build up an appetite."

Tamsyn nodded, her eyes shining as she spread mustard on her sirloin. "We'll be going back to Spain soon."

"Good," he said laconically. "I'll be glad to shake the dust of this place off my feet. And so will the woman. But what of the Penhallan?"

"I think I have to let it go, Gabriel," she said, keeping her eyes on her plate. "Will you mind?"

His face darkened. "You do what you wish, but I intend to see to those gutter sweepings, lassie. But I'll do it in my own way and in my own time. It won't affect your plans."

Tamsyn was silent. She knew she couldn't stop him. For Gabriel it was a sacred obligation, and he'd feel the baron's eyes on him until it was done. But Gabriel's vengeance must not affect her own confrontation with Cedric, and for that reason she would face her uncle alone. Gabriel's temper was too uncertain, and if he came across the twins while he and Tamsyn were visiting with Cedric, there would be no way to prevent him from dealing with them on the spot. And then there would be witnesses to the inevitable bloody mess, and Cedric could lay charges, and Gabriel would probably end up on the scaffold in Bodmin jail.

But he would never permit her to go alone, if he had the faintest inkling of such an intention, so he must believe that her love for Julian St. Simon had superseded the need to exact her parents' vengeance.

"So we'll fetch the woman and be back to Spain, then?" Gabriel resumed, a slight frown in his eye.

Tamsyn nodded and took a gulp of coffee. "But not until the morning. I wish to give the colonel a little present first, something to remember while we're gone."

Gabriel raised an eyebrow. "Not something requiring my help, I assume."

Tamsyn smiled. "No, I don't think so, Gabriel."

"Then I'll bide here. Mine host has a decent enough cellar, and I daresay I'll find some congenial company."

"Well, will you come with Cesar to Audley Square at daybreak? I'll slip out through the window again and meet you in the mews. We'll ride back to Cornwall, collect our things, and come back with Josefa."

Gabriel nodded. Such an unorthodox departure didn't strike him as peculiar; it was the way they were accustomed to doing things in the mountains. However, something about this change of plan disturbed him. It wasn't in character for the bairn to abandon a mission with such insouciance.

Tamsyn wiped her plate clean with a hunk of bread, finished her coffee, and stood up. "I need to change and fetch some money, Gabriel."

He reached into his pocket for the key to his room. "Top of the stairs, on the left."

In the bedchamber Tamsyn changed into one of her cambric gowns and swapped her riding boots for a pair of jean half boots that wouldn't be nearly as effective in the rain and the puddles. She shoved her riding clothes into a cloak bag to take with her, put a billfold and a purse of coins into a reticule, examined herself in the spotted looking glass with a critical frown, then returned to the taproom, trying to remember not to stride.

Annie was clearing the table and nearly dropped the tray at the transformation. "Oooo," she said. "Yer not a bloke!"

"No," Tamsyn agreed. "But you're still a pretty lass."

"Oh, wha' a cheek," Annie said, bridling. "You got

no call to play games like that . . . takin' advantage of an innocent girl."

"I wasn't taking advantage," Tamsyn pointed out logically. "Since I'm not a man, how could I have been?"

Annie sniffed and returned to the kitchen with her tray.

Gabriel was still sitting at the table nursing a refilled tankard. "You're away, then?"

"Yes." She bent to kiss him. "I'll see you at daybreak."

"I'll be there."

Tamsyn raised a hand in farewell and went outside into the rain-swept gloom of London Town.

She returned to Audley Square in the early afternoon. Belton opened the door and found himself face-to-face with a conventionally dressed young lady. If it weren't for her distinctive hair, he would never have believed it was the same person who had left that morning. "Please, could you send someone to bring the parcels from the hackney?" she asked, just her eyes visible over the armful of packages she held.

"Let me take those, miss." Belton moved to relieve her of her burdens.

"No, no," Tamsyn said, afraid that the old man would drop them onto the wet steps. "But there's more in the coach."

Belton called over his shoulder, and a stalwart young man in a baize apron and leather britches emerged from the kitchen regions. He glanced curiously at the young woman clutching her packages, then went out to bring in the rest of her purchases.

"Has his lordship returned?"

"Not as yet, miss. I expect he's gone to one of his clubs. Usually does of a morning, when he's in town."

"Good." That suited Tamsyn. By the time Julian returned, she would be ready for him. She started up the stairs. "Have those packages brought up to his lordship's apartments please, Belton, and could you send up two wineglasses and a corkscrew?"

The stalwart young man trotted after her, his arms filled. "Put them on the couch," she instructed, dropping her own on the coverlet. "Thank you. And could you light the fire, please? It's such a miserable day." She waited as he raked ashes, laid kindling, and struck flint on tinder. The wood caught, a plume of fragrant smoke arose, and a flame shot up the chimney.

The lad carefully laid on logs, then stood up, wiping his hands on the seat of his britches just as a red-cheeked girl of about thirteen came in through the open door with the glasses and a corkscrew. She, too, couldn't hide her curiosity as she glanced covertly at his lordship's extraordinary visitor. A right little trollop, no better than she ought to be, old Mrs. Cogg in the kitchen had opined. Maisie had never before met someone who was better than she ought to be.

"Wonderful." Tamsyn offered a somewhat distracted smile as the lad departed with a jerky bow, followed by the girl; then she flew across the room and locked the door behind them. She stood tapping her front teeth with a fingertip. How long did she have?

It took fifteen minutes to lay out her carefully selected picnic. Vintage claret, dainty shrimp barquettes, smoked oysters, dressed crab, strawberry tarts, and fresh figs. Nothing that couldn't be eaten with the fingers.

The fire was crackling nicely now, the candles were lit, and the room, despite its oppressive furnishing, felt quite cozy. She threw off her gown, thrust it into a corner of the armoire together with her half boots, underclothes, and the cloak bag with her riding britches. Then she shook out the gown that had taken her hours to select. The blonde silk lace shimmered, soft and lustrous in the candlelight. She slipped it over her head, and the delicate material, the painstaking work of a dozen Chantilly-lace makers, caressed her naked body, as sensuous as a spring breeze.

She stepped up to the cheval glass and examined herself. The gown had cost a small fortune, but the effect was everything she'd aimed for. It was as demure and virginal as a bridal nightgown. The wide, exquisitely edged sleeves reached her elbows, drawing attention to her delicately rounded forearms and tiny wrists. Her neck rose slender and graceful as a swan's from three tiers of lace ruffles, and her almond-shaped eyes were huge and luminous, their deep violet startling against the creamy pallor of her face and gown, the silvery sheen of her hair.

Experimentally, she fastened a band of white velvet ribbon around her hair. The effect was astonishing. It accentuated the air of childlike innocence that was somehow not what it seemed.

Tamsyn turned slowly, examining herself in the mirror. Her bare feet peeped from the embroidered lace hem, and the material drifted down her body, the lace so fine that her skin glimmered beneath.

She felt as she had when she'd planned her Aladdin's cave, as seduced by the game as she knew Julian would be. Her loins were moistening, her nipples hardening, and her spine tingled.

She unlocked the door, cast one final look over the

inviting table, and curled up in a massive black-leather armchair beside the fire.

Julian, after a relatively satisfactory session with the prime minister, had repaired to Horseguards to see what old friends and colleagues he might usefully find, and then to the Admiralty to discover what ships were sailing to Lisbon in the next week. A frigate, escorting a convoy of merchant shipping, was due to set sail from Portsmouth under a Captain Marriot by the end of the following week, and it looked like the likeliest passage he would find. The captain would need to be officially informed that he'd have four passengers on the voyage, and Julian would need to get the requisite instructions from the appropriate admiral, but that wouldn't take more than a day or two.

Feeling very cheerful, Julian went back out into the drizzle, to where a damp urchin was holding Soult. The lad caught the sixpence with a cheeky grin as his lordship mounted, and ran off, biting the coin to test its mettle as if he couldn't believe the largesse.

Julian rode home, left his horse in the mews, and entered the garden through the gate. He glanced up at the window of his bedchamber. It was closed against the rain, but light shone warm and welcoming from within.

An involuntary smile crossed his eyes, and his heart jumped with pleasure at the thought that Tamsyn was waiting for him.

He entered the house through a side door and strode upstairs, encountering no one, which didn't surprise him. He never entertained at home and was so rarely in residence himself that Belton and Mrs. Cogg managed to run the house with the help of a lad for the heavy work, and a kitchen maid. Most of the rooms were kept under holland covers anyway.

He entered his bedroom and then stopped. Tamsyn was a tiny figure in shimmering pale lace framed against the heavy black leather of the armchair, swallowed somehow in its depth. Smiling, she uncurled herself and stood up.

"Have you had a trying day, milord colonel?" she said softly, coming toward him. "I've prepared a picnic for us."

He stared at her, his breath suspended. Dear God, she was wearing a ribbon in her hair! And the gown, so demure and yet so unutterably wicked. She looked as virginal, as innocent, as a child in the schoolroom, but her skin glowed in luminous promise beneath the material that stroked over her hips and outlined the soft swell of her breasts, the hard, dark tips of her nipples.

His head swam as she stepped closer to him and lifted her face in sweet demand for a kiss. Still speechless, he bent his head and kissed her lips.

"Will you take off your sword?" she said, stepping back before he could put his hands on her. "It's such an ugly, great thing and so unrestful."

Unrestful. This woman was the most unrestful he'd ever encountered! But her hands were unbuckling his sword belt, lifting it away from him with a grimace of effort. And it did look absurdly large and menacing beside her delicate fragility. *But she was neither delicate nor fragile!* He watched in bemusement as she placed the sword carefully in the corner of the room and turned back to him.

"May I help you with your boots?"

In the same trance he sat down in the chair she'd just vacated. With a little frown of concentration, she straddled his lap with her back to him and hauled on his left boot. The curve of her backside, opalescent beneath the spider's-web covering of the gown, was impossible to resist. He placed his palms on the damask globes, and the heat of her skin seared his hands.

"I'm trying to concentrate," Tamsyn said as the boot came off. "I have to do it like this so I don't get mud on my gown."

"I'm not objecting," he murmured, finally finding his voice as he smoothed the gossamer material tightly over her bottom. "I'm sure you're supposed to wear something underneath this."

"That rather depends on where one's wearing it," she said with a grunt of effort, falling back onto his lap, sitting on his hands as the second boot came off. "There." She tossed it to the floor to join its fellow. "Now, shall I take off your coat, and then I'll bring you a glass of wine and a smoked oyster."

"In a minute," he said.

"Of course," Tamsyn said meekly. "Whatever you wish to do is what I wish to do."

"Now I've heard everything," Julian observed, but he was smiling. Whatever game this was, it was one he was more than happy to play. He moved one hand to encircle her waist, holding her firmly in place, while his other hand slithered beneath her, the tips of his fingers inching into the cleft of her bottom until she wriggled with a little gasp. Finally he let her go. "I don't want to tear this gorgeous virginal garment . . . at least," he added, "not just yet. So you'd better get up."

Tamsyn slid off his knee, shaking down the gown. "Whatever you wish, my lord." She went to the table and poured wine into a glass. She brought it over together with a platter of smoked oysters and, with a shy smile, sat on his lap again. She held the wine to his lips, then began to feed him the oysters. "Do you like them?"

"Mmmm," he murmured with his mouth full, distracted by her slight weight on his thighs, the scent of her skin, the impossibly shy smile, the deceptive purity of the blonde lace. "I think I'm going to enjoy this game."

Her eyes widened in hurt innocence. "A game? This is no game, my lord. I wish only to please you. I wish to do whatever you wish me to do."

She held the wine up to his lips again, then took a sip herself, before placing the glass on the table beside the platter of oysters. She swiveled on his knee until she was nestled against his chest, her body curled against him.

She was like a small bird, her heart beating against his shirt front. Vulnerable, frail. And it didn't matter that he knew she was neither of those things. It didn't matter that he knew her to be a fierce and uncompromising, tempestuous bandit. For the moment she was all sweet innocence, and she was driving him wild.

She kissed the pulse in his throat, and her body shifted on his lap, an infinitesimal movement that nevertheless brought the blood surging into his loins. Her voice was musical as she murmured soft words of passion to him, weaving threads of enchantment around him, and it took him a minute to hear exactly what this innocent, fragile little creature was saying. There was nothing in the least sweet and virginal about the words; they were the hungry, earthy words of passion and need that riveted him with their brazen sensuality, shocked him to his core as they dropped from the soft lips of this shyly smiling girl.

"You siren," he whispered on a low throb of desire. She nibbled his lip, delicate little bites of the most exquisite sensuality, and her eyes were closed. Again she moved on his lap, but this time with more purpose so that she captured his erection between her thighs.

"Lift your skirt," he demanded, his voice now a rasp of need.

Obediently, she raised herself just enough to pull the lace up over her hips. Her fingers moved on his waistband and his aching flesh sprang free. He caught her waist and swiveled her on his lap so that her back was to him. He slid his hands beneath her bottom and lifted her just sufficiently to drive into the pulsing warmth of her belly.

Tamsyn drew breath at the power of his thrusting flesh, rocking her on her perch, pressing against her womb, impaling her with his pleasure. He held her buttocks with bruising fingers as the whirling conflagration caught her, swept her up, exploded in her belly so she thought she was flying apart, and she heard his cry against her back as he yielded himself to the fire.

Flame crackled in the hearth, a candle spurted. Julian slowly came back to the room. Tamsyn had fallen back against his chest, lying as weak and weightless as a wounded bird.

"Sorceress," he accused with a feeble chuckle when he could speak at all.

Tamsyn smiled weakly. "I can play many parts, milord colonel."

"Don't I know it." He kissed the top of her shining head. "And now I'd like you to feed me some more oysters."

"I am here only to serve you, my lord," she said demurely, sliding off his knee. "Your word is my command."

Julian stretched luxuriously, and a slow, lazy smile

played over his mouth. "I can think of many commands, buttercup. I foresee a long night."

It was a very long night, and Tamsyn had been asleep for barely half an hour when her internal clock woke her just before daybreak. Julian was deeply asleep, sprawled on his stomach beside her, his red-gold hair thick on the pillow.

She slid out of bed, barely disturbing the covers, and crept out of the bed hangings into the dark room. She was used to moving around at night, and her eyes accustomed themselves quickly to the darkness. The remnants of their picnic still sat on the table, and the heavy furniture was disarrayed. She smiled reminiscently as she dressed hastily in her riding britches. The colonel's commands had involved a fair degree of gymnastics on occasion.

She was ready in five minutes, then sat down at the secretaire to write him a note. Somehow she had to produce a convincing reason for sliding off in the night without telling him. Maybe he wouldn't have insisted on coming back to Cornwall with them . . . but he might have, and she didn't want him anywhere in the vicinity when she tidied up her loose ends with Cedric Penhallan.

Milord colonel:
We have to return to Cornwall to collect Josefa and the treasure, and Gabriel has something to do for himself. We'll return here two weeks from today. I know you have work to do in London, so I didn't want you to feel that you should have offered to come with us. Two weeks today, I shall be yours to command again. Besos.

She read it through quickly. It would have to do. If

he was vexed that she'd disappeared as abruptly as she'd arrived, then she would make it up to him when she returned. At least he would have something to remember in the meantime.

She rolled the paper and with a little smile tied it with the ivory velvet ribbon she'd had in her hair. Then she tiptoed back to the bed and placed it carefully on the pillow beside his head.

Julian mumbled in his sleep and turned onto his back, his arms flung wide. Tamsyn resisted the urge to push aside the unruly lock of hair and press her lips to his broad brow. He slept like a soldier, she knew, and the slightest touch would waken him.

She crept out of the room, hurried down the stairs in the silent house, into the book room at the rear. She flung up the low window, scrambled over the sill, and dropped to the soft, damp earth beneath.

Gabriel was waiting in the mews, holding Cesar's reins. He greeted her with a nod. "All well, bairn?"

"All's well." She sprang into the saddle. Five days should see them back at Tregarthan. Her confrontation with Cedric would take no more than an hour or two. The horses would need a day to rest. And then they would return, and she would concentrate all her forces on the bastion that was Colonel, Lord Julian St. Simon.

And if she failed to breach the walls, then she'd settle for what he could give her for as long as he was prepared to give it.

It was broad daylight when Julian awoke. He read the note in disbelief and growing anger. For hours she'd played the most elaborate game of seduction, showing him a side of herself he wouldn't have believed possible. But she was *still* a goddamned brigand! Why couldn't she be simple and straightforward? Why in the world would she slide out in the middle of the night to do something as simple as fetching her luggage and Josefa?

Uneasiness prickled his spine. Why would she? Not even Tamsyn thrived on unorthodox maneuvers to the extent that she'd choose to leave like that without some good reason.

And he could think of only one reason: she didn't want him with her on the journey. She'd given him a night to remember, while deliberately planning to slip from his bed and be on her way while he was asleep. It made no sense at all that she would do something that devious when she was simply going back to Tregarthan to collect Josefa and her treasure.

Despite her denial, was she going back to try one last time to discover something about her mother's family? Had she perhaps found a clue that she wanted to follow up before finally leaving England?

From what he knew of Tamsyn, it made more sense that she would try to finish what she'd come there to do than that she would meekly give it up because he'd asked her to. Oh, he believed she intended to return to Spain with him. But she was going to do something first.

Damn the woman for an obstinate, devious hellion!

And he couldn't go after her until he'd completed the formal arrangements for their passage from Portsmouth. If he was really persistent, prepared to hang around in corridors waiting for an audience, prepared to push ruthlessly through the obstructive layers of the bureaucracy, he could probably have the documents in his hand by the end of the day. But he couldn't then start his pursuit at night, so he would lose twenty-four hours.

Why was he so uneasy? He frowned, staring around

the disheveled room in anxious vexation. Even if she had some idea about the Penhallans, the worst that could happen was that she would face Cedric and he'd humiliate her with his scorn. What could possibly happen in twenty-four hours at Tregarthan? And she had Gabriel with her.

Chapter Twenty-four

"I WISH YOU WEREN'T GOING BACK TO SPAIN," LUCY SAID disconsolately, sitting on the windowsill in Tamsyn's tower room. "I was really looking forward to sponsoring you for the Season."

"It was a rather sudden decision," Tamsyn said, buttoning her shirt, trying not to show her impatience.

"But what about your mother's family? Don't you want to find them anymore?"

"Your brother persuaded me that it wasn't really a good idea. They probably wouldn't know what to do with me if I *did* find them, and I probably wouldn't have anything in common with them, anyway." Tamsyn tucked her shirt into the waist of her riding skirt and hooked it up, wishing that Lucy would cease this catechism and find something else to do. Gabriel had gone to Fowey for the afternoon. He'd offered no reason and she hadn't asked. If he'd gone after the twins, it was his business, just as her uncle was hers. His absence gave her the opportunity to ride to Lanjerrick and see her uncle, but Lucy was wasting precious time.

"Are you going back with Julian because you're his mistress?" Lucy spoke in a sudden rush, her cheeks flushed, her china-blue eyes unnaturally bright as she gazed intently at Tamsyn.

"Oh." Tamsyn sat down on the dressing stool with a rueful grimace. "How did you discover that?" She picked up a riding boot and thrust her right foot into it.

"We heard you one evening," Lucy said, her flush deepening. "And we . . . well, we saw you in the corridor. Julian was chasing you."

Tamsyn grinned, remembering the occasion. "Why didn't you say something before?"

"I . . . we . . . we thought it would be indiscreet. Julian obviously didn't want anyone to know, because he's usually so cool with you, and . . . oh, dear, this is so embarrassing." Lucy half laughed as she pressed her hands to her flaming cheeks.

"No, it's not," Tamsyn said stoutly, pulling on her other boot. "But I don't think your brother would like to know that you know, so you will make sure Gareth doesn't bumble into a confession, won't you?" It explained Gareth's winks and innuendos and the sometimes calculating look she'd encountered. He was probably sizing up his chances of stepping into Julian's shoes should they become vacant, Tamsyn thought with an inner grimace.

"Of course Gareth wouldn't say anything," Lucy declared a touch defensively. "He's not indiscreet."

"No," Tamsyn said, unconvinced. She could well imagine Gareth's approaching Julian with a hearty masculine laugh and a wink and the invitation to share the juicier aspects of his liaison. But she could as well imagine Julian's response, and if Gareth could imagine it, too, then he would hold his tongue.

"Well," she said, "that is one reason why I'm going back to Spain."

"Do you think you'll marry Julian?" Lucy was frowning now, nibbling her bottom lip.

Tamsyn swiveled on the stool to face the mirror as she tied the crisp linen stock at her neck. "Do you think I'd make him a good wife?" she countered lightly.

Lucy didn't immediately reply, and Tamsyn wished she hadn't asked. Then Lucy said, "If you love him, then of course you would. Do you?"

"Yes." She turned back to the room. "But I doubt your brother thinks I would make an appropriate Lady St. Simon."

"Well, you are rather . . . well, rather unlikely," Lucy said slowly. "But I don't think that should make any difference."

Tamsyn shrugged into her jacket. A full description of exactly how unlikely she was would require several hours of explanation that Lucy would find hard to credit. "Mistresses usually don't become wives," she said casually. "Lucy, I have to run an important errand, so you must excuse me. I'll see you at dinner." She went to the door and opened it invitingly.

"Where are you going?" Lucy, with obvious reluctance, prepared to leave the room. "Shall I accompany you?"

"No, because I intend to ride Cesar, and there isn't a horse in the stable that you can ride that would keep up with him." Tamsyn smiled to soften the statement. Lucy was a dreadful horsewoman, and Tamsyn suddenly vividly remembered the moment outside Badajos when Cesar had shied and the colonel had grabbed her bridle. She'd been furious, and he'd explained that he was used to being on the watch when riding with his sister.

Lucy pulled a face but didn't argue further. "I'll see you later, then."

"Yes." Tamsyn waved from the door as the other woman trailed rather mournfully down the corridor to her own room.

Tamsyn closed the door with a sigh of relief and began to gather things together.

Copies of the documents Cecile had given her went into the pocket of her cloak; the locket was around her neck, as usual. The original documents were hidden in a jewel cask in the armoire. She thrust her pistol into the waistband of her skirt and strapped knives to each calf over her britches.

She didn't expect this meeting with Cedric Penhallan to turn violent. But just in case, she was prepared, both physically and mentally. Her head was clear, her heart cold and determined and filled with vengeance. She was going to drop like a bolt from the blue into the vicious, orderly world of Cedric Penhallan. And she was going to claim her mother's diamonds as the price of her silence. It could be called blackmail, of course, if one was being a particularly fussy stickler for ethics, but she was dealing with an attempted murderer . . . and goodness knows what other crimes he'd committed in the interests of ambition throughout his long career. It was simple justice. And besides, the diamonds belonged to her.

An inconvenient little voice trilled that Julian would say it was still blackmail, however you painted it. But he was safely in London and never going to find out.

Josefa came bustling in as she was putting on her hat, a rather dashing tricorn. The Spanish woman was wreathed in smiles and hadn't stopped smiling since they'd returned with the glorious news that they were going home. She rushed around the room, picking up

Tamsyn's discarded afternoon gown, scolding her nurseling for her untidiness, but her smile unwavering.

"Josefa, I'm going for a ride, if anyone wants to know. I'll be back by five o'clock at the latest." Tamsyn planted a kiss on one shiny round cheek and left the room, running down to the stables.

Five minutes later she was on the road to Lanjerrick. She and Gabriel had ridden over one afternoon a few weeks before, to get a sense of the extent of the Penhallan estates, but they hadn't entered the grounds. The gray stone house stood on a promontory overlooking St. Austell Bay and was easily seen from the road. It was a house of turrets and gables, with a steeply pitched roof and transomed windows. Tamsyn had taken an instant dislike to it, finding it forbidding after the soft, golden warmth of Tregarthan.

She turned through the stone gate posts and rode up a weed-infested drive. Apprehension and excitement prickled along her spine as she left the road behind her and rode deeper into Penhallan land. This was Cecile's home, the place where she had spent the years of her growing. Had it changed much in the last twenty years? Had she missed it much? Tamsyn realized she'd never given that question any thought. Cecile had always seemed so joyful in her life that it was hard to imagine she had any regrets. But perhaps sometimes she had thought of her childhood home with nostalgia, as Tamsyn thought now with an ache of longing of the mountain villages and the icy peaks of her own childhood.

The drive opened out into a gravel sweep, and the house loomed, ivy covered, the stonework cracked in places, its windows curiously blank, like blind eyes. It struck Tamsyn as strange that a man as rich and powerful as Cedric Penhallan should neglect his property. When

Cecile had talked of Lanjerrick, she'd described its magnificence, the grand parties, the weekend shooting parties, the endless stream of guests. But there had been women in the house then. Now there was only Cedric and the vile twins. Presumably they didn't notice the air of neglect.

She rode boldly up to the front door and dismounted. As she did so, the door opened and a liveried flunkey in an old-fashioned powdered wig stepped out. "You have business here?"

"Yes, I'm come to call upon Lord Penhallan," Tamsyn said cheerfully, tethering Cesar to the stone pillar at the base of the steps leading up to the front door.

The flunkey looked momentarily nonplussed. Taking advantage of his uncertainty, Tamsyn swiftly mounted the steps. "Would you announce me to the viscount?" Without waiting for a response she pushed past him and stepped into the hall. An expanse of black and white marble tiles stretched to the staircase, and light came from a series of arched diamond-paned windows along one wall. As she stood looking around, curiosity now superseding her apprehension, a pair of greyhounds leaped out of nowhere and raced past her.

"Walters, what the devil are you doing?" An irascible voice rasped from the rear of the hall. "Close the bloody door, man, before the dogs get out."

The door banged shut behind her, and the two dogs sloped back into the shadows.

"Who in the name of the good Christ are you?" the same voice demanded. Cedric Penhallan came forward, glaring into the gloom. Then he stopped as he saw his visitor clearly.

Tamsyn raised her head and looked her uncle full in the face as she had done at the party at Tregarthan. She saw, as then, a choleric countenance, flat black eyes, a shock of iron-gray hair, a beaky nose above a fleshy mouth. A massive, powerful frame beginning to run to fat. Her scalp lifted as she felt that aura of menace flowing around him, and for the first time she felt fear.

Cedric stared at her. The minutes passed, and the only sound in the room was the scratch of a dog's claws on the tiles. "Who are you?" His voice was suddenly quiet, a strange light enlivening his hard eyes. He knew the answer but he wanted it spoken.

Tamsyn stepped closer to him on a sudden surge of exultation, banishing her fear. He knew and yet he couldn't believe what he was seeing. "Good afternoon, uncle."

"Good God, it's St. Simon's doxy!" Before Cedric could respond, the slurred voice of Charles Penhallan came from the stairs. He held a wineglass in one hand and his eyes were unfocused. "Look what we've got here, David. The little whore's come back for more." He laughed and came down the stairs, only then seeing his uncle.

"Beg pardon, sir. But what's St. Simon's harlot doing here?"

"Don't be any more of a fool than you can help," Cedric said coldly. He jerked his head at Tamsyn. "Come in here."

She moved to follow him, aware that David had joined his brother on the stairs. It was very fortunate Gabriel was not with her. They were both regarding her with a lascivious, drunken interest. She glanced up at them. "What a pretty pair of cowardly sots, you are, cousins. Have you had fun with any little girls recently?" Then she followed Cedric into a large paneled library.

"Where have you come from?" He spoke from the sideboard, where he was pouring cognac with hands that weren't quite steady.

Tamsyn didn't answer the question, saying instead, "I look very like her, don't I?" She felt rather than heard the twins stepping into the room behind her.

Cedric tossed back the contents of the glass. "Yes," he said. "The very image of her. Where is she?"

"Dead. But she lived rather longer than you'd intended." Tamsyn was beginning to enjoy herself; all her fear had gone. She glanced again at her cousins, who were standing by the door, gawping in incomprehension. "Long enough to ensure that you will pay for what you did to her." A cold smile touched her lips. "Was it really necessary to send her to her death, uncle?"

"Your mother was a very difficult woman." Cedric refilled his glass. He seemed almost amused. "She intended to ruin me . . . to bring disgrace on the name of Penhallan. If she'd been just a silly chit, I could have brought her to heel. But Celia had an iron will . . . hard to believe, really, to look at her. She was such a little thing."

"What's St. Simon's doxy got to do with us?" David asked, sounding petulant in his drunken confusion.

"Are you?" Cedric asked Tamsyn with the same amusement.

She shook her head. "Certainly not. I'm a Penhallan, sir. Penhallans are not whores, are they?"

His color deepened, and his breath whistled through his teeth, but his voice when he spoke was as neutral as before. "So just where does St. Simon come into all this?"

"He doesn't," she said. "He knows nothing about it."

"I see." Cedric stroked his chin. "I suppose you have proof of your identity?"

"I'm no fool, sir."

"No . . . no more was your mother." He laughed suddenly, sounding genuinely entertained. "Fancy that. Trust Celia to come back and haunt me. Curiously enough, I miss her."

"I'm sure she would have been touched to hear it," Tamsyn said dryly.

He laughed again. "Sharp tongue, just like hers." He turned back to the decanter and again refilled his glass. "So what do you want?"

"Well, I had in mind the Penhallan diamonds," Tamsyn said pensively. "They were Cecile's and by rights should come to me."

"What's she talking about?" Charles demanded.

"Hold your tongue, you idiot!" Cedric surveyed her over his glass. "So she continued to call herself Cecile. Dear God, she was stubborn."

Apparently he wasn't going to challenge her claim. Tamsyn was puzzled by the amicability of an encounter that should have been bristling with hostility. "You don't dispute the diamonds are mine by right?"

Cedric shook his head. "No, most certainly they're yours if you can prove you're Celia's daughter."

"I have the locket. And signed papers."

He shrugged. "I'm sure you have ample documentation. Enough to ruin me, of course, if the story of your mother's disappearance was made public."

"Precisely." It still didn't feel right, but she couldn't put her finger on what was making her uneasy. She knew she had a cast-iron claim, so why should it feel wrong that Cedric would acknowledge it? He was an intelligent man, not given to wasting energy on futile causes. "Actually," she said, "I don't really need the diamonds, I have plenty of my own. Cecile made rather a good marriage, you see."

Cedric threw back his head and guffawed. "Did she, indeed?"

"Yes, but I doubt it would have met with your approval."

"So you don't need the diamonds, but you want them?"

"As you said, they're mine by right. Either you make reparation to my mother's memory, or I shall send a story to the *Gazette* that will have the entire country humming."

"You can't let her get away with this!" Charles lurched forward, some of the sense of what was being said finally penetrating his buzzing brain. "It's blackmail!"

"Oh, well-done, sir," Cedric applauded. "Such perspicacity! You'll take a glass of champagne with me, niece, to seal our bargain."

It was statement rather than request, and Tamsyn's eyes narrowed. "I don't believe so, Lord Penhallan."

"Oh, come now, let us at least strive for civility," he chided. "Your mother was always gracious in victory. She never failed to carry off a situation with finesse."

He was right, Tamsyn thought with a stab of pain. Cecile would have won her victory and taken a glass of wine with her brother. She'd have slipped the diamonds into her pocket, shaken his hand, and left him with a smile.

She inclined her head in graceful acceptance.

"Then, if you'll excuse me a moment, niece, I shall fetch up a bottle of something very special. Your cousins, I'm sure, will do their best to entertain you."

"Yes, I've tasted your ideas of entertainment once before," Tamsyn said coolly to her cousins as their uncle left the room. Gabriel could have them later, for now she would exercise a little revenge of her own. She put one leg up on a chair and slid the knife out of its sheath, then did the same with the other. Thoughtfully, she turned back to the twins; she held the knives by their points between the thumb and forefinger of each hand, just as her father had taught her.

Their eyes widened as they saw her face and saw what Cornichet had seen when she'd come for his epaulets. Then both knives came spinning, arcing through the air, and the twins howled as much in shock as in pain as the two points neatly buried themselves in their right boots, piercing the leather as if it were butter to lodge between two toes. Charles and David stared down in disbelief at the quivering knife handles, shock rendering them momentarily mute.

"You're fortunate I'm in a forgiving mood," Tamsyn said blandly. "I doubt you'll find too great a wound when you remove your boots." And they still had Gabriel to deal with, but she'd spare them that knowledge.

"Good God!" Cedric exclaimed from the doorway, taking in the scene. His nephews were struggling for speech like two gobbling turkeys, their eyes darting in disbelief from the shivering knife handles in their boots to the coldly smiling woman who had thrown them.

"I owed them a favor," Tamsyn said as the two men bent like automatons to pull the knives loose.

Cedric raised his eyebrows. "Of course, I'd forgotten that you'd already made their acquaintance."

"Yes, I had that pleasure some weeks ago," Tamsyn said. She moved swiftly and twitched the knives from the twins' slack grasp. She examined the points. "Not much blood at all, really. The baron would have been proud of me."

"The baron?" Cedric sounded fascinated.

"My father," she said, wiping the knife tips on her cloak before returning them to their sheaths.

"I should really like to hear more," Cedric murmured. "But, unfortunately, there won't be time." Turning his back, he eased the cork off the champagne bottle. It came out with a restrained pop, and there was a fizzy hiss as he filled four glasses.

"I trust you don't object to drinking with your cousins?" He turned back and handed her a glass. "They're an unworthy pair, I know, but unfortunately one can't choose one's relatives."

"Perhaps not, but I'm afraid I do object to drinking with cowardly scum." Tamsyn took the glass, but her eyes, like violet ice, challenged Cedric.

"Then we won't do so," Cedric agreed equably, leaving the two glasses on the tray. He raised his own, his expression still faintly amused. "To Celia."

"To Cecile." Tamsyn sipped the wine, imagining Cecile doing the same. Cedric drained his glass and she followed suit.

"So if we could conclude our business, uncle, I'll bid you farewell." She smiled as she put the glass on the table, but something strange was happening to her face. Her mouth wouldn't obey her brain. The edges of the room were blurring, a gray haze swimming toward her. Cedric's face danced in the mist before her eyes, suddenly larger than life; his mouth was opening and closing. He was saying something but she could hear nothing.

Imbecile! Overconfident, too clever by half! Cedric had invoked the one person who could get through her guard. Cecile. And she'd fallen for it in her haste and her arrogance, and her certainty of the rightness of her cause.

Gabriel! But the words were stuck in her brain. . . .

Cedric bent over the crumpled form. He found the locket around her neck and opened it. For a long moment he examined the two portraits; then he closed it and let it drop back between her breasts. He removed the pistol from her waistband and the knives from their sheaths, observing, "A young woman who clearly comes prepared."

He stood up, murmuring with a degree of regret, "A pity, my dear . . . but blackmail was a bad idea. You and your mother knew how to go too far." He looked across at his dumbfounded nephews, his lip curled contemptuously. "She was worth four of you. Now, get rid of her."

"I b–beg pardon, sir. What . . . what should we do with her?"

"Cretins!" It was a bark of angry derision. "What do you think you should do with her? Get rid of her! Remove her! Take her out to sea and drop her overboard! Just make damn sure she's not alive to tell this tale or any other." He threw his large bulk into an armchair and watched morosely as Charles bent over the inert figure.

"And do it before she comes to," he said abruptly, seeing the way Charles's hands moved over Tamsyn's body. "Don't you think to start playing with her. She's a damn sight too clever for the pair of you. . . . If she comes to, she'll run rings around you."

Charles flushed darkly, but he picked up the limp figure. "Should we take the *Mary Jane,* sir?"

"We could row out and drop her off Gribbon Head,"

David suggested, one eyelid twitching with the shocks and anxieties of the last half hour. "With the crab pots."

"She'll make a tasty morsel for the crabs." Charles laughed, and his eyes were full of greedy malevolence as he looked down at her pale face. "Don't worry, sir, we'll make sure she doesn't come back here again."

"Do it right," Cedric said wearily. "That's all I ask."

Chapter Twenty-five

"WHERE DID SHE SAY SHE WAS GOING?" GABRIEL STARED AT Josefa, slow anger beginning to burn in his eyes. The woman stood her ground, although her lip quivered a little.

"She didn't say. Just that she was going riding and she'd be back by five o'clock."

Gabriel glanced up at the clock on the stable wall. It was past six. "How did she seem to you? What kind of mood was she in?"

Josefa frowned, considering this while Gabriel tapped his foot with growing impatience on the cobbles. "You know how she is before an engagement," Josefa said finally. "Her eyes were bright, she wasn't thinking of anything but what she was doing. You know how she is," she repeated.

"Oh, yes, I know," Gabriel said grimly. "I'm a fool! I *knew* she wouldn't have given up on the Penhallan." He spun on his heel and bellowed in a voice to shake mountains, "Saddle my horse again."

"But where is she?" Josefa quavered.

"Causing trouble," Gabriel said softly, his eyes sharply focused. "Alone. And those filthy swine are there. . . . Hurry up, lad!" he snapped at the groom struggling with the girths of his horse. Impatiently, he pushed him aside. "I'll do it." His large hands were surprisingly deft on the straps, and then he leaped into the saddle and galloped out of the stableyard.

The horse pounded the lanes between the high hedges, sensing his rider's urgency. Gabriel rode low in the saddle, his fury at Tamsyn for deceiving him mingling with dread. She wasn't back when she'd said she would be; therefore, something had happened to her. She was clever and a good fighter and she didn't in general make mistakes, but this issue was an emotional one. To make matters worse, she was worried that the colonel would discover her secrets, so she was acting in haste, and Gabriel didn't trust her to keep a clear head. One slip, one piece of carelessness, was all it would take to destroy one woman up against the three Penhallans.

His horse swung around a corner and then shied into the hedge as it came almost eyeball to eyeball with a massive black that seemed to have come out of no-where.

Gabriel hauled back on the reins. "Madre de Dios, Colonel, where did you spring from?"

Julian didn't answer. The expression on Gabriel's face sent a shiver of apprehension down his spine. "Where the hell are you going in such a hurry, Gabriel? And where's Tamsyn?"

Gabriel had no time to consider whether it would be in Tamsyn's interests to reveal her secrets to this man. He could do with another pair of hands, and the colonel's were the hands he would have chosen if he'd had the choice. "Lanjerrick, in answer to both questions, Colonel, and you'd best come along. I don't know what we're going to find."

"God's grace, but I thought as much!" Julian's skin

was clammy, and a cold premonition curled in his belly. "She found out the Penhallans were her family."

"She's always known it," Gabriel said shortly, setting his horse to the gallop again.

The cold, hard ball of premonition grew as he turned Soult in the narrow lane and caught up with Gabriel.

"What do you mean?" Julian rode neck and neck with Gabriel. "Since when has she known it?"

"She's always known she's kin to the Penhallan."

Julian absorbed this in silence, the rhythmic pounding of Soult's hooves on the rutted lane sounding in his blood. Why wasn't he surprised? "She knew before we left Spain?" He seemed to need clarification, although the picture was forming with hideous clarity.

"Aye. She's set on revenge for what they did to her mother."

"What kind of revenge?" he asked dully as the pieces fell into place and the true extent of her deceit and manipulation took clear shape. And the true extent of his own gullibility. So desperate to believe in her essential honesty, in an innocent purpose behind her need for his protection and the shelter of his roof. But there was no essential honesty, only a cold and calculating seduction with a black core of lies. Lies she'd been telling from the moment she'd laid eyes on him.

"She was going to ruin Cedric for what he did to her mother . . . expose him in public. But then she decided she couldn't expose him without your finding out, Colonel, so I'm guessing she's just gone for the Penhallan diamonds. A much simpler revenge . . . and the bairn would have it that they were her mother's by rights and therefore now hers." Gabriel shook his head. "She's diamonds aplenty, of course, but she has a powerful sense of justice . . . always has had."

"And a powerful sense of justice is reason for theft?"

"Och, she's not out to steal them, man. She'll persuade the Penhallan to give them to her. She holds some powerful secrets against him."

"Oh, I see. Blackmail," St. Simon said in the same flat tone.

"In a manner of speaking. But she believes she's only doing what the baron would have done himself if he'd lived long enough."

"Such a wonderful parental example," Julian said with bitter sarcasm. "So you're telling me she's gone to Lanjerrick to blackmail Cedric Penhallan into giving her the family diamonds? Does she think Cedric's simply going to hand them over for the asking?" He laughed in scorn.

Gabriel's mouth tightened. "The man's capable of murder, and she knows it. She'll be prepared. But she should never have gone alone!" He drew a harsh, ragged breath. "If those gutter sweepings are there, she'll be one against three of them. They've put their hands on her once—good God, man, you've known them for what they are! You know what they're capable of doing to her?"

So she'd heard that story too. Was there anything she hadn't discovered? Was there ever a moment since they'd first met when she hadn't been plotting and planning, using him? In London, when she'd been lying beneath him, entrancing him with her love play and her soft, lascivious movements, and the luminous glow in her eyes, and the power of her passion . . . at every moment she'd been pursuing her own lawless, deceitful course. And he'd believed in the truth of her emotions. God help him, he was beginning to find it hard to ignore his own.

Was she intending to leave him once she'd completed
her little blackmail? But no, of course not. She needed
him to get her back to Spain. She needed him, the blind
dupe, to arrange passage for them all. She needed his
escort so she could travel with all the safety and trap-
pings of a guest of the British army. And when she was
safely home again . . . why, then she would leave
him. She would no longer need him. Had she intended
to steal out into the night like the lying thief that she
was? Leaving him without a word of explanation?

Abruptly a flash of fear pushed through his corrosive
anger. He thought of the twins, of what they would do
to her if she could be rendered helpless. And Gabriel
said they had put their hands on her once already.

"What do you mean, they've put their hands on her
already?"

Gabriel told him the story. "But they're mine, Colonel. Don't you forget that."

"I have my own scores to settle," Julian said harshly.
"First with the Penhallans . . . and then with Tamsyn."

Gabriel glanced sideways at him in the pale light of
the crescent moon. The colonel's face was tight and
angry, but there was sorrow behind the anger . . . the
sorrow of a man finally giving up a fight, finally facing
unpalatable facts. And it filled Gabriel with deep fore-
boding. But he could think of nothing to say to repair
the damage. Tamsyn said she loved the man, but she'd
created this situation, and only she could put it right.
Once she was out of whatever danger she'd walked into.

"I'll be going first with the Penhallan," Gabriel declared, dropping low over his horse's neck, spurring the
animal to increase his speed as they approached the out-

skirts of Lanjerrick land. "But I'll happily share the pleasure with you, Colonel."

"We'll go across the cliff top." Julian turned his horse aside, through a break in the hedge. "I've no mind to approach through the front door on this errand."

Gabriel followed, and they galloped across the flat turf of the cliff toward the gray house, looming unkempt and unlit out of the darkness.

"Just a minute!" Julian hauled back on the reins. "There's a light down in the cove. Who would be taking a boat out at this time of night? It's too dark for crabbing."

They drew rein at the head of the cliff and looked downward. A lantern flickered and wavered on the beach below; the surf crashed and boiled against a rocky outcrop at one side of the cove, before tumbling in a line of foam along the shore.

"We struck gold, Colonel," Gabriel murmured, swinging off his horse. "I think that's the scum down there."

"I believe you're right." Julian too dismounted, and they tethered their mounts to a scraggly thornbush, bent out of shape by exposure to the blasts of the sea wind. He was filled now with a calm, cold determination. He wanted Tamsyn in his hands, and he would unleash the full force of his bitter hurt . . . his deep contempt for her lying, cheating, blackmailing soul. But perhaps she wasn't down there on the beach. It was always possible she had carried off her coup and was on her way back to Tregarthan with the Penhallan diamonds tucked in her shirt.

But somehow he knew that wasn't the case.

Gesturing to Gabriel, he inched over the cliff top and found the narrow ribbon of path snaking down to the

beach through the scree and scrub. It was hidden from
the beach by a cliff overhang at the very bottom, and
when they reached the overhang, they dropped soundlessly onto the sand, ducking behind a rock to observe
the scene.

The twins were sitting on the sand, and a fragrant
curl of blue smoke rose from a cigar David was smoking.
Between them was a bottle of cognac. Pulled up at the
shoreline was a rowboat. They were talking and laughing in low voices, and Julian felt the skin on the back of
his neck contract. He'd heard that sound before. He'd
seen them like this. Relaxed, satiated. Taking a break
before they returned to the cringing, battered little girl
who had lain on the grass in front of them.

He stared in cold dread, expecting to see the glint of
silver hair against the sand, the diminutive figure, pale
and naked, her torn clothes scattered over the ground
where they'd been stripped from her body.

But he could see nothing in the wavering light of the
lantern on the sand, or the weaker light of the moon.

Gabriel had drawn a knife from his belt, and his gray
eyes flickered sideways in a silent message. Julian nodded, his hand closing over his pistol.

They slipped, two powerful wraiths, from the con-
cealment of the rocks and approached the two men.

Tamsyn lay in the bottom of the boat, her nose
pressed to the gunwales as she fought wave after wave of
nausea. The drug Cedric had given her was wearing off,
but her head was still muzzy and the nausea was almost
impossible to control. She fought it grimly, dreading the
thought of lying in her own vomit, trussed as she was
like a Christmas goose. Her hands were tied behind her
back and then roped to her ankles. She'd still been unconscious when they'd done that, but not later . . .

when they'd pawed her, opened her shirt, lifted her skirt . . .

She closed her eyes tightly and hung on through another wave of sickness. So far that was all they'd done. She'd given no sign that she was conscious, and they were going to wait until she came to before they really settled down to enjoy themselves. Charles's drunken slur played in her head, his lewd chuckle as he said that there was no pleasure in necrophilia. David had muttered something about the governor, and then he too had laughed and put his hand roughly inside her shirt. Then they'd left her and she'd heard them on the beach, talking and laughing. They'd come over several times to look at her, and she'd stayed inert, her face pressed against the rough wood of the gunwales as her mind slowly cleared and she tried to think how she was to get out of this particular pickle.

It seemed as insoluble as the situation with Cornichet. Whether rape was a softer alternative to flaying was something she cared not to debate. Her death was the ultimate intention both then and now. If only she didn't feel so sick . . . but, then, perhaps if she vomited all over the loathsome twins, they'd find her too disgusting even for rape.

It was a possibility. They'd have to lift her out and put her on the sand, since presumably the narrow and awkward shape of the rowboat didn't lend itself to leisurely violation. And presumably they'd have to loosen her bonds. And then, if she was violently sick, it would take them off guard, and if she had some room to maneuver, maybe she could do something.

It was a forlorn plan but all she had. She lay still, listening, waiting for a change in the tempo of their voices, a footfall in the sand that would indicate an approach.

What she heard was a soft, sighing sound, a thump, a shuffling of sand. Then footsteps. Tamsyn struggled onto her back. Moonlight shone on her white face, where beads of sweat dewed her forehead and the hard lines of the timbers were imprinted on her cheek.

Julian was looking down at her. How had he come to be there? His body was very still, and his blue eyes were hard and bright and questioning, and she could feel his anger and his resentment in every aching bone of her body. Tears of weakness sprang to her eyes as she lay still, gazing up at him. Now he knew everything. His knowledge burned in his eyes and scorched her with his contempt.

Then Gabriel came up beside him, and his warm, loving anxiety poured over her. "Och, little girl, how could you do this to me?" he said, bending to lift her.

But abruptly, Julian pushed him aside. "Leave her to me." It was a harsh command issued on a ragged breath, but Gabriel took a step back.

Julian bent over her, slipped his hands beneath her, and lifted her up. The motion, the change in position was too much. With a groan Tamsyn turned her head away from his body and vomited miserably onto the sand, splashing his boots.

"I'm sorry," she whispered. "I knew it would happen the minute I moved."

"It doesn't matter," he said, and the gentleness of his voice surprised them both. He set her down on the sand, and she rolled onto her side, retching feebly while he cut the ropes that bound her. When she finished, he wiped her mouth with his handkerchief and took the twins' bottle of cognac from Gabriel, hovering anxiously beside him. "Have a swallow of this."

She took a gulp, and the fire burned down her gullet and into her heaving stomach. And miraculously, the queasiness began to abate. She wiped her damp forehead with the back of her arm and looked helplessly up at him. His features were granite, but his eyes were confused.

She turned to look at Charles and David, lying still on the sand. "Are they dead?"

"No, just resting after a knock on the head. Have they touched you?" The question was almost dispassionate, but now his eyes were livid.

She shook her head carefully. "Not much. They were waiting for me to come to. Cedric put something in the champagne . . . I don't know what it was. I don't know how long I've been unconscious. But it wasn't dark when I was in the library."

"It's close to eight o'clock now." He turned away from her, as if satisfied that she was sufficiently recovered to dispense with his attention. "What do you think, Gabriel?" He nudged the still figure of Charles with his toe. "They won't be out for long."

"How about we strip 'em naked, put 'em in the boat, and send them out to sea?" Gabriel said promptly. "They'll probably get picked up sometime tomorrow, more's the pity, but what a sight they'll be!"

"You'd have to row the boat," Tamsyn pointed out. "And then how would you get back to shore?"

"Swim," Gabriel said with a grin. "I'll row them out beyond the headland. The tide's going out, it'll take them a goodly way out to sea by morning."

"You'll be swimming against the current, and it's strong around here," Julian pointed out.

"So am I," Gabriel said, still grinning. "You going to help me strip them, Colonel?"

"With pleasure."

Tamsyn watched as the twins were rendered white and naked on the sand. They both stirred and groaned as Gabriel tugged off their boots.

"Funny thing!" Gabriel frowned. "Seem to have hurt their feet in exactly the same spot."

"Yes," Tamsyn said. "I owed them a favor."

Julian's eyes darted toward her as she sat on the sand. He fought the persistent and exasperating amnesia that had swept over him first when he'd seen her lying in the bottom of the boat, and she'd gazed up at him in silent, anxious plea, and his heart had turned over with joy that she was alive, and he'd forgotten his hurt and anger in his joyous relief and the need to hold her in his arms.

Coldly, he turned away from her to help Gabriel heft the inert figures into the rowboat.

Tamsyn shivered, but the night was warm and the chill was within her. She'd seen his eyes, and she could read his thoughts as if they were an open book.

Gabriel stripped to his long woolen drawers and helped the colonel push the boat into the lapping surf, then sprang over the side and fitted the oars into the rowlocks. David stirred, groaned, and his eyelids fluttered. "Go back to sleep, laddie." Gabriel tapped him gently on the jaw with his heel. It had looked to Julian like the lightest of touches, but David fell back again, inert.

The power of this unpredictable giant was not to be minimized. "You're not intending to kill them, are you?"

Gabriel shook his head, saying cheerfully, "A day in

the broiling sun on the open sea will do nicely, Colonel. I'll even leave them an oar, if you like."

Julian looked at the naked bodies and thought of them bobbing on the open sea under the midmorning sun, waiting to be found by a fishing boat. It was a pleasing prospect. "Leave them one," he said.

Gabriel nodded. "And you'll take the little girl back home."

"I'll not deny her the shelter of my roof for another night," Julian stated flatly. "After that, since your business is done here, I imagine you'll have no further need of my hospitality."

Gabriel frowned in the moonlight; then he said neutrally, "Leave my horse where he is. I'll collect him and my clothes when I get back."

Julian stepped back to the sand, watching, hands on his hips, as Gabriel pulled strongly toward the opening of the cove. Then he turned around. Tamsyn was sitting on a rock, her hands clasped lightly in her lap, her head bent as if she were looking for something in the sand.

She raised her head, and her eyes were large and strained in her pale face. "So you know everything now."

Julian raised an eyebrow. "I can't believe that," he drawled. "There are no more secrets, no more illicit little plots percolating in your devious mind? You'll have to forgive me if I find that hard to credit, Violette."

"Oh, there's one secret," she said dully. "But only one, and you might as well know it. I love you. I love you so much it hurts. And I'll never love anyone else in the same way."

Her hands fell to her sides. "There, now," she said. "That's all of it. I've tricked you, and I've used you. I've lied to you, and I've rearranged your life to suit my own

purposes. I forced you to leave Spain, and I'm the illegitimate daughter of a Penhallan and a robber baron.
But I love you with my heart and soul, and I'd give my
last drop of blood if you ever needed it."

She stood up. "But of course you won't ever need it,
so I'll go now. And you need never fear that our paths
will cross again." Turning from him, she began to walk
back across the sand.

"You omitted to mention puking all over my boots
in that catalog of wrongs," Julian said.

Tamsyn stopped. She turned slowly. "I suppose
you're entitled to that," she said. "Entitled to mock.
Why should you believe in my love? Anyway, it's a poor
thing. I know it can't excuse or make up for what I've
done to you."

"Dear God," he said. "I'm assuming this extraordinary show of humility was brought on by that drug
Penhallan gave you. I trust its effect isn't permanent."

It was too much! All Tamsyn's sorrow and weakness
went up in a puff of smoke. She was not going to walk
out of his life a broken reed. Colonel, Lord Julian St.
Simon was going to have something else to remember
her by. "Oh, you despicable bastard! You are an unmiti-
gated cur!" She swooped down, grabbed a handful of
sand, and threw it at him. Darting sideways, she picked
up the empty cognac bottle. It flew through the air and
caught him a glancing blow on the shoulder, before
rolling onto the sand.

"*Diablillo!* Virago! Termagant!" Julian taunted, grinning as he ducked one of Gabriel's boots.

"*Espadachín!* Brute! Bully! Unchivalrous pig!" she
hurled back, searching for another missile. "You can't
even accept an apology gracefully!"

Julian dived for her, bringing her down onto the

sand. He felt extraordinary, struck by a blinding epiphany. He'd been reborn in some fashion, his hurt and anger vanished in the mists of incomprehension. It no longer mattered how or why this had all started. What mattered was the now. She loved him. He *did* believe her, every word of her declaration. He believed it because he knew it was how he felt himself. He'd fought the knowledge . . . he'd been fighting it for weeks . . . and now he'd lost the battle. She was a lawless, unethical, manipulative, illegitimate half-breed, no possible wife for a St. Simon, and he didn't give a damn.

Scissoring her legs with his own, he pinned her arms above her head, subduing her with his weight. "When did you decide you loved me?"

"Weeks ago," she said, lying quiet now beneath him, reading the light in his eye, a trickle of incredulous hope beginning to seep into her veins. "But I knew you didn't think you could love me in the same way, although I knew that you did . . . and I was hoping that when we were together in Spain, maybe you could learn to look into your heart. But I still had to deal with Cedric . . . it was something I felt I *had* to do . . . for Cecile, and for my father. But I gave up my big plan to ruin him publicly, because then you'd have known the whole story, and I thought you'd be unhappy to discover how I'd been deceiving you."

"Unhappy, eh? You're a mistress of euphemism," he declared with a wry quirk of his lips. "But maybe you can find a euphemistic explanation for blackmail? Just to enable me to live with it, you understand."

"It wasn't blackmail, it was restitution."

"A little better. Keep trying."

"The diamonds were my mother's," she said quietly,

and finally told him the full story. "It was only justice," she finished.

"Only justice," Julian mused, his body still pinning her to the sand. "I suppose I can live with that. A woman with a fine sense of justice, not a blackmailer at all." He nodded judiciously. "Yes, I think I can live with that."

"You're very heavy," Tamsyn said. "I don't want to puke all over you again."

Julian with a muttered exclamation promptly rolled off her.

"I have to go back to Lanjerrick." Tamsyn sat up. "My sense of justice hasn't been appeased . . . and Cesar is still there."

Julian got to his feet and pulled her up. "Then let's pay your uncle a visit."

"You don't have to come with me."

"Oh, but I do," he said. "I too have a very fine sense of justice."

"You don't mind too much that I have Penhallan blood?" she asked hesitantly as they climbed the path to the cliff top.

"Oh, I hardly think so," he responded with a dry smile. "Your kinship with a murderous viscount is probably the most respectable thing about you."

Cedric was in the library, cradling a brandy goblet, morosely awaiting the return of his nephews, when there came a violent hammering on the front door. He sat up abruptly, listening to the servant's footsteps on the marble tiles, the sound of the bolts being drawn back on the front door.

Then the library door was flung open, and Julian St. Simon stepped into the room, Celia's daughter behind him.

"The cretins bungled it," Viscount Penhallan said wearily. "I might have known they would." He gestured to the decanters on the sideboard. "Help yourself to a drink."

"I wouldn't risk it in this house," Tamsyn said tartly.

"Oh, there's no fear with the cognac, or the port," her uncle said, leaning back in his chair, regarding her through narrowed eyes. "Did you kill them?"

"No." Julian poured himself a glass of cognac.

Tamsyn helped herself to an apple from a fruit bowl. "Not all Penhallans are murderers, uncle." She scrunched into the apple. "Where's my horse?"

"That magnificent beast is in my stables," he said. "I congratulate you, he's a superb animal."

"A present from my father," she said through a mouthful of apple. "I told you Cecile made a good marriage."

"So you did." He turned his head against the cushions and let his gaze rest lazily on St. Simon. "So how can I help you, St. Simon?"

"All in good time," Julian said calmly, leaning back against the sideboard, long legs stretched in front of him, casually crossed at the ankle. He took a critical sip of his cognac.

"I've decided you can keep the diamonds," Tamsyn said. "I'm going to do what my father would have wanted and tell the world every last detail of your infamy . . . including what you tried to do to me. I couldn't do it before because the colonel didn't know the whole story, but now he does. . . ." She paused, catching Julian's raised eyebrows. "You do agree that I must do this, don't you?"

"Who am I to question the baron's wisdom and wishes?"

"If you really don't wish me to . . . if it will involve you in scandal, then I won't," she said slowly. "I'll just settle for the diamonds instead. But that would be blackmail, and I know you don't approve of that."

"Blackmail?" he queried, his eyebrows disappearing into his scalp.

"Restitution. I forgot that was what we're calling it," she said lamely.

"And a fine sense of justice, if you recall."

"Yes, that too."

"So you're going to do what your mother threatened to do twenty years ago?" Cedric held out his empty glass toward Julian, who pushed himself away from the sideboard and brought the decanter over to him. Cedric nodded his thanks. "Is that so?"

"Yes."

Cedric inclined his head and took a deep draft of brandy. "Then if we've concluded our business, perhaps you'd get out of my house."

"Certainly." Julian put down his glass and walked to the door. "But just one more thing . . . a mere formality, but one should observe the proprieties, as I'm sure you'll agree." His smile was sardonic as he offered his host a small bow. "Since it appears that you're Tamsyn's nearest male relative, however much she might regret that fact, I suppose I must ask your permission to pay my addresses to your niece."

"So long as you don't expect me to walk her down the aisle," Cedric said equably. "You may both go to the devil for all I care."

"Thank you, sir." Julian bowed again. "Come, buttercup." He swept her out of the room ahead of him.

"Do you really wish to marry me?" Tamsyn demanded in a fierce whisper as they crossed the hall.

"Apparently," he said affably. "Unless it's simply my social conscience that insists I make an honest woman of you . . . but, then," he added thoughtfully, "I probably shouldn't set my sights too high."

"Cur!"

"Brigand!"

Epilogue

MADRID, CHRISTMAS, 1812

A LIGHT SNOW WAS FALLING, A FINE POWDER SETTLING ON the winding road approaching the city across the plain. The wind sharpened and a gust lifted the carpet of snow, sending it in a rolling drift toward the gates.

The corporal outside the guardhouse shivered and turned up his collar. He stuck his head into the frowsty warmth of the guardroom. "Looks like someone's coming, sir."

The lieutenant turned from the charcoal brazier where he'd been warming his hands and stepped outside. A small group of horsemen was approaching, white wraithlike figures in the drifting powder.

"Spanish saddles," the lieutenant said, clapping his hands together. "Looks like the brigadier's lady. I'd know that horse anywhere."

The four horses surged out of the snow and drew rein at the guard post. Two of the riders were unremarkable, but a third was a giant oak of a man astride a massive, rawboned stallion. Beside him rode a small figure astride a magnificent milk-white Arabian.

"Good evening, Lieutenant." The Arabian's rider

spoke English in a faintly accented female voice that made the corporal stare.

The lieutenant, however, showed no surprise. "Evening, ma'am. You're just in time for the Christmas ball at the duke's headquarters. Started about an hour ago."

"Perfect timing." Tamsyn flashed him a smile. "I hope you're not on duty all evening."

"I drew the short straw," he said with a rueful chuckle. "But the lads will bring us some Christmas cheer later."

"Who was that?" the corporal asked as the four riders rode on into the city.

"The brigadier's lady," the lieutenant said. "Oh, but of course, you're a Johnny Raw. Only been out here a couple of weeks, I was forgetting."

He went back into the guardhouse, stamping the snow off his boots. "Lady St. Simon," he elaborated as the corporal followed him. "She rides with the partisans, acts as liaison between them and the commander. The big chap's her bodyguard, goes by the name of Gabriel. Watch out for him if you catch him in his cups. Mostly he's as gentle as a lamb, but when he's had a few, he's a devil."

"Brigadier, Lord St. Simon's wife?" the corporal said in astonishment. "A partisan?"

"That's right." The lieutenant was enjoying the man's amazement. "Quite the pet of the regiment, she is. Reckon we'll all be glad to see her back." He chuckled. "She should have reported in four days ago, and the brigadier's been worried sick—makes him a right martinet."

Brigadier, Lord Julian St. Simon was at this moment trying very hard to be polite to his partner in the quadrille. The ballroom in the large mansion occupied by

the Duke of Wellington was hung with greenery wilting
in the oppressive heat. The warmth from the fires blazing in massive open hearths at each end of the room was
augmented by myriad candles flaring in branched
candelabra. The scent of perfume and pomade and
ripely overheated flesh was almost overpowering as the
officers of the Army of the Peninsular and their ladies
forgot the privations of summer campaigning and enjoyed the social pleasures of winter quarters.

Julian, however, was not enjoying himself, despite the
fact that his partner was one of the belles of the regiment. The Honorable Miss Beazley, well aware of the
reason for her partner's monosyllabic conversation, was
understanding and kept up a light flow of undemanding
small talk, occasionally reminding the brigadier of a step
in the elaborate dance when he became more than ordi-
narily absentminded.

The clock had just struck nine when the double
doors to the ballroom were flung open, letting in a draft
of refreshingly cold air from the hall. There was a whirlwind rush of movement as a small figure hurtled across
the dance floor.

Brigadier St. Simon dropped his partner's hand as his
wife, still in her riding britches, leaped into his arms
with a cry of jubilation, her legs curling around his
waist, her arms fastening around his neck as she kissed
him.

Vaguely Julian was aware of the immodesty of her
position, of how clearly her limbs were outlined in the
tight britches. His hands cupped her bottom, holding
her up against him, her mouth devoured him, and his
head spun with the weakness and dizzying joy of relief.

"Passionate little filly, isn't she?" Wellington murmured, clearly enjoying the spectacle. "Nice lines."

"I think perhaps I should take Julian's place with Miss Beazley," Tim O'Connor said with a grin. "She looks somewhat abandoned." He strode onto the floor and gracefully swept the brigadier's neglected partner back into the formation.

Julian, still clutching his clinging wife, stepped hastily off the floor. *"Where have you been?"* he exclaimed when she'd released his mouth for a minute. "I've been out of my mind!"

"There was snow in the passes . . . some of them were closed," Tamsyn said, sitting back on his supporting hands, smiling into his face. "And we had a couple of skirmishes . . . not serious ones," she added hastily, seeing his face darken.

"You gave me your word you wouldn't take part in any combat."

"I didn't participate," she said. "Ask Gabriel." She brushed his lips with her own.

"I shall." He still sounded a little grim, but Tamsyn, who knew how difficult it had been for him to accept her return to partisan activities, simply kissed him again.

"Dear God!" Julian suddenly came back to a full sense of their surroundings. "What are you doing dressed like this in the middle of a ball? You're shameless!" But he was laughing now with pleasure as he moved his hands to her waist and swung her away from him, setting her on her feet.

"Would you have preferred it if I'd spent an hour changing into something respectable before letting you know I was back?" Tamsyn demanded, pouting with mock petulance.

"No," he stated. "If you'd delayed a minute, I'd have wrung your neck."

"That's rather what I thought," she said with a grin,

turning to the man who had come up behind them. "Duke, I have a dispatch from Longa. He's moving into France with some of his raids now."

"I'm glad to see you back safe and sound, Violette," Wellington said. "I hope I shall now regain the relatively undivided attention of your husband." He raised his eyeglass and examined her with an air of enjoyment. "An unusual costume, ma'am, for a formal ball."

Tamsyn gave him a wry smile. "My apologies, Duke. But I couldn't wait to see Julian, and since he was here amusing himself without a thought for me, I had no choice." She turned reproachful violet eyes upon her husband. "Dancing with the beautiful Miss Beazley, sir! I was cut to the quick."

Julian shook his head, pursing his lips. "You're sailing very close to the wind, buttercup." With one swift movement he swept her up under his arm. "Excuse us, gentlemen."

"It's not fair that you should call me buttercup when I can't call you milord colonel anymore," Tamsyn protested as he carried her out of the ballroom and out into the snow.

"Life is full of inequities, my dear."

"And this is one of them," she grumbled. "I hate being carted around like a sack of potatoes. It's not in the least dignified."

"But then you're not a very dignified sort of a person," Julian pointed out as they entered the narrow town house where they had their own quarters.

"Not at all a suitable wife for Lord St. Simon, I suppose." She wriggled in his hold to push open the door to the bedroom at the head of the steep flight of stairs.

"On the contrary. A perfect wife for Lord St. Simon." Julian dropped her facedown on the bed.

"A woman whose nearest male relative is the focus for the biggest scandal to hit London in a century?" She rolled onto her back, her smile quizzical.

"Lord St. Simon couldn't imagine a more perfect wife," he repeated with mock solemnity.

Tamsyn opened her arms. "As it happens, Lady St. Simon couldn't imagine another husband. And at the moment she is *very very* hungry for love, *mi esposo*."

He smiled, and the teasing light was gone from his eyes as he came down onto the bed beside her. "You will never go hungry for my love, *querida*."

"A love for all life," she declared, tracing his mouth with her fingertip.

"Is there another kind?" He clasped her wrist and sucked her fingertip between his lips, his teeth lightly grazing the pad.

"The baron and Cecile didn't think so." She smiled, her eyes growing languid under the sensual caress.

"Sensible pair, your parents," he observed judiciously, turning her hand and kissing her palm. "A love for all life, sweetheart, and no holds barred." His tongue stroked over her palm, darted between her fingers.

"No holds barred," Tamsyn murmured, savoring the promise behind the laughter in his bright-blue gaze. "Now, that sounds most enticing, milord brigadier."

"We aim to please, ma'am."

About the Author

JANE FEATHER is the nationally best-selling, award-winning author of *Valentine, Velvet, Vixen,* and many more historical romances. She was born in Cairo, Egypt, and grew up in the New Forest, in the south of England. She began her highly successful writing career after she and her family moved to Washington, D.C., in 1981. She now has over a million books in print.

Next from the best-selling, award-winning
Jane Feather

VANITY

on sale December 1995

Read on for a preview of this tantalizing
new historical romance.

The crowds had been filling the streets since before dawn, jostling for the best places along the route to Tyburn, the luckiest finding spots around the gibbet itself. Despite the light snow and the raw wind, there was a holiday atmosphere: farmers and their wives, come in from the country for the entertainment, sharing the contents of their hampers with their neighbors; children dodging in and out of the throng, chasing each other, collapsing in squabbling heaps to the cobbles; sharp-eyed townsfolk, lucky enough to have houses along the route the cart would take from Newgate, shouting their prices for a seat in the window or on the roof.

It promised to be a spectacle worth paying for, the execution of Gerald Abercorn and Derek Greenthorne, two of the most notorious gentlemen of the road, who'd terrorized travelers across Putney Heath for the better part of a decade.

"You'd think if they could catch them two, t'other wouldn't be 'ard to get," a rosy-cheeked woman mumbled through a mouthful of pigeon pie.

Her husband took a bottle of rum from the capacious pocket of his greatcoat. "They'll not nab Lord Nick, woman, you mark my words." He took a hearty swig and wiped his mouth with the back of his hand.

"You seem very confident, sir," an amused voice said behind him. "What makes this so-called Lord Nick harder to catch than his unfortunate friends?"

The other man tapped the side of his nose and winked significantly. "He's clever, see. Cleverer than a barrel of monkeys. Give the Runners the slip anytime. They says 'e can disappear in a puff of smoke, he an' that white 'orse of 'is, jest like Old Nick, the devil 'isself."

His interlocutor's smile was slightly mocking as he took a pinch of snuff. He made no response, however. He was close to the front of the crowd and, standing head and shoulders above the majority of the spectators, could easily see the gibbet over the surrounding heads. All trace of a smile was wiped clean from his face as he heard the low rumble of excitement from Tyburn Road that indicated the approach of the cart with the condemned men. Using his elbows, he pushed through the crowd, ignoring the curses and complaints, until he'd reached Tyburn Tree.

John Dennis, the hangman, was already positioned on the broad cart stationed beneath the gibbet. He brushed snow from his black sleeve and peered through the now fast-falling flakes, watching for the arrival of his customers.

"A word with you, sir."

Dennis jumped and looked down from his perch. A man, unremarkably dressed in a plain brown coat and britches, fixed him with a gray-eyed, penetrating stare. "How much for the bodies?" he asked, drawing out a leather purse. It chinked richly as he rested it against the palm of his other hand, and Dennis's eyes sharpened. He examined the man closely and saw that although his clothes were plain they were well-cut and of excellent cloth, his linen was spotless, although without frills, and his hat was liberally adorned with silver lace. His sharply assessing gaze encompassed the fine soft leather boots with buckles that he immediately recognized as real silver. Highwaymen, or at least Mr. Abercorn and Mr. Greenthorne, clearly had well-to-do friends.

"Five guinea apiece," he said without a moment's consideration. "And three for their clothes."

The stranger's lip curled and an expression of acute distaste flickered over his countenance, but he opened his purse without another word.

Dennis leaned down, extending his hand and the man in brown counted the gold coins into his palm. Then he turned and beckoned four burly carriers, leaning on their carts on the outskirts of the crowd. "Convey the bodies to the Royal Oak at Putney," he said without expression, handing them a guinea each.

"Like as not, we'll 'ave to fight the surgeons' messengers for 'em, guv," one of the four said with a leering wink.

"When they're safely at the Royal Oak, there'll be another guinea each," the man in brown said coldly. Turning on his heels, he made to push his way back through the crowd. He'd done what he'd come to do, ensured that his friends' bodies would not end up on the dissecting table under the surgeons' knives, but he had no stomach to see their deaths.

He made fair progress until he reached the middle of the crowd; then the noise swelled from the Tyburn Road, heralding the imminent arrival of the prisoners from Newgate, and he found he couldn't take another step as the excitement rose to fever pitch around him and the throng pressed ever closer to the gallows. Resigned, he stood still, bracing himself against the buffeting as the crowd jumped on tiptoe, pushed and pulled, cursed and shouted, jostling for a better view.

"Take yer 'at off, woman!" The raucous yell was accompanied by a none too gentle shove at the monstrous confection of straw and scarlet-dyed feathers.

The irate owner, a florid-faced carter's wife reeking of gin, swung round and launched a stream of Billingsgate obscenity that was answered in like form. The man in brown sighed and tried to close his nostrils to the stench of alcohol and unwashed humanity as the atmosphere heated up despite the still falling snow and the vicious wind. Something brushed against him, he felt a fluttering against his waistcoat, and he was instantly alert. He clapped his hand to his waistcoat, knowing what he would find. His watch had gone.

Furious, he stared around at the sea of eager, panting faces, eyes glowing with excitement, mouths ajar. His livid gaze fell on an upturned face beside him, standing so close to him a wisp of cinnamon-colored hair brushed against his shoulder. It was the face of a madonna. A perfect, pale oval, with tawny gold eyes set wide apart beneath a smooth, broad brow; luxuriant dark brown eyelashes fluttered and her beautiful mouth quivered in distress.

Suddenly a loud voice bellowed, "Take care of your pockets! There's a bleedin' pickpocket around!" and a chorus of indignation rose in the close air as people patted their clothing, felt through pockets, and discovered that they too were missing sundry items.

Almost instantaneously, the girl standing beside him swayed, moaned, and sank downward. Instinctively, he caught her up before she could be lost in the sea of legs and heavily booted feet stamping on the cobbles. She hung limply against him, her face even paler than before, perspiration pearling her forehead.

Her eyelashes fluttered and she murmured, "Your pardon, sir," before she collapsed again and began to slip through his hold.

He hauled her upright, maneuvering her into his arms, and turned to push his way out of the crowd. "Let me pass. The lady is swooning," he declared repeatedly, the harshness of his voice having some effect so that at last he managed to make his way to the rear of the throng, who were now taken up with the spectacle at the scaffold. He'd reached a relatively empty space when the great roar from the crowd told him that the cart had been driven from beneath Gerald and Derek, leaving them swinging from the gibbet. His expression grew grimmer and his eyelids dropped for a second over eyes that were gray and cold as arctic ice.

"My thanks, sir," the bundle in his arms murmured in a faint voice as the girl stirred. "I have lost my friends in the crush and I was so afraid I would be trampled. But I'll manage very well now."

Her voice was surprisingly deep and rich. Her velvet cloak had fallen open as he'd pushed through the throng, revealing a simple gown of fine muslin, a discreet white fichu at the neck as befitted a modest young lady of good family. Her hands were buried in a velvet muff. She gazed up at him and offered a tremulous smile when he seemed disinclined to set her down.

"How do you intend finding your friends?" he asked, looking around pointedly at the seething press of humanity. "They could be anywhere. This is no place for a gently bred young woman to wander alone."

"Pray don't let me trouble you further, sir," she said. "I'm certain I shall find them . . . they'll be looking for me." She moved in his hold and he detected more than a touch of determination in her efforts to free herself.

Suspicion flickered in his brain as he thought of the sequence of events. It had all been very convenient . . . but surely he was wrong. This sweet-faced, honey-voiced innocent couldn't possibly have been light-fingering her way through the crowd.

Philip's face sprang unbidden to memory. Philip as he had been as a child. Angelic, gentle, coaxing, innocent little Philip. Neither of his parents would hear a word against their darling . . . not his parents, or his nurse, or his tutor, or any member of the household where young Philip ruled supreme.

"Put me down, sir!" The girl's now indignant demand brought him back to the present with a jolt.

"In a minute," he said thoughtfully. "But let us first devote some attention to finding your friends. Where exactly did you lose them?"

"If I knew that exactly, sir, I would have little difficulty finding them again," she responded tartly. "You have been very kind and I know my uncle will be very grateful to you for rescuing me. If you give me your name and direction, I'll ensure that a reward is sent on to you." She wriggled again with serious purpose.

He tightened his hold, hitching her higher up against his chest. His voice was suave as he protested, "My dear ma'am, you insult me. It would be the act of a dastard to leave such an innocent girl to fend for herself in these circumstances." He looked around him with an air of anxious interest. "No, I really must restore you personally to your family."

He glanced down at her again. The hood of her cloak had fallen back and snow was gathering on the glowing brown hair coiled smoothly around her head. Her expression was one of acute exasperation, banishing all trace of the helpless swooning maiden in distress. "Perhaps, if you told me your name, we might make some inquiries," he suggested gently.

"Octavia," she said through gritted teeth, praying that he'd be satisfied and set her on her feet. Once on the ground, she'd be free and clear in a second. "Octavia Morgan. And I do assure you, there is not the slightest need for you to remain with me any longer."

He smiled, convinced now that he was right. "Oh, but I believe there is, Miss Morgan. Octavia . . . what an unusual name."

"My father is a classical scholar," she responded automatically, her mind now working swiftly as she finally understood that he was playing with her. But why? Was he intending to take advantage of her present vulnerability? On the whole, he didn't strike her as a man likely to ravish a young lady in distress. He looked and spoke like a gentleman, although his plain garments and unpowdered hair indicated someone who didn't inhabit the Fashionable World.

But if not that, why wouldn't he let her go? The fruits of her morning's work were concealed in a pouch tied around her waist and lying snugly against her thigh beneath her top petticoat. It was reached through the slit in her dress that enabled her to adjust the position of the whalebone panniers when moving through a narrow doorway. He couldn't possibly feel the pouch, even holding her as he was, but it was time to bring this dismayingly intimate encounter to a close.

Her hand came out of her muff and she drove the heel of her palm into his chin, jolting his head back. At the same time, she twisted her head and bit his upper arm hard.

He dropped her like a hot brick, and she was up and running, weaving through the crowd with a desperate agility, but she knew he was on her heels, a silent, deadly pursuit. She ducked into an alley, gasping for breath, hoping she'd given him the slip, but then she saw him advancing on the mouth of the alley, a look of set purpose on his face.

She plunged out of the alley and back into the rowdy crowd that was beginning to disperse. The mood was now quarrelsome and voices were raised in streams of abuse, fights erupting as knots of people struggled to get out of the square. A rank of chairmen touted for custom as the throng eddied past them and Octavia headed for the line. She glanced over her shoulder, praying that her pursuer had followed her into the alley, but he was still behind her, keeping pace with her, pushing through the crowd, seeming not to hurry and yet somehow gaining. There was a relentlessness to this dogged pursuit and her heart began to thump, the first tremors of panic fluttering over her skin. She had his watch. If he'd guessed and was intending to capture her and bring her before the magistrates with the evidence still about her, then she'd be facing the hangman as surely as the two unfortunates whose deaths had just provided the crowd with such an amusing morning.

Her hand slipped through the slit in her skirt, feeling the laden pouch. The tapes beneath her petticoat fastened at her back and were impossible to reach one-handedly through the slit so she couldn't untie the pouch and throw it from her at this point even if she wished. And she didn't wish. It would be a cowardly waste of a morning's work. There was enough to pay the rent, redeem Papa's precious books and buy his medicine, and put good food on the table for a month to come. And if she gave it up, those heart-stopping, nauseating moments of terror that accompanied every artful brush of her fingertips would have been for nothing.

Resolutely, she withdrew her hand and slithered sideways through a noisy family group bewailing the disappearance of a child. They closed up behind her, arguing violently. The rank of chairmen was almost ahead of her now . . . three more steps . . .

"Shoreditch!" she gasped to the leading chair and moved to step inside as one of the two chairmen held open the door.

"No, I don't think so, Miss Morgan." A hand closed over her shoulder as the quiet voice spoke, gently mocking, behind her. "You see, I really do feel I have a duty to see you safely restored to the bosom of your family."

She was caught. But he couldn't know for sure that she had his watch. She was hardly dressed like a common thief and the only evidence he had was that she'd been standing beside him when the cry of "pickpocket" had gone up. She turned to him with a haughty toss of her head. "Sir, I find your attentions unwelcome. I trust you won't oblige me to summon the constable."

Amusement glittered in the gray eyes bent with such mocking solicitude upon her. "On the contrary, ma'am. Perhaps I should summon him for you."

"You goin' to Shoreditch, lady, or not?" the chairman demanded truculently before she could gather her wits to deal with this very deliberate calling of her bluff.

"Most certainly I am." With relief, she turned again to enter the sedan chair.

"No," her infuriating companion said in the same affable tone as before. "No, I really don't think so." Taking her arm now in a grip that meant business, he drew her away from the line of chairs. "You and I are going to have a little talk, Miss Morgan."

"About what, sir?" she snapped.

"Oh, I think you know," he said equably. "A little matter of private property and public assaults. But let us get out of this crush."

She seemed to have no choice, but at least there was no more talk of constables. Maybe he'd be satisfied with the return of his property and that would be an end to it. She said nothing, offering no further resistance as he swept her along before him through the gradually decreasing crowd.

Suddenly the atmosphere changed. The mob began to push and shove with greater force and a panicked murmur ran through their ranks. Voices were raised in warning and the murmur of panic became a full throated roar.

" 'Od's blood," Octavia's companion swore as he identified the roar. He tightened his grip on her arm. "Trust the press gang to know where to find good pickings. We have to get out of here before they run amok."

Octavia lost all desire to free herself from her companion, who was suddenly her only anchor. Her feet were swept from beneath her and if he hadn't dragged her against his body she would have gone down to the cobbles. The whole mass of humanity surged forward, men, women, and children screaming as they fought to get out of the square and into the surrounding streets where they could run freely. An army of cudgel-wielding sailors headed by a group of naval lieutenants poured into the square from the Edgeware Road, rounding up men and boys indiscriminately as they swept down upon them, inexorable as a tidal wave. Women's sobs and cries of protest as their husbands and sons were torn from their sides rose above the angry, frightened roar of the frantic crowd.

The press gang wouldn't take up a gentleman, and Octavia's captor was undoubtedly a gentleman, but their danger lay in being swamped by the crowd. The screams of the trampled rose, high-pitched with anguish, then faded into long, drawn-out groans of pain and despair as the heedless feet kept coming, kicking and stamping on fallen bodies.

Octavia lost all sense of direction; she was aware only of the strong comforting grip on her arm as they were tumbled along on the tide. She could see nothing except chests and arms until something flashed across her sideways vision.

"Over there!" she yelled, trying to make herself heard above the tumult. She darted sideways, lowering her head and pushing like an enraged bullock toward the deep doorway that had caught her eye. Her companion added his own bulk to the process, carving a path sideways through the throng until they were huddled in the doorway and the tide was sweeping past them.

"Thank God!" Octavia leaned against the door at her back trying to catch her breath. Her hair had come loose from its pins and her fichu was torn, exposing the creamy swell of her bosom. Her companion's gaze slowly drifted over her disordered appearance and abruptly she pulled her cloak tighter around her, covering her dishevelment, aware of the weight of the pouch lying heavily against her thigh.

"You have sharp eyes, Miss Morgan," her companion observed calmly, leaning beside her, watching the passing stampede. "We'll stay here until it's over."

"I presume you too have a name, sir," she said in an attempt to recapture her earlier assurance.

"Oh, most certainly," he agreed, taking a japanned snuffbox from the deep pocket of his coat. He flicked the lid and delicately took a pinch.

Nothing else was forthcoming. Octavia tapped her foot on the stone lintel. "Am I to be told it, sir?"

He looked at her, one eyebrow quizzically raised. "I confess I hadn't given the question any thought. However . . ." He bowed, managing an elegant flourish in the confined space. "At this moment, Lord Nick is at your service, Miss Morgan."